FULL-THROTTLE SPACE TALES #4

SPACE HORRORS

Edited by
David Lee Summers

FLYING PEN PRESS SCIENCE FICTION

www.FlyingPenPress.com

Space Horrors: Full-Throttle Space Tales #4, shelve in Science Fiction
Flying Pen Press Science Fiction
First Edition, first printing, continuous printing on demand
First date of publication: October 2010
Editor: David Lee Summers, www.davidleesummers.com
Cover Designer and Cover Art: Laura Givens, ArtDirector@FlyingPenPress.com

ISBN: 978-0-9818957-6-5

Flying Pen Press Science Fiction is an imprint of
Flying Pen Press LLC
20000 Mitchell Place, Suite 25
Denver, CO 80249
www.FlyingPenPress.com

All Flying Pen Press titles, imprints, and distributed lines are available at special quantity discounts for bulk purchases for sales promotion, premiums, fund raising, educational or institutional use.

Space Horrors compilation copyright ©2010 Flying Pen Press LLC
Cover copyright ©2010 Flying Pen Press LLC
Poetic Justice text ©2010 Alastair Mayer; Listening text ©2010 Anna Paradox; The Walking Man text ©2010 Glynn Barrass; Natural Selection text ©2010 Simon Bleaken; Oh Why Can't I? text ©2010 CJ Henderson; Last Man Standing text ©2010 Danielle Ackley-McPhail; Anemia text ©2010 David Lee Summers; Chosen One text ©2010 Dana Bell; Sleepers text ©2010 Selina Rosen; Divining Everest text ©2010 Patrick Thomas; Into the Abyss text ©2010 Dayton Ward; Salvage text ©2010 David B. Riley; The Golem text ©2010 Judith Herman; In the Absence of Light text ©2010 Sarah A. Hoyt; A Touch of Frost text ©2010 Gene Mederos; Wake of the White Death text ©2010 Lee Clarke Zumpe; Plan 9 in Outer Space text ©2010 Ernest and Emily Hogan.

All material is original to this volume.

All rights reserved. No part of this book may be reproduced in any form or by any means without the express written consent of the Publisher, excepting brief quotes used in reviews. For permission to reproduce any part or the whole of this book, contact the publisher.

Flying Pen Press Science Fiction, Flying Pen Press, Full-Throttle Space Tales and the flying pen nub logo are trademarks of Flying Pen Press LLC.

This is a work of fiction. Names, characters, places, and incidents are the products of the authors' imaginations or are used fictitiously. Any resemblance to actual events, locales, or persons, living or dead, is entirely coincidental.

Library of Congress Control Number: 2010931956

Manufactured in the United States of America and in the United Kingdom
Printing by Lightning Source Inc. and Lightning Source UK Limited

FULL-THROTTLE SPACE TALES #4

SPACE HORRORS

FULL-THROTTLE SPACE TALES

Title List

#1: Space Pirates
Edited by David Lee Summers

#2: Space Sirens
Edited by Carol Hightshoe

#3: Space Grunts
Edited by Dayton Ward

#4: Space Horrors
Edited by David Lee Summers

#5: Space Tramps
Edited by Jennifer Brozek
(September 2011)

Things that go bump in the night...

Simon Bleaken's "Natural Selection": A naturalist travels to a world to study a species of beetle-like aliens. When one of the creatures attacks another, the entire colony turns on the aggressor. How will such aliens view the human that has appeared in their midst?

Judith Herman's "The Golem": A young girl named Kayla is on a voyage through space with her family. In the hold, she makes a friend—a magical entity animated by a prayer. Can Kayla's new friend save her from an abusive father?

Patrick Thomas's "Divining Everest": Major Hans Benedict and the 142nd Starborne travel to a planet run by vampires to investigate a distress call. However, the vampires may not be the most frightening creatures on the planet Everest.

Danielle Ackley-McPhail's "Last Man Standing": Miners land on a world where a microscopic lifeform voraciously feeds on iron—including the iron found in the human bloodstream.

Ernest and Emily Hogan's "Plan 9 in Outer Space": The problem with spaceflight is that it takes a long time. One crew decides to alleviate the boredom by remaking Edward D. Wood's classic zombie film *Plan 9 from Outer Space.* However, their filmmaking is interrupted by real zombies!

These and more stories await inside...

It's always night in space!

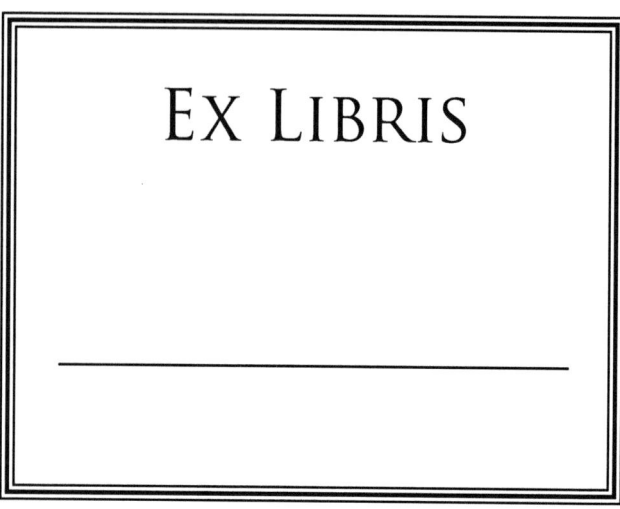

Whoever fights monsters should see to it that in the process he does not become a monster. And if you gaze long enough into an abyss, the abyss will gaze back into you.
—Friedrich Nietzsche

There are nights when the wolves are silent and only the moon howls.
—George Carlin

Where there is no imagination there is no horror.
—Arthur Conan Doyle, Sr.

In space, no one can hear you scream.
—Promotional tagline for the movie *Alien*

Table of Contents

9 Introduction — David Lee Summers

11 Part I: Man's Own Inhumanity
    13 Poetic Justice — Alastair Mayer
    21 Listening — Anna Paradox
    39 The Walking Man — Glynn Barrass

57 Part II: Alien Menaces
    59 Natural Selection — Simon Bleaken
    73 Oh Why Can't I? — CJ Henderson
    89 Last Man Standing — Danielle Ackley-McPhail

113 Part III: Seductive Vampires
    115 Anemia — David Lee Summers
    133 Chosen One — Dana Bell
    141 Sleepers — Selina Rosen
    155 Divining Everest — Patrick Thomas

173 Part IV: The Spirit Realm
    175 Into the Abyss — Dayton Ward
    193 Salvage — David B. Riley
    205 The Golem — Judith Herman

219 Part V: Shambling Zombies
    221 In the Absence of Light — Sarah A. Hoyt
    233 A Touch of Frost — Gene Mederos
    247 Wake of the White Death — Lee Clark Zumpe
    269 Plan 9 in Outer Space — Ernest and Emily Hogan

279 About the Authors

Introduction
David Lee Summers

Greetings. My name is David Lee Summers and I will be your host as we journey into the darkest reaches of space.

In addition to being a writer and editor, I'm an astronomer employed by Kitt Peak National Observatory to operate telescopes. I spend most of my working nights staring up into the cold vastness of space and I can tell you that space is scary. We know of a planet with an atmosphere that would crush you to death if the sulfuric acid rain didn't take the skin off your bones first. We know of a moon that frequently turns itself inside out because of volcanic activity. There are bursts of radiation that would cook a human, even inside a shielded spaceship. What's more, all of that happens just within our solar system.

It gets even scarier if you go outside the solar system. You'll find supernovae, the largest explosions known to man. There are objects that eject matter at nearly the speed of light. There are stellar corpses that weigh more than the sun, but would fit on the head of a pin, producing gravity so powerful it bends the fabric of space itself.

Earth is a very comfortable place when you start looking out into space. Even so, we know that Earth is a fragile protector at best. An asteroid could crash down on us and destroy all life as we know it. A distant supernova could unleash so much radiation our atmosphere would not shield us. Earth itself is geologically active, and we know that a super volcano could form, wiping out much of the life this planet has so carefully nurtured. Even without those disasters, we know that our sun is mortal and will die one day. Beyond our basic drive to explore, we have good motivation to brave the dangers of space and look for other places to settle.

This anthology looks at the kinds of dangers we might encounter in space. In some cases we might face frightening alien menaces. In other cases, we might create dangers through the use and misuse of technology. A number of the stories in this anthology are set on sleeper ships, where humans are put to sleep and cryogenically suspended so they can survive the long distances between stars. Perhaps this is not surprising, since I think many people relate to Edgar Allan Poe's words, "Sleep, those little slices of death; Oh how I loathe them." One could argue that cryogenic suspension is the most technologically viable means we have of turning ourselves into the "undead."

In other stories, we look at other kinds of monsters in space. We imagine zombies, vampires, and wraiths. Although these creatures are hopefully imaginary, they hold power for us because they represent what happens when our humanity is ripped away from us. That seems all too likely when humans seriously confront the vast, frightening realities of the universe. However, facing horror provides a certain kind of hope. It allows us to confront the issues right up front so we can hopefully defeat the dangers real and imagined that we might encounter when we travel to the stars.

So, buckle up, it's time to go full-throttle into the future and meet the dangers head-on.

Part I:
Man's Own Inhumanity

Poetic Justice

Alastair Mayer

The sleeper ship *Raven* sliced the icy, inky trans-Plutonian darkness a light-year out from Earth.

"Come on, Trevor, old man, you've had plenty of sleep, two years in fact. Time to wake up." Joe Fontano's voice carried a note of forced cheerfulness.

Trevor Montgomery heard and resented the words. He resented being woken up, and resented the cheery tone when he felt like death warmed over. Hibernation wasn't supposed to be like this. He felt as though he'd had a tormented night's sleep instead of waking up alert. It ought to be as though he'd just laid down. He opened his eyes, then squinted against the glare. "Turn those accursed lights down!"

"They are. It's dark in here, you're just not used to it. But I have to do this." Fontano held up a small flashlight and shone it in Trevor's eyes; first the right, then the left.

"Ow, damn you!" It felt like a laser.

"Sorry. Your pupil response is good."

Trevor blinked away the after-image of the flashlight. He looked around. Yes, the hibernation vault did have an almost Stygian gloom to it, now. Fontano gestured at the multi-colored graph on the nearby display. "Your vitals are okay. You don't have freezer burn."

"Freezer burn? I was not supposed to be frozen." Trevor scowled. The hibernaculums were supposed to maintain body temperature at four degrees Celsius, well above where ice crystals could form. He'd helped design them himself.

"That was a joke. Lighten up, you're the first live human I've had a conversation with in months." Fontano suddenly smiled. "Hey, at least I didn't tell you to chill out."

Trevor scowled again. Fontano was ill-suited for this work, always playing the fool, never taking things seriously. How had he managed to stay sane those months alone? He himself had that to look forward to now.

The *Raven*, like all sleeper ships, carried its hundred passengers and dozen crew members in cold sleep. This artificial hibernation reduced life support requirements to something manageable for the decade-long trip between stars. In rotation, each crewmember would take a turn awake for six months at a time to oversee the ship's systems, then revive his replacement. The ship's life support reserves allowed a week of overlap with the two of them awake, to ensure no after-effects from the hibernation and to provide time for the shift hand-off.

Trevor examined the display of his vital signs. Fontano had been correct about them looking normal, but that was only the present status. "My head aches, it's throbbing. Are you sure my blood oxygen was normal?"

"If you can trust the sensors." Fontano said, and grinned. Trevor had designed them. "I was okay when I came out of hibernation—" he broke off and coughed. "Well, except for the cough. Must have been the cold and the dry air."

Trevor glared at him. The humidity in the hibernaculums was controlled.

"Cold temperatures won't give you a cough, not unless they didn't sterilize everything properly." But Fontano did look a bit pallid.

"Whatever. Look, let's get you up. Can you sit up? Get out of that thing?"

Trevor sat up slowly. He didn't feel the strain he had expected. The ship's "gravity" was artificial, the result of constant acceleration at one-tenth of Earth-normal gravity. The problem with standing was balance, not strength, but he soon adapted to it.

"Well done!" Fontano applauded briefly. "We'll have you doing cartwheels down the corridors in no time."

Trevor looked forward to the end of the week; to when he would put Fontano and his abrasive manners and loud-mouthed humor into hibernation; to when he would have the ship blissfully to himself.

The following days dragged wearily on.

"The way I see it, Trevor, is that with two of us awake we only need to do half the work each. We can split the tasks."

"Your math is impeccable, of course," said Trevor, his hint of sarcasm lost on Fontano. "But to what end? I need to review all the ship's systems, and you are supposed to check that I still remember how after my time in hibernation. Although I will grant you that the latter task is hardly necessary."

"Of course it's not necessary. Oh, I'll double check you on today's work, but the rest of the week ... pfah." Fontano waved a hand airily. "Then we can have more free time together. We can talk, or play games. I have a deck of cards."

Trevor shuddered. "Why, that would be delightful." It would not, but he could tolerate it for a week. "But first we must get our work done. Where are you in the inspection rotation?"

The inspection of the ship's systems was largely make-work, something to keep the awake crew member busy. The ship's internal sensors and self-diagnostic routines should discover any problems before a manual inspection would. Human attention should only be needed if something actually needed replacement or repair. But the inspection routines kept the crew's skills honed, and there was always a chance that a fault could arise in the fault-detection systems themselves. If a serious problem developed, additional crew could be revived from hibernation to assist.

"The top floor," said Fontano.

"Top floor?" The phrasing was unfamiliar to Trevor.

"You know, all the way forward. Under acceleration that's 'up', so the top floor. Then there's the forward deuterium tanks, the middle floors are the wardroom and bridge. The hibernation vaults are the cellar. Cargo and aft tanks in the sub-basement and engines in the sub-sub-basement." Fontano grinned. "See, it makes perfect sense."

"I do see. Did you devise this nomenclature or was it something you inherited from Lucerne?" Roger Lucerne had preceded Fontano in the awake rotation.

"Pfah! Lucerne is an ignoramus. He's got no imagination. I came up with it." Fontano beamed.

"Ah, well then. By all means, let us proceed to the top floor and begin our inspection."

By the fourth day, Trevor estimated that he'd suffered through a thousand of Fontano's stupid little jokes or half-witty sayings. He didn't know which was worse: performing all the inspections with Fontano double-checking him, as per procedure; or splitting the inspection work between the two of them, leaving that much more unassigned time during each day. Trevor would have been perfectly content using that time to work his way through the ship's extensive library of books and videos, but Fontano was always yammering on about something, or telling stupid jokes. Knowing that it was temporary, Trevor bore this as best he could. But sometimes he had to get away.

"I'm going down to the cellar to inspect the hibernaculums." Trevor said, tossing his handful of cards on the wardroom table as he got up.

Fontano looked up from his own hand. "Your hand is that bad, eh? Ha, ha, ugh!" His laugh turned into coughing. He caught his breath and began to gather up the pile of cards on the table. "We already did that inspection. Are you losing your memory?"

Trevor shook his head. "No, we did the standard inspection. That's all very well as far as it goes, but you'll recall that I helped to design these hibernation chambers. I just want to do a more detailed inspection, to satisfy my own curiosity. No, don't get up, I don't need any help."

Fontano shrugged. "All right, suit yourself. The damn cold makes my cough worse anyway. Ha, 'suit', and we were playing cards. Get it?" He started to lay the cards out on the table for solitaire.

Trevor rolled his eyes as he walked from the wardroom.

It was cold and gloomy in the hibernation vaults. The hibernaculums themselves were individually refrigerated, but the vault itself was kept cool and dark; there was no point in wasting energy. Trevor had no intention of examining every one of the chambers, he would just do a few at random. But there was one in particular that he intended to check.

He located the hibernaculum and looked longingly through the transparent cover at the figure within. Even in cold sleep she was radiant. He touched a display panel and it lit up, displaying a brief status report and the occupant's name: Eleanor Montgomery.

Working with precise movements, Trevor Montgomery removed the screws from a service panel cover and then set the cover on the deck. Revealed within the hibernaculum's machinery, amidst an orderly array of wires and plastic tubes, was the system's master control processor. Trevor took a small hand-held computer from one pocket and a cable from the other, then used the cable to connect the hand-held to the maintenance port on the hibernaculum's processor.

He spent several minutes reviewing data on the handheld's display, periodically punching in commands and reading the results. He began to mutter under his breath. Finally, deliberately, he unplugged the cable and replaced the panel cover, muttering all the while.

He stood up and turned to look around the vault. It was as gloomy and quiet as it had been earlier. He turned back to the casket he'd been working on, and gazed once more upon Eleanor. He clenched a fist. "I will have my revenge."

"Fontano, you're scheduled for hibernation today." Trevor stepped into the ward room and held up a small device; a hypospray. "Your sedative."

"Already? I'm starting to enjoy this. You know they made a mistake, planning for only one person awake at a time. The time goes so much more quickly with two."

Was he insane? "Well, but that would put twice the drain on the ship's life support, we would run out of consumables."

"Oh, I know that. It's just…" his voice trailed off.

"You don't want to go back into hibernation?"

"It's cold. The hibernaculums are like coffins." He stared off at nothing. He coughed his annoying cough again, then he turned and grinned. "Still, I guess I won't die of sleep, eh?"

"No, Fontano, I promise you won't die of sleep."

"I just worry that I'll dream." He held up a hand to forestall Trevor's interruption. "No, I didn't last time. But, my next shift is in five years. Can you imagine, lying there dreaming all that time? Or worse, having nightmares?"

"Nonsense, you won't know a thing. You will be in suspended animation, you know that." Trevor paused, as if considering. "I'll tell you what, though. I can give you a stronger shot of sedative before prepping you for hibernation. You'll be out before you go under." Trevor held up the hypospray and twisted a dial on it, increasing the dose.

Fontano looked relieved. "Yes, I'm just a little nervous about going back under."

"Not to worry. Although you're the expert." He held the hypospray ready.

"What? You know far more about the hibernation systems than I do."

"I merely meant that you've already put someone under on this trip. I have only done it in the lab," Trevor said as the injector hissed its contents into Fontano's arm.

"What? Oh, yes, right. I thought you meant something else."

"That you revived Eleanor for a few weeks and put her back under too? Yes, there is that."

Fontano's eyes widened in surprise, then his eyes rolled back and he slumped to the deck, unconscious.

"Yes, there is indeed that," said Trevor coldly. He picked Fontano up, not a great burden in the *Raven's* low acceleration gravity, and carried him down to the hibernation vaults in the "cellar".

Fontano awoke while Trevor was prepping the hibernation chamber. Good, Trevor had judged the dosage properly.

Fontano looked about himself wildly, looked up through the transparent cover of the hibernaculum, and struggled briefly against the straps holding him in place. He groped for the strap release button but there was only a hole in the plastic where the button should be.

"Trevor, you? What?"

"Ah, you're awake. How fortunate."

"But, what is going on? Is my hibernation over? What happened to Lucerne, why are you waking me up?"

"Oh no, your hibernation has not begun."

"What? But … But the straps!"

"Ah, yes. I had to remove the release button. My apologies for not doing a neater job and covering that hole, but I might want to replace the button later. After you're asleep."

Fontano squirmed then relaxed. Slowly a look of comprehension crept over his face, and he struggled again. "Trevor! What you said before, about Eleanor, that's crazy!"

"Is it? You hid the signs well enough. Nothing in the main logs, nothing on the ship's internal monitors."

"That's because nothing happened! Let me out of here and let's talk about this."

"Oh no, I cannot let you out. It is time for your hibernation. Besides, there is nothing to talk about. I know that you are very good with computers, no doubt you edited the logs. Most of them, anyway."

"I didn't touch the logs. What are you talking about?"

"Please don't insult my intelligence. Did you think I wouldn't check the detailed logs on my own wife's hibernaculum? Was it she who told you to modify that log too?" Trevor held up a screwdriver to show Fontano. The other hand held the service panel cover for a hibernation chamber.

"What are you talking about?"

"The internal event log in the control unit. Each chamber has its own processors, and they talk to the ship's computers." He waved the panel cover. "Not that you can see it from where you lie, but this one is from yours, by the way."

A shiver ran through Fontano. "I don't know what you're talking about. I never touched Eleanor's hibernaculum, or any logs."

"Then why did the event log show a reset?" Trevor shook his head. "You thought you had wiped the memory so it would appear to be a glitch, but I went digging into the backup memory. You revived her because you wanted company. Was she a willing accomplice or did you force yourself on her?"

Fontano shook his head wildly. "That's crazy talk. Yes, there was a power glitch, that's in the ship's main log too. But I didn't revive anybody! I don't know what you saw in the backup memory, maybe a ghost image, bad data. Let me out and we'll check out the other systems."

Trevor had been bent over the internals of the hibernation unit as Fontano talked. He stood up and looked at Fontano. "An amusing story. Now let me tell you one. What I'm doing here," he said as he turned back to the service panel, "is reprogramming your hibernaculum."

"Reprogramming?" There was an edge of hysteria to Fontano's voice.

"Yes. I'm afraid you won't be going to sleep before the temperature in there starts dropping. In fact—" he paused to make a delicate adjustment. "In fact, you won't be going to sleep for quite a while. I gave you a stimulant to wake you up just now, and the hibernation chamber will maintain that. You might be awake for days. Of course, I had to flush the Hybernazine reservoir."

"Trevor! You can't do that!"

"Oh, don't worry about the life support reserves. Your little glass casket there will drop the temperature and oxygen levels just as though you were hibernating. The rest of the ship will be fine."

"No!"

"No? You're probably right, you probably won't be awake for days.

Once the hypothermia and hypoxia sets in, you'll go right to sleep." He replaced the cover on the service panel and began tightening its screws. "But don't worry, you won't dream."

"For the love of God, Trevor!" Fontano struggled again against the straps, squirming violently on the bed of the hibernaculum.

"Yes," Trevor said, "for the love, anyway." He secured the last screw then switched off the interior light on the hibernaculum. He turned to leave the hibernaculum storage area. At the vault door he paused. He could still hear, although faintly, the sounds of Fontano's struggles and screams for help. Trevor shook his head. A loudmouth to the last. He closed the door and latched it.

Listening

Anna Paradox

My cargo loader called in sick three days before launch.

"Selene, I've been grounded." Neil looked pale on the screen in my cabin. "Health inspection says I have the flu."

"The flu? Where did you pick that up?"

"Probably some tourist who couldn't put off their vacation on Luna just because they had the sniffles. I was down in Luna Mall taking Ivy to dinner a couple weeks ago. Earth inspection must have let another one through."

"Damn, Neil. I hate replacing crew on short notice."

"Don't I know it. Plus now company regs will keep me grounded at least four weeks without pay."

"Will you be all right?"

"Course I will. I just hate missing the run."

"Have Ivy or the boys caught it?"

"Not so far." He coughed dryly. "I'm on house quarantine. A couple weeks in the bubble on rest and fluids, and I'll be fine."

I frowned. "Neil, make sure you go to the clinic if you feel any worse."

"What can they do that we can't do at home? Just save me a place for the next run. I'll try to get a local temp placement and see you when you get back."

"You know I will, Neil. Get well soon."

"Give the ol' red planet some footprints for me."

I put in the call to Human Resources with misgivings. Our plasma drives would carry us to Mars in forty-one days. We were scheduled for ten days at Deimos Port, then the return trip. The twelve crew of *Copernicus VII* relied on one another. Neil had been a steady and proficient cargo manager for six years. Three months is a long time to spend on a small ship with a stranger. This close to launch, I'd have to take whoever HR had available.

HR promised me a replacement later in the day. I told them to have him meet me at Dock D for an interview. They reminded me that just cause must be demonstrated to turn down a posting.

I suited up and went to give *Copernicus* a walk around.

She was a fine ship of the line, sitting tall and proud on her engines on the Luna plain. We'd attached the crew airlock yesterday. The captain and I boarded first, through the long, airtight corridor from the underground facilities of Dock D. Company security checked us through as usual. Dave, the first engineer, was on board, and the other two engineers would follow later in the day. I'd expected Neil today, too, to begin inspecting and loading cargo through the big tunnel to be attached this afternoon.

The trap door to Dock D for the cargo arm was closed. We'd open the cargo doors to receive the arm after I had a loader. I ducked under the crew walkway. Everything looked good. *Copernicus'* name stood in bright red letters on her smooth silver skin. The fence was in place and unbroken. Nothing out of place. I leaned my helmet against the ship, taking in her normal buzzes and echoes. Then I gave her a reassuring pat, let myself back in the inspection airlock, desuited, and went to see the captain.

Captain Aldrin Larsson's door was open. He looked up from his immaculate desk when I knocked, and waved me in. "Complications already," he said.

"You've heard about Neil?"

He shook his head. "Grounded?"

"Regs and flu."

"Bad break. Do the best you can for us with the replacement. Like you always do."

"Thanks."

He tapped the screen on his desk. "No, I meant this. Headquarters is displacing our passengers for a bigwig. They want us to join the suites to accommodate the owner's son. Apparently he's going to Mars to oversee operations, and we get to give him the ride."

I considered what we'd need for forty days of formality. "So, dinners with the captain every night and butler service for breakfast and lunch?"

He scrolled down. "That's odd—actually, no. Says he is recovering from anti-agathic surgery, and will want his privacy. Plans to bring on his own food and keep to his room."

"I won't rely on that."

"Good plan. Sort it all out." The captain ran a hand through his thinning sandy hair. "I'll send the formal apology to the bumped passengers and a get well note to Neil. Has the third thing gone wrong yet?"

It was an old joke between us: troubles always come in threes, like my ex-husbands or his children. We exchanged small smiles, and I said, "Not yet. I'll keep a watch for it."

I sketched a salute at him, although the company said we were no longer military, and took my leave.

We had two passenger suites, side by side. Normally, each room held four bunks. Weight matters when accelerating to reach another planet. It was rare someone felt rich enough to pay for an entire room, much less two. We could unbolt all but one of the bunks, open up the door between the rooms, and add a table and a couple chairs. I wrote out the instructions for the ground crew, and called them in. We'd planned to take precious metals as our discretionary cargo to Mars. I cancelled it, and arranged a ton of canned luxury foods instead.

Then it was time to interview Neil's replacement. I took the crew walkway back through security to Dock D.

I had a few minutes with his file before Timothy Harvey joined me. He'd been with the company for two years, and had done fill-in work on ships for seven months of that. Only one long trip. Born on Earth, came to Luna just before the company hired him, mostly worked in company warehouses. The supervisor comments were all the non-committal generalities that either meant he hadn't stood out or the writers wanted to avoid a lawsuit. They weren't much help.

I stood to shake his hand when he came in. He was younger than I expected, slightly heavy with light green eyes. "Pleased to meet you. What would you like me to call you?"

He slid into the chair across from me. "Tim's fine."

"Thanks, Tim. I'm Selene Terrell, vice-president of *Copernicus VII*. HR offered you to replace an ill crewman of mine for our trip to Mars."

"Yes, ma'am."

"How did you like your last trip to Mars?"

"It was fine." He became more animated for a moment. "The food was a little monotonous near the end."

"It does get a little dull when the fresh foods run out. Why did you decide to come to Luna?"

"I had a friend, said the company was hiring, and it was good pay."

"What was his name?"

"Her name was Mae. Mae Ilahoto."

"It says here you're single. Anyone you are likely to miss while we're in transit?"

He shook his head. "No one in particular. It's only three months and video calls are almost as good."

"I find the lag makes them a bit unsatisfying."

"It won't be a problem."

I clicked the point inside my pen. "Here, catch."

He fumbled a little, but didn't drop it. I remembered Neil's grace and fast reflexes as he caught a falling box, and sighed inwardly. But there was nothing here that I could legitimately object to. I held out my hand for the pen. "Good enough. Welcome to the *Copernicus VII.*"

His hand was a little clammy when he shook mine goodbye. I wiped my palm on my pants after he left, and hoped for the best.

Back on the ship, more crew had boarded, and I let them know we'd be having a new cargo manager this trip.

"Flu?" asked Kate Heinish. "I hadn't heard of any on Luna."

I frowned. As ship's surgeon, she usually knew of new infections on Luna. We kept close tabs on them—both because they could spread rapidly through our closed air systems and because they were rare. Since we'd built the Lunar ecology from the dirt up, we'd been able to leave most pathogens on Earth. That meant the Luna-born were often more susceptible to the ones that came through. Flu should have been news.

"Do you think Neil might have misdiagnosed?"

She nodded. "But you know they won't change their minds in time for him to join the flight."

"That's true." Health inspection would quarantine him on suspicion at least four days, and we launched in three. I put it out of my mind.

I checked in on Tim several times a day during loading, and it seemed to go fine. Newton and Mare, who assisted Neil pre-launch, knew how *Copernicus* liked her balance. And if Neil would have packed the holds a little more elegantly and efficiently, it was still good enough.

Invictus Sadad, the owner's son, boarded through security with his face bandaged. His luggage came through the cargo doors, an entire cartload. Tim crashed the cart into the corridor wall while bringing it to our guest's cabin. Later, the captain asked, "Think that was our third trouble?"

"Maybe. If it was, we got off light. Mr. Sadad hasn't complained."

"Good enough," he said.

I called Neil at T minus 2 hours, and he said he was feeling better. And so we launched.

Halloween fell one week into our trip. I woke from unsettled dreams, thinking I'd heard something—a scrape and a thump. Those sounds didn't belong on my ship. Was it part of the dream? I dressed quickly, and went to walk the corridors of *Copernicus.*

There was nothing unusual in the hall outside my cabin. We offer what privacy we can, but air must flow throughout the ship, and metal walls ring on impact. We twelve crewmates slept in shifts, four at a time. The steady growl of the engines, the hum of the air pumps, and the talking and moving of the crew make a steady background to our journey. Meals create a bit more sound, and if the engineers need to hammer or a couple fights, we all know it. That bump and scrape—if I'd really heard them—didn't belong.

And my footsteps should echo just so in the corridor. Instead, they were muffled. There was something around the corner.

I spotted the photocell near the floor, tripped it and jumped back. A scarecrow jumped towards me, bouncing into the spot where I would have stood.

I called Dave directly. "Dave Callahan, come to corridor C immediately."

"Ah, Selene, I should have known you would find it. Can't we leave it longer?"

"No. Come."

He arrived rushing. "Selene, it's just a Halloween joke."

"Really? What's that?" I pointed to the blade in the scarecrow's hand, dripping with a black ichor.

"What?! I didn't put that there, Selene, I swear." He reached his hand toward it, and I knocked it away.

"Don't touch it. We'll have Kate analyze it. That blade would have cut me in the stomach."

"Selene, you know I'd never hurt the crew."

"Dave, we've been shipping together for five years, and each year you've done something more elaborate for Halloween. I don't know what to think. Confine yourself to quarters until further notice."

"But—"

"No, I mean it, and now. You don't want to give me any more reasons to be mad at you."

He met my eyes, then nodded and left. I called Kate to examine the evidence.

Kate sniffed the knife, and frowned. "That's vaguely familiar, but I can't place it. It'll take me a while to analyze this. I'll let you know as soon as I can." We worked together to take the knife out of the scarecrow and drop it into a sterile container without touching it. It had been crudely shoved through the hand of the scarecrow.

The scarecrow was a mechanical marvel. Dave had used some of his own clothes over a wire frame, and would no doubt be able to reuse most of the parts again later. A paper hat and a few tufts of straw completed the illusion. For the moment, we carefully gathered everything and took it to the clinic.

"Will you be able to get fingerprints?"

"I don't know. I don't have any special powder or training for that. It may be easier to get DNA." She set the canister on the spectrograph table and began to open the lid. Before she could finish, an alarm went off, with flashing lights and loud blaring.

"What is it?" I yelled, covering my ears.

Kate went to the readout, pressed a few buttons, and tightened the lid again. The light continued to flash, but the sound stopped. "Ricin! That should never have made it past the security scanners."

"How did it get on my ship?"

"That doesn't make sense. It's one of the substances the security

Listening

scanners particularly check for. My spectrograph is set for wide scale analysis, so it didn't go off until it detected a dangerous concentration. But the security scanners react to one part in ten million—someone would have to encase it in steel, then scour the exterior, then sterilize what they cleaned it with and do it two or three more times. And then we'd want to know what was hiding in the steel. This should never have made it on the ship."

"Unless someone turned off the scanner. I knew I didn't trust Tim Harvey! I—"

"Ms. Terrell, I need you on the bridge."

"Selene, we have a problem in the galley."

The two voices broke through the intercom at once. "Kate, lock yourself in and guard this. See what else you can find out, and I'll be back as soon as I can."

I heard the bolt slide behind me as I ran for the bridge. Bridge was a fancy name for the room barely bigger than a closet where Captain Larsson and a co-pilot could guide the ship and check her status. "Captain?"

"I've found something odd in our vector. We're behind course, consistent with the ship weighing 600 kilos more than our manifest. It's subtle, but there."

"I have another reason to suspect our new cargo loader. That alarm was Kate discovering ricin, which is on the terror list. He must have shut off the detector to bring it on."

"Take Marco and detain him. Somehow."

I nodded. *Copernicus*' builders had wasted no space on a prison. I'd find a way.

"And be careful."

"Always."

I began calling up security information. Harvey had to be in his room. We had cameras on multiple independent circuits. We could trace every source of heat on the ship. Nothing human-sized could be out of place.

I listened, too. Nothing out of the ordinary. Until Mare's voice came over the intercom. "Selene, I really think you need to see this in the galley."

It was on the way. I called Marco directly and asked him to arm himself and meet me there.

Marco covered a cough as we met at the door to the galley. I went in first, since his big frame made any space in the ship feel crowded. "Mare, what is it?"

She pointed at a strange mushroom in one of the chilled produce bins. "I know this wasn't here last night. I'd have said something."

"What is it?"

"It's an amanita. It's deadly! That shouldn't be on the ship at all."

Something niggled at me, and behind me, Marco coughed again, harder. I leaned over the drawer.

The amanita called attention to itself with its bright red spotted cap. It would be very hard to miss. It was distractingly out of place. I looked at the rest of the produce. Just barely visible, once I turned my gaze from the deadly mushroom, was a fine powder scattered over the rest of the produce.

I pulled open the next drawer, and saw the powder there, too. "Have you eaten any of this?" I asked Mare.

"No," she said. "I saw the mushroom and worried."

"I did," said Marco. "Randy and I had breakfast an hour ago. And I don't feel so good."

"Marco, go to the clinic, now. Mare, don't let anyone else eat until we check everything. We need to call everyone—except Tim Harvey—and see who has eaten."

I called Kate first. "Kate, we have a possible poisoning situation. Have you eaten since dinner?"

"No, I was on my way when you called me about the scarecrow."

"Good. Don't. Marco's on his way, and we may have more for you."

"What about evidence security?"

"Preserve it if you can. But save lives first!"

"I understand," she said.

"Good. Out."

I called the captain next. He hadn't eaten. Dave hadn't eaten. Randy wasn't answering calls, and neither was Inoko. Quill said she'd had a snack six hours ago, but felt fine. I told her to go to the clinic anyway. Everyone else seemed in the clear.

I hesitated over calling our passenger. True to his word, he hadn't left his cabin since the start of our trip. Why would he have started now?

After a moment, I called him and lied. "Mr. Sadad, this is vice-president Selene Terrell. We are running a drill. As part of the drill, I

Listening

need to know if you are in your cabin."

"Why, yes, Ms. Terrell, I am."

"And have you left it for any reason in the last eight hours?"

"No, I have not."

"Thank you. I'm sorry to disturb you."

"Oh, not at all. Not at all."

I closed his line and went to find Randy and Inoko.

Copernicus is a small ship, and I had full security displays running on my specs. It took me only a few minutes to find each of them lying in a pool of vomit, unresponsive. Randy was in hydroponics and Inoko was in his cabin. Newton, and Gottfried, still able bodied, helped me carry them to Kate's overcrowded clinic.

She had multiple lines running to Marco, who looked pale. She told Quill to stand up and make room for Randy and Inoko. We only had three beds in the clinic.

She began attaching lines to Randy and Inoko.

"What do you know?" I asked.

Kate's eyes slid to Marco. "Not much, yet," she said. "I'll do what I can."

"Tim Harvey has a lot to answer for. Quill, stay here and do what Kate tells you. Gottfried and Newton, you're with me."

I unlocked the security cabinet, and we took sidearms and body armor. I knew Gottfried could handle himself under fire, so I asked him to lead.

Everything would go so much easier if Tim Harvey would open his door. But I knew he would have heard running in the corridors and Kate's alarm. The question was, was he listening?

At his door, I had Newton stand off to the right, on the hinge side, and Gottfried step to the left. Then I took a breath and knocked on the door. "Tim, I need to talk to you."

"Just a minute."

I stepped back, out of the line of the door, and waved Newton farther away, too. Then we heard the bolt move, and the door swung open.

Harvey's eyes widened when he saw the armor and sidearm. He started to close the door again, and Gottfried rammed it open with his shoulder.

"Just step back, Tim, and let us in."

"What is this? I haven't done anything!" He retreated into the room, hands in front of his chest.

"Haven't done anything?" I advanced on him. "Tim, you're the cargo master. There are things on this ship that shouldn't be here. That means you did it."

"I swear, I didn't think it would cause any harm. He just said…" Then he grabbed for something under his bunk, and Gottfried shot him.

With a taser. None of us are fools enough to shoot a projectile in the fragile confines of our ship. Tim Harvey stiffened and then slumped. I checked his heartbeat and breathing—both fine.

"Gottfried, restrain him." We had safety ties in our belt kits. "We'll get our answers when he comes to. Don't touch anything. There may be traps or antidotes in here. But we'll need to search very carefully. The two of you take turns watching him. Call me if he wakes up. Otherwise, I'll be back in four hours."

They nodded their acceptance. I left them, with the profoundly uneasy thought that I was overlooking something.

Back at the clinic, I asked Kate if she could step out for a minute.

"How are they, really?"

"I'm doing everything I can. I've pumped their stomachs, and Marco's bulk seems to have diluted the effect a bit, but I just don't have the tools I need. It's—it's going to be touch and go for a while yet. I haven't even been able to isolate the poison yet."

"Not amanita?"

"No, amanita's effects are different. Flu-like symptoms…" her eyes widened, and the other shoe dropped. "Oh my god. Neil," she said. "Flu-like symptoms, followed by apparent recovery, followed by organ failure. We've got to call him."

"I'll do it." I hesitated a moment. "If the poisoner had an antidote with him, would you be able to recognize it?"

She thought. "Maybe. There's only so much I can do now, so I'll start on the chemical analyses. If we knew, it might help."

"Good. The knife, too—it could be part of the puzzle." There was a scraping sound from the ceiling above us. I cocked my head. "Did you hear that?"

"Hear what?"

I listened a moment more. It wasn't repeated. "I'm not sure. Do what you can, and call me if you need me. I'll call Neil."

I made the call from my cabin, composing myself as best I could through the two minutes of lag to connect with Luna. Ivy answered. "Selene, is that you?"

"Yes, Ivy. Neil needs to go to the hospital right away."

I waited two minutes, and she put her face in her hands. "Selene, it's too late. He died this morning."

"Ivy, I am so sorry. We found amanita on the ship today. Have the coroner check for it."

I waited. She looked up and said, "What does that mean? Is the ship in trouble?"

"Yes, we have some trouble. I'm—"

In a wash of static, the connection went dead. Then I heard the scream.

It's worse when a man screams, somehow. In all the dramas, women scream, high-pitched and frantic until it seems less real. This was real—strangled terror from the front of the ship. I threw open the door and ran to the bridge.

Captain Larssen had fallen half onto the floor. Blood flowed from his chest, and there was a thing perched upon him, stabbing him again and again.

I took careful aim and hit it with the taser, as short a burst as I could manage.

"Se-selene," the captain burbled. I moved closer, to hear him. "There's another problem with nav. Check—check the stars. And tell my kids I love them."

There was so much blood around him. I leaned in, to begin first aid.

"Behind you," he breathed.

I twisted, and saw another of the things clinging to the ceiling. It leaped, and I fired, and it fell.

When I turned back, Captain Larssen's eyes were frozen. I saw now that one of the stab wounds had exposed and pierced his heart, and knew it was too late.

Then I saw the hole under the pilot console, with another of the things inside it. Aiming the taser at it, I began backing away. Three feet, four feet, five... "All crew, stations! We are under attack. Repeat, crew, stations. We are under attack."

The thing made a scraping sound as it leaped for the air duct. I heard it scuttling away.

Then I heard the dry chuckle over the intercom. "That won't help you, you know. This is my ship now."

"What do you want?" I yelled back.

"Oh, you'll know soon enough. You'll all know."

I heard our passenger click off the system. I had blown it. The pattern was there, and I missed it. The obvious scarecrow, and the hidden and poisoned knife. The blatant amanita, and the deadly subtle powder. The clearly guilty cargo master and the man who had never shown his face. Which meant...

I ran for Harvey's room. I heard thumpings and zapping and yells as I arrived. Then Gottfried opened the door. "There were six of them. They got Harvey and Newton."

I looked in at spattered blood and fallen bodies. Then I took a blanket off Tim's bunk and gingerly gathered up one of the scorched things. "We're not beaten yet. Let's get Dave to take a look at this."

We exchanged our tasers for fully charged ones at the security locker. Then we went down to Dave's door.

Dave opened at my knock, fully suited and armored. I hoped that our guest wouldn't know that, to *Copernicus'* crew, "stations" meant suit up, armor up, and stay in place. If he didn't know where to send his pets, we might gain a little time.

"Dave, you're cleared."

"I figured."

"I have something for you to look at." I opened up the blanket. "What are we dealing with here?"

He moved the blanket to a table, and poked at the thing with a long screwdriver. It didn't move. Then he took a knife from a holder on the wall and sliced along the thing's back.

It didn't bleed. The black, glistening skin parted to reveal gears and circuits. Dave peeled the skin away from one of the legs and bent it with the screwdriver.

"It's a highly transformable six-legged robot in a jellied matrix. Looks like smart metal legs—can shrink and extend by a factor of four. Same for the tail, with the integrated blade. These..." he brushed the screwdriver across the mandible-like protrusions at the front "...are fine manipulators, and this is an ocular assembly. Antenna here." He pointed out a globe and a stick above the mandibles. "Quite the elegant piece of engineering, really."

"How does it get its orders?"

He peered at it. "I don't see any sound sensors. So they probably come in through radio."

"So, our guest can't speak its orders?"

"No, he probably can. I'd guess he has a transmitter that takes his commands and resends them as radio. He seems the type."

"How much does it weigh?"

Dave hoisted it experimentally. "About half a kilo."

"The ship's six hundred kilos over manifest. The captain discovered it this morning. So, he could have twelve hundred of these things."

"Probably half that. My guess is, they need some support."

"And he had some other materials to smuggle on board," added Gottfried.

"Right. In any case, that's still too many for us to take out one at a time. Dave, would they be susceptible to gas? Ultrasonics?"

He shook his head. "Gas, definitely not. They don't breathe. Ultrasonics—we could get them one at a time with that—not good enough. Nope, what we need for these is a ship-wide EMP."

"Wouldn't an electromagnetic pulse fry the ship systems too?" asked Gottfried.

"Yeah," Dave smirked. "But I can fix it."

I looked him in the eyes. "Are you sure? There's no rescue for us if you're wrong."

He looked more serious for a moment. "I'm sure. Really, Selene, I promise."

"Set it up, then. And keep yourself alive. You just became our most valuable player."

"I'll stay here," said Gottfried.

"What are you going to do?" asked Dave.

"I need to talk to Kate. She has patients, and we don't want to surprise her with her equipment going out. Then I need a button, so I can trigger the EMP at a time of my choosing."

"And then?" asked Dave.

In five years of long hauls, you learn about the people you ship with. I knew what he was asking, and I knew how to tell him.

"And then I'm going to listen to our guest. With extreme prejudice."

The clinic had gone into quarantine shut down. I suited up before passing through its airlock. With sealed ducts and double doors, it would be the safest place on the ship.

It was a little crowded inside. Mare had joined Quill and Kate, and with all three beds extended, once I came in, it was elbow to elbow.

"The galley's not very defensible," said Mare.

"Good choice," I said. "How are they?"

"All unconscious now," said Kate. "I think—I think an antidote would be our best chance."

"If he has it, I'll get it from him. Kate, I need to understand him. What do we know about this bastard?"

Quill answered. "This might help. His father is 168 years old. He's got the billions to pay for it, and the rejuvenation treatments work great on him. Our boy—he's only sixty-four. And judging by how long he's stayed in his room—I don't think the treatments worked so well for him."

"He likes poisons," said Mare. "The amanita, and the ricin, and whatever was on the food."

"Which I still haven't been able to analyze," said Kate. "But get this—along with the ricin, there was asphalt and formaldehyde in the mixture on the knife. Both used as embalming fluids at various points in history."

The pattern clicked together. "Thank you. That does help." I took a deep breath. "Get ready. In a little while, there will be an electromagnetic pulse. Dave says he can put the ship back together afterwards."

Mare drew in her breath through her teeth. "He'd better. We can't stop this ship without the computer."

"And I'm still hoping…" said Kate.

"Hope, pray, and watch your back," I said. Then I let myself out the airlock.

"Here's your button," said Dave. "Just push this, and I'll have job security for the next three weeks."

"This is no time for humor," said Gottfried.

"It's always time for humor," said Dave.

"Selene, do you want me at your back?"

"Not this time, Gottfried. It'll be easier to talk my way in alone. You two take care of each other."

"You take care."

"I always do."

Then I took off my suit and put it away. I clipped the button to my chest, underneath my shirt. I put the taser in the small of my back. I thought briefly of the days when Captain Larsson and I served on a military ship together. Then I walked to the door to the guest quarters, my hands open and in front of me.

"You win, Prince Sadad," I said. "This is your ship. You can have everything you want."

"What do you know about what I want?"

"You said we would know, in time. So tell me."

That dry laugh came again. "There's nothing that can stop what I want now. My other servants have sabotaged your drives and poisoned your food. You will all die here."

"You are right. You have completely outplayed and outthought us. You hold our lives in your hands."

"Yes! I am like a god to you!"

I pressed my hands together, and bowed to the door. "Do you not want me to bow to you in person? It is right that I should lower myself before my god."

He laughed, harshly. "Why not then? You may enter."

I opened the door, and bowed again, taking in the scene through the corners of my eyes. He'd hung purple velvet curtains along the walls, and dozens of his pets clung to them, pointing their eyes and bladed tails at me. He sat on the edge of his bed, only his face and hands visible, and those wrapped in bandages. He wore the circlet with the rearing cobra on his bandaged brow, and held the scythe and lash.

I bowed again. "It is good to look upon you, Prince Sadad. I am glad to see who I will serve—in this life and the next."

The bandages around his mouth wrinkled horribly. "You know who I am, then?"

"You are the king who rules beyond the veil."

"Yes! I am the ever-living one! Not my father! No matter how he simpers and takes whores to his bed. He let my mother grow old! He let me grow old!"

"All this is nothing to the kingdom beyond the veil."

He quieted. "Yes. I shall rule, and you shall serve me. This ship shall sail forever into the void, and you will serve me forever."

"I bow before you, oh king." I paused. "But mighty king, these ones around me, they cannot die. So they cannot serve you beyond the veil. And the other humans—they have not yet chosen to serve you. Do you not want servants who follow you by choice? Give me the antidote, and we will serve you of our own free will—this life and the next."

I was close to him now, and I saw his eyes slide, so quickly, towards a box on the table. Then he laughed. "You are a clever one. I shall keep you the longest. When all the others have crossed to await me, you and I shall share this potion of immortality." He put a hand down and caressed a different box at his side. But I knew him now, and I heard the lie.

"You honor me too much," I said, clapping my hand to my chest. All around me his pets fell from the curtains as the pulse spread through the ship. He reached for something, and I grabbed my taser and shot him.

He fell backwards with a cry. I prodded him with the taser first, then checked for a pulse. There was none. The treatment must have weakened his heart. "So much for your immortality," I said. Then I took the box on the table to Kate.

"I think this one is the antidote," I said.

"We haven't got a lot to lose," she replied. "And our guest?"

"Heart stopped when I tasered him."

She nodded, and tested the pearly fluid in the flasks inside the box in vitro first.

Then she gave it to Inoko. After an hour, she gave it to Randy, and the next day to Marco. And in time they woke.

There was lots of clean up, of course. Dave hadn't been exaggerating when he said three weeks to fix the electronics. We scrubbed where we needed to, and gave Captain Larssen and Newton Barelo and even Timothy Harvey last honors. I found the security video, and watched Harvey turn off the scanner and the scales as Sadad's agents loaded his luggage. He'd done nothing worse than that, and three men had died of it.

At some point, Sadad had tricked the ship into nudging us above the plane of the ecliptic. But we recalculated the fuel use, and Dave and Gottfried made some smart adjustments to the engines, and we limped into Deimos port, two weeks late and heartily sick of the foie gras and caviar from our shipment of luxury foods.

The Walking Man

Glynn Barrass

A dream of flying through space, through mindless vacuums without suffering the fetters of metal machines or recycled air.

But was it a dream? There seemed something far too real about it, but also, something far too ethereal, for he was moving more swiftly than the laws of physics allowed.

Plus, the planets were too uniform in size and location, like a child's science room diorama. Still, they rushed towards him at incredible speeds.

First came Jupiter, then Saturn and Uranus. He swooped between and past these three to fly towards Neptune at a speed unimaginable.

The exhilaration made him want to scream aloud.

There was no air in space, hence, no air for his lungs to exhale with, but then, why could he feel the wind rushing through his hair?

The black depths bore no answer, the stars winking a secret knowledge they dared not betray to this usurper so unnatural to their abode.

Neptune's bright blue orb began to engulf his vision now, blindingly bright; its presence felt warm and wholesome.

Then came darkness.

Voices, harsh and filled with mockery, awoke him from his dream.

Dreamworld space to nightmare reality, only death could seem more painful.

Sidal opened his eyes. Laying on his side, he found himself facing a wall. He was in the place where he'd fallen asleep—in the brig of the Walker. It was dank with intermittent shadows because his jailers had chosen to leave the overhead light on. Just a little more torture that way.

He turned onto his back, feeling the rough bunk against it. There was light to blink by and he did so while his eyes adjusted.

In the meantime, his jailers continued to taunt.

"Sir?" Lieutenant Commander Gantz was polite even in his dementia, "I have a report that reads that after much torture and degradation, all crew members that you deemed friends or were on friendly terms with, have been thrown into the Walker's leg gears, alive."

"Including the captain," sniggered a voice he still didn't recognize.

"Screw you!" screamed Sidal, jumping from the bunk towards the wire grate mounted in the door's lower half. He gave it a hefty kick. The door vibrated loudly and was accompanied by sounds of scuffling as his jailers backed away.

A few seconds of silence, then dull cackles from without.

His actions, quite unbecoming of the second in command of the machine he was trapped within, were the result of two full days of imprisonment without food or water, and the taunting.

Knowledge of the captain's death made it his ship to captain, or his vehicle at least.

The crew called it the Walker, or the Walking Man. Sidal called it a walking prison. And no one was taking any orders from him.

The Walking Man—a 275-foot tall automaton powered by hydraulic pumps and pistons—was a survey vehicle that traveled across the desert wastelands of Mars. Until that is, the machine changed its course unexpectedly, followed by a bloody mutiny perpetrated by officer and subordinate alike.

Sidal, once Commander Sidal, was one of the survivors, although he didn't know what others, if any, were left now.

The captain was dead, obviously, and he'd watched Lieutenant Üstemen die with his very own eyes.

This had happened in the mess, Gantz mutinying alongside two junior lieutenants and the majority of the lower hands.

The slaughter had been swift and meticulous; Sidal still shuddered upon recalling it.

Thankfully, he had other things to focus his mind on.

Still, the knowledge of yet more death angered him to the core.

He calmed himself down and set to it.

Climbing to his knees, Sidal scooted left, away from the door till he was beyond the grate's view to continue the task he'd begun a day earlier: trying for freedom.

This task was to be accomplished by levering up one of his cell's floor plates. The only one congenial to looseness was the plate to the left of the door, and working on it while shielding his work had proven difficult.

At times, his captors had been cognizant that he was doing *something*, but not entirely sure *what*.

Times like this.

His back forming a shield to his actions, he utilized a slim metal ruler, the only item he'd had in his pockets upon capture, to slowly but surely lever up the square floor plate.

"What ya doing there?" asked Gantz.

"Naughty things," his unknown companion replied.

The ruler, tucked between the plates, was about to reach another corner. Slow, tedious work as it was, the corner's freedom might provide leverage enough to pull the plate right off.

A sudden shudder racked the room around Sidal. The floor vibrated painfully as he struggled to stop himself from falling.

Still, he nearly lost the ruler to the gap. Squirming painfully to retrieve it, his grabbing ripped the ends of his fingers and snapped a long sliver of resin from the plate, but the ruler was saved.

He stared around the room in shocked surprise.

The shuddering diminished, back towards the Walking Man's usual, gently vibrating gait. Sidal's heart beat frantically.

"Sir?" called the unknown voice. "I have it on good authority that the Walker has just trampled to death a medium-sized colonist carrier."

"Say about two hundred souls down?" Gantz added. "And Gusev City comes next … aren't your wife and kids there?"

"Why you…"

In one swift movement, Sidal found himself retrieving the sliver of resin before spinning towards the grate. He only realized what he had done when his jab elicited a loud shriek from the other side.

He shuffled back. The sliver of resin, pallid yellow in color, shook a little before disappearing through the grate.

The screaming continued.

"Aw gawd, my eye!"

It appeared Sidal had hit his unknown jailer in the eye.

Turning to the floor panel, Sidal realized that the injured man's bawls might give him the opportunity to remove it faster.

Adding imperative was the dreadful thought of the Walking Man's threatened assault on the city. Escape from his cell was his first necessity. His second, gaining control over the deadly machine around him.

"Bwah! Get the keys, I wanna kill 'im!" The unknown voice screamed.

"Here, let me help you," Gantz said, followed by a high-pitched screech that shook Sidal, almost to the core.

It was opportune though; he'd reached the edge of the plate.

Beneath lay a wedge of darkness and a crawl space.

The screaming ended. Sidal heard a noise at the grate, accompanied by a low moan from the man he'd blinded.

He strained at the panel. The freedom beyond grew nearer, millimeter-by-millimeter.

A slick, flopping sound caused Sidal to turn and see something disgusting: a disembodied eye dangling loosely from the grate. Coated in a pink membranous tissue, it hung suspended from a misshapen, fleshy trunk.

The eye was cobalt blue. It dripped milky white fluid to the floor.

Gantz was giggling now. "Why I eyes ya!" he said. "All the live long day."

The other man groaned and said, "Aw you bastard, that hurt!"

"But can the eye see?" Gantz said, his tone more serious now.

Sidal grimaced at this sick madness and turned to the panel. His arms began to shake as it bent from his exertions.

"I see him!" the unknown man exclaimed. "He's trying to escape!"

The shock of hearing this made Sidal grit his teeth as he pushed harder than he'd thought possible.

The unknown man continued, his voice filled with panicked rage as he screamed. "Get the keys! He's escaping!"

Two events followed; the first was that the panel Sidal had been worrying at snapped forward with a thunderous crack. The second: Sidal lost his equilibrium and fell headlong into the hole he'd uncovered.

Six feet he fell into the bowels of the Walking Man. Landing face down, his forehead slammed onto a dusty metal floor that smelled thickly of oil.

Momentarily filled with sparks, his vision cleared and then he was on his hands and knees, shaking purpose back into his throbbing, bleeding head.

His nose dripped blood down onto the floor beneath him. Wiping it, he experienced a second of eye-watering pain but was soon up on his feet and off in a running crouch to escape the square of light lying beneath his escape route.

Sidal did not know where he ran, his bearings lost ever since he'd awoken within the cabin-turned-cell.

He thought it likely he was somewhere around the machine's lower torso. He would know for sure as soon as he reached a wall—or ran into one in the darkness. This thought had him slowing down, for he'd already nearly been knocked out by his fall, as his bloody nose attested. Doing so again would not be conducive to his survival. So he jogged with his hands raised before him, almost running straight into a girder as a result, and as there were still no signs of pursuit he decided to walk it. His jailers must still be having trouble finding their keys, he assumed.

His hands found a curved wall. So he was where he thought he'd be. One consolation.

Sidal followed the wall like a blind man, a hand held out and in constant motion as he searched for a handhold. He knew there would either be a ladder or hatch somewhere along the wall.

As he walked, he glanced intermittently towards the square of light he'd escaped from. It disappeared intermittently as girders got in the way, but he saw no signs of pursuit from that quarter. Perhaps his jailers were just too deranged to bother chasing after him. Sidal wasn't taking any chances.

He sped his gait and soon enough his hands reached a raised area and a handle. This avenue to freedom opened after a few panting tugs but creaked loudly, echoing through the dank space behind him as Sidal opened it up to light.

The light wasn't overly bright, but after the near darkness he found himself needing to squint regardless.

Pulling the door tight behind him, he opened his eyes fully to find he stood beneath a corridor circling the machine's torso, on a floor between its inner bulk and its outer shell. The floor plates above lay checkered with grids of light, making the dusty space surrounding him conducive to vision.

He was getting somewhere.

Again following a curved path, albeit in the opposite direction from where he'd entered, Sidal followed the tunnel looking for something to help him climb up.

He found it soon enough.

A thick-gauged pipe jutted up from the floor on the tunnel's outer side, following the curve and looking about the right height to assist his climb.

Climbing onto it, Sidal balanced himself precariously, feeling its warmth radiate through the heels of his boots. He reached to the nearest grate-bearing panel and pushed.

It held fast. Sidal's resulting *tut* invoked answering echoes around him. Louder echoes followed as he started punching the panel, his frustration growing with the strength of his assault until the panel popped off, clattering away above him.

Then silence, punctuated by Sidal's panting breath.

But no sound of pursuit, and after half a dozen deep, calming breaths Sidal jumped, pulling himself up through the hole and into the lighted corridor above.

He replaced the panel. Remaining in his crouch he examined the white, plastic-coated walls around him, starkly bright from the array of lights lining the ceiling.

There should be an elevator somewhere along these walls.

This pause caused him to consider his situation further.

Sidal had been so wrapped up in escaping his cell, he hadn't actually considered his plan once he had escaped. This freedom, as he followed the curve of the corridor, lay all around him.

All he could think of was to find more survivors, and if their numbers warranted such action, take back the Walking Man. Gusev City required warning regardless, and the radio equipment lay in the control room, up in the head.

He needed weapons then, but doubted the armory had been left unguarded.

Sidal found his train of thought interrupted. He paused mid-step. He'd come across one of the machine's oval-shaped intercom systems. Straddling the right-hand wall, one of its lights flashed.

A survivor?

Rushing towards it, he retrieved and put on one of the ear-mike headsets before examining the illuminated button.

The card beneath it read *Infirmary.*

He pressed the button, hesitantly.
Silence greeted him.
"Hello?"
More silence.
He was about to try another button when a variety of bumps and curses had him repeating his request.
"Hello?"
"Who's there?" Came a rasping whisper.
"Sidal," He replied, trying to place the other voice.
The judder of a throat being cleared was quickly followed by a voice he recognized as that of the chief medical officer, Doctor Casper.
"Heh, yeah, whatever." Casper sounded hesitant, suspicious even. "Sir, are you sane?"
Sidal stared around the corridor before nuzzling himself into the booth.
His voice became a whisper as he said, "I am ... but what about you?"
"Yeah. Well you sound okay. Heh. What's your status?"
"You first," Sidal retorted.
"Me? I've sealed myself in the infirmary, emergency viral protocols and such ... a load of crazy bastard crewmen are on the other side of the door trying to force their way in."
Sidal experienced déjà vu. Maybe the doctor *was* on the level.
The armory lay near the infirmary. Sidal questioned the doctor about this.
"That'd be suicide, they're bristling with guns out there. Are you feeling okay, sir?"
Sidal's confidence in the doctor's sanity was bolstered a little more.
"Done something to my nose," he replied. "Trouble breathing but it's nothing urgent. You?"
"Heh, I feel okay that you're okay."
Sidal found himself looking around again. He put it down to justified paranoia.
"Doctor you sound a little…"
"Stress induced morphine consumption," Casper interrupted. "I highly recommend it in my situation."
Sidal shook his head, but pitied the man also. He'd been in that situation.
"But what's your diagnosis, Doctor? What on Earth's gotten

into the crew?"

Casper was quiet for a few seconds, then emitted a strangled sound that may have been a laugh.

"You know the brain-computers, the scrubbed ones in the Walker's head?"

"Yeah?" Sidal did not like the way this was going. Casper's next words confirmed his suspicions.

"Well ... one of them's turned bad, been possessed by something ... evil."

"What? That's insane!" *Are you insane, Doctor?*

Casper snorted. "Any other explanation as to why this is happening?"

Recalling the incident with the eyeball, Sidal nodded. Then he recalled something far worse.

"They told me it's heading towards Gusev City. To destroy it!"

"Crap! This thing'll smash the place to shreds." Casper fell silent, then, "You have to get to the head, cripple the machine, destroy it."

It sounded like a plan, perhaps the only plan. Sidal sighed and rued the loss of the armory.

He tapped his fingers on the side of the booth, wondering where he could obtain a weapon. Then reflecting on Casper's possession theory, he asked, "How do you know so much anyway?"

Casper cackled. "I captured Ensign De Guevara in here, she was as crazy as the others but I managed to persuade some information out of her."

"So is there a cure to this insanity?" Sidal crossed his fingers.

"De Guevara's dead now, I dunno. Kill the brains and there may be a chance."

Sidal, wincing at this, said, "Why aren't we affected by this thing?"

A longer silence, the longest yet. He was about to repeat his question when Casper finally answered.

"Heh, my honest medical onion? Luck."

Your honest medical what? thought Sidal. "That'll do," he replied aloud, shaking his head. "I'm off, Doctor. Speak to you when all this is over."

"You're a brave man, sir. Good luck."

Sidal replied in kind before removing and replacing the headset.

"Doped up and as mad as a hatter," he muttered, heading away from the booth. *But is Casper right?* It was too incredible to imagine, but the doctor was correct in one respect: The Walking Man *had* to be stopped, and as the machine's only surviving high-ranking officer, it was his duty to stop the behemoth in its tracks. Assuming that nobody stopped *him*.

Somewhere along the curve would be an elevator; he hoped it wasn't guarded.

It wasn't, as a few dozen yards of walking proved, but there was someone in front of it. Even from a distance they appeared wrong. Closing in, Sidal found himself gagging at the sight.

A human form lay sprawled atop the white-paneled corridor, dressed in white but smothered in red. Pooled in blood, the floor plates around her lay crimson also.

A female ensign, partly uniformed, lay there eviscerated from her navel right up to her breasts. The latter shuddered to the Walking Man's progress.

Sidal halted before her, shuddering also. It was a disgusting sight, made more intense by the red slashes brutally criss-crossing her face.

He still recognized her though. Ensign Olgier. *Good officer.*

Her uniform lay a red ruin, the torn-open shirt revealing organs and intestines unfurled. One look was enough to tell him that her death had been both ugly and violent.

What terrible madness had the crew embraced? *I have to stop this thing.*

The elevator lay ahead and to the left of Olgier. Sidal noted this only partly as he stared across her ruined form, back towards her face. Within that face, slick with crimson, her eyes bulged like glazed gray marbles, her blonde hair lying red at the roots.

Sidal gulped and held the gorge back, glad that the damage to his nose hindered the intensity of Olgier's abattoir stench. Stepping past her he noted absently that one of her shoes was missing, a slender foot wrapped in pink pantyhose brushing his leg as he skirted around her.

Making a wide diversion around the accumulated pool of blood, wet still and reflecting the overhead lights, he saw his shadow fall across her and stopped in his tracks.

No.

He couldn't leave her like this, not dead and molested beneath the unforgiving brutality of the neon lights.

Removing his shirt, he kneeled and laid it upon her face and chest. He then turned towards the elevator dressed in only his pants and vest.

The elevator unit bore a cylindrical silver door. To its left was a panel consisting of eight square buttons. He pressed the topmost and the elevator whined into life; it would take him directly to the head.

Sidal thought about his lack of weapons then considered the corpse behind him. He clenched his fists. The elevator stopped whining and fell silent. He pressed the 8 button again. Nothing happened.

He was about to press it again when a shuffling noise made him freeze mid-reach. Then something wet took hold of his leg. A sound of slick shuffling followed.

Sidal closed his eyes. The voice he heard poured ice into his veins.

"Sir, could you help me put my bits back in?" it said, sounding both garbled and obscene.

Involuntarily, he opened his eyes and began to slowly turn his head.

The voice continued. "I can't get it all pushed in."

He completed his turn to find his shirt crumpled at his feet, stained red beneath the hand latched onto him. The other hand rose towards him limply.

It flopped into the blood with a smack and a splash. Sidal jumped. Her head raised, Olgier stared up from a shredded visage that still succeeded in portraying a pleading sadness.

Numb with shock, he utterly missed the distant but closing footsteps.

"Sir? Commander Sidal?"

His face transformed into a mask of grimacing horror.

"Sir?"

The footsteps grew closer.

Olgier's face changed now, forming a torn up grin of slashed gums and blood-slicked teeth.

"Here! He's Here!" She screamed, her grip on his trouser leg growing tighter.

Sidal snapped out of his stupor with a shudder. Olgier shouted again and he finally took note of the closing footsteps.

He tried freeing his leg. Failing, he pulled harder. The footsteps grew closer. Olgier laughed.

Sidal kicked her in the head, twice, and finally she released him. He started to run away from the elevator. Olgier's voice, mewling from between broken teeth, was quickly overtaken by far louder voices and the sounds of stamping feet.

Following the curve, he ran with no clear goal. He was considering going under the floor again when he spied the handle attached to an outer wall panel.

In a few quick, panicked movements it was open, then closed again with him behind it. He now stood on a narrow ledge with a sheer drop behind. Gripping the inner handle, he held his breath. The footsteps grew closer.

And closer, then they were past his position and off around the corridor. Ensign Olgier had fallen silent too. He felt as glad of this as the fact that his pursuers had lost his trail. *Probably just playing dead again though*, he realized, waiting in ambush for the next sane sucker to blunder her way.

It was insane. And madness was one thing, but the reanimation of the dead? Impossible. But Sidal had more important things to consider right now, like survival.

The ledge was wide enough to accommodate his feet but hardly allowed room for movement. Behind him stood the outer shell of the Walking Man and between his ledge and this: a curve of darkness. And if the machine lost its stability even a little he would find himself tumbling through this darkness to his death.

With this in mind he started moving right from his entry point, quickly but carefully shuffling around the curve because he knew that somewhere ahead would be a ladder leading up the Walking Man's trunk.

The fear of falling or discovery took their toll with every step as flashing images of the terrors he'd witnessed reappeared in the darkness. Then his knuckles slapped something new: the tubular edge he wished for. Though replacing the ledge with a hole, Sidal still made silent thanks for the ladder's existence. He mounted it with care and began to climb.

The machine's stability gained even more importance now. Even the Walking Man's gently rocking footsteps unnerved him as he ascended through the darkness. Taking floor by floor, his hands sweaty on the rungs, more than once he found himself having to stop to wipe them before continuing.

Sidal's journey took an age, perspiring in the darkness. No signs of pursuit though, and he only knew that he'd reached his destination when his head hit an obstruction.

It was a hatch, and if his suspicions were correct, it would either lead into the head or to one of the shoulders flanking it.

Discovering his location was simply accomplished by reaching into the darkness to his left. His fingers found an array of nebulous objects, including the eyes and rubber skin of a bulbously shaped oxygen mask. This meant that the Martian atmosphere lay above him, ergo: he was beneath one of the shoulders.

Sidal would've preferred the head, but he was at least nearing his goal. His mission of destruction to avoid destruction was almost over.

He slipped on the mask one-handed. Turning a knob on, the nose flooded the mask with metallic-tinged air. Exploring the area provided another useful discovery: the rubber-gripped handle of a flare gun. He tucked this into his pants. It could be used as a weapon, at close range.

Again one-handed, he began turning the hatch's handle, using the other to maintain a tight grip on the ladder.

Two counterclockwise rotations and it lay unlocked. Sidal shoved the hatch up and open to flood the space around him with icy cold air and light.

The sweat on his body turned cold. Sidal blinked and adjusted to the abrupt change in atmosphere as he completed his ascent towards the Walking Man's shoulder.

The air was freezing. He shivered and wrapped his arms around himself as he quickly took account of his bearings.

He found himself standing upon the machine's left shoulder. He'd climbed out facing its rear.

A pink sky surrounded him, the dim blob of Sol hovering in the distance half-concealed by purple-hued clouds. It looked beautiful to eyes used to walls and artificial light. The metal beneath his feet lay rusty and strewn with sand.

Sidal turned, crouching a little to accommodate the machine's slowly plodding movement.

He'd turned to the Walking Man's head, darkly silhouetted against the sky. Huge and uncouth in dimension it resembled an Easter Island Tiki head.

The thick-lipped, heavy browed profile rocked gently to the movement of its legs, as did Sidal. He took a quick look to his left, seeing a rocky brown landscape beyond which lay his family and Gusev City, before heading for the hatch on the Walking Man's neck.

Without the benefit of an environment suit Sidal gave himself mere minutes before succumbing to the unforgiving Martian atmosphere.

The Walking Man

Thankfully, he needed far less than that.

Rushing across the Walking Man's barrel-like trunk he was soon at the hatch, unscrewing it while attempting to ignore the ice forming across his back.

Two counterclockwise rotations and it stood unlocked. Sidal opened the hatch to a space gray with half-light. A few seconds later and he was again inside the Walking Man.

Sidal retained his mask; it helped contain his panicked breathing. Still his heart beat like a drum. Closing the hatch as quietly as possible, he turned back to his goal—a huge, perfectly formed cylinder sitting snug within the machine's misshapen head. The roof of this bore the brains of the matter, literally.

He looked left, right, then up. The restriction of his mask made him doubly careful as he walked right until halting at a ladder.

An elevator stood a little further around, but operating this would bring undue attention, he was sure.

He took a deep breath, wiping his hands against his trousers before beginning his ascent.

His climb was a hesitant one. He felt unsure of his surroundings even though he had spent the majority of his daily life in the room above. Since the plague of madness had begun, all bets were off.

Reaching the top of the ladder, which lay between a gap in the handrail surrounding the control room, it appeared to Sidal that nothing had changed. True, the Walking Man's brainpan, a lower, squatter cylinder at the center of the one he had just mounted, obscured much of his view, but still, the consoles lining the handrail beyond, and the chair-mounted telescopes facing the machine's lozenge-shaped eyes, betrayed nothing untoward.

Climbing into a crouch, he edged slowly left until catching sight of his first signs of life.

Two ensigns and two officers stood before the central control panel, facing straight ahead and ignoring all but the view before them. Noting this with relief, Sidal crept towards the brainpan, wary to avoid nudging the pipes twisting out towards the consoles.

A few seconds later and his hands were on its rim. He raised his head over it. His heart pounding loudly against his ears, he forced his breath to slow as he stared into a sluggish pool of thick, pinkish liquid.

Deep within this, five pink disembodied brains hung suspended, rocking gently within its viscous depths.

After taking a wary look towards the pilots, he proceeded to pull himself higher, leaning over the pan for a closer examination.

I have absolutely no idea which one of these is the 'bad one,' he thought with apprehension. *I'm going to have to kill them all.*

Sidal reached towards his belt buckle. *Let's hope the flare gun's enough.*

He didn't know what, if anything, gave his presence away, certainly he thought he had been moving stealthily enough, but as he pointed the gun into the brainpan a loud 'crack' preceded a gaping hole in his chest. Sidal gaped down at this momentarily before feeling weak all over. He tipped into the pan with a splash he barely heard. His vision turned black.

The change came as soon as he touched the liquid. It was something miraculous.

The pain disappeared. He couldn't even feel his body. But he could hear voices, in his head, psychic intrusions from only one, unimaginable source.

Thirty-two minutes till contact with Gusev City.

Some of us are not in concurrence.

Suggest change of course then.

Tried that thirteen times. Will try again.

Three voices, two male, one female.

Non-concurrence, still, the female voice said.

Unconnected brain in proximity, a valuable tool in ceasing this operation, one of the male voices said.

Then Sidal could see again, but he wasn't in the brainpan.

Instead, a wide expanse of space lay before him, outer space. By the looks of things he was in his very own solar system, but he was a giant now. Looking down he discovered he now bore the form of the Walking Man, gigantic and static in the ether.

He wasn't alone.

The huge, ringed form of Saturn lay before him, tilted on its side and spinning on its axis. To his right lay deep darkness, and to his left? He turned from Saturn to see Venus and Mercury, small in the distance and flanking Sol's glowing orange orb.

This is a dream, he said.

Of course it is, said a voice behind him.

You're seeing a representation of our forms, the female voice, Venus said.

While you're here you can help us retake control, boomed Saturn.
And kill the one that wants to murder your city, Mercury continued.
But how do I?
Turn right, think your body right, said the voice behind him and Sidal obeyed.

This movement sent the other celestials out of view, bringing him into contact with the invisible voice's source.

It was Mars. Mottled orange and black, he glowed with power.

I'm here to help you, he said. *We're all here to help you,* the others added as Sidal found himself moving counterclockwise until only the black depths of space lay visible.

He's in the outer rim, Saturn said. *Lurking there with death on his mind.*

You can do it! Venus said enthusiastically. *Just think yourself forward.*

Kill the bastard, kill him dead, said Mars.

We believe in you! Mercury said.

We concur, the others added in unison.

Sidal concentrated on the void and a moment later he was speeding through darkness spotted with intermittent stars.

He saw nothing but continued regardless. His force of will pushed him through the ether and towards…?

You're being attacked again, Venus cried.

We're trying to stop them but you need to speed things up, Mars added, his tone loud and forceful.

A tiny gray blot appeared. As it grew, his stomach curdled.

It pervaded badness thoroughly, something dark within the darkness.

The emanations, invisible though palpable, pushed forcefully but Sidal pushed back.

Dull pinks became visible within the gray, making the planet appear blotchy and disease ridden. It exuded a pure, baleful evil.

Pluto: the brain gone bad.

Close enough to touch the unwholesome orb, Sidal reached out, and froze.

His metal hands, thick-fingered and huge, hovered over Pluto and although they twitched, they could do naught else.

Pluto laughed, a sinister, demented sound that reverberated through the darkness.

Sidal, attempting to speak, found his throat clogged up.

He gasped, his mouth opening to disgorge a cloud of viscous red, shifting and curling through the ether.

A voice broke through the silence, Saturn. *You've been shot*, he said, plainly and without aplomb. *You won't last much longer.*

Pluto cackled.

Sidal looked down, trying to reach those few extra miles to crush away Pluto's unwholesome life.

His fingers twitched, then fell still.

They've shot you five times now, said Venus.

You're dying but you can still help us fight it. This was Mercury. *Use your mind to join us.*

What do I do, what do I do? His anxious words blew a tunneling hole through the blood cloud.

Open your eyes, Mars said. Sidal obeyed.

Something strange but miraculous happened, and it was no illusion.

A landscape view of sandy orange desert lay before him, far beneath his feet as he stepped across the Martian vista. His huge legs made short work of this uneven panorama, as he received a picture-perfect view through the eyes of The Walking Man.

He *was* the Walking Man, lumbering and gigantic, heading towards Gusev's doom in incessantly loping steps.

Gusev City, her towers, spires and domed roofs, lay silhouetted against a horizon turned dark ruby with night.

Sidal strode ever closer.

He tried to stop, willing himself to a halt. Nothing happened. A tumorous, unwelcome presence cackled.

We've tried that, Venus said sadly.

But its control is too strong, bemoaned Saturn.

There's only one option if we want to save the city, Mars said. *Help us start the rocket boosters. Send us right into space.*

Sidal balked. *We're not built for space travel! Not with human occupants still inside.*

It's a sacrifice I know, but thousands, more even, will be saved, Mercury replied.

What do I do? Gusev City's closing, twinkling lights added panicked imperative to his words.

Hold on. Saturn said, *they're trying to fish your body out.*

Concentrate on your feet, Mars said, *imagine them igniting.*

The Walking Man

While we seal the brainpan, the others added.

Sidal concentrated.

And a shuddering roar filled the landscape. The Walking Man froze mid-step as the fuel in its calves sent whirlwinds of smoke and sand tearing up from the soles of its feet.

We're going up! Venus said with enthusiasm.

Gusev City sank beneath Sidal, replaced by blood-red sky. He panicked mid-air, but could not move to illustrate it.

Where will we go?

He realized now that he wasn't speaking with his mouth, but with his mind, and had been for some time. His body was dead, he concluded.

And you peed the tank when you died, Venus moaned. *How undignified!*

His head touched purple cloud cover, breaking it asunder as he rose ever higher.

The red surrounding him deepened, darkening to black.

Where will we go? he repeated.

To explore the Universe! The voices replied in chorus, all except for one.

Pluto's tumorous presence remained sullenly silent.

Sidal experienced an invigorating freedom as the Walking Man escaped the Martian atmosphere. He saw stars twinkling in the darkness near the Tannhäuser Gate.

Infinite space! He thought and smiled.

And the red globe of Mars, ever diminishing beneath his feet, dwindled away, in safety and in peace.

Part II:
Alien Menaces

Natural Selection

Simon Bleaken

For Jane McCaa

The beetles were feeding again. Breaking and crushing loose chunks of rock with their sharp mandibles and extracting the metal ores within; digesting them to reinforce their own metallic brown elytra that glinted with a dull luster in the late afternoon sunlight.

Nearby, crouching on the edge of a low grassy ridge, a micro-definition camera clutched excitedly in her hands, Rebecca Aaron watched these unique creatures in rapt fascination, even though she had seen them feed countless times before. She lifted the small recorder to her bulky breather unit, dictating into it between snaps of the camera, knowing that the beetles wouldn't react to her presence.

"The native coleoptera are the largest of their kind I have ever seen," she noted. "Their adult size is roughly equivalent to that of a small dog; measuring on average between fourteen to eighteen inches in length, and eight to ten inches in width. Their larvae are each at least the size of a mouse. Like the beetles back on Earth, they have the characteristic sheath-like elytra and complex chewing mouthparts; and their larvae are sedentary blind grubs, with the typical three pairs of legs on the thorax."

Clicking off the recorder she edged forward, spellbound as these huge but harmless giants wandered around their nest site—something more common for ants than beetles; yet these coleoptera seemed to have an intricately developed social structure. But that was only part of the appeal of these incredible insects—there was so much about them that was unique and unknown, so much still to document and understand of their complex biology. She couldn't deny it, she was hooked.

Shifting closer and lying flat against the damp terracotta soil, she angled her camera at the closest insect, trying to capture as many varied images as she could get, hoping for some insight into their behavior that had so far eluded her.

One of the smaller beetles, clearly a juvenile, lumbered over to her, exploring. She flattened her hand, allowing the beetle to roam across it, the bristly legs tickling and probing her skin. Its powerful mandibles flexed and clicked, but Rebecca wasn't concerned. She'd quickly learned in her months of study that they were absolutely harmless, despite their fearsome appearance and incredible strength; she could even walk barefoot amongst them in safety. Metal ore was the only thing that interested them, and while she didn't yet understand how they managed to draw sustenance from it, she had discovered that they seemed to ignore processed metals and alloys altogether.

It still astounded her that the prospectors and settlement scouts who had visited this world back in the thirties had deemed it valueless, just another rock not worth the effort of terraforming. That decision had been made mainly because the ores and minerals it contained were of no use for industrial purposes. The fact that the air was slightly toxic and required the use of filtering masks to breathe had also played a major part in discouraging settlers from coming here.

So much the better, for Rebecca had no love for the human race.

Although her life and career as a zoologist derived from her deep passion for studying the myriad forms of life that were constantly being discovered on newly charted worlds, coleoptera and arachnids especially, her heart remained cold toward her own species; noisy, destructive, and self-centered humanity, moving and spreading like a cancer through the stars. It angered her to think that after having torn up, squandered, and abused the Earth's precious natural resources, they had now started doing the same to the other planets in the universe. It also enraged her that the prospectors who had found this world, and the scientists who had traveled with them, had assessed the indigenous giant beetle population as worthless and unremarkable. To her, although they were clearly creatures of limited intelligence, they were far more intriguing than most people she had known, not to mention preferable company—never talking too much, never criticizing, never breaking promises or letting her down. With her beetles it was a straightforward case of "what you saw was what you got", pure and simple. And what she saw was as close to a slice of heaven as she had ever experienced in this cold, godless universe.

That was when she'd arranged to come out here. She'd been

surprised with the speed at which her research grant had been cleared, having expected the usual tiresome delays at the dithering hands of bureaucracy who reveled in gift-wrapping all requests in red tape. She suspected it had something to do with the fact that her colleagues at the Zoological Institute had never gotten along with her. Deep down, even Rebecca had to admit that with her single-minded drive and burning obsession to achieve results at the exclusion of all else, she wasn't the easiest of people to get along with. She had managed to put more than a few noses out of joint along the way. Her colleagues themselves—a group for whom she had little time and even less respect, had called her a bitter and jaded cynic, incapable of warmth and compassion. Some had even remarked—when they thought she was out of earshot—how sorry they felt for the beetles, having to put up with her.

Rebecca honestly didn't care what they thought. After all, Dian Fossey hadn't been truly appreciated in her own time either. The best people never were.

It was getting late now. Growing shadows began to creep across the land as the sun set in the blood-red sky. Reluctantly, Rebecca slipped her camera into its case and set off through the dense brown vegetation that covered the planet; picking her way through glistening leaves and vines slick with moisture, surrounded by small clustered clouds of buzzing insects, the earthy smelling mulch squishing damply underfoot. The humid, sticky air made her t-shirt feel clammy, and sweat darkened the areas under her armpits and down her back, but she barely noticed, having long grown used to such discomforts.

The planet itself had no official name—just a basic seven-digit coordinate code, but she had taken it upon herself to name her new home. She had chosen Karisoke, in honor of the study site where Dian Fossey had worked for twenty-two years studying mountain gorillas. For although Fossey had lived and died long before Rebecca had been born, her work, life, and sheer dedication to her chosen field had been a major source of inspiration.

Halfway to the habitation module, Rebecca stopped, looking out over a small gorge at the lush tropical plant-life and massive savannas of Karisoke, hearing the cries, calls and hooting wails of the animals forming the planet's complex ecosystem. Somewhere deep in the vegetation she could hear something ponderous picking its way along, its clumsy progress sending flocks of wild flying creatures winging into the sky with angry, startled shrieks. The setting sun cast a glossy reddish sheen across the foliage, making it look as though the leaves and grass were awash with blood. Large floating seeds and spores drifted lazily in the air like oversized dust motes. The tropical beauty and solitude of this world never failed to strike her with awe. It was a place full of wild, dramatic splendor; but the savage efficiency of the natural world had always appealed to her. Little was wasted here, everything had a purpose and a reason for being—a link in the great and fragile ecosystem. It had taken her a while to get used to the sight of brown vegetation, so different from the chlorophyll green that populated her own world. But then, so much here had taken time to grow accustomed to at first. The sky was always a deep orange-red during the day, turning a dark and moody purple-black when it rained. The night was much darker than on Earth, with no cities to cast light pollution. There was also no moon to reflect the light from the system's sun after dark, leading to some of the darkest nights she had ever seen—but allowing the stars in all their beauty to shine through; not that she could pick out any familiar constellations from here, although they were all still out there: Orion, Taurus, Canis Major, The Big Dipper. She was just seeing them from the wrong angle to make them out.

Yes, this stunning world was hers alone, as were the beetles, and it was a great joy to her not to have to share it. Nor was that likely ever to change, since most people tended to cluster on the nearest habitable planets closest to Earth. For despite the way it had been popularly fictionalized before commercial space travel became a reality, the truth had quickly hit home to the people of the Earth: space was a big disappointment. Interstellar travel was long and tedious, lacking amenities and comfort. The under-supplied colonies were cramped, difficult to maintain, and often rife with crime and racial hostility. Space had also opened up hitherto unknown diseases and viral pathogens, and had found new dangerous animals that made the scorpions, rattlesnakes, and black widows of Earth look harmless by comparison. Yes, the novelty had quickly faded, and few were curious enough to brave the discomforts to travel beyond the overcrowded colony worlds.

Arriving back at her battered habitation module, she let herself inside the inner-lock, and purged the outside atmosphere before removing her breather and stepping into the artificially purified and filtered environment. Overhead fans turned lazily, beating back the stifling humidity.

She pulled the clasp from her dark hair, and ran a hand through it, shaking it down around her shoulders. Kicking off her boots, she switched on the light and powered up her computer terminal, ready to record the day's findings and store them onto a DHT chip. As she slipped in a spare chip and keyed in her observations for the day, she glanced up with a smile at the small web in the corner of the room.

Incy was out and about.

She stood, stretching wearily, one hand lazily brushing an errant strand of hair back behind her ear; then leaned over, peering closely at him. He was truly a handsome specimen, even for a common house spider. Eight long, slender legs delicately balanced on the web, avoiding the sticky snare-lines; pedipalps carefully feeling and sensing the world around it. Like coleoptera, arachnids never ceased to amaze and impress her. Unlike the stumbling progress of humanity who took years to develop, grow and learn as they limped clumsily toward adulthood, spiders were born with the knowledge of how to spin webs and hunt. They were survivors, and had followed humanity—first as they explored the planet Earth, settling even into arctic research stations and remote settlements—and then, finally, on the giant leap into space. Incy, as she had named him, must have traveled with her inside one of the storage crates, for there were no natural arachnids on Karisoke.

"How's your day been?" she asked jokingly, taking care not to disturb the web as she spoke. It seemed unlikely that the sealed and filtered air supply of the habitat would provide an opportunity for any flies or tropical mosquitoes to get inside the living space to feed Incy. But sometimes they did manage to get in—possibly through the airlock with her when she returned home each day. Sometimes she would catch some for him, and release them near his web, so that they flew in as they escaped the confines of her container.

Outside, there came the first faint rumbles of thunder, and large dime-sized drops of rain began to slap against the roof of the habitat. Rebecca turned the switch on the lamp units, brightening the crowded interior, as the rain began to lash down upon the world outside in unbroken sheets of water. The steady *hissing* spray drowning out all other sounds, drumming on the roof and windows, forming a constant background sound, as she finished her reports of the day's observations and reviewed briefly the notes she had taken on her tenth day, when she had caught and dissected one of the beetles—a task she had painfully regretted, but one which had been invaluable in providing some clues to the remarkable life-cycle and digestive process of these remarkable insects.

Finally she sat back in her chair with an exhausted sigh, rubbing her eyes with her fingers, feeling the first tell-tale signs of a headache starting there. She pushed back the chair and stood, stretching her aching back, making slow lazy circles of her head and hearing her neck click as she did. It had been a long day, tiring but rewarding. Despite the weariness that settled upon her, she felt alive and connected to the planet around her, a sense of home and belonging that she had never felt on Earth. Hard to believe she had only been out here two months now. Sometimes it felt as though she had always known this place. As if the planet Earth had been nothing but a crazy, chaotic dream of noise, pollution, and heaving masses of ignorant and annoying human beings.

Outside the rain continued to *hiss* against the habitat, a continuous and unceasing white noise that some might have found irritating, but that she merely found soothing. If it hadn't been for the toxic air outside, she might have peeled off her sweat-stained t-shirt and muddy khaki pants and simply walked outside, enjoying the coolness of the air and water as it washed the accumulated grime and sweat from her skin. Instead, she would settle for a regular shower in the tiny, cramped cubical that was barely large enough for her to squeeze into.

Nights were quiet here on Karisoke, away from the rush and bustle of colonized worlds; although they were never fully silent, filled as they were with the furtive rustling, hooting, and bellowing of life in all its myriad forms, getting about the business of living, hunting and self-perpetuation. But while others might have found the isolation, and lack of a social nightlife distressing and even maddening, Rebecca welcomed it with open arms. Had it been a physical, tangible thing she might very well have wrapped herself in it like a thick, warm blanket. She had no need for human companionship; out here she was free and the world was hers to savor and enjoy. The breather spoiled the illusion a little, but the magic of the atmosphere was unsullied. She still recalled vividly the first night, when Karisoke had welcomed her with a spectacular meteor shower that lit the night sky like a hundred blazing streamers of fire as the meteors burned up in the lower ionosphere, victims of air friction. Although she had not seen anything quite like that since, each night never failed to offer her something new and wonderful—from the sunsets that simply dazzled her with their overwhelming beauty, to the nocturnal mating of what had seemed to be some kind of native fireflies.

Tonight however, it seemed the regularly scheduled show had been canceled, due to rain.

That night she had trouble dropping off to sleep, the headache had hit with full force, suddenly and sadistically transforming itself from a nagging ache into a full-blown skull-cracking migraine. The paracetamol patch she had administered had done nothing for it.

She finally fell asleep in the still hours shortly after midnight, when the rain had petered off to a fine drizzle. The last sound she heard was the trickling of water from the roof of the habitat, and her dreams were filled with vivid memories of the river by the house on Earth, where she had lived as a child.

The next morning, she knew as she opened her eyes that her simple headache of the night before had been nothing less than the vanguard of a full-blown virus. Her whole body felt chilled to the core, and her head throbbed madly, the pain seemingly centered behind her aching eyes. At least there was no sign of the usual sore throat that normally always accompanied such things, and that left her feeling as if each swallow contained broken glass and sandpaper. She rolled weakly onto her side, drawing back the blind and peering out, her sensitive eyes flinching at the intense brightness of the light. The rain had completely stopped, and the ground and vegetation sparkled with a reddish sheen in the sunlight.

A sudden dizziness overcame her as she swung her legs out of the bed and stood up, and she sat heavily back down. She rested for a few minutes with her head in her hands, hair flowing down over her fingers, as she waited for the sensation to pass. She had drugs and medicines aplenty in her supply case, so finding something to ease the discomfort wouldn't be hard, but it was damn inconvenient when she had been looking forward to a full day in the field with her beetles.

She slipped on a fresh t-shirt and then grabbed her thick jacket—something she had brought with her, but never yet needed on this tropical planet. Still she felt intensely cold, and walked slowly to a mirror. Her own face, ghostly pale and shivering, framed with her disheveled morning hair stared back at her. *God, I look terrible*, she thought. Suddenly an intense shiver raced through her and she grabbed the edge of the counter as the habitat seemed to spin and churn around her. She squeezed her eyes shut, then stumbled desperately toward the small, enclosed bathroom as the intense urge to vomit welled up within her. She barely made it in time, and after the distasteful deed was done, she sat on the floor with her arms wrapped around her, shivering. Perhaps today would be better spent indoors after all, she decided.

Three hours later, after taking some of the high-strength permaxical from her medicine cabinet, she began to feel a little more in control of herself. The shivering had subsided, as had the nausea, although the damn headache stubbornly refused to leave and pulsed like an evil heart beating right behind her eyes. She spent the next hour staring out the window, at the clouds drifting lazily overhead, and watching the arboreal creatures soar and wing above and around the tree line. Finally she decided enough was enough—she felt better now; not a hundred percent, no—but certainly up for a visit to her beetles, although she would give her usual morning jog a miss. Besides, it was maddening to be stuck inside the habitat, even if she did have Incy for company. The filtered air in here always seemed stale, as though something wholesome had been removed during the purification process, and she had never been much of an indoor person anyway.

Rebecca actually began to feel a little better as she trudged slowly along the path she had marked, back toward the beetles' nest. The breather unit seemed a little heavier today, her steps were slower and lacked her usual enthusiasm, and her limbs felt like clumsy lead weights—but it was good to be outside and roaming freely.

She gazed out across the gorge as she passed it, a habit that she had developed since her first day, for the view was always breathtaking. Today, a low ground mist covered the area, adding a mysterious, hazy quality to the landscape as it swirled. Above this came the screeching chorus of the arboreal creatures interspersed with the rustling and grunts of other animals hunting and feeding in the tall ferns between the trees. She waited there for a few minutes, her breathing calmer and her head, despite feeling like her sinuses were stuffed with warm cotton wool, felt a little more focused. Then she continued, as fast as her uncooperative limbs would allow, on toward the nest site.

She settled down on her favorite rock overlooking the nest. As she had expected for this time of the day, the nest was a hive of bustling activity—but she quickly noticed some kind of commotion among a small group of the beetles not too far from where she was sitting. Standing clumsily and almost overbalancing, Rebecca crept closer, wishing her head didn't feel like it was spinning quite as much. A group of about ten to fifteen coleoptera had surrounded a single member of the group, who was standing over the torn carcass of a juvenile. Judging by the dark blood staining the mandibles of the larger insect, it had been responsible for the death of the younger one. Rebecca watched with captivated interest. During her observations she had witnessed a few fights—possibly struggles to assert dominance or leadership, but had never witnessed one of the beetles actually kill another before.

What happened next took her completely by surprise.

With a speed, coordination, and ferocity that startled her, the surrounding beetles charged toward the singled-out individual, the light glinting from their metallic chitinous forewings as they converged and began tearing into the victim, stripping away its shiny brown elytra in a ruthless attack. Then, as quickly as it had started, it was all over, and the beetles all withdrew as one. Rebecca edged closer still, putting one hand out against a nearby rock to steady herself, caution giving way to curiosity as she leaned forward to get a better look. To her astonishment the singled-out beetle was still alive, but its hard protective casing had been totally removed, and the remaining coleoptera were now gently herding it towards the edge of the nest site, while yet more gently carried away the remains of the slain juvenile.

Rebecca felt a flutter of excitement as she watched the proceedings. This had never been expected, not behavior of this kind. Had she just seen what she thought she had seen? Had they just punished one of their members for murdering another? By removing his protective shell, they had in essence left him defenseless to the elements—and now they were clearly casting him out of the nest site.

Just wait, she smiled to herself, momentarily forgetting her own physical discomfort. *When those idiots at the institute read about this, they're going to be kicking themselves.* But suddenly that same thought chilled her, and the smile slipped from her face. If she told them, they'd want to send more people out here to assist her. *I think I'll hold off on submitting this, at least until I make some more observations. And that,* she thought smugly, *could take months.*

By the time she got home, dusk had settled on the land, and she collapsed onto her bed, totally exhausted. She curled onto her side, not even bothering to get undressed, and fell into a deep and delicious sleep.

In her dreams she was back on Earth, heading into the imposing glass and steel headquarters of the Zoological Institute to hear the final decision regarding her request to transfer to Karisoke to study the indigenous beetle population there.

She stepped inside and carefully removed her breather unit, and the protective membranes from her eyes, storing them in the container of cleaning solution she always carried with her. The pollution levels of the Earth had grown to such an extent that such measures were required. She moved briskly down the hallway from the stark metal reception area, past rooms where biologists and scientists were busily scurrying about in their white lab coats, like frantic mice locked within a maze too vast and insidious for them to see or comprehend. Within minutes she was being admitted into the main meeting area on the administration level, an ugly room of stark modern efficiency; gleaming glass, chrome and steel, dark varnished woods, and shiny marbled flooring. An artificial kingdom ruled by flawed and blind people. Self-elected gods in a shrine of plastic and polymers, ruling their judgments over the natural world they had secretly forsaken.

This is it, she told herself bitterly. *They're going to deny my request. They know how much I want this, so they'll keep me from it.* She knew they disliked her—said she was too outspoken; accused her of clinging to ideas and beliefs not suited to the modern age. She had no time for their opinions, and no desire to listen to their pompous debating—but the truth was, if she had any hope of getting to Karisoke, she needed their approval.

That had been the day they had all surprised her, and allowed her to go...

When she awoke the next morning, it was to an agony which made the previous day's illness seem like a dress rehearsal. It was a little before dawn when she opened her eyes, aware that her whole body was shivering—despite the fact that she was drenched in sweat. She threw the damp, wrinkled sheets aside, and staggered to her feet—almost falling to the floor as another wave of dizziness swept over her. Each breath she took was like inhaling a lung-full of burning acid, and her clammy skin looked horribly yellowed with the clear signs of jaundice. *No way is this just a simple viral infection,* she thought, slumping down into her chair before her computer terminal. She reached over and grabbed the front of the medicine cabinet, thankful it was well stocked to last until the next supply vessel arrived to bring her fresh equipment. She applied three Taslodex patches to her arms, slightly more than the recommended average dose, but she was far from caring about that, and slumped back with her eyes closed. As she rested, she tried to figure out what might be causing this sudden illness. However, as far as she could recall she had neither been bitten nor stung by any of the flora or fauna here, nor had she been outside without a breather unit. Her fruits and vegetables were grown inside a separate hydroponics unit attached directly to her habitat, and the air and water running into them were filtered and purified. Surely there was something she was missing, but what? The beetles? No, that was unlikely. She'd studied them closely for two months now, and there was nothing harmful about them, they certainly contained no toxins...

She opened her eyes an hour later and realized she had fallen asleep in the chair. Her neck was stiff, her aching body wracked with shivers, and her damp clothes were pasted to her clammy skin with sweat.

She climbed gingerly to her feet, intending to take some Permaxical to augment the Taslodex patches she had applied earlier, before slipping into bed. However, she froze with her hand resting on the medicine cabinet, staring into the corner of the habitat.

Incy lay curled in a tight ball on the surface of the desk just below his web.

She didn't have to touch him to know he was dead, and at the sight of him a dreadful suspicion crept into her mind. Walking stiffly and slowly, she passed along the small sectional corridor leading into the hydroponics bay and opened the door. When the door slid aside she stared in numb shock, her worst suspicions becoming a cruel reality before her eyes. The plants in the bay, transported as seeds from Earth, were turning brown and wilting. Their leaves were starting to shrivel, horribly imitating the way Incy had curled in death.

There was no doubt now. There was a breach somewhere in the habitat and toxic air from outside was steadily leaching in.

She hurried back into the habitat, stumbling against the desk as her legs gave way beneath her. The urge to defecate suddenly came upon her, a sensation like a small tornado was churning within her bowels, and she barely had time to scrabble her way into the small bathroom before a stinging stream of waste came pouring from within her.

When she at last emerged from the bathroom, pale and shivering, her vision starting to blur and her stomach feeling no less stable than it had a few moments before, the first thing she did was reach for the breather. It was the only thing she could do. Maybe once she stopped breathing the unfiltered air, the side-effects of her exposure to the toxic atmosphere would pass. Then she could set about finding and sealing the leak into the habitat.

But as her fingers closed around the breather, it crumbled in her grip, breaking into several brittle plastic and metal fragments that clattered to the floor. Puzzled, she grabbed the spare breather lying beside it—but again, the same thing happened. At the sight of this, the despair and the miserable agony became unbearable and she sank to her knees, sobbing in bitter frustration.

It's not fair! Why the hell is this happening? She drove her fist down onto the desk, pounding the surface until the rage within subsided, trying not to give in to the terror that followed in its wake.

Something scuttled quickly across the floor, catching her attention, and she looked up in time to see it scurry beneath her bed.

Rebecca watched it with confused and mesmerized horror, convinced for a moment that she must have been seeing things. Then it hit her. It had been one of the coleoptera that she had been studying—but what had it been doing so far from the nest? She had never seen any come this far before.

A quick relocation of her bed revealed a large opening in the habitat wall, the edges of which had clearly been torn open by the sharp mandibles of the beetles—yet the metal, being processed from various alloys, had simply been discarded on the ground and not consumed.

Why would they...?

Then another terrible thought hit her, and she hurried outside, staggering and almost bent double as a sharp cramp cut through her. Her bowels opened again before she could stop herself, and she collapsed onto the dark soil, tears blurring her eyes.

When she finally made it around the other side of the habitat, she opened the protective panel covering the air filter system, and peered inside. The whole unit had been shredded and torn apart, the twisted fragments littered the floor of the compartment—and in the far wall was another hole, again large enough for the beetles to squeeze in through.

It was then that the true state of things came slamming home like a sledgehammer blow. With no breathers, no air filter—and not enough spare parts to completely rebuild the damaged unit, there was no chance at all to survive. The next supply vessel wasn't due for months, and the Zoological Institute wouldn't grow suspicious when she didn't report in, because Rebecca had a noted habit of going for long periods without contacting them.

For a long time Rebecca simply knelt there, staring at the ruin that had once been her lifeline. She had been advised not to come by the institute, or at least to come with a team, but she had refused; her own antisocial preferences winning out over common sense. She had refused the extra equipment they said she needed. She wanted to show them she didn't need them or their ways. And now this had come of it.

She raised a trembling hand to her mouth, her body and senses suddenly numb and cold. The world around her seemed too bright all of a sudden—too starkly defined and in colors that seemed unreal and garish. The world began to sway like the deck of a boat on a stormy ocean, but she squeezed her eyes tight and fought against the urge ... *the need* ... to vomit.

The desperate scream that had been building within her all this time now broke free; a hoarse, ragged scream of terrified, hopeless, misery. The disbelief and a sense of sudden loneliness, unlike any she had felt before, overwhelmed her like a foul and stinking cloud of fetid darkness; sapping her spirit and threatening to send her mind and sanity tumbling into a churning helter-skelter of senseless chaos.

For now there was nowhere to go, and nothing to be done.

When the supply ship arrived two months later, there was no sign of the habitat in the clearing. Only a few remaining fragments of twisted metal remained, sticking up out of the ground like the bones of some long dead corpse. Only after digging and poking around the underbrush did the rest of the habitat turn up—in fragments scattered throughout the bushes and buried beneath the damp terracotta soil.

Rebecca Aaron's body was found shortly afterward, not far from the clearing, badly decomposed and heavily picked over by animals to the point of being virtually unrecognizable. In the curled claw of bone and rotting flesh that once had been her hand, they found a single battered DHT chip, badly corroded by the elements and caked with dirt. Much of the chip was corrupted beyond repair, except for the last handful of entries—mostly observations from her last few days of study. But along with them, the members of the Zoological Institute also found her final message when, her body slowly dying from the poisonous atmosphere against which she now had no protection, she had fought against her sickness to record her own fate:

"It's getting cold. The roof is leaking, and the floor's flooded. It's hard to keep writing—fingers are trembling so bad I keep missing the keys. There's a burning in my stomach now. It's getting hard to breathe, too.

"The beetles are outside. I can see them in the fading light. Jesus, they're just *waiting* out there, not even moving. There must be hundreds of them—looks like the whole damn lot of them. At least, all the ones from the nest I was studying anyway. I think they're watching me. I think they know what they've done ... stripped away my protection, leaving me vulnerable ... just like that outcast beetle that I saw. Sounds crazy, but that's what they're doing. Did I once say I thought them unintelligent? What the hell was I thinking? What was I seeing—what was there, or what I wanted to? I can't believe I never saw that in their nature, their complex social order, so unlike the normal behavior of coleoptera. God, I was so stupid!

"...They started attacking the habitat today, tearing into it with those mandibles of theirs, ripping chunks out of it like it was paper! I crawled out, and they let me go—right through them. Those little bastards even cleared a space for me. I tried to get a few of them as I went ... but they're too fast for me. My whole body is burning up. I think my eyesight's going. Everything is so blurry now.

"I can't keep writing. Fingers can't find the keys too well at all now. Power cell in the portable terminal is fading. I'll save what I can to DHT. I hope they don't break that apart too. It's so cold here. I think I'm just going to sleep for a while now. Just a little while.

"One last thought keeps running through my head though. It should be funny, but it's not. I keep thinking how my colleagues wanted to see the back of me, and how they pitied the beetles for having to put up with me.

"Jesus, where did it all go wrong?"

Oh Why Can't I?

C.J. Henderson

> "Sing, everyone sing;
> Sing, everyone sing;
> All of your troubles,
> Will vanish like bubbles,
> Sing, everyone sing."
> — Italian folk ballad

It crossed the edge of the galaxy without warning. When it arrived at a point where someone did notice, it was discovered there was no stopping it. Indeed, for those unfortunates in its path, there was not even the possibility of understanding it.

The thing, of course, in the previous galaxies which it would have called home if it had possessed intelligence enough to do so, had consumed many worlds over the millennia—some containing sentience, some not. The entity, whatever it was, was not a picky eater. All it required for sustenance was matter in any form. Asteroids, comets, free-floating cosmic ice, galactic dust particles, oh, and planets. It did enjoy planets.

Round and large, filled with elements and all manner of goodness. Skies thick with water vapor, mountains covered with green, fields overflowing with scrub and vines and grasses. Oh, and oceans—how it dearly loved water. Brimming over with swimmers and plants and things somewhere in between the two.

Things that flew in the skies, that swam the seas, lumbered across the ground, these were delicious treats, like tiny grains of sugar sprinkled across an otherwise somber slab of oatmeal. The swallower of worlds loved their taste. It was only the sometimes aftertaste of certain rare planets which left it somewhat unsatisfied. All the screaming, the wailing and the panic, the fear and terror, those worlds crawling with higher life forms, those could be so disturbing—a nuisance, really.

But, it could overcome. It could endure. After all, in the shallow recesses of its stunted consciousness, it realized that one had to accept the good with the bad. The problem was thinking creatures, which once consumed, upset its delicate balance. It did not enjoy their mental recriminations, their self-absorbed, overwhelming need to complain over their unexpectedly abrupt deaths.

But, what else was it to do, it wondered. Since the time of creation it had chewed its way across the universe, consuming life, assimilating the sweet and varied chemical composition of whatever might drift within its path. Not a being possessed of very developed cognitive skills, the thing let the piece of a thought pass—as it always did. Some planets were tasty and that was that, and some were tasty, but talked back to it the next day. It was the way of things. There was nothing to do but press on.

As the entity allowed itself to be pulled along by the currents of space, it threw itself into slumber. The swallower knew it would awaken, as always, when the next meal presented itself. And, with luck, by then the recently acquired, and highly annoying, four hundred voices screaming within its mind would be dissolved, and it would be able to feed happily once more.

"Could you repeat that, sir?"

Captain Alexander Benjamin Valance, commander of the Earth Alliance Ship *Roosevelt,* stared at the face on his com-screen. He knew he had heard the words correctly, realized there was little chance his equipment could be so selectively faulty as to be capable of distorting random words within a sentence. Still, there was a part of him that hoped such a thing was possible.

"I could sing your orders a cappella, Captain, but it wouldn't change them any."

"No, sir," answered Valance, his tone crisp, if still the slightest bit dazed. "I'm certain it wouldn't. Although, it would make such moments more interesting."

Admiral Jeffrey Mach was shorter than many career officers who reached the Navy's upper echelon. He wore a beard always bordering on non-regulatory length, and understood that when you were sending the best and the brightest off toward almost certain doom, that allowing them a moment of near-insubordination was not only acceptable, but recommended. Pursing his lips to acknowledge Valance's comment, he raised one eyebrow as a warning against any further line-crossing, telling the captain, "It might at that. Perhaps we'll get the chance to test your theory when you return."

"I do appreciate the admiral's highly optimistic use of the word 'when,' rather than 'if.'"

"I try to stay positive, Captain. As you might wish to do yourself. Are there any questions?"

Valance could think of several, but none he cared to voice. Rather than risk his superior's further displeasure, he answered simply, "No, sir. I believe my orders were straightforward enough."

"Listen, Al ... I know this is a raw deal. We should be sending a fleet, and we are. But well ... you know politics ... we have a responsibility to the Forgeen. They've already lost one world, we've got a treaty, and yours is the closest ship we've got. We just can't get anything else there in time, and we've got to get something in between their homeworld and ... and whatever it is that's coming."

"I understand, Admiral," responded Valance, meaning his words. "It's what we sign on for."

Both men stared at each other over their comlink for a moment. Separated by some twelve light years of space and two decades of age, they both knew the elder no more enjoyed handing down a death sentence than the younger enjoyed receiving it. With a final salute, though, the pair broke their connection and returned to their respective tasks. Time, after all, was not standing still.

And neither was the horror making its way toward the Forgeen homeworld. Valance allowed himself a small sigh, then prepared to alert his crew to the almost certain possibility of their upcoming demise.

"Tell me I didn't hear what I thought I just heard. There's a pack of Delbickie's Frosted Pink Tobacco Chews in it for anyone that can convince me."

The speaker, Chief Gunnery Officer Rockland Vespucci, better known to his shipmates and pit bosses across the Confederation of Planets as "Rocky," had good reason to doubt his hearing. The shipwide announcement just made by his vessel's captain was enough to throw any swabbie for a loop. Possibly three.

"To do so, even for the dubious joy of receiving a free pack of

Delbickie's Frosted Pinks, would be to do you no favor. We all heard the same message, I do believe."

The words of Machinist First Mate Li Qui Kon, most often referred to by the rest of the crew as well as tube and wire jockeys everywhere as "Noodles," left his friend rolling his eyes as well as reaching for another beer. Pulling the remnants of the six-pack of JingleTime Stout out of his reach, though, Technician Second Class Mark Thorner waggled his index finger in the gunnery officer's face, reminding him, "Now, now, you know better than that. No depressants to be self-administered after a Stations 10 alert."

"Yeah," added Quartermaster Harris, knocking back the last of his Indiana HicUps longneck, "after all, when a to-stations call is that depressing, who needs to add on to it?"

"Hey," said Rocky, still unable to move himself out of his chair, more from depression than inebriation, "anything worth doing is worth doing right."

"Then perhaps," interjected Mac Michaels, one of the top Grade A members of the *Roosevelt's* egghead division, "we might want to get ourselves squared away and attempt to meet this approaching nightmare with a touch of competence. I don't know, call it a change of pace."

"Hey, listen," snapped Rocky, his defensive hackles rising up of their own volition, "we're plenty competent, when it comes to dealing with things even a quarterway normal. But this, I mean … *this* … this ain't what anyone I know's gonna be callin' normal any time soon."

"He does have a point," admitted Thorner.

And, so did they all, each and every one of them. Around the mess hall, the gathering of suddenly no-longer-off-duty sailors began to push themselves up and out of their seats, preparing to throw themselves at their latest excursion into the unknown—a movement toward which none of them were looking forward. Of all the assignments ever handed to the *Roosevelt,* this was the most colossally unbelievable.

One of their allies, the mainly agrarian, and largely defenseless Forgeen System, had called for help. One of their outer planets, apparently, had been consumed. Not blown apart, not shredded, not sliced, diced, cubed, or vaporized. It had been, the Forgeen ambassador swore, eaten.

A rambling, impossible space anomaly, a thing some fifteen thousand standard miles across, had floated into the Forgeen sphere of influence and wrapped itself around one of their worlds. The planet had been called Xiube, a place entirely given over to the cultivation of grains and marine life. It was a profit sphere, a world with very few inhabitants, every inch possible of its surface having been given over to agricultural commerce. When the unknown critter had finally unrolled itself, not so much as a spare set of atoms could be found of Xiube, its four hundred some growth specialists, weather functionaries, farmhands and the such, any of its twenty-seven billion sea creatures, its wheat, clover, bamboo, frill hedge, keblir vines, et cetera.

It was gone. All of it. Just as the Forgeen had said.

And now, the obviously not-yet-sated thing was on the move once more. This time headed for D'frok, homeworld of the Forgeen—a giant of a planet with some seventeen natural satellites, as well as four artificial ones. Every one of them packed with beings—some fifty-six billion residents all in all. Each and every one of them terrified out of their minds as their evening news programs did their best to grab ratings by endlessly broadcasting just how desperately hopeless their situation was.

Historical records, once cross-referenced against all those available from throughout the Confederation of Planets' one-hundred-and-fifty-eight members, revealed the creature to not be completely unknown. It had been discovered, in fact, after all available data had been culled, that the entity had been cutting its way across the galaxy in a somewhat straight line for several hundred standard years, apparently entering the Milky Way at, what the jokesters at Earth Alliance HQ referred to as, the "ass-end of the wrapper."

Chocolate-treat-related nonsense aside, this intel had left the rough and readies of the *Roosevelt* more than a touch apprehensive. First off, as big as their ship was—large enough to comfortably hold a complement of ten thousand Navy personnel—something over fifteen thousand miles across sounded at least a trifle bigger. Second, the facts at hand stated that this head chef for the Interstellar House of Wipe-You-Out had been doing so for millennia, without the slightest interference. This meant that no space-faring race had ever been able to do anything about it in the past, except perhaps the precision military maneuver generally known as get-the-hell-out-of-the-way.

Hoping to be able to manage a slightly better showing, especially considering that not doing so meant death and destruction to quite a few innocent Forgeens, Captain Valance immediately set his maintenance and technical crews to making certain every weapon they had was up to standards. The pounders, the whisperers, even the forward particle accelerator affectionately dubbed "the lightwave motion gun" were all brought on line, every recoil circuit checked, each cross beam tested, every toggle oiled.

Sadly, what normally would have been enough to draw the crew together in white-hot camaraderie, was in this instance only heightening their tension. Up and down the length of the *Roosevelt,* its men and women were growing tense, frightened. Desperate.

It was hard to blame them.

They had been sent on a suicide mission, and everyone knew it. They were the stop-gap, the noble gesture. As whispers and murmurs ran along the great ship's grapevine, darkness filled the minds of its crew. The thing could not be stopped. Not by them. Not by just one ship, no matter how big. They were doomed, and they knew it. Hell, they were supposed to know it.

And with that knowledge came the creeping fear. It was one thing to be sent into battle against hopeless odds, the lone ship sacrificed to cover a retreat so the fleet could survive. That meant glory and an honorable death. But that was not where the *Roosevelt* was headed. They were headed down the gullet of a voracious, intergalactic paramecium. They were fish food, leftovers, the soon-to-be joke of the fleet.

Although, even that much they could have held out against. The *Roosevelt's* complement were the finest Earth had to offer. They were tough, well trained, and ready to die for their world. But, many of them were wondering, was dying all they were being asked to do this time? What exactly was going to happen to them? After all, they were not being requested to simply be blown apart—no. They were being asked to be eaten. Dissolved, digested, rendered down to their basic atoms. What, nearly half the crew was wondering in less than half an hour after the announcement, did that actually mean?

What was this inconceivable thing toward which they were headed? Would it store their memories, absorb their souls, keep each individual consciousness prisoner within its vast, unknowable reaches? Would their minds be tortured throughout eternity, or would their bodies be used as fuel, an endlessly slow, painful dissolving which would leave them screaming for eons?

Such speculation had been kept in check due to a welcome combination of luck and scope. So far, none of them had been asked to accept anything so mind-bogglingly fantastic or hideous. No creature met, no world uncovered, no race or life form upon which they had happened defied explanation to such an extent as to be beyond comprehension.

Now, that had changed.

Now they had been ordered to throw themselves against some sort of impossible space vampire, a ravaging eating machine so spectacularly, sky-blottingly large it could be seen while still in space by those it would consume. Now they were being asked to offer up more than just their lives—suddenly, their souls were in the balance. And, it had to be admitted, with that being the case, the crew of the *Roosevelt* were not reacting as well as might have been hoped.

Valance included.

The captain forced himself to walk the corridor from his cabin to the bridge with a steady, casual motion. He would not betray the dread he was feeling, would not allow the creeping fear gnawing at the back of his mind to show in his face. That was his job, to rise to the occasion. To bear the burden of command. He did not assemble a false smile on his face, did not try to convince his crew he did not understand or share their panic. Such was too hard a mask to maintain, and unfair.

"One step at a time," he thought, nodding to each he passed in the passageway. "Just take it one step at a time."

No, he told himself, his responsibility was to prove that it was possible to hold oneself together. Those he saw with moisture in the corners of their eyes he did not reprimand. Those he heard muttering prayers he did not chastise. They would snap to when needed. When it came time to fight, they would do so with courage. And when it came time to die, they would do so with honor.

As Valance glanced around the bridge, standing in the doorway without actually stepping inside for a moment, he set his mind in order. They were not coming back. There was no hope. Still, there were lives counting on them. Billions of them. And then, suddenly, something he had read as a child flashed through the captain's mind. It was some sort of fantasy story—men in loin clothes and wizards and the such. He could not remember the title, the author, even the name of the main character, but he did remember what was important—

"If it bleeds, it can die."

"What, Captain?"

To the amazement of Communications Officer Feng, Valance looked at her and smiled. Giving her a jaunty tilt of his head, he moved to his command chair, ordering her to patch him through to the entire ship. When she responded that the channel was open, Alexander Benjamin Valance addressed his crew.

"As if I had to tell you, this is your captain speaking. A look at the latest projections shows we're going to be on top of this thing in less than an hour. So, I thought we should get our game face together."

From stem to stern, heads turned, attention was riveted.

"I know a lot of you are scared. Why not? It's a scary thing they've asked us to do. But, some of us have been scaring ourselves, and that, ladies and gentlemen of the *Roosevelt,* we do *not* need. Do you understand me, people? That is something we ... do not ... *need!*"

"Oh yeah," said Rocky, hope beginning to scratch its way through the depression which had settled in his chest, "the captain's goin' somewheres with this."

"Ahhh," responded Noodles, his eyes fixed on the speaker above their heads, "you think?"

"So this thing is big. So it's something we've never seen before. Every time we turn around we keep stumbling across things we've never seen before. That no one has ever seen before. But ... nothing we've found so far has been able to stop us, so what is it that's making us all so certain this goddamned bacteria from Hell is going to be able to?"

Around the ship, nerves began to unwind, shoulders began to straighten.

"And let me remind you people of something, our orders were to stop this thing. Not to whine and moan, not to lie down and let it roll over us. Keep this in mind, ladies and gentlemen, nobody said you were supposed to *die* today—*nobody!*"

In the fighter bays, in the engine rooms—everywhere—sailors began to turn to one another, heads nodding, grins replacing despair.

"You were given a job ... to protect fifty-six billion lives. Now, I don't know what a Forgeen looks like. I don't know what they eat, how they make love or what it smells like when they fart. But, I'm willing to bet they love each other. That they love their children. And, when that goddamned son'va bitchin' thing fills their sky, I'm willing to bet they're going to know fear."

Throughout the *Roosevelt,* fingers tightened into fists.

"Well, we're the only hope they've got. Maybe we can't stop this thing, but then, maybe we can. The simple truth is we won't know until our guns bark and the smoke clears. And if we can't kill it, maybe we can hurt it. Maybe we can change its mind, drive it off, get it to chase us somewhere else."

"Captain's right," Harris said to Thorner, giving him an elbow to the ribs, "we were giving up without a fight."

"All I want to remind you people of," snapped Valance, "is that we have a duty, and that we have more than one way to fulfill it. So, grease the long rods, you monkeys. Check out your fighters, fire up the shields, and swab the damned decks, because we're on a hunt, and we're going to throw everything we have at the enemy until it's nothing more than an intergalactic pancake!"

From the rear mine launching facility, to the very tip of the forward shuffleboard tournament hall, a thunderous cheering burst forth from every throat. Some forty-three minutes later, the crew of the *Roosevelt* would discover whether or not their own personal spatula was big enough to do the job required.

The first sighting of the approaching creature did nothing much to help spread calm throughout the crew. As deep spacers, they were accustomed to seeing massive things framed against the blackness of the void. But, these were always moons, comets, planets, stars. Rarely in their travels had they even come up against other ships much bigger than their own. But, the thing centered in the ship's monitors now was not a ship or any other kind of inanimate object. It was alive.

No one color could be attributed to it. Vast areas of the thing were a sallow purple, others black, red, green—more. None of the colors were vibrant. They surged beneath the beast's outer skin, pulsating, sometimes mixing one with another. None of the continual combinations did anything to improve the monstrosity's looks.

"Primary weapons in range, Captain."

"Heat 'em," ordered Valance, "but let's just keep the array ready for now. We don't want to give away our entire hand right at the beginning." Turning toward his tactical unit officer, the captain gave the redhead a nod, saying, "Send out a few teams, Acampora, mix the payloads. Let's see what this thing does."

"It's still a great distance off, Captain," answered the woman. "They're only going to have fuel to get there and get back."

"That's all we need, Lieutenant," snapped Valance. "They're not going out to mix it up against enemy fighters. They're dumping payload so we can assess from a distance. Now move 'em out."

In only seconds, some ninety fighters were streaking through the black, headed for the creature. The first wave in broke across a several thousand-mile stretch of the beast, raking it with laser fire. The second wave went right up the middle of the same sector, dropping nuclear payloads. The last thirty ships strafed the outer edges of the sector, blasting away with combination missiles, dropping everything from napalm and shrapnel bombs to chemical and corrosive weapons.

As the ships turned to make their run back to the *Roosevelt*, Valance and Mac Michaels studied the data coming back to the ship from the various tagged sensors dropped during the attack. Pursing his lips, the science officer sighed hard, then said, "Not even slowing down, sir. Speed and heading constant. Like it didn't even notice us."

Valance nodded. Silent. Tight-lipped. While he pretended to be concentrating on the forward screen, the captain darted looks at the rest of the bridge crew from the corners of his eyes. All of them were feeling the strain. He could see their nerves tightening. Knowing he had to do something quickly, Valance said, "All right, much like we figured, light weapons don't have much effect on this gorilla. Let's up the ante, then. Whisper guns, mark central mass. Mr. Michaels, provide coordinates. Full beam dispersal…"

Sweat beaded across every forehead not already soaked.

"On my command…"

Everywhere, chatter ceased. Prayers were offered.

"*Fire!*"

The *Roosevelt's* fourteen forward particle weapons sliced the darkness, varying rays of pink, green, and yellow boiling through space. Striking in a ring around the seven hundred square miles of surface area above their target, the beams tore across the flesh of the beast, all moving inward toward the center of what Valance and Mac Michaels hoped was the creature's heart. And, while the devastating attack continued, before damage assessment could be made, the captain ordered, "Pounder batteries, zero the mark. Battery commanders, commence firing!"

The pounders, the ship's planet busters, had been gathering projectiles during the entire race to head off their target. The pounders were normally used against orbiting bodies. The mass drivers would launch a captured asteroid or meteor at high speed toward a target, then let the planetary body's gravity take over, pulling the object in hard and fast. The resulting damage was usually catastrophic.

Their target this time, of course, was not a planet, but long range observation had revealed that due to its incredible size the beast did have its own gravitational field. Whether or not it would be sufficient to cause itself damage—that remained to be seen.

"First volley within a hundred thousand miles, Captain."

"Release the second volley."

As the next brace of pounders released their payloads, the first sped on toward their target. No one on the bridge broke the mounting silence as the initial salvo shattered the creature's personal atmosphere. The thing's gravity grabbing hold of the projectiles, their speed nearly doubled as the beast dragged them closer, embracing their promise of destruction.

"Second volley entering atmosphere—"

"Fingers crossed, everyone—"

And then, the thousands of tons of rock, ice, and iron slammed into its target. Massive renting holes burst through the creature's outer skin, driving deep enough into the horror to release great, thousand mile arcs of fluid pumping madly. The bridge crew held their breaths, waiting for a reaction, and then, the second volley hit.

Michaels' science team had planned the attack to pound at what was hopefully the monster's most vulnerable spot. The fighters were sent in to attack its fringes, to draw attention away from the core. Then, after the whisper beams hopefully broke open the thing's flesh, the pounders were released to fall in two circles—the first broad, the second tighter, more focused. As the second volley struck, sending more geysers of blood and bile into the air, cheers went up across the *Roosevelt*. Taking no chances, however, her captain commanded, "Half a job done is nothing accomplished. Mr. Rockland…"

"Aye, sir?"

"Fire the lightwave!"

Prepared since before the creature had been sighted, Rocky punched in the final three codes needed to begin the lightwave motion sequence. Deep within the *Roosevelt,* its massive protonic engines began to siphon off energy for the attack to come. The lightwave gun was the ship's most powerful weapon, but it was also its desperate last chance. Capable of disrupting the gravity of a gas giant, of collapsing an entire solar system's logical motion, it was humanity's ultimate weapon of mass destruction.

"Weapon ready, sir," snapped Rocky, his finger poised above its detonator.

The only problem was, once fired, the *Roosevelt* would not be capable of independent movement for several hours. The decision to use the lightwave motion weapon was never one made lightly. Indeed, it had never before been made in combat.

"Is target locked, Mr. Rockland?"

"Target is locked, sir."

Which meant, if the lightwave motion burst did not destroy the creature utterly, or at the least incapacitate it, then the Forgeen, and the *Roosevelt* along with its crew, were finished.

"Then *fire!*"

Valance's order, it would later be determined, was given a mere 2.43597 seconds too late.

Even as Rocky's finger descended, at his observation post, Mac Michaels began to notice an odd reaction taking place across the surface of the creature. With the majority of the steam beginning to dissipate, his long-range sensors were finally able to send back visual images worth examining. As he did so, the science officer raised both eyebrows. The first eyebrow was lifted due to perplexity. The second out of horror.

"Oh crap—"

Was all the science officer could blurt before the lightwave motion gun was engaged. As its overwhelming payload of destruction raced through the darkness, gobbling up distance at the speed of light, across the surface of its target, the creature's skin was mutating, bonding—rebuilding itself.

"All hands," announced Valance, his voice edged with both hope and doom, "brace for motion backwash."

The golden dazzle of accelerated light slammed into the monster with force enough to not only stop its forward motion, but to force it backward for the first time in its entire existence. However, that was all it did. As the impact flash faded from the screens, to the horror of the crew, the beast appeared unaffected.

"Mac," asked Valance with an even tone desperate to shatter, "what? Give me a 'what?'"

"It, it seems to have ... scabbed over, sir. The wound—the fluid release, we thought we hurt it, and we did. But it seems all we did was bring its defenses on line. Scanners indicate the scab is the density of adamantium, running a solid mile deep."

"And *that* was enough to stop our beam?"

"It didn't stop it, sir. It deflected it. And, since the bonded area runs to around a depth of five miles around the impact point, well…"

"Yes, Mr. Michaels?"

"At least we know the thing works … ah, sir."

No one spoke. No one breathed. All any of the crew on the bridge did was stare at the screen, at the image of the terrible thing hanging in space. The living being that had just survived a direct blast from the mightiest weapon ever assembled by Earth science.

"It does seem to have stopped moving, sir," offered one of the sailors on long-range duty. "Perhaps we did more to it than we realize."

"And perhaps, Mr. Rennie, it's just trying to decide how to proceed," responded Mac Michaels, glowering at the ensign under his command.

"Well, goddamnit," snapped Valance, "then it's one up on us, because that's what we should be doing!" Not waiting for anyone to respond, the captain depressed his comlink and addressed the crew.

"Now hear this. We have apparently stunned the beast, but that is all. I have no idea how much time we have before it begins to move again, either toward Forgeen or us, but in that window of opportunity, if *anyone* thinks they have a good idea, *now* is the time to sing out with it."

For a moment there was no response to the captain's request. And then, Ensign Rennie, going as pale as a man could without actually fainting from blood loss, pointed toward the forward screen, whispering:

"Th-Th-The … it … it's moving."

As all eyes turned, dread etching them open, unblinking, bulging from the dawning realization that what they were viewing might possibly be the last thing they ever witnessed, all could see Rennie was correct. The thing was moving once more. This time, toward the *Roosevelt.* A number of the bridge crew began to tremble, several shed tears.

"*No!*"

As all heads turned, hope springing wildly into hearts across the bridge, Communications Officer Feng turned to her console and began flipping switches. Focusing both the *Roosevelt's* messaging systems and translation programs into a tight beam aimed at the monstrosity beyond, she hit her transmit button, then sang;

"I don't want to die,
Although I'll admit we're beaten,

I'm telling you this from the heart—
No one here wants to be eaten."

"What in the wonderful world of color is she doin'?"

"Of course," said Valance, ignoring Rocky's question. "Of *course!*" Snapping his fingers, the captain shouted, "She's the Communications Officer. She's doing her job—she's trying to communicate!"

"By singin'?"

"We're sorry that we shot you,
To see you bleeding made me sad.
We want you to be our friend,
Not someone who's all mad."

"She's not making up the best lyrics, sir."

"Who cares," Valance snapped at Michaels. "It's the feeling she's putting into them, the heart—listen to her. She's trying to explain us. She's—"

And then, the captain went quiet.

Staring into Valance's eyes, Rocky whispered to Rennie, "Oh yeah, that's the look. Here it comes."

Slamming his fist against the arm of his command chair, Valance let out a hopeful whoop. Ordering Michaels to patch all the ship's com systems into Feng's console, he broadcast to the rest of the ship: "Yeoman Feng is attempting to teach fifteen thousand miles of angry space-faring Jell-O that sentient beings are worth something. She's looking to get through to it with song, the most basic emotional tool our lizard cortex ever created. Any of you that know how to sing, help her out."

And with those words, it started.

"You must remember this—"

"We all live on a yellow—"

"Born free, as free as—"

From every corner of the ship, from the forward batteries to the mess hall...

"Roll out the barrel—"

"Moon over Rigel 7—"

"Row, row, row yer boat—"

In a hundred languages, and five times as many keys, some ten

thousand voices unleashed the story of humanity.
"I am the very model of a modern Major-General—"
"Fairies wear boots and you better believe—"
"We are the champions—"
They used light opera and heavy metal. They sang country western ballads, rock & roll and parodies. They sang of their homes...
"I'll take Manhattan—"
They sang of their hopes...
"To dream the impossible—"
They sang of their loves...
"Oh, the yellow rose of Texas—"
And, none of it seemed to work. Relentlessly, the horror moved on toward the ship, sliding ever closer, undeterred. Unforgiving. As the image of the nearing monstrosity began to fill the observation screens, voices by the dozens, by the hundreds were silenced. What, their owners' minds asked, was the use? It was over. They were finished. It was inevitable.

But, on the bridge, one voice did not fail.

Having given off trying to make songs up, Yeoman Feng reached into her past and pulled forth the one collection of notes and words that could stop any force thrown against it. Her voice small and trembling, she sang of need. She sang of hope.

Closing her eyes and filling her lungs, she sang of something that might be behind the moon, or beyond the stars. She sang of a place where there was no trouble, one she was not certain existed, but that could be found by happy little bluebirds.

And, although the bleeding, revenge-seeking creature approaching the *Roosevelt* had never before heard a human voice, did not know what a rainbow was, or why one might wish to go over it, something within its staggering bulk began to stir—to awaken.

To comprehend.

Then, Feng sang—

"Why, oh why, can't I?"

And, the entity which had only a few minutes earlier shed its first drop of blood, followed that sensation by shedding its first tears.

It was some days later that Rocky and Noodles sat in a quiet corner of the mess hall with a few others of the crew, including newly promoted

Lieutenant Feng. Knocking back another long gulp from his Ballards Bitters, the Gunnery Officer announced, "I've said it before, and I'll say it again, ain't nobody gets to see shit like we do."

"Not very eloquent, Mr. Rockland," said Feng, grinning wide, "but eminently correct."

"So, Mac," asked Noodles, "you've got the captain's ear. What's the word? What are they going to do with our playmate?"

"You mean Caesar. That's what command's named the intergalactic fried egg that almost ate the *Roosevelt*—"

"And us along with it."

"Amen to that."

Taking a swig from his own high-voltage refreshment, Michaels added, "Oh, you guys'll love this. Seems the Confederation of Planets cut a deal with it. Turns out swallowing down thinking beings gives our new pal psychic gas. But, it can't tell one planet from another. So, we're putting together a team that will simply lead Caesar across the galaxy, directing it to dead worlds, asteroid belts with no useable resources, comets that have become a hazard to navigation—"

"Hey," offered Harris, "they could take it to that sargasso of space junk that makes getting around our own system such a nightmare."

"Good call," answered the Science Officer. "First place they took him."

"You know, it's kind of sad."

"What do you mean, Feng?"

"What I mean is, Caesar was happy enough, millions of years, just floating along, eating anything that came his way. No worries ... then—bang—he meets us, next thing he knows, he's like janitor to the galaxy."

"One day you're a god," observed Rennie, "the next you're just pushing a broom."

"The horror," joked Noodles. "The horror."

"Man," replied Thorner, "consciousness really *is* a bitch, ain't it?"

And, with that, the conversation turned to other things, as conversations always do. Some left the table, others replaced them. They did, after all, have duties to perform. Much like Caesar, and any other being the universe has ever known unfortunate enough to develop language skills.

Last Man Standing

Danielle Ackley-McPhail

The *Caliphus* landed on the moon MineCorps had designated A-RCK-01 amid a cloud of fine, rust-colored particles. Dust was everywhere, invasive. If not for the high-grade ion field protecting the surface of the ship and its various venting and intake systems, they would already be in trouble. From an impartial viewpoint, it was a spectacular effect: an aura of red dust limning the ship from ten inches past the buffer. The crew, however, was ill at ease, left to imagine the total encapsulation they could only view in swirling fragments on the monitors.

Tom Henry was beyond concerned. As the mission engineer, he, more than anyone else, was aware that the ionic drive was not designed to combat such a constant assault. The particles made him uneasy. For lack of a better word, he thought of the matter as dust, but it didn't move right; it appeared slick, almost greased as it slid along the ion field like it was trying to get through. He held back a shudder. This was bad. Their orders were to set up dirtside and stockpile ore until the star-freighter *O'Connor* arrived. Not only was that not currently possible, but every instinct he had was screaming at him to lift off immediately, and the contract be damned.

"Your assessment, Mr. Henry?" Captain Jared Troy asked, rising from the chair and coming to stand at his shoulder.

Tom ran a series of computations before responding. The data scrolling across the monitor reinforced his concerns. "The dust storm extends beyond the range of our hull sensors. I can't pinpoint when it will end. We're okay for now, but we have twenty to twenty-five standard hours before the system is overwhelmed if it maintains this density."

Captain Troy straightened and turned toward the rest of the crew. "You heard the man, suit up and get out there, you rock hounds. This has become a hit-and-run extraction."

"Sir," Tom interrupted. "I don't know what this storm will do to their suits, or the equipment." The moon was large, with three-quarters Earth-standard gravity and an oxygen-rich atmosphere, but the chemical composition of the air was not friendly to humans.

Troy's mouth twisted in annoyance. His eyes narrowed and he leaned back over the console. "Planetary evaluation ruled out a corrosive atmosphere and did not register anything over a level-one bacterium, correct?"

"Yes, sir."

"So, the worst we should be facing is some dirt, yes?"

Tom looked away, his expression tight. He focused on the monitor and by sheer will forced his voice neutral. "It would seem so, Captain."

But he didn't believe it.

Troy moved across the deck to the hatch. "Donovan," he called into the to crew compartment. The foreman, climbing into her EVA suit, looked up, her expression closed as she continued to slide on and seal her gauntlet. "Sir?"

"Here's where that mech unit of yours proves its worth. Get it out there pounding rock ... and double the crew while you're at it, we can't risk the Chomps so get the extra men running sack relay," he ordered. "I want a constant stream of ore feeding into the cargo bay at all times."

Kate Donovan nodded sharply in acknowledgement as she tugged her helmet into place over her short bristle of dark brown hair, her jaw worked as she toggled her comm active: "Anything else, sir?"

"Check-in is half standard. We don't know how much time we have so monitor your systems closely. Any sign of malfunction is to be reported immediately."

Two-thirds of the mining crew scrambled to comply, the other four remained huddled around the monitors, makeshift markers changing hands as they made book on everything from the time the ion shield would fail to how much ore would end up in the hold before it did.

Tom Henry kept his eyes locked on his station monitor; already sections of shield sensors showed signs of strain. He continued to watch, his lips moving silently in prayer.

Kate Donovan regularly worked side by side with her crew. In part, this was to make sure no one slacked or took unnecessary risk to secure a bonus, but it was also so she could watch Jean-Paul Marot's back. She had to—no one else would. Not even Jean-Paul Marot. The titanium-plated ass had a death wish.

No one else aboard was aware their new mining mech was actually a cybernetic prototype. To them he was just another bit of hardware. Only Kate knew, and by contract she couldn't reveal to anyone there was a human soul beneath the chassis. It had been a hard contract to win and though she had wondered at the reason for the odd clause when she'd triumphantly signed the deal, she also hadn't realized how hard it would be to keep silent. Jean-Paul did his best to act the part of inhuman mech, but in a hundred little ways he betrayed his humanity, even if she was the only one to realize it. She had lost count of the thoughtful ways he'd helped her out on shift, both with tricky tasks and unforeseen mishaps. He'd even saved her ass a time or three.

She followed close behind as he passed through the waiting decontamination unit and headed down the ramp to the planet's surface, pickaxe in his right robotic hand, massive jackhammer held casually in the other. Red dust swirled disturbingly around him the moment he was past the ionic shield, adhering to the flexible Kevlar-fabric laminate that sheathed his frame. He unconsciously swiped his optics clear across his arm as no mechanical being would have and headed for rock.

"*Hey, JP,*" Kate subvocalized across her comm on his private band, "*not too far. There's plenty of surface ore close to the ship. Start with the port-side outcrop there while I organize Troy's bucket brigade.*"

He didn't acknowledge her command verbally, but set to breaking up the easy-access payload that had placed this moon at the top of MineCorp's A-list. She toggled the comm to the crew frequency and started barking orders to the rest of the shift workers. In short order, sacks of dust-covered iron ore were being ferried into the hold.

Everyone earned out their bonus that day. They were beat. Everything was red with dust—right down to the men. Between the mech and the extra men, the ship's holds were full before second shift was halfway through and the crew even managed to set up the steel storage hoppers on the surface and started filling them. Once those were full they would be shuttled to the *O'Connor* on its arrival. For now, the entire crew was calling it quits for the day. As the final hold hatch closed, Tom keyed the sequence to lock the ship off from the decon unit. When it was secure, he remotely extended the vent shaft until it pushed through the ion shield. A clever one-way valve on the end of the shaft kept the moon's atmosphere from contaminating the ship.

"Okay, Donovan," he commed the foreman. *"You and your 'hounds are cleared for decon."* He felt his tension ease a bit as the monitor displayed the men and women piling back into the ship with their gear. The mech unit was the last aboard. Once it cleared the walkway, Tom spoke over the crew frequency: *"Please stand clear of the closing door, decontamination commencing."*

Directed jets of air dislodged particles of foreign matter from the crew while fans in the duct system sucked the contaminants down the flexible vent shaft and ejected it past the ion shields before retracting back into place. Then, though all of the crew had been through the process before, Tom issued the standard warning for the next stage of decontamination: *"Please close your eyes in preparation for low-grade irradiation."* As the final stage completed, Tom Henry ran a scan on the chamber before sounding the all-clear and initiating the release sequence.

Several of the returning crew, including Donovan, were in the process of loosening the seals on their environment suits as they waited for the hatch lock to disengage when a low curse transmitted across the crew frequency. One of the men had dropped his pick. He seemed to sway as he bent to retrieve it, then crumpled to the floor.

"Shit!" Donovan's startled voice came over the comm. *"Do not release your seals!"* she ordered the rest of her crew as she moved toward the miner.

Tom immediately keyed the interrupt, setting off the automatic alert, and reversing the release. It looked like John Palmer, but it was hard to tell. He wasn't out cold, but he remained flat on the deck as Donovan conducted an eyes-on inspection.

Tom's earlier unease returned as he watched the monitor. There was no sound feed currently active in the chamber, but it was clear from her expression that the foreman reprimanded the crewman. Tom switched on the intercom and the internal recorders. "Donovan, report."

She looked up, her navy blue eyes darkened by the displeasure clearly visible through her faceplate. "Mr. Henry, please send a medtech to the decon quarantine unit. Crewman Palmer apparently sustained a suit breach in the field. Injury appears minimal, but shows signs of dust contamination." Her words propelled Tom's tension to another level all together. Bad enough the potential of some foreign contagion, worse, in Tom's opinion, that Kate Donovan was at risk. He sent the order to medbay and continued to monitor the decon unit.

"Aw come on, boss, it's barely even a scratch!" Palmer interrupted. One hard look from Donovan and he cut off his protest.

"Not a word, Palmer," she growled as she helped the man up. "Safety protocol exists for a reason. You will observe it from here on out or it will be my boot kicking you out the door. Am I understood?"

Tom watched as she turned and scanned the room. Her face tensed, concern overshadowed by anger as she clearly noted those that had breached the seals on their protective suits. With a nod toward quarantine she spoke to her crew in a controlled voice. "Okay, Palmer, Simms, Chou, Colman ... pick a bunk and get your butts inside. The rest of you, remain suited." She then turned to face the monitor.

"Mr. Henry, please reinitialize decon procedure," she requested, closing the door behind her as she entered the quarantine cell next to Palmer's.

Jean-Paul watched as his single link to humanity closed herself in what potentially could be her coffin. That shouldn't matter, but even after the repeat decon completed he remained facing her cell.

Miners were a superstitious lot. If they ever learned of his past, those standing around him would as likely as not shove him off the ship; out with the bad penny, and all that. If anything happened to Donovan they wouldn't have to. He'd tried to keep distant, but in the silence of his mind he considered her a friend. A dangerous thing, in his experience ... for the friend. All too often, people in his proximity ended up dead. One accident after the other had left him the last man standing. The first had landed him in this mobile metal suit. The second landed him in hell as the suit forced him to take another's life to preserve his own ... and he could do nothing but comply. That chemical command was the first thing he'd forced the Corporation to deactivate, when he'd sued them to become a free agent, but the damage had been done. In his own mind it had cost him the last of his humanity. That was one of the reasons he'd become a roamer, taking only short-term contracts before moving on to another crew. Less time for his shitty luck to kick in, less opportunity for people he liked to pay for it.

This time the strategy had failed him. He suspected it was because

Donovan reminded him very much of Chloe Kendall, the last friend he'd allowed himself since he realized what kind of monster the Corporation had created in him. His hand unconsciously tightened on the haft of the pickaxe until the sensors in the "fingertips" registered a deformation in the metal.

"*Go on, JP,*" Donovan cut into his thoughts. "*It's just a precaution. We'll be out of here before the O'Connor hits orbit.*"

For the first time in almost a year, Jean-Paul spoke, if only over his private frequency: "*Quarantine is seventy-two hours, the O'Connor arrives in forty-eight.*"

"*So I suck at math! Get out of here, we'll be fine!*" She waved him away with the gauntlet she'd just removed. "*And don't forget to run a systems scan as soon as you hit your bay. I want a full report, even if I am on forced down time.*"

Jean-Paul brought his pick hand up in salute before he slowly turned and left the now-empty decontamination unit, then passed the harried medtech on his way through the main service corridor that ran the length of the ship. JP silently moved through the crew compartment toward his own bay only to have his preservation mixture flood in chemical-response to the ever-present betting markers transferring from hand to hand.

It took him a lot of effort to resist tightening his grip with the anger and further damaging the equipment.

Kate heard the chatter over the crew frequency long before she received word from anyone on the command staff.

The *O'Connor* was delayed by a meteor outburst. The trail was far-reaching and heavy with particles, obstructing the entire distance between the star-freighter and the *Caliphus*. Their flight crew was waiting for the shower to pass before continuing on to A-RCK-01, where the star-freighter would take up a geosynchronous orbit above the mining site until its massive cargo holds were full.

It could take many standard days for the route to clear. This delay could cost them every bonus written into the contract. Not to mention the hefty penalties that would be levied against them if they fell behind schedule. Tom Henry warned her in a private message that Captain Troy ordered the crews back on shift in between dust storms. The captain hadn't the decency to inform her himself. She was glad they were still making some progress but with her trapped in here things were running less than smooth.

Rising from her bunk, Kate moved to her computer access, first checking for any messages from Tom or reports from her assistant foreman before checking on Palmer's status. He'd been put through the full spectrum of diagnostic testing, but all results were negative for any identifiable contagion or foreign antibody. The miner mostly slept, complaining about feeling weak and tired. The medtech suspected the onset of anemia and was treating Palmer accordingly, but protocol demanded the four of them remain in quarantine the full seventy-two hours. Time was nearly up.

"Hey, Mac, you have a timer set out there or something?" she called out over the open intercom as she settled back on her bunk. "It's not like one of us is going to up and keel over in the last ten minutes."

She saw the medtech look up from his most recent batch of tests and cock his head. "Let me see if I remember the phrase properly … safety protocol exists for a reason…"

"Yeah, yeah, talk to my ass, why don't you?" she groused back. Every person on the ship had overheard her comments to Parker. She was the first to agree, but the only things she was showing symptoms of were boredom and frustration. Outside this ship was a site they'd contracted to mine and in her head was a clock counting down to their deadline. Her eyes never left the monitor.

Finally, Mac Taylor punched a few keys on his system and pushed back from his chair. Moments later the lights on the monitoring sensors lining her walls blinked out. Kate was up and waiting at the door to her cell before the hermetic seal parted. As she pushed through into the decon unit proper, the doors to either side of her swung open as well. She turned and scanned her crewmen; Simms, Chou, and Colman looked a little twitchy, much as she herself felt, but otherwise hale. Palmer … he looked like something was biting into him hard. Pale and tense, with an odd blue cast to the whites of his eyes. A sideways glance at Mac, who didn't seem fazed, was only marginally reassuring.

"We cleared for duty, then?" she asked.

"Except for your buddy Palmer here, yeah. Need to build up his iron levels a bit before you send him out on shift again."

Kate nodded and turned to her crewman. "You got lucky, John. You go get fixed up, and while you're on medical leave, you be sure to read your procedures manual, am I understood?"

With a disgruntled look at drawing quarter pay, Palmer nodded and followed Mac from the chamber. Kate turned back to the others. "Well? What are you waiting for? You've just had a three-day vacation … get to work!"

The three of them groaned as they preceded her out of the decontamination unit. It was damn good to move further than eight full steps in a row; it was even better to walk out under her own power, with the freedom of the ship and beyond still open to her. Kate headed for the crew compartment to catch up on the status of the operation. There was only so much she could run by wire.

"Hey," she called out as she entered the chamber from the main shaft. "I see an awful lot of loafing going on here."

Her comment was met by laughs and groans and shouts of "Look who's talking!" All of it was good-natured. It was like breathing uncanned air after the isolation of quarantine.

She swept a sharp glance around the room, her eye gleaming. "So, who took the book on me?" More groans, followed by dirty socks and empty meal packs lobbed at Tom Henry, whose cheeks were amusingly flushed at being caught out. Strange, he usually stayed out of the betting.

Glancing at Tom, Kate allowed the warmth she felt to show in her eyes as she indulged in a faint smile, her first in three days. "You, sir, can afford to buy me a steak, then." More laughter and the subtle air of tension in the compartment dissipated. Tom looked stunned, though pleased, and slowly nodded, but she was already moving past, going to check on Jean-Paul.

"It's not there," a voice called from behind her.

"What?" Kate turned and spied Captain Troy standing in the command deck hatchway.

"It's not there," the captain repeated. "I sent it out with the shift. Your crew was falling behind."

Kate ate her response to that criticism, merely nodding in acknowledgment as she pivoted and headed for her equipment locker, all the while expecting Troy to summon her back. She didn't like him or the risks he took with her people, but she was a contractor on this job and he was the boss. That meant she had to play nice; which also meant she stayed as far from his proximity as she could manage. She breathed a little easier with each step she took away from him.

Then she heard the sound of boots behind her, and the clang of another locker opening nearby. She looked over into Troy's reproving gaze and actually had wistful thoughts of quarantine.

"Hey, JP, coming at your back, with company." The subvocal voice coming over his comm, combined with the familiar address, triggered a complex chemical response the moment Jean-Paul heard it. Relief, pleasure, warmth; it was hard to focus under the bombardment. He carefully put down the equipment he was using and pivoted around.

It was a mistake on several levels. First, what machine would halt its given task randomly? Second, why should it matter to him that Kate Donovan was well and out of quarantine? Machines did not have friends. JP endlessly had to remind himself that. He had a practical reason for being glad to see her, though. In her absence, Captain Troy had been running Jean-Paul nonstop like a piece of heavy equipment still under warranty. The chassis could take it, but JP's brain was getting loopy, making it hard to manage the servos and gyros that controlled his mobility and balance; more than once he caught himself swaying. No small concern when you were a 300-pound metal behemoth surrounded by frail men of flesh. What was more he'd started getting a few low-level alerts from his exoskeleton's monitoring system.

Kate came up to him and looked him over before turning to scan the mounds of ore waiting for the rest of the crew to catch up on stowing it. Without a word she walked over to the storage bins and peered inside.

"JP, how long have you been out here?" she asked across his private frequency.

He remained silent. It wasn't like she really needed an answer to know he'd been out here too long, and talking to her was a bad habit to get into.

"You pig-headed ass!" she hissed, before turning to Captain Troy. "Thank you, sir, for your diligence on my behalf during the quarantine period." Her tone was carefully neutral. "Things appear nicely ahead of schedule here. If your inspection is complete, I need to run some *mandatory* maintenance on the JPM unit. We can't have it breaking down, not with the nearest repair facility light-years away."

Jean-Paul had the urge to laugh without the means to do so. Troy's face was nearing puce in color, but there was no way he could argue. As if there were no question, Kate turned and headed back toward the *Caliphus*. With extreme care, JP followed.

"What the hell!" Kate's hands clenched and unclenched reflexively as she stared at the diagnostic report spit out by JP's charging and maintenance station. There were half a dozen warnings. Nothing serious, but definitely all of a sudden. Best to start with the simplest issue first.

"You've got a problem with your ground wire." Moving to the indicated section, she detached the protective Kevlar skin and opened the access panel so she could eyeball the situation. "Hmm ... must have been a defective batch, looks like some of the copper coating is worn away. The steel core is starting to oxidize." Taking a can of compressed air, she blew away the corrosion to get a better look at the situation. Then she noticed another spot on a nearby O-ring. In fact, anything that wasn't titanium seemed to have sprouted rust. There wasn't much, and it wasn't bad, but it was disturbing. Better to replace it all now before the situation got worse. A trip to the spare parts locker uncovered sufficient replacements. She was even able to swap out most of the corroded bits with titanium, rather than the older steel alloy.

"Okay, pal, I'm going to have to power you down for maintenance." A sound came from JP, short, sharp, and cut off, but she didn't need to hear it to know he was very unhappy with this part. "Don't worry, it shouldn't take long."

Maybe it was her imagination, but the silence that met her reassurance seemed thick with displeasure. Couldn't be helped, though; she couldn't do this kind of repair with his system active. She shut off the system, then waited for the power to drain from the exoskeleton before starting the repairs. With care, she reached in and disconnected the ground wire first. As she was extracting it, the intercom squawked an alert.

"Aw, *shit!*" Kate swore as the sound startled her, causing her to jerk back. A sharp pain went through her arm as some internal part of the cybernetic unit gouged her hand. This was the very reason she'd deactivated her comm. Fool that she was, she hadn't thought to kill the intercom as well. Her breath hissed out as she gritted her teeth against the pain.

"Donovan, report!"

A few more curses ensued before she managed to extract herself from JP's inner workings. Heading for the intercom, she slapped the toggle active with her uninjured hand as blood dripped from the other. She quickly wrapped it in a clean rag from a pile she had nearby.

"What?" Her tone was less than civil and there was a long pause on the other end.

"You're needed in medbay immediately."

How convenient; thanks to them, she had a need to be there. "Give me ten minutes."

"But…" the tech protested. Kate heard the slightest thread of panic in the word. There were some frenzied sounds in the background. Probably some rock hound got a little juiced up. Well, they would have to wait.

"I said ten minutes. It's the best you're getting." She released the toggle and returned to JP, quickly, but carefully replacing the ground wire. She would have taken the book on that one. Finished in Guinness record time, she closed the access panel and powered his system back up.

JP made a sound that was almost a gasp as his sensors and motor functions were restored.

"Sorry," Kate said in a rush. "I'm not done yet, emergency. Didn't want to leave you in limbo. Be back as quick as I can." Not waiting for an answer—it wasn't like he'd talk to her anyway—she flew from the compartment and down the corridor leading to medbay.

It was probably nothing, she told herself, but as she neared the medics' domain there was an ungodly shriek, followed by several crashes. Cursing and thuds continued to pour down the corridor.

"Aw, crap!" Maybe not quite nothing…. She picked up her pace until she was full-out running, grabbing the edge of the open hatch and sling-shotting herself into the compartment. Her breath caught in her throat and she stopped short at the sight of Palmer. At first glance he looked like someone had put a dusty shipsuit on one of those terracotta warriors from ancient China and then brought it to life. But when she saw his face, it was less serene than taut and hard like granite, etched in agony. He could barely stand straight as he tore at the med supply cabinet, frantically trying to get it open, as Mac and the other tech fought to restrain him. Each time he moved a cloud of dust particles swirled in the air around him.

"John!" Kate yelled.

Palmer's thrashing efforts stilled as he turned to look at her, his gaze a curious mix of hatred and terror and pleading. "Make it stop," he groaned. Now that he wasn't flailing around she could see that his body trembled and his teeth had cut through his lip. The blood marking his face was more brown than red, barely visible against the dust permeating his skin.

"Please," he begged.

Before anyone could move, Palmer tensed, his back arching as a high, thin gasp fought its way from his throat. His eyes rolled into his head as he crumpled to the floor.

Kate looked up and met Mac's panicked gaze. "What the *hell* was he doing dirtside without a protective suit?" she asked.

Mac gave a twitching shake of his head, and then another, but managed nothing more. Next to him, looking like she'd been on the losing end of a prize fight, Medtech Eva Sanchez wore a haunted expression as she brushed a bit of dust and blood from her cheek. "He hasn't been outside. He hasn't left medbay."

A tremor shook through Kate Donovan as she looked down at her fallen man. He was as red as the crew that just came off shift, and way too still. Her breath coming just a little quicker, she knelt beside him and started to feel for a pulse. Eva's hand darted out and smacked hers away.

Kate gave her a cutting look. "Like it isn't already too late for that." She reached out again, placing the tip of two fingers against Palmer's throat. It took a lot of effort to leave them there long enough to be sure he was gone, before drawing them back. When she did she couldn't help rubbing at the slick, oily sensation of the dust on her skin as she tongued her comm active to the captain's private frequency.

"Troy," she hailed, "we have a problem."

Having drawn monitoring duty, Tom Henry was alone on the command deck when the captain hurried through the hatch, clearly a man with a purpose. Clad in a full environmental suit, Troy had a large rucksack over each arm and another on his back. They were jammed full of supplies, with meal packs and other necessities sticking out the top of each of them.

Tom swiveled in his chair and waited expectantly. He could feel the puzzled expression creep across his face.

"Seal off the command deck, Mr. Henry, and prepare to lift off."

Without realizing it, Tom came to his feet. "Sir, there's a double-shift crew still dirtside!"

The look on Troy's face burned along Tom's nerves like dry ice on bare skin. "Want to join them?"

"I don't know what's going on, but you are not stranding those men." Tom squared his shoulders and braced himself.

There was a mad glimmer in the captain's eye and there was something off about their color.

In two strides, Jared Troy was at his side. Before Tom could react, the captain grabbed him by the shipsuit and raised a cutting torch to within an inch of his head. Troy's finger was on the switch. Tom tensed and prayed the frantic working of his jaw would be construed as a nervous response to the situation. He triggered the comm frequency assigned to Donovan and subvocally sent one word across the link: *"Help!"* Something must have betrayed him, though. Jerking him sharply off balance, the captain shoved him toward the hatch. With the torch still to his head, Tom dared not resist.

"On second thought, I'll cover lift off myself."

The captain thrust Tom from the compartment with enough force to send him sprawling. Before he could gain his feet, the hatch closed and he heard the locking mechanism slide into place. Tom tried the manual override, but Troy had used his executive code to lock down in siege mode. Already the ship rumbled and groaned as her flight system was powered up. There was no way to stop it now. While the designers had factored in the potential for mutiny, none of them had ever considered a scenario where it was the captain hijacking the ship.

A quick roll of his tongue across his lower jaw triggered every frequency aboard ship. "Code Red! All crew return to ship, secure for lift off! Move it, people, now!" It didn't matter that Troy heard right along with everyone else; the crew had to be warned.

An incoming message across Donovan's frequency: *"What the hell's going on, Tom?"*

"You tell me! Troy's gone rogue, he's holed up on the command deck ... he's initiating immediate launch, without everyone on board."

Silence, thick and heavy.

"Palmer's dead."

"What?!"

"He's dead ... cause unknown."

It was like hitting a wall. That peculiar feeling a person gets when their grip on consciousness or reality slips, like everything is detached, muffled, safely distant; the mind lying to itself. "Oh, shit!" The words were hollow, like they came from the far end of a tunnel, even though the voice was his. A worry for Kate was the only thing crisp and clear to him.

"Shake it off, Tom. We have to get those men back on board before it's too late."

There it was—something to focus on. "Yeah, I'm heading for the external hatch."

But it took him too long to get there. As he ran, the *Caliphus* rumbled and shook. At some point ahead of him, a man screamed as the engines engaged, forcing the hatch to close automatically. Tom reached his target moments too late. The first thing he saw was a wide crimson streak running the length of the wall panel that served as the mass-deployment ramp. At the base of that wall a crewman lay in a crumpled heap and a growing pool of blood. Two others stood close by, frozen in horror at what had just happened.

Cursing, Tom scrambled for a supply locker near the panel, pawing through it until he came up with an extra-long plastic zip tie. He moved to the injured man and looped the strip around the stump where the foot had been severed, yanking it tight until the blood ceased to pump across the floor. Staring in stunned silence at the bloody streak, Tom got the impression the crewman had made a leap for the ramp once it had already begun to close and could not clear his foot in time. It also occurred to him that there were only three miners in the compartment, leaving five men unaccounted for.

"Anyone else make it back on board?" he asked, praying the others had just ignored procedure and left the decontamination unit. But the two men standing shook their heads, guilt shadowing their eyes.

Jared Troy had a lot to answer for. Tom prayed those stranded had been far enough from the blast zone when the engines fired. Their environmental suits contained hydration packs capable of sustaining them for up to a week with strict rationing. They also contained a nutrient solution that would hold them at least as long. Assuming they'd been clear of the lift off, there was the chance of rescue.

"Okay," Tom said, setting those thoughts aside for now. "We have a situation. You two are to remain suited until cleared by medical. Everything else will be explained when we're safe in orbit. Now help me get your friend strapped into one of those quarantine bunks, then secure yourself for launch." It was difficult to stand, let alone move against the forces of lift off, but they all managed to strap in.

"*Donovan,*" he sent over the foreman's private frequency. "*We only got three. One of them needs treatment for a traumatic amputation."*

She cursed quite impressively. *"Better than none. Troy can't leave orbit as long as that meteor cloud is in the way ... that will give us some time to salvage this situation. Meet me in medbay once the ship reaches apogee. We need to plan."*

"The unmitigated bastard!" Kate seethed as she paced medbay waiting for the last of the crew to arrive. With her were the four off-shift miners, the two medtechs, and Hal, the third member of the flight crew, in charge of navigation. JP crouched in the med-chem shower, the only space out of the way and large enough for him.

Her head whipped around as Tom Henry entered medbay, followed by the rest of the miners on board, the injured man supported between his suited crewmates in a chair carry. The medtechs scrambled to assist, but Kate's attention was riveted on Tom. She glanced at the intercom by the hatch before speaking. The activation light was dark.

"He's diverted all systems control to the command deck and cut us off from the interstellar comm. Can you get us in?"

Tom's brow furrowed as it took him a moment to process what she'd said. As he did, his gaze ran over her, lingering on her bandage, while barely meeting her eye. She saw relief flicker across his expression as he nodded his head. "Yeah, it will take some time, but Troy doesn't know enough to keep me out all together."

"Good, get on it," she said. "We have to warn the *O'Connor* not to dock with the *Caliphus,* not until we know there's no danger."

Tom was just turning toward the systems substation in the corner when Mac called out from across the room, his words muffled slightly by the mask covering his mouth and nose.

"Donovan! We have trouble!"

Kate, with Tom right behind her, hurried across the bay where the medtechs were working on the injured miner. They'd just started cutting him from his suit, all except the injured leg. Kate grabbed a mask and slipped it on before she rested her hand on Mac's shoulder, leaning around him for a look. She hadn't been able to tell who the injured man was when they'd first brought him in, still suited and slumped over. She saw now that it was Bobby Fletcher, the new man on the crew. *Just a kid, really,* she thought, and she ached for him as she glanced at his mangled ankle. Something struck her as she took in the color of the drying blood, echoing a memory she couldn't place.

And then he looked at her.

His eyes flickered open and he looked right at her. Pain filled his gaze and the whites of his eyes had a decidedly blue cast to them. Kate's breath caught as he shut them again and a rust-tinged tear escaped, leaving a trail in the faint dust she hadn't realized coated his tan skin. Then the memory clicked: just like Palmer, only much faster. His body began to twitch with increasing violence. Seeing that, Mac and Eva scrambled, forcing Kate back as they grabbed the edge of the gurney and shoved it into a quarantine cell similar to the ones down in decon. They then slammed the hatch shut and triggered the lock. From there they moved to their diagnostic stations. Not bothering to sit, their fingers flew over the keys as they darted around the room from system to system.

In Bobby's cell, a nozzle in the wall released a cloud of gas. The man went still, with only his chest rising and falling gently as power lights flickered on indicating the cell's monitoring sensors had been activated. Nothing else was done to care for his wound or make him comfortable.

"What are you doing?" Kate demanded. "You can't just leave him like that!"

She heard the rest of her crew get to their feet and come to stand behind her, grumbling ever louder as the medtechs went about what they were doing without responding. Stalking forward, Kate was about to yank Mac around when Tom intercepted her, laying his hand on her arm. He said nothing, but there was a sad, almost frightened look on his face. She glared at him and pulled away. "Why are you stopping me? It is their duty to take care of that man!" Kate was furious. She didn't know Eva for nothing, but Mac ... she'd gotten to know him, to like him. It made no sense that he would ignore Bobby's suffering.

Mac spoke over his shoulder, his voice tight and strained, his eyes never leaving his monitor. "There's no more to be done..."

"No more to be done?!"

Eva's head snapped around, her expression livid. "He's already dead, Donovan, all but the dying, just like Palmer, and so are the rest of us if you don't get off our backs and let us try and figure this out. We need to know what's going on in there now, before it's too late. "Now everyone out of here! Why don't you do something useful, like figure out how to regain control of the fucking ship!"

Tom's arm slid around Kate, and Mac's voice murmured over her private frequency. *"He's in no pain, Kate, we made sure he's in no pain."*

She recalled the gas that had filled the chamber and nodded, though the medtech couldn't see the motion with his attention still completely on the monitor. Whirling away from Tom—and the sudden, uncharacteristic urge to curl into the protective shelter of his arms—Kate motioned for her people to follow as she left medbay.

JP was already waiting in the corridor. Not caring if the others would see it as odd, she touched his arm briefly, knowing the sensors there acted much the same as nerve endings. He wouldn't admit to needing the comforting touch, but she did. Jean-Paul was her friend, and though he wasn't in danger of infection the same way the rest of them were, she realized at that moment that he was just as much at risk: stranded and alone, should anything happen to the rest of them, left waiting to die a much slower death.

"Come on," she spoke aloud to those following. On impulse, she reached back, this time taking Tom's hand in hers, pulling him along. "We need a plan."

So far Tom had regained read-only access to the system via a generic service code, but that was all. And it was all he was likely to get, unless he cracked the captain's command code, because Troy had registered a charge of mutiny against each of the crewmembers with command access, automatically locking them out of the system. None of them had anticipated that. They were currently holed up in one of the storage compartments because everything else was blocked to them.

Tom continued to stare at the monitor, wishing he could accomplish more, particularly as Kate stood with her hand on his shoulder watching everything he did. Sadly, the truth remained; he wasn't a professional hacker. He knew some tricks, but that had only gotten them this far.

"Can you get us a read on what Troy's up to, at least?" Kate asked, pulling Tom from his thoughts. "Maybe slave this monitor to his so we can tell what he's up to?"

"Not ... quite ... not without him realizing it, but something close." It was brilliant, actually. And he hadn't thought of it. Tom shook his hands loose and rolled his head from side to side, desperately trying to relieve the tension in his neck.

"Okay, here we go..." He punched in the codes for remote diagnostic viewing starting from the time he went on shift until now and there it was, a complete list of the commands Troy had entered since taking over the ship. As the list scrolled, Tom felt the bile rise from his stomach and creep into his throat. *"Kate..."* he sent over her private frequency. *"Kate..."*

"What?"

He pointed at the screen. *"He's preparing to vent the ship."*

Kate sat down hard on a crate beside him. *"He's nuts! He'd go right along with us, wouldn't he?"*

Tom shook his head, running his finger along several very canny commands the captain had entered. *"He's already isolated and sealed the command deck. The only ones sucking vacuum will be us."*

"Environmental suits..."

Tom shook his head and nodded toward the far end of the storage compartment, where Hal and the miners were looking for any consumables among the stored supplies. *"He's locked us out of the crew compartment. The only suits we have are already in use."*

A nearby stack of crates went crashing to the deck as Kate shoved herself to her feet and vented a bit of anger with a well-placed fist. She kicked a few more for good measure. "You done?" he asked out loud.

"It's been a bad day, okay?" she growled through clenched teeth.

He had to smile at her. "Don't worry, it's not over yet." Tom patted the crate for her to sit back down. Apparently she was curious enough to comply.

"Now, pay attention here," he told her, going private once more. *"We're locked out of the command systems, but it never occurred to Troy to restrict maintenance."*

He shot her a smile that had to be just a bit smug as he typed in several commands. *"To vent the ship requires the coordination of several interconnected programs, each one responsible for a different stage of the process. This is to prevent accidental venting. It also means that if one of the programs fails to complete its part, none of them can do their job..."* With a flourish, he hit the final key.

"I've just started the next system on a self-diagnostic, and scheduled each of the others to begin their own scan, offset by ninety minutes each."

"Done preening?" Her words weren't precisely encouraging, but her expression was both relieved and impressed.

Tom smiled back at her a bit sheepishly, before he took a chance, leaning closer and murmuring just loud enough for her to hear: "What can I say? Engineers don't often get to show off for the pretty ladies." He watched her flush, but she didn't take the bait ... yet.

"How much time did you just buy us?"

"These systems are pretty complex. Likely about eighteen hours. Enough time for us to come up with a mechanical workaround."

Kate smiled, and for a brief moment all of Tom's tension fell away. "My hero," she murmured.

Dare he risk that he was reading her wrong? Tom reached out to brush a finger lightly across her lips. Kate watched him do it but didn't protest. He was about to lower his mouth to hers when she jerked back and grabbed his hand, holding it up to the light.

"Shit..." She whirled away and disappeared out the hatch before Tom even knew what was happening. Puzzled, he looked down at his hand only to notice a faint smudge of red dust on his finger.

"Shit..." Tom slammed his fist into a nearby stack of crates.

It was clearly still a bad day...

...And it wasn't over yet.

Kate sat on a gurney in medbay staring at the faint tremors running through her hand. Nerves, that was all ... so far, anyway. She imagined that if she stared hard enough, she could see her pores exuding dust. The machinery in the background beeped a bit more vigorously.

"Stop getting yourself all worked up."

The hand Kate had been watching fisted. "Then tell me what we're facing here, Mac. And what you can do about it..."

"Well, you're infected. I suspect we all are, but I can't say to what degree without testing the others. Let's get them down here and see where things stand, then I can brief everyone."

"But..."

"It's in the air, Donovan. We're not talking *if*, we're talking how far along. Getting everyone together isn't going to make a bit of difference."

Kate nodded, but her hand clenched tighter. She accessed the crew frequency and ordered everyone to medbay, then sat back and waited. It wasn't long; Tom was the first through the door. She couldn't meet his eye but was aware, comforted even, as he perched beside her on the gurney, not touching, but close. JP was the last; he moved to the space directly behind her gurney and crouched into his version of sitting. At her back, where no one could see, she briefly felt his robotic hand reach out and lightly touch her shoulder, as a friend would.

"Everyone settle in and listen," Kate raised her voice, sounding steadier than she expected she would. "Mac's got something to say."

They all turned to look at the medtech expectantly. Mac leaned over his keyboard and brought up a view from the external sensors, he then turned and looked each of them in the eye. "It's not dust, it's an airborne organism.

"It doesn't meet any of the organic profiles on record so none of the sensors or diagnostics picked it up. Planetary evaluation didn't catch it because their rovers are made of titanium. The organism feeds on ferrous iron, any source … from raw ore to hemoglobin, it doesn't matter, as long as it's oxidized. Initial warning signs are similar to those for anemia. In the final stages, intense internal pain and what appears to be dust exuding from the skin." He turned and tapped a few more keys. The live feed was replaced by a medical slide none of them had the background to identify. He tapped another key and the slide split, the two sides disturbingly similar but for color and some variation in the cellular structures.

"The one on the right is a healthy blood sample. The left side is an infected one." When Mac turned to face the group Kate was struck by his somber expression. "Both of these were taken from Fletcher. The first when he was placed in the decon quarantine unit, the second … moments before he died."

There were gasps and curses from the group, and several of the men stood up as if there was something to fight. Kate just went kind of numb. "But, that was just a matter of hours. Palmer took days to even show signs."

She flinched as Mac turned his gaze back to her. There was such sorrow in his eyes. "Eva thought it was a matter of saturation. You breathe it in and there's not much there. Your body can fight it off a while, like you would any airborne infection, until it gets a foothold. If it enters directly through the bloodstream, it attacks and multiplies too rapidly for the white blood cells to combat it. The larger the wound and the longer it's open, the more contamination there is, the quicker the body succumbs. Other conditions also affect the rate of decline."

Mac's voice caught as he finished the last statement.

When Kate had first arrived, she'd assumed Eva was resting. Now, she wasn't so sure. Coming off of the gurney, she moved in front of him, where he couldn't avoid her. "Mac, where's Eva?"

The medtech flinched but continued with his briefing as if Kate wasn't there. "In extreme cases where the infected party has a chronic or temporary iron deficiency, such as anemia or rapid blood loss, the organism attacks the iron-rich organs of the body."

"Mac?" Kate tried again.

He continued to ignore her, stepping around her and moving to the pharmaceutical cabinet across the room. Unlocking it, he drew out several large bottles and one smaller one, which he set to the side. Pulling empty prescription pouches from a nearby shelf, he divvyed the bottles among them until he had ten identical bags of large oval brown pills. He tossed one to each of the men.

"Iron pills. Take two now and then one pill twice a day until we find a way out of this. The organism is apparently lazy; it continually goes toward the most easily accessed iron first. This should slow things down."

Kate had enough. She got right in his face and barked: "Mac!"

He stopped still. Didn't look up. When he spoke, she could barely hear him. "She's dead, Donovan ... just like Palmer ... just like Fletcher ... and just like Captain Troy ... And so are you, unless you start taking these."

He handed her the bag of iron pills and the small prescription bottle he'd taken out earlier. She turned it over and read the label, her brow drawing down in confusion. Hormone supplements? Kate looked up and trapped Mac's gaze. And then he spoke, only over her private frequency. *"She had her period, Kate ... she just ... had her period, and now she's dead. She didn't even know."*

And then he said aloud, "Take them."

Kate's hand closed reflexively over the prescription bottle. In a woman's normal cycle there was heavy iron loss. Kate shuddered. With a nod she popped the bottle open and took her first dose dry while he watched.

Satisfied, Mac stepped around her and back into the midst of the group.

"Wait..." she called out, spinning around to face him. "Did you say *Troy* is dead?!"

Mac looked over his shoulder and nodded. "He's what broke this, gave us a comparison we needed to isolate what was going on. That's how we found out it will attack the organs. The captain had a history of anemia. He thought he was safe in his suit, but by then it was too late. Because he was in his suit, the medical system automatically tracked his basic biometrics; from nearly start to finish we had a complete profile. Long enough to learn exactly what it does to us ... long enough to learn the organism dies very quickly without oxygen..."

"Funny, that," the navigator, Hal, growled out. "...so do we!"

If she hadn't been looking in their direction, Kate might have missed the look on Tom Henry's face at Hal's outburst. The look was familiar, just like that little *ah-ha* moment back in the storage compartment. "Tom? Whatcha thinking?"

"I have an idea..." he said. "But first, Mac, how many resuscitation ventilators do you have on board?" Kate thought she saw where he was going with this; ever since the invention of the original Draeger Pulmotor back in 1907, resuscitation ventilators were standard equipment for all mining operations.

A glimmer of hope returned to the medtech's expression as he glanced toward the back of medbay where a ward of twelve beds was laid out. Each had a ventilator built right into the bulkhead above it. He slowly nodded his head as he answered: "Enough."

"Excellent ... is there a master switch capable of activating them all at once?"

Mac nodded, approval clear in the set of his features.

"So," Tom went on, turning back toward the men. "Before the bug got him, Troy initialized a full atmospheric vent on the *Caliphus*..."

Anger kindled in the men's eyes, tightened their jaws. Kate shifted nervously and Tom darted a look in her direction, giving her a bit of a wink.

"Kate and I managed to stall the process, but it's still in place. If we put that process back on track we can purge the organism from the ship."

"What about us?" one of the miners asked. "Mac said we already got it."

"Well..." and here Tom looked nervous, "we'd have to go down with the ship, so to speak..."

The uproar was deafening. As the miners surged forward Tom stood his ground. Kate moved to his side, as did Mac, but the deciding factor was JP, who rose ominously from his crouch.

"Listen to the man," he commanded everyone in the flat, mechanical voice only Kate had heard until now.

"Oh my God! You spoke!" she sent over JP's private frequency.

"Not now!" he shushed her, and sheepishly she had to agree. She was just so stunned. "Go on, Tom," JP prompted out loud.

Tom didn't look nearly surprised enough in Kate's opinion, as he continued outlining his plan. "If Mac puts each of us under beforehand, when the ship vents, we will suffocate, no pain, no awareness. We program the ventilators to activate two minutes after the ship has been purged. Ventilators come on, we come back from the dead ... no more bug."

Silence, then Mac cleared his throat. An uncomfortable sound, an unhappy sound.

"Won't work, Tom ... the ventilators aren't the type of thing you can program. There is a master button, but it has to be manually operated."

Tom swore softly beneath his breath, only to surge once more as he leaned forward, that gleam back in his gaze. "I'll wear a suit ... push the button myself, then when you come around, Mac can do the same for me..."

Mac was already shaking his head. "There's no way to ensure all the organism is vented that way. You'd just be resetting the clock, eventually we'd reinfect."

"Damn it," Kate said, gripping Tom's arm in support. "There has to be a way to make this work!"

No one said a word. From one face to the other there was some degree of uncertainty, lost looks, and fear. Someone shifted. Someone else coughed, until someone smacked them.

"I can do it."

Everyone turned to look at JP, only they didn't see him; they saw a machine, something Kate was heartily fed up with.

"So sue me," she told Jean-Paul subvocally, before she deliberately violated her contract.

"Crew," Kate spoke into the stunned silence, a serene smile on her face, "I'd like you to meet my friend, Jean-Paul Marot, he's a cyborg."

In the end, they'd cancelled all the diagnostics Tom had scheduled except for the one that had been running. That had allowed them time to get everything set. The crew was strapped in and JP was anchored into place in front of the main medbay computer. Two buttons were marked in front of him: one to sedate the crew, the other to revive them. In ten minutes, the venting process would complete. It was time for him to press the first button.

The flashback hit with the force of a comet, leaving Jean-Paul disoriented. He swayed, his consciousness once more doubly trapped: his physical form within a tomb of fallen rock and as a passive observer in his own brain unable to stop the events unfolding against his will. Once more he saw himself reach out, saw the battered and bloody form of his foreman clinging doggedly to life, saw himself slide the end of the umbilical into his friend's neck, stealing Franklin's chance of survival. Saw the blood forever on his own "hand."

For the first time since his encapsulation, Jean-Paul Marot managed a vocal scream. It was pitiful. It came out in a low, constant tone, reminiscent of the ancient time of television and the sound broadcast when a station went off the air.

Not again. Please, God, not again, he thought, the plea held a frantic edge as he felt his mind crumble at the prospect of what he had to do. *What if it didn't work? What if some of them ... all of them, don't come back?* He was drowning in chemical despair at the risk of being responsible for even more deaths, this time by conscious decision. For God's sake, he'd volunteered! If this did not work, he would well and truly be a murderer. The "scream" increased in volume and intensity until something slapped the side of his brain case.

Tom Henry had extracted himself from his resuscitation ventilator and come up beside him. JP focused on the rage twisting the man's expression. "The longer you take, the more they suffer, the more chance some of them won't survive; either hit the godamn button or get out of my way."

"But you'll die." His monotone vocals did not convey the anxiety this caused Jean-Paul.

"But *she* won't ... not if *I* can help it." Tom's voice was thick with conviction, flavored with disgust at Jean-Paul's hesitation.

And there it was, the real reason JP had volunteered.

"Go back to your bunk, my friend." JP answered. "It's time to sleep."

He waited, his titanium finger on the button, as Tom hooked back up.

The last thing Jean-Paul heard as he killed them was Kate's slurred voice over the crew frequency: *"You still owe me that steak, Tom Henry."*

Part III:
Seductive Vampires

Anemia

David Lee Summers

I sat up late, well past the hour that should have been lights out for me, pouring over a volume of Edgar Allen Poe's short stories. On the table next to me, a largely ignored comp screen displayed telemetry of the Starship *Ramoth's* cryogenic life-support units. I—Gwen Morris—was the engineer in charge of those cryogenic units, and like Poe's detective —C. Auguste Dupin—I had a mystery solve.

The *Ramoth* was a colony ship bound for a planet orbiting the star Sigma Draconis. There were approximately five thousand people aboard the *Ramoth*—almost all of them cryogenically suspended in a cylinder rotating around the ship's central core. The sleeping colonists really didn't care about the gravity provided by the rotating cylinder, but it sure made life easier for the crew of twenty that remained awake to look after them during the seventeen-year voyage. The core of the ship was its massive engine, a Bussard Ramjet that scooped up interstellar hydrogen for its nuclear fusion reactor and propelled us toward Sigma Draconis at three-quarters the speed of light.

A tone sounded from the computer and I quickly marked my place in the book and set it aside. Turning to face the computer, I nodded as I saw a familiar caution indicator. Each cryogenically suspended person's circulatory system was hooked up to an external pump that assisted the heart and constantly monitored the blood for such things as oxygen content and toxicity. One bank of ten people just tested anemic. The computer had already initiated corrective procedures and within a few hours their red cell count would be perfectly normal. I had seen exactly this same behavior once a week for almost two years. It happened in a different bank of cryogenic containers each time and the incidents were always minor. The computer always corrected the incidents, just as it should. The problem was, there was no reason it should be happening at all.

I brought up a video that showed the affected cryogenic containers and commanded the computer to show me the video stream starting twenty minutes before the warning. It was like looking at a video of a morgue. Ten motionless bodies in transparent cylinders were illuminated by wan, reddish light. After watching for about five minutes, the view flickered and wavered. I'd seen this before and it made me think of a power fluctuation. However, when I checked the computer logs from the time of the fluctuation, all indications were that power levels were rock steady.

Yawning, I looked around at the bookshelves that lined the walls of my cabin. I turned back to the computer and tapped the book on the table next to the monitor. I felt like I would be a disappointment to a detective such as C. Auguste Dupin. Sure, I had learned when these cases of anemia would develop, but after two years I still could not predict where or why. Because the cases were all minor and the computers always compensated, the captain did not consider the problem a priority. However, he didn't mind me looking into it. After all, unless something broke down, I had little to occupy me—aside from my reading—for seventeen years. Thinking that suited me just fine, I stood, stretched, and climbed into my cot and turned out the lights. I would consider the problem more after getting some sleep.

The next day, I donned my coveralls and went to the galley. I stopped just long enough to eat a bagel and swallow some coffee before proceeding to the bridge. I was running a bit late—not that it mattered much, since schedules were pretty relaxed on this voyage. When I arrived, the captain was typing on his computer console. He said he was going to document the voyage and turn it into a novel. Somehow, I didn't think it would prove to be a very exciting read. The navigator was checking the ship's course and the ship's doctor was scanning the sensor logs from the cryo chambers.

"Hi Gwen," said Doctor Neaux. The doctor enjoyed watching old movies and was especially fond of the James Bond films from the twentieth century. "I see we had a case of anemia in section F-94 last night."

The captain looked up from his console and I could feel his eyes upon me. "It looks like systems compensated, just as they have in the previous cases," I reported. "I'm still trying to find out the cause."

The captain turned his attention back to his monitor.

Anemia

"It would be good to figure this out," said the doctor. "I worry about this problem getting worse."

I nodded. "So do I." With that, I turned my attention to my console. I performed a routine systems check and confirmed that everything was as it should be. Before signing aboard the *Ramoth*, I had been in charge of cryogenically frozen animals at a farm facility. The actual work was really not all that different from what I did aboard the starship. However, the farm owners were demanding and required that I spend long hours on the job. It paid well, but I never seemed to have much free time to enjoy my real passion of reading. When I saw that my company, American Agricorp, was planning to start a farm colony on Sigma Draconis II, I really wasn't interested at first. I certainly had no desire to be cryogenically frozen. However, I soon heard that they needed a small crew to run the ship while the colonists slept. They needed people who were loners by nature and would remain stable during the seventeen-year voyage with little to do. In return, we would get a plot of land to retire on and do whatever we wanted when we arrived at Sigma Draconis. All I had to do was keep the systems working and maintain a clean record during the voyage.

Several generations ago, my ancestors had been homesteaders around Springer, New Mexico. There's very little in that part of the country, even today. I think the genes that allowed them to be successful farmers and ranchers in that lonely part of the country had been passed down to me. I didn't mind having a few people around, but Earth really was getting too crowded and it always seemed there were too many demands on my time. Aboard the *Ramoth*, there was time enough at last to read and enjoy life. In some ways, I did not look forward to the day this long voyage would come to an end.

I stared at my console for several minutes, trying to figure out an approach to solving the problem of the anemic colonists. Finally, I ordered up a schematic of the ship and instructed the computer to plot each of the locations where the anemia was noted in the order they occurred. Each successive point was plotted and vanished. It happened just fast enough that persistence of vision allowed me to see two or three of the previous points just as a new point appeared. I'd done this exercise before, but so far, I could see no pattern. The cases of anemia seemed truly random.

Frowning, I started thinking about my procedure. The schematic I was using viewed the ship from the top. On a hunch, I commanded the computer to display the ship from the side and I reran the sequence. I didn't see any more indication of a pattern than I had before.

The navigator, Jennifer Wong, stepped up next to me and watched the patterns of dots as they appeared. "Hey wait a minute." She reached over and stopped the display. "Mind if I try something?"

"Go right ahead." I scooted my chair back so she had easier access to the keyboard.

Jennifer had a background in astronomy and mathematics and I gathered she liked to solve puzzles in her spare time. She displayed a few different combinations of dots against the profile of the ship. Each time, she shook her head. However, on the sixth time through, she came up with a pattern that even I recognized. There, superimposed against the ship was a pattern of dots in the shape of the constellation Orion. "Those are the cases that happened between October 15 and December 17 last year." She plotted up another group. I recognized the Big Dipper plus a few other stars. "Ursa Majoris," she declared.

I took over the keyboard and plotted up the last ten points. "Do you recognize that?"

She shook her head even as she continued staring at the schematic. Finally, she deleted a few points. What was left looked like a zigzag. "It looks like your anomaly is working its way through the constellation Cassiopeia."

"Can you tell where the next case of anemia is likely to occur?"

"That's easy," she said. "Only one star left." She superimposed a plot of the constellation Cassiopeia over the schematic, then lined the stars up with the dots. She pointed. "Section C-57."

My mouth dropped open as the implications of what Jennifer had just pointed out to me struck home. Not only was the pattern predictable, it was intelligent. I could see two possibilities. Either someone had programmed a virus into the system, which somehow caused the anemia, or someone was doing it in real time. A search of the life support systems should find the former. If that gave no results, I would be waiting in Section C-57 in a week's time to see who showed up. "Gotcha," I said.

Four days later, I was working on the bridge when a shadow fell across my console. I gasped and turned. The captain was standing over me with his hands behind his back.

Anemia

"Sorry, sir. I didn't hear you step up."

He waved my apology aside. "The shipboard network seems slow. I was wondering if it's related to the tests you're doing."

"I'm afraid so. I'm running deep level scans of the network to make sure a virus hasn't infiltrated our systems."

He frowned. "We have programs that do that on a regular basis."

"They don't really perform the deepest level scans and they can miss things," I countered. "There's evidence of something strange going on. I really don't want it to get worse and bite us."

The captain took a couple of steps back toward his chair, his head down, apparently in thought. "How much longer will you need for these tests?"

"Another day, two at the most," I responded. "I haven't found anything so far."

"Very well, but unless you find evidence of a bigger problem, I don't want you to continue draining ship's resources." He looked over to Jennifer Wong. "You have the bridge. I'll be in my quarters."

"Yes, sir," said the navigator. When the captain left, Jennifer stepped up to my station. "Any chance this could just be a bug in the code?"

I shook my head. "I've run simulations before. Nothing that causes a change in the colonist's blood count has cropped up."

"What about a hardware failure? Maybe it's just coincidence that these things seem to be happening in a pattern. After all, we only identified three patterns that looked like constellations."

"I've checked the hardware. I've examined all of the systems that glitched, but I haven't seen any sign of a problem. All the filters and gaskets have been fine. There's been no sign of leakage that I can determine." I sighed. "I just can't think of a reason unless someone's deliberately tampering with the system."

"Why would anyone do that?" asked Jennifer.

I sighed. "I really have no idea."

She patted my shoulder and I flinched. She quickly withdrew her hand. Her eyes told me she was sorry that she had violated my personal space. "You should probably call it a day, soon. The scans you're running won't be finished until tomorrow, anyway."

I nodded, realizing she was right. I stood and stretched stiff muscles. "I'll see you tomorrow, Jennifer," I said.

"Get some rest."

I left the bridge and made my way down the corridor to my quarters. Stepping in, I looked around at the books on the shelves. I had finished my collection of Poe's short stories and considered starting the poems. However, I felt like I needed more inspiration to solve the problem I was dealing with. I turned to C. Auguste Dupin's literary successor, Mr. Sherlock Holmes. It had been years since I first read those adventures. I grabbed one of the books at random. It was *The Case Book of Sherlock Holmes*. I made myself some tea and settled in to read "The Adventure of the Illustrious Client." The story reminded me of one of Holmes' admonitions to Watson, "You have seen, but you have not observed."

Sitting the book aside, I took a sip of tea and decided to take a walk. I retrieved my tool belt and flashlight just in case I needed them and went to the elevator at the far end of the deck containing the crew quarters. I took the elevator to F-deck and stepped out.

Surrounding me on all sides, floor to ceiling, were crypt-like cryogenic containers. The light was kept low to conserve energy. As I progressed among the colonists lying in death-like slumber, I found myself reflecting on the name of the vessel. *Ramoth* was an homage to one of the dragons of Anne McCaffrey's Pern novels. Moreover, Ramoth helped to rediscover that dragons are capable of time travel. It seemed a good name for a ship subject to relativistic time dilation while traveling to an alien world in the constellation of Draco the dragon. However, as I made my way through the dimly lit corridor surrounded by corpse-like bodies, I couldn't help but think of more villainous dragons such as Smaug from Tolkien's *The Hobbit* or the dragon killed by Saint George. The problem was, if I was in a dragon's lair, why did I feel it unlikely I would find treasure at the end of my journey?

I stepped up my pace until I came to the ninety-fourth bank of cryogenic containers. I performed a cursory visual inspection. Everything looked as it should. I saw a few scratches around the screws of the blood filtration unit, but those could have been caused by me during my recent inspection. Even the quick-connect coupling where the doctor could draw blood samples was shiny and spotless. Realizing there was nothing more to learn here, I returned to the elevator.

On a hunch, I decided to stop off at C-deck and check the 57th bank of cryogenic units. As I stepped down the corridor, I thought I saw something move. I shone my flashlight toward the cryogenic

Anemia

containers, but only saw the sleeping forms of colonists. The movement must have just been some dust, or perhaps one of the light bulbs developed a flicker. My heart started beating a little faster despite my reassurances to myself and I stepped up my pace as I moved down the corridor.

At last, I arrived at my destination. The control panel and support systems looked identical to the ones in section F-94. Just as I was about to leave, I realized there was something slightly different about this unit. The quick-connect coupling where the doctor could tap in and draw blood wasn't exactly the same. Whereas the one on F-94 appeared shiny and new, as though it had been used recently, this one was just a little blackened and dull from oxidation. There was nothing unusual about that, except that it told me the connector on F-94 had been used recently and the one here had not been touched in some time. I wondered if the doctor had taken blood samples and decided to ask him. As I turned and stepped back to the elevator, I felt as though I was being watched.

The next day, I saw Dr. Neaux as he was leaving the galley.

"Have you been taking blood samples from those patients who've been testing anemic?" I asked.

He shook his head. "I haven't really seen a reason since they're already tested through the life support systems. Aside from these minor cases of anemia, I haven't seen any indications of a problem."

I pursed my lips. "I was just wondering if it was worth an independent check, just to make sure there isn't an equipment malfunction related to these cases of anemia."

He inclined his head and finally nodded after a moment. "Perhaps you're right. It wouldn't hurt to do a quick check." He turned and proceeded toward the medical bay while I continued into the galley to eat my breakfast.

After breakfast, I went to the bridge. The deep-level virus scan revealed no problems. I thought about repeating the scan, but looked over my shoulder and saw the captain. It was likely that running another scan would not only be fruitless, it would just annoy my crewmates. Besides, after my sojourn the night before, I didn't think the problem was in the computer anymore. The best explanation was that someone was drawing off blood. However, I still had no idea why.

I spent the rest of my shift checking and adjusting the life support systems as necessary. Everything was behaving as I expected it to. At the end of the day, I ate a quiet meal in the galley and then returned to my quarters. Opening my volume of *The Casebook of Sherlock Holmes* to the contents, my eyes fell on one of the titles: "The Adventure of the Sussex Vampire." I decided that was the next story to read.

Two nights later, I finished work early and went to my quarters. By my best guess, a case of anemia was due to strike section C-57 that night and I wanted to be ready. I thought about checking out a pistol from the armory, but that would require the captain's permission. I would have to explain to him why I thought I needed a sidearm to confront what was, most likely, a technical malfunction. Likewise, I thought about asking either Jennifer Wong or Dr. Neaux to accompany me. However, even if some crewmember was drawing blood from the cryogenic units, the amount was small enough that I guessed the person was more likely weird than dangerous. That seemed plausible since most of us that opted for a life of near-solitude on a starship for seventeen years were considered at least a bit weird by the people we left behind on Earth. Still, I made sure I had a good-sized wrench and screwdriver well within reach on my tool belt.

I went to the elevator and descended to C-level. The red lights cast their usual, eerie glow. I thought about activating the bright, white fluorescent lights, but decided against it. If someone was hiding, it would alert them to my presence. I made my way down the corridor. Again, I thought I saw movement. I shone my light in one of the cryogenic cylinders and saw a young woman just out of her teens. It was easy to imagine her turning and opening her eyes, even though I knew people in cryogenic suspension could not move.

Swallowing, I turned and continued down the corridor. When I arrived, I inspected the cryogenic control units. All was the same as a few days before, except…

The quick-connect valve was shiny.

I ground my teeth. Whoever was behind this had already been there.

A faint squeak, like the rubber of a shoe against the metal deck caused me to swing around. There, in my flashlight beam, was a man. His eyes were closed and he stood absolutely motionless. He wore the same coveralls that every colonist wore. His stomach and chest were still, as though he wasn't breathing. By all appearances, he seemed to be a person from one of the cryogenic containers, except that he was vertical, propped up against the bank of electronics instead of horizontal and in a transparent cylinder. He must have fallen out, or been removed.

"Where did you come from?" I mused aloud.

His eyes popped open. "Section D-13," he said. "I'm surprised you hadn't noticed before now."

I dropped my flashlight and fell back into the cryogenics containers behind me. My heart hammered in my chest and I fumbled for my screwdriver.

"That won't be necessary," he said. "I mean you no harm."

"Who are you?" I asked.

"I am called Jaeger," he said.

"Are you responsible…"

"For drawing a small amount of blood from the odd cryogenic unit?" He shrugged, as though the answer was obvious.

"What is this, some kind of test?" Despite his earlier assurance, I finally drew the screwdriver and brandished it in front of me.

"Test?" His eyebrows furrowed.

"The pattern of drawing blood from the cryogenic units—the pattern like constellations."

He took a deep breath and let it out slowly. "Not at all, Miss Morris," he said. "It was not a test. It was merely a mnemonic so I could remember where I'd been. I was really trying to make the pattern appear random. Apparently I wasn't clever enough." He took a step forward, but stopped when I held the screwdriver up. "I really am quite impressed that you were able to predict where I would appear in only two years' time. I underestimated you. I thought my work would go unnoticed much longer than it did."

"Why are you siphoning blood from the cryogenic units?"

"I consume it."

His tone was so natural and matter-of fact, that chills went up my arms. "What are you, some kind of vampire?"

He shrugged again in that same non-committal way that seemed to imply the answer should be obvious. Jaeger inclined his head and though he was several feet away, I felt him in my personal space, just as Jennifer Wong had been when she touched me a few days before. "It occurs to me that there might be a better way to live than trying to steal the blood I need periodically."

"What do you mean?" I asked.

"I think you can work it out." He smiled and I realized that his canine teeth were surprisingly long and sharp. "I did not set you a test before, but I'll set one for you now. I assume you realize that I'm at the end of one of my patterns."

I nodded. My intuition screamed that I should jump this guy, try to take him out. He was obviously a stowaway—and a mad one at that.

His smile turned gentle, and I felt comforted, as though he had caressed my cheek even though he was still more than an arm's-length away. "You have two beautiful eyes. A coronet, such as one worn by the northern kings would complement them nicely." He turned and I watched him walk down the corridor. I tried to give chase, but found myself frozen in place. When he turned the corner around a bank of cryogenic units, I could move again. Carefully, I made my way to the junction in the corridor where he disappeared. Jaeger was nowhere to be seen.

I backed away from the junction, into the elevator and went up to the crew decks. Once I was safely inside my cabin, I locked the door for the first time since the voyage began.

The next day, I didn't leave my cabin, even after first watch began. The captain signaled on the intercom. "Are you feeling all right, Gwen?"

"I'm fine, sir. I think I have a lead on what's going on with the anemic crewmembers. May I have the day to investigate further?"

"You may," said the captain. "But, I wish you had called the bridge to let me know."

"Sorry, sir," I said. "I'll report once I've put the information together."

There was a non-committal grunt and the captain disconnected. I stared at the speaker for a moment and then turned my attention to the computer. I brought up the crew manifest and looked at the information regarding section D-13. Sure enough, unit three was occupied by a man named Klaus Jaeger. I then pulled up telemetry on unit D-13-3. It indicated respiration, heart action, everything that would lead me to believe that a person was there. I then went back and checked the telemetry from the time I was talking to Jaeger in the hall. It appeared

D-13-3 had been occupied at the time. The answer was simple enough, my "Jaeger" was a stowaway who had borrowed a name from one of the crewmembers. I felt somewhat reassured. I was more comfortable as a detective figuring out the motives of a human weirdo than as Gwen Morris, vampire hunter. I might have been the descendent of cowboys, but I didn't even own a Bowie Knife like the one used to slay Dracula in Bram Stoker's novel. Whether detective or vampire hunter, I decided I should check container D-13-3 for myself.

I showered, dressed, donned my tool belt, and took the elevator down to level D. Even though it was no brighter on the lower decks, it somehow seemed less ominous than the night before. I quickly arrived at section 13. To my surprise, the third cryogenic unit was empty. I opened it and looked inside. A makeshift computer board was wired in. There was a pulse generator to simulate a regular heartbeat and computer chips that would simulate respiration and other autonomic functions. I shut down the unit and yanked the board from the cryogenic cylinder. It was time to tell the captain what I'd found.

I arrived on the bridge a few minutes later, wielding the computer board I had pulled from the cryogenic unit. "Captain, I think we have a stowaway."

The captain looked up at me and scratched the stubble on his chin. "Oh?"

I sat down at the controls for the ship's main display and brought up the video from the night before. It showed me as I walked into the camera's range. I saw my shocked reaction as I realized that someone had already been to unit C-57. I turned, searched with my flashlight, dropped it, and backed away ... apparently from nothing. Somehow no video of Jaeger was recorded during our conversation. Unfortunately, there were no microphones on the lower decks, so all the video showed was me apparently talking while wielding a screwdriver against empty space.

I felt the skeptical gazes of the captain, Doctor Neaux, and even Jennifer Wong on me. I shook my head. "I don't understand what's going on. The video's been altered somehow. I saw a man on the lower decks last night." Turning, I held up the computer board. "Someone wired this board into unit D-13-3. Come down with me and I'll show you."

The captain's eyes darted between the video screen and me. Suddenly his eyes widened and a sly smile appeared. He nodded. At first I was relieved, because I thought perhaps he realized the video could have somehow been altered. Then, I realized that his reaction was likely far more selfish. Something interesting had finally happened on the voyage—an incident he could include in his memoir. Even so, he stood and straightened his jacket. "Yes, let's check this out. Ms. Wong, you have the bridge." He turned his head. "Doctor, please accompany us."

I led the captain and the doctor down to level D. As we approached unit 13, a chill crept up my spine. Going numb, I let go of the computer board. It clattered to the metal deck, chips scattering several directions at once. Klaus Jaeger lay in unit D-13-3. I looked inside the tube next to him. There was no sign of the bare wires where I'd ripped out the makeshift computer board less than half an hour before. Everything was just as it should be. "I ... I ... I don't know how to explain," I said.

The captain took in a breath and let it out slowly. "Gwen, I think you've been working a bit too hard. You need to take a break."

"Captain..."

"Gwen, you're relieved from duty pending further notice." With that, the captain turned and walked back to the elevator.

"I'll walk you to your quarters," said the doctor, reaching out to take my elbow.

"No thanks." I pulled my arm away. "I know how to find my room."

"Suit yourself." The doctor followed the captain and I saw the doors close on them as well as my nice comfortable retirement. Next to me, I thought I saw a slight grin form on Klaus Jaeger's face.

I spent the next few days in my quarters, coming out only to visit the galley, grab a quick meal and return. On the fifth day, there was a knock at my cabin door.

"Come in." My voice sounded like sandpaper rubbing against itself.

Jennifer Wong stepped through the doors. Her sad brown eyes reminded me of a puppy I once owned. "I've been worried about you. How are you doing?"

"I've been trying to calculate how many years I'll have to work after we land at Sigma Draconis before I can afford the dream house they were going to build me." I turned my monitor around so Jennifer could see. Displayed on it were the architectural drawings of the home I'd submitted to corporate headquarters before we left. It was a lavish house with a grand library right in the center to hold all the books I had in my cabin plus the ones in storage—all the books I might not get to read now.

"Relief from duty is hardly the end of the world," said Jennifer.

I snorted. "You know the contract as well as I do. Any black mark on our record means they don't have to honor the contract. They don't have to build the house for me. They don't even have to give me retirement after we land. Being relieved from duty was one thing, but the captain also put my absence from the bridge that morning on the record as well."

"We've got fifteen years before we land." Jennifer tried to smile reassuringly. "In that time you could get a commendation that might cancel out this action."

I saw her point, but still I couldn't see how I could dig myself out of the trouble I'd somehow gotten into. If everything worked as it should, I saw no way I could distinguish myself enough to earn a commendation. If something broke, repairing it would be my job—nothing worthy of special note. Even more frustrating was that I had gotten into this trouble by following procedure and trying to do the right thing. I couldn't hide the frustration and tears began to flow.

Jennifer came close and put her arm around my shoulder, trying to comfort me. I've never really liked being touched and that was just too much. I stood up suddenly and Jennifer dropped to the floor like a sack of potatoes. I wanted to say something to ease the hurt I saw on her face, but I was too conflicted inside to find the right words. Looking up into the mirror, I saw my face and realized that I looked much angrier than I felt. I tried to soften my expression, but I fear it was too late.

Jennifer stood and straightened her coveralls. She put on a brave face, but didn't smile. "If you feel like talking, let me know. I'll be happy to drop by." With that, she stepped briskly out of the room without giving me a chance to say anything further. The hurt I caused her just compounded my frustration. I put my face in my hands and more tears flowed. This time there was no one to comfort me.

Two days later, I realized that Jaeger was due to visit one of the cryogenic units for more blood that evening. I had been giving thought to his riddle. He said I had two beautiful eyes and that the coronet of a northern king would complement them. A search of constellation names on the computer told me there was a constellation called Corona Borealis—the Northern Crown. That must be the constellation. Two beautiful eyes suggested he would start at unit I-2. Jaeger had gotten me into this mess. I wanted to learn more about him. As far as I could tell, the captain had not restricted my freedom of movement around the ship at all, so I went in search of the stowaway.

He was standing in front of unit I-2 when I arrived.

"I don't believe in vampires," I declared when I saw him.

"I never asked you to."

"Then what are you?"

"Very old and lonely." There was a sadness in his eyes as he said that.

"How old?" I asked.

"I was already two centuries old when I first heard Robert Bussard give a lecture about the principles of the ramjet."

I shook my head. "You heard Robert Bussard...? He lived over five hundred years ago. It took that long for us to get that far with space travel."

"I know." His expression did not waver and I could sense he was earnest. "I've been waiting all that time for an opportunity to travel amongst the stars. When I heard that American Agricorp was going to start a farming colony on Sigma Draconis, I went to work for the company with the hope of being selected as a colonist. The most difficult part was distinguishing myself on the night shift."

"Why the night shift?"

"Because sunlight has always been toxic to me." He shrugged.

"What would you have done when we reached Sigma Draconis?"

"I suppose I hoped that since Sigma Draconis is a slightly different spectral type than our sun, I might be able to walk about during the daylight."

I inclined my head. "The problem is, you don't know for sure."

He shook his head. "Aboard this ship, I've been able to move around whenever I want for the first time in almost seven centuries. Can you imagine what that's like?"

I folded my arms across my stomach. "You say you don't ask me to believe you're a vampire, but everything you are telling me indicates that you think you are."

He smiled slightly at that observation. "What about the evidence you've seen so far? I don't show up on your video cameras, for instance."

"I know vampires aren't supposed to have reflections. What does that have to do with video?" I was growing impatient with this game.

"Same principle," he said with a toss of his hand. "I can bend light around myself. Don't ask how it works, I can't explain it any better than you could explain how you blink, breathe or swallow without choking. It just happens. It's a good defense for a predator."

"It's not perfect, though," I observed. "I could see a ripple when you moved."

"It's also not all that effective if you look right at me as you did a week ago." He pointed up at the camera mounted on the wall. "It would be much harder to fool the camera if I stood right in the line of sight."

I nodded. "That's all fine and good, but I gather you gave me a clue about how to find you for some other reason than explaining how you manipulate light."

He nodded. "Over the years, I've grown accustomed to being alone, but that doesn't prevent me from being lonely from time to time. I sense the same in you."

I thought about Jennifer's visit a couple of days before. I thought of her touch that was too familiar for comfort. I also thought of my hurt when she stormed away. I had wanted her to stay. I just didn't want her to be too close. "How do I know I would want you for a companion?"

"I don't believe you can know that, yet," he conceded. "However, I have the ability to change you. You could be free of your mortal coil. You could retire when you desire, no longer bound to the authority of others unless you chose to be."

I turned my back on him. "It seems too good to be true" I stepped away a few paces. "Besides, I'm not entirely sure I believe you."

"We are only two years into this journey," he said. "You have fifteen years to decide."

When I turned around, he was gone.

The next morning, the captain dropped by my cabin. "How are you feeling?" he asked.

That proved to be a difficult question to answer. I was still hurt because people didn't even try to understand what I'd seen and had disciplined me when I did nothing wrong. My thoughts were also absorbed by Jaeger, who I thought really must be a vampire. At the very least he was more compelling—and more frightening—than anyone else on the ship. "I'm not really sure how I feel," I admitted at last.

The captain's eyes narrowed, as though evaluating me. "Do you feel like returning to duty?"

I frowned at that. "I never felt like I needed to be relieved from duty in the first place," I said honestly. "I feel like I've been disciplined for doing the right thing."

The captain pursed his lips and looked down at his folded hands. "Gwen, I've reviewed the video from the other day several times. I'm afraid I see nothing but you standing in front of a cryogenic unit talking to yourself. The doctor agrees that it looks like you were on the verge of a nervous breakdown." He sighed. "I don't believe I made the wrong decision. You needed some time off."

"Maybe that's true," I said. "But you also gave me a demerit for being late that day. You've never done that before."

He closed his eyes and was silent for a moment as though summoning some inner resolve. "You've been late a lot—more than any other crewmember. I had to give you a demerit or risk being disciplined myself."

"These disciplinary actions are going to affect my contract."

"I know, and I'm sorry about that. I'll talk to them, see what we can do." I didn't sense much hope in the captain's voice. He shuffled his feet for a moment and cleared his throat. "Is there anything else I can do for you?"

"I think you've done all you can, sir." My voice was tight.

The captain nodded. "Then I'll see you on the bridge tomorrow morning." With that, he turned and left my cabin.

I stared at the door for a time after he left. There was no apology, no attempt to understand. Maybe the captain would help, maybe he wouldn't. I'd have to see what happened over the next several weeks. Finally I turned my attention to the computer monitor. It was a plot of the ship. Superimposed on it was the constellation Corona Borealis. I knew where I'd next see Jaeger.

A year later, I sat in my cabin reading *The Vampire Lestat* by Anne Rice. I enjoyed the novel despite the fact she got a lot of the details about vampires wrong. There was a knock at the door. A moment later, Jaeger stepped in. "Ah, good," I said as I marked my place in the book. "I have a fine unit of O-positive picked out for us this evening."

"That sounds lovely." He held the door open for me as I stepped out into the corridor. We strolled side-by-side toward the elevator.

Really, my job hasn't changed that much over the years. I used to tend cryogenically frozen livestock. That's what I've returned to doing, especially after the rest of the ship's crew died. The only one I miss is Jennifer Wong. She really was a good soul, but she didn't have a good sense of personal boundaries. That was especially true the night she finally realized all the things I had said about Jaeger were true and she tried to shoot me with a pistol from the armory.

With Jennifer gone, it took me a while to figure out how to change the ship's course, but I did manage it. We'll miss Sigma Draconis II by a few billion miles and continue on into interstellar space—just Jaeger and me, blissfully free of the dangers of sunlight.

Chosen One

Dana Bell

A faint stale breeze assaulted my nose while I slept, smelling of unwashed bodies. Humans are such stinky creatures unlike us felines who instinctively keep ourselves clean. After all, we wouldn't want our rightful prey catching our scent and scampering away.

My ears twitched slightly as a sudden, silenced high-pitched squeak invaded my hunt and play dreams. I lifted my head from where it had rested on my black paws and listened for the sound again. Hearing nothing, I stretched, being careful not to wake my human companion. She'd had a hard day distributing the few supplies she'd gotten in from the last Earth supply ship. Most of the miners were understanding, but there's always one or two who aren't and they made my human's life a bit more interesting.

I hopped down to the uneven stone floor and up on the narrow ledge of the "window". It wasn't really. It's just a hole in the asteroid wall and my human—Leslie is what she calls herself—put up a cloth-covered board for me—"her" male feline. Sitting down I pushed aside the rough cloth and peered out into the hallway.

I blinked my green eyes, thankful I could see along the darkened way. No humans were up oddly enough, though there always seemed to be someone about, and the strange silence caught my attention. All I could hear was the usual *whopf, whopf* of the air and water recycling pumps.

Glancing back, I knew it would be a long while before Leslie was up and about. She'd burrowed deep into her sleeping bag like a serpent in a blast hole. I jumped down and sniffed the outcrop under the window. There was blood, a few bits of skinny tail hair, and an odd scent that seemed both familiar and not. A burning started in my nose and I backed away, using my paw to try and clear the stench away.

I sneezed several times and finally the offensive odor cleared. My back arched and I hissed. A dead one was here. One of the long-lived ones touched with the ancient blessing of Bast. Or maybe it was more of a curse. Among my kind it was spoken of both ways.

Leslie groaned and I looked back up at the window. Maybe I should go back inside and lie beside her. When I did that, she'd settle down. You see, my human came out here after the terrible Race and Class Wars. I don't remember much about them since I was but a youngling and had more important things to think about, like using the zero-G litter box correctly and keeping my dignity while floating in the air.

But my human, she lost her entire family in the war. Many living out here in the asteroids had. They'd settled among the twirling rocks to escape the terrible memories and try to scrape out a living by mining the minerals and precious stones, like the flashy politicians back on Earth said they could. Not that many have hit it rich. Most make just enough to pay the taxes on their claims and buy a few supplies.

My head popped up as a leathery sound snaked over the rock. The tunnel serpents were dangerous and deadly. They weren't native but an odd variation contrived by some gene expert to keep down the population of the skinny tails. Not that it had worked. Instead, the creatures had escaped and liked to den close to the humans, sending many of our companions to the final sleep. And so, we felines hunt them and send the serpents to a swift and final end.

Well, as quick of an end as we allowed. What fun is food if we don't get to play with it first?

I scrunched down and began to track the noise, rubbing my side against the smooth rock, trying to be silent as I slowly stalked my prey. Around a corner, the red, white, black, and aqua snake coiled, its velvet tongue lashing out at another of my kind.

No, not my kind, I corrected myself as the rotting stench touched my sensitive brown nose. I sneezed and jumped back just as the serpent swung toward me and struck. I heard its head rattle against the unstable boulder barely missing me.

The stinking mass pounced, sinking deep canine-like fangs into the scaly flesh. I watched in horror as the long body flopped, causing pebbles to skitter scatter over the floor. Finally, the snake stilled, its tongue slithering out of its mouth, a few green drops of its venom splattering on the stone.

"It's dead," the other told me. "You should take more care."

"You shouldn't be here," I hissed back. My body trembled. Though I had heard the stories, none had prepared me for the true appearance of the creature. Short cropped tan fur scattered with black spots, towering above me by at least a full head, ebony claws extended making an *erch* noise as it moved.

It lifted a giant paw and casually licked the serpent blood mixed with green venom away. When the necessary washing was done, it stared at me with round yellow-red eyes.

"I am nothing to fear."

"You're so ... big." I could think of nothing else to say.

"We are the first ones. Not contaminated by the touch of humans."

It sounded almost condescending. As if by choosing to companion with Leslie, I was less than it was.

"I saved your life this night. Remember my favor well." It bounded away and I stood staring after it. How could a feline so large, be gone so quick?

When morning came, I wondered if I had indeed encountered one of the favored ones of Bast. I awakened as was usual, lying beside my human. She smiled at me and rubbed behind my ear. I closed my eyes halfway and purred for her. Leslie fed me my breakfast of dried sea dweller and I lapped my water to rid myself of the salty tang.

As was normal, she went to the trading post to haggle with the few stragglers who would come in today to see if there was anything left. I think she said she had a case of unmarked soup, several boxes of crackers, and a package of cookies she was saving special for someone.

I again sat in the window watching the humans hurry by. Not that I cared what they did with their day. I just enjoyed the few who stopped to give me a friendly pet and sometimes sneak a treat they'd secreted in their pockets.

Old George always brought me a green sharp-scented treat I loved to roll in. I heard him say he grew it for all the cats (I really don't like that word) and he felt we deserved it for all the de-rodent work we did. Most of the humans just rolled their eyes, but he'd wink at me like he knew I understood.

Of course, several of us lived with him, so I suspect he knows we do.

He came by as was normal and pulled the cotton bag out of his pocket. I saw something hanging out of his other pocket and batted at it. When he turned, I flattened my ears against my head.

"Just a dead snake," he reassured me, taking some of the scented stuff on his fingers and running them over my fur. "Found it down the hallway there. Quite peculiar." He shrugged. "See ya later, Blackie." He trotted away.

Blackie. He always called me that. Leslie called me Shadow. My true name is—no, I mustn't even think it. The ancient one might hear, or so the legends say, and then have power over me. I can't allow that.

I lost part of my day in a haze of pungent leafy enjoyment and took my normal nap on my human's bed. Upon waking I bathed myself yet again—no self-respecting feline is ever dirty—ate a few bits of the dry stuff Leslie left for me, drank more water and prepared to go off exploring again.

Quickly, I checked the small room for any unwelcome guests. Finding none, I padded out and down the rock-hewn hallway. I had to dodge uncaring human feet several times. Many don't watch out for us and I don't remember how many times my tail or paws have been stepped on. They don't even apologize and that is truly offensive.

Finally, I got to the trading post.

Old George was there and he had the snake spread out on the old board counter. Leslie was sitting on a barrel watching. I jumped up and batted at the dead serpent.

"Shadow, be careful!" Leslie warned as she tried to move me away from it.

"It's quite dead," George said. "Though, I don't think any of the cats killed it."

I wish he'd stop calling us cats.

"Why do you say that?"

"Normally, when a cat kills it, the neck is broken and it's partially eaten." He turned the intact snake over. "This one has a wound on it and when I tried to give it to Bossy—" Bossy lives here in the post. She's the oldest of us and tells us stories about Earth. It's from her I heard about the ancient ones "—she only hissed and tried to scratch me."

"Shadow doesn't seem to be afraid of it."

"He ain't claiming it neither." George scratched his shaggy dirty hair and grimaced. Maybe he'd figured out he was dirty and needed to bathe. "Strange."

"I just hope it doesn't mean we have yet another pest to deal with." Leslie shook her head. "I'm getting tired of us figuring out how to fight one problem only to have another crop up."

"It's called life, my dear girl."

"If you say so." She quickly ran a hand over my back. "What do you need, George?"

I ignored them as they discussed what he needed, what Leslie actually had, and all the details of the transaction they finally agreed upon. Old George put the serpent back in his pocket and ambled away.

Over the next few cycles, several tunnel serpents and skinny tails were found all over the asteroid. The other felines avoided the kill spots, but I found myself drawn to them, sniffing the odd scents and sneezing out the sharp hurt until I no longer needed to.

I'd told the others about my encounter with the ancient one. Bossy had stared at me with her one good eye. The other she'd lost in a fight with a skinny tail.

"You've been chosen," she'd told me.

"Chosen?" I hadn't understood.

"The stories say," she'd continued, "the ancient ones select one of us."

"For what?"

"I do not know. A chosen one has never come back and told us."

Quite honestly, I didn't know whether to be concerned or not. So, I continued my days of sleeping, eating, bathing, hunting, being petted, and receiving treats from the humans. What else is there in the life a feline?

Perhaps I should have paid more attention to Bossy's warning. Or perhaps, I should have known there was little to fear.

For when it happened, I had been hunting under the many metal moving parts of the air pump station. The skinny tails seem to like it in here. There're so many places they can hide and we felines have a hard time catching them when they dart in the narrow places we can not squeeze our flexible bodies into.

I had cornered a skinny tail and had made ready to pounce, only to feel a sharp pain in my head. I shook it and my vision blurred as drops of heavy red fell over my muzzle. The tang of hot blood touched my tongue and I sensed it was my own.

The skinny tail wiggled toward me its beady black eyes keenly watching. Its sharp little teeth plunged into my paw and I yowled in torment. I tried to swipe at it and break its neck, but my paw would not obey. Heavily I fell, my head smacking into something hard. I heard a *kkk* and knew I would not rise nor be able to stop the nipping teeth tearing at my body.

That was the last I remembered.

When I awoke again, I found myself lying on a soft bed. I heard the *sprrrr, sprrr* of water nearby and I suddenly found I longed for a drink. Shakily I got up, surprised to find my body intact and not in pain.

I blinked, raising my head to gaze around. Above, a gauzy fabric waved in the wind attached to marble columns covered in bright colorful designs. All around I could smell the delightful pungent tang of my favorite green plant. Surrounding my furred bed was a soft, fine powder I had never seen before.

Carefully I extended my paw and touched the powder, quickly withdrawing it when the substance spread under my touch. I wasn't sure I liked it, but I was so thirsty.

The powder was soft under my paws and though not easy to walk upon, it did not impede me to my destination. I lowered my head to lap at the clear water, feeling the liquid revive me in a way I could not express.

"So you've awakened, warrior."

I had not heard the female approach. I jumped back and whirled to face her, my black hair puffed up along my spine.

"You're in no danger here." She sat down and blinked her green-yellow eyes at me, her bushy spotted tail draped over her paws.

She looked like the ancient one. She had the same tan fur and black spots, but she wasn't as large as he had been.

"You are welcome in my temple."

"Your temple?"

A deep amused purr rumbled from her chest. It was then I noticed the odd gold circle about her neck.

"I am Bast, warrior."

Bast! I pushed my belly onto the powder and lowered my head. I must pay proper respect to the goddess.

"You died in honor, warrior. There is no need to crawl upon the sand as would an adder.

She rose. "Come. There is a matter yet to be resolved."

I got to my paws. The sand clung to my belly. I'd have to clean it off later. I followed Bast beyond the place where I had awakened to an open dwelling of many smooth stairs and golden columns. Standing on each side were humans in thin clothing, their heads bald and odd markings on their faces.

"My priests who have chosen to serve me in the afterlife," she explained.

At the top I stopped. Bast strolled to a pile of fur and took her place. All around her were other felines. A mass of browns, blacks, whites, and so many other colors, I could not sort them in my mind.

Bast's head turned and the ancient one I had encountered joined us. My heart began to pound as if I had hunted well and now was the time of play.

"So, he has passed beyond," the ancient one said.

"He has," Bast agreed. "Yet, the debt has not been repaid."

"It has not." His yellow-red eyes looked at me. "Unfortunate."

"Perhaps not. Warrior," Bast summoned.

I dared to approach her.

"You owe a debt to this, my favored one. Would you choose to repay? Or do you intend to dwell here with me?"

"I have already passed beyond." I did not understand the choice offered.

Again her chest echoed the purring laugh. "Humans have legends of us."

I still did not understand.

"My offer stands."

"I can release him," the ancient one offered.

"No. This one has always had great promise."

"And if it was my wish to repay?" I almost feared her answer. I thought she would return me to my damaged and tortured body.

"That was burned by your human."

"So how?" I did not understand how such a thing was possible nor how she'd known my thought.

"I bestow my favor on many." Her tongue darted out and touched the muzzle of the ancient one. "Besides, humans need to be reminded of their proper place. And ours as well."

"And that is?" I still didn't truly understand.

"We were worshipped once, warrior. So we should be again. Now, is it truly your wish to repay, warrior?"

"It is."

"So be it." Bast came to me and stole my breath.

"Sure looks like Blackie," Old George said as he rubbed my head. I nipped at his fingers. He had my favorite leafy smell on them.

"Well, we both know that's not possible." Leslie scratched behind my ear and turned away to shelf the new shipment of supplies.

"Poor ole boy."

I saw Leslie wipe liquid from under her eye. "Well, at least you didn't see the body." She shuddered. "It was horrible."

"Smart thing you did burning it."

"It was the best thing."

"Where'd you find this fella?" His hand ran the length of my back.

"Captain of the supply ship found him in the hold. Knew I'd lost mine and offered him to me."

"Smart man."

"Guess so." She sighed. "I miss Shadow."

I jumped down bored with the conversation. It was time to hunt and I had in my mind to find the skinny tail who had ended my first life. Bast had promised me my revenge and the goddess always kept her word.

Padding out on the familiar stone, I was joined by the ancient one. The other felines saw us coming and darted into hiding spots until we passed. They knew we were no longer like them.

"I found the skinny tail," the ancient one told me.

"Good. I want to play with it for a long time before I kill it."

"As is proper."

"So, I have another debt to repay."

"You will have a long time to do so. And I am patient, youngling."

I knew his words to be true. For as Bast told me, humans have many legends of us and the one they scoff at even as they speak it, is truth. We do indeed have nine lives and I have another eight to repay the ancient one before I return to Bast and her temple.

I just didn't know that I'd live them as a chosen one—a vampire.

Sleepers

Selina Rosen

It wasn't so much that he'd done it that beat at the corners of his conscience but that he'd known he shouldn't have even as he was doing it and he'd done it anyway. So he'd gone into space not knowing what was waiting on the other side to get away from all that this very destructive behavior pattern of doing things he knew were wrong had brought him only to realize too late that you couldn't change *who* you were by changing *where* you were.

He had rationalized at the time that it was the only way, but wasn't that what he had always done? Hadn't he always done just what he wanted and then rationalized that he didn't know or that it was all he could have done when it all went horribly wrong?

And it was always a bunch of crap. It was crap now because he had known better. He'd known there *was* another way and just like always he'd done what he wanted instead, because he didn't like reality.

But he didn't know, he couldn't have known, that they would wind up like *this*.

He'd been rudely awakened from his forced and monitored sleep by a drug and adrenaline cocktail constructed to have him up and moving in mere minutes. There was a horrible sound he knew only too well from months of training that meant the crew had been awakened to deal with some problem with the ship.

He was to be the physician for this group of colonists all destined for a new life on a planet the humans called Paradise. The Earth's sun was going supernova right on schedule, and for the last few hundred years the planet had periodically sent groups of colonists to Paradise to save the human race as well as all other plant and animal life forms from extinction.

Joseph had never really wondered why they called the new home world Paradise. He wasn't an idiot; he knew. As long as things on Earth were good, as long as doom wasn't just around the corner, few people—at least few you'd want to be the future of mankind—were lining up to get on a space ship that may or may not make its one-hundred-year flight, to maybe land on a distant planet that may or may not be all that habitable. Add to that being put to sleep that whole time without knowing for sure whether you'd really wake up on the other side, and the only way they could convince "intelligent" people to go was to sell them the idea that this other world was perfect and that it was worth all the risks which ... Well they didn't wind up with all that many smart people. Mostly they wound up with people whose lives were so horrid they were more than willing to take the risk that anything would be better than what they had.

Of course as it became more and more apparent that the sun really was going to turn into a huge black hole and suck their solar system into it, more and more people would be fighting to get on board, but Joseph had left hundreds of years before that would happen.

Joseph's life had been a mess and he'd been more than willing to chuck it all to start over fresh somewhere else. If he never woke up ... Well, he never woke up, and what a great way to commit suicide. He wouldn't know what hit him.

It wasn't till he was rudely awakened and heard that siren that he began to doubt his decision.

The rest of the crew had also been awakened from their hibernation. They were all running around trying to don their uniforms and helmets in the small room where oxygen still smelled more like ozone than atmosphere—the pumps having just been turned on to flood the small cabin. The gravity system also was just coming on line and they were all but floating as they tried to put their suits on to go face whatever it was they had to face.

"What's wrong?" Joseph called to the captain as they both tried to get into their suits, still not quite awake. Then Joseph could feel the shot of adrenaline and drugs the machine had given him really kick in. It was disconcerting and made him instantly nervous, but he was also wide awake.

"I don't know any more than you do and won't till I get to the bridge," the captain said.

By the speed with which he and the rest of the crew finished putting on their suits and ran towards the bridge Joseph knew the drugs had caught up with them as well. The captain made a quick check to make sure they were all in their suits and then he opened the door and suddenly it hit Joseph—he had no idea how long they'd been asleep. It might have been a hundred years; it might have been fifteen minutes. Neither his body nor his brain seemed to have any idea how much time had passed.

He didn't get to go to the bridge with the others. His job was to go to the main cryo chamber and make sure that the machines keeping the rest of the colonists alive and suspended stayed on line. It didn't serve the mission for them to have all been awakened with the rest of the crew. There was no need to have three hundred people running around when only six were needed to handle the bridge. So he was in fact part of the crew, but while it was their job to steer the ship through any hazard they might have encountered, his only job was to make sure the passengers got to Paradise alive.

He had made it to his destination before the rest of the crew made it to the bridge. He went to his console, checked his monitors, and everything seemed in order. He had just finished his initial checks and learned that one hundred years to the day had passed since he'd last climbed on board this ship when the crackle inside his helmet told him he was going to have to listen closely to hear what was actually being said.

"It's all right. We've just gone into orbit around Paradise," the captain said, an air of relief in his voice.

Joseph felt more than relief. Everything was going exactly as it was supposed to. He and the rest of the crew were supposed to be awakened as they went into orbit—he to make sure everything in the cryo chamber stayed copasetic, the rest of the crew to prepare to land the ship. Soon he would be reborn—have a whole new life on a whole new world. He felt real excitement for the first time in years. He had ceased to be important on Earth. Life had gotten hard and boring all at the same time and he had just needed to get away from everyone he knew. Those closest to him hated him, some not without good reason, but the others just because he had let them down in one way or another. Now they were all dead, Earth was only astronomical moments from obliteration, and he would have a whole new life. A new chance to accomplish all the things he'd always wanted to do, but had never been able to stop from slipping through his fingers.

Then Howard, the first mate, said the last thing Joseph wanted to hear, "Something's not right."

Then the whole ship rocked. Joseph found himself spinning across the floor, looking for anything to hang onto and not finding it. He was slung against the far wall into the front of a cryo tank. His right hip hurt but he quickly assessed that he hadn't broken anything and he crawled back across the floor—in case the ship might lurch violently again—pulled himself up his console and now carefully hooked his safety harness to the anchor wishing he could kick his own ass for his stupidity.

"What the hell was that?" Janice, the senior tech cried out.

"It felt like something hit us," Howard said.

"Of course something hit us numb nuts," the captain cursed. "Find out what. Are we in an asteroid belt? Is another ship firing on us? Did something snap off of us and hit us? Get the sensors on line and get us some visual of what's out there. Someone do something."

The sound of panic in his voice and the fact that the captain didn't have a clear idea of how to do any of the things that needed to be done didn't put Joseph at ease.

There was nothing from the rest of the crew for awhile, which also didn't make Joseph very optimistic about his future. Then there was the sound of brand new alarms going off. These different from the first—no doubt these meant there was damage

Something was wrong with the light in the chamber. He thought at first it was a result of coming out of cryo-sleep. They had told them it could take their eyes hours to completely adjust, but when he looked at the face screen in front of him the light seemed fine. It was some sort of ... Well something in the air.

"We've got a hull breech!" Simpson the engineer yelled.

"Hey guys!" He started touching the button on the side of his helmet that would let him be heard by the others. "There is like this strange glowy gold dust looking stuff in the air."

"Yeah I see it too," Brian the other tech support guy said.

"It's just dust. We've been traveling in space for one hundred years. Things got dusty the ... Well whatever it was that hit us it stirred up the dust," the captain said.

"I said we have a hull breach!" Simpson bellowed, this time an edge of panic to his voice.

Joseph knew what that meant. There couldn't be dust in the ship; it was air tight. There hadn't even been any oxygen in here; there was nothing to make dust, so that meant this stuff was coming from outside. You didn't have to be an engineer to know that wasn't good.

"I don't give a damn about a little dust. I just want to know what hit us, if we're safe to land, if the breach is going to suck us all out into the vacuum of space!" the captain shouted.

And that was when it happened. It looked to Joseph like the dust went right *into* the supply lines that fed the cryogenic tanks. Like it was sucked in there. But that couldn't be because the system was closed, completely closed. Nothing could get in.

Yet that was exactly what it appeared to do. It was like it soaked right into the plastic tubes and then just surrounded the bodies inside.

He watched in awe trying to decide whether anything he was seeing was real or if it was all just a trick of his eyes caused from being in cryo goo too long and only having minutes to be forced awake by chemicals.

Then the alarms changed again and he didn't have to ask why because this alarm he knew as well as the emergency alarm. This one meant the cryochamber was failing; something was wrong.

He started punching buttons and twisting levers, reading the monitor and trying to get the power back to the right systems.

"Captain, the main cryochamber is failing..."

"Deal with it. We're under fire!" the captain yelled back. The ship rocked violently again, but this time with his safety line on Joseph was just thrown into the console and was able to stay on his feet during impact. Still, it didn't help his injured hip any.

"I'm trying to contact Paradise now." The captain sounded slightly more controlled.

Joseph looked with panic at the instrument panel going nuts and the monitors spilling information he didn't want to see and that he couldn't read fast enough and all he could think was that things hadn't been so bad back on Earth.

He looked over at one of the tanks just as the eyes of the person inside opened. That was not supposed to happen. In the main chamber the passengers were being awakened in their goo. They were all drowning all around him. He had to find the fault in the system and fix it.

But it was too late. He'd known it had been too late even as his fingers worked their magic over the keyboard, even as he fixed the fault and brought the systems back on line he'd known. Even when the monitors said everything was normal and all the passengers' vitals were fine, he'd known it was a lie. It couldn't be that simple.

"You all right down there, Doc?" the captain asked. It took a minute for his voice to even register. "I said you all right down there, Doc?"

"I ... I'm fine. Everything seems to be all right now. I nearly lost everyone in the main chamber, though. Still don't really know why I didn't."

"You went off line for a couple of minutes. I thought maybe we'd lost you. We just hit a couple of asteroids. We have made first contact with Paradise station and they are expecting us and ready to guide us in. They said most ships hit the asteroid belt. Find a seat and buckle down. We'll start landing sequence in less than thirty minutes. They tell me we're in for a rough landing."

They hadn't been wrong about the landing, and Joseph wasn't the only member of the crew to throw up as soon as they popped their helmets. The air was breathable but felt thin to Joseph and smelled of rotten eggs indicating high sulfur content.

He wanted to just embrace his new world and these new people he was meeting but something just felt off to him. Not that he could really put his finger on it. He kept telling himself it was paranoia left over from the drug and adrenaline cocktail the machines had pumped into him, but he just couldn't shake the bad feeling he had.

The people of Paradise that came to welcome them seemed genuinely warm and glad to have them. The colony itself spread far and wide in every direction and he could see farm land mixed in with homes and businesses as if the two belonged side by side. There were trees and plants of every Earth variety and in fact if it didn't smell so bad he wouldn't have been so sure he hadn't landed right back on Earth. Except everything was very clean and obsessively orderly and just like he couldn't quite get over the bad smell he couldn't quite get over his feeling of impending doom.

"Everyone feels a little off when they first land." The guy looked to be about forty, of medium height and build, with a full blond beard and long blond hair tied back in a neat pony tail. As if reading the confused look on Joseph's face he smiled and added, "Dazed and confused. It's part of being asleep for a hundred years and then waking up on a strange planet. It's enough to put anyone off, and then of course our gravity is heavier than Earth normal and our air is slightly different. Safe of course but different. My name is Jeremy. I am the leader of this unit and these are my aides Franklin and Karen."

Franklin was a dark-headed fellow of about five-six and about thirty while Karen was a slightly older woman of about five-four with a broad smile and mousey brown hair. Except for being impeccably groomed they were all just average-looking. Nothing really outstanding about any of them, just people, Joseph didn't know exactly what he was expecting but it wasn't anything as mundane as this. Even their clothing—plain tan jumpsuits with straight lines—didn't look quite right to Joseph.

"It usually takes a few days to feel like a human again," Jeremy explained.

Franklin laughed, though Joseph couldn't pretend to know why. He also didn't know why goose flesh broke out across his forearms when they all smiled at once and started leading them towards a vehicle parked only a few feet from their craft. Jeremy was probably right. It was all just the after effects of sleeping longer than he should have lived while standing in goo suspended in animation more dead than alive for over a hundred years.

"Ah ... What about the passengers?" the captain asked, and Joseph wondered that he hadn't even thought about them. After all, he was in charge of waking them up.

Jeremy smiled reassuringly from his average face and said simply, "We've found it's better if the crew has twenty-four hours to adjust from the disorientation you're all experiencing before waking the sleepers."

The quarters they were given were beyond clean and very orderly. Each of the crew was given an eight-by-eight room with a bed in one corner and a closet in the other. There was a common bathroom for them to share that had a shower, a toilet, and a sink.

All very minimal, very efficient, very clean.

They all took long showers then changed into the plain tan jumpsuits their hosts had left out for them to wear. Joseph's skin felt tingly and raw like he had a sunburn and when he looked into the mirror in the bathroom—there were none in their private rooms—he could see that his skin was very red. The rest of the crew was the same so he assumed it had something to do with the whole cryogenic process. He gave everyone quick physicals and didn't find anything obviously wrong with anyone, and in fact his hip was the worst injury any of them had picked up in their few minutes of excitement before landing.

Karen came and led them down a long hall to a room with a long table with several chairs around it. There were about a dozen people there besides the three they'd already met—all equally well groomed and wearing the same thing they now wore. They were all very quiet. Food was brought out that looked just like what they normally would have eaten on Earth—a piece of fish, a salad, some cooked beets.

"Thank you for your hospitality," the captain said.

"It's the least we can do for those who bring new members to our flock," Jeremy said.

Joseph didn't like the sound of that. It felt to him like they had landed in the middle of some strange religious cult. As he looked around at the other members of the crew he could see the same apprehension on their faces that he felt. It might have just been what Jeremy said—that the whole experience left you feeling a little out of sorts—but as they got further and further from their sleep and the drug cocktail, Joseph was feeling more and more like something just wasn't right, not less so.

And what if he was right? What if something was wrong? There was absolutely nothing they could do. The ship they'd landed in was only built to make a one-way trip. He started to eat the food in front of him and found it had very little taste, like it had been cooked without any spices. He suspected that was also a hold over from their cryogenic sleep and tried to convince himself that everything was fine.

It was hard because no one was talking to them.

"Joseph had some trouble with the cryo chamber coming in," the captain said, obviously as uncomfortable with the silence as Joseph was and just trying to make conversation.

"Really?" Jeremy said without looking up from his meal.

"Yes, we almost lost everyone in the main chamber; in fact I'm not sure there won't be trouble waking them. Not sure all of them actually made it." Then Joseph started telling them all exactly what had happened even though none of them quit eating or even looked up at him. He felt the sweat start to gather on his face and he had to work to hide his nervousness.

When he'd finished his tale Jeremy just said, "I'm sure they're all fine. This has happened every time a ship comes in, something to do with the asteroid belt. No one has ever died. We're all fine."

Were they? Were they really? They certainly looked fine but there was something just not right about the way they all just sat there, the way everything was so tidy and perfect.

Why weren't they talking to them, asking questions? He expected them to be asking questions about Earth. None of these people had ever lived on Earth, but it was their planet of origin. He wondered that they didn't seem interested in learning about what had happened since the last ship landed at all.

Maybe they were shy, maybe they didn't care. Maybe their ancestors were like Joseph and they were just glad to get away from Earth. Maybe they'd been raised hearing stories about how much Earth sucked and didn't care what was going on there.

As they finished their meal and headed back to their quarters, Joseph wondered at how tired he felt. It seemed weird to him that he should be so tired after sleeping for a hundred years. He was a doctor and he knew all the medical reasons why, but the side of him that was just a normal guy still thought it was odd.

Just outside the door to their quarters, Jeremy stopped and turned slowly around to face them. He smiled and Joseph's blood ran cold. There was something unnatural about that smile. "Our tradition is to give the captain and the crew leadership of all the others in their ship. Housing has been prepared for all of you just east of Paradise. Tomorrow you will go as a group to your ship, awaken your sleepers, and go there together to embrace your new life."

The captain looked a little confused. "Joseph is the only one needed to awaken the passengers."

Jeremy frowned then but didn't look angry. "We have found that it's better if the crew meets the sleepers. It brings home the idea that they are in charge. Having leadership brings order. Obviously you had the highest leadership qualities or you wouldn't be the crew."

Joseph didn't like being forced into a leadership position. That was what had caused all of his problems on earth. Still he wasn't going to argue with this guy who creeped him out more by the minute.

Joseph fell right to sleep but kept having the same nightmare over and over—that guy in his cryo tube opening his eyes, he just couldn't have lived.

He woke up with the captain shaking him and found that the rest of the crew was all standing in his very small room. "What the…" Janice moved to hold her finger over his lips.

"Look, does this place seem right to you?" the captain asked in a whisper.

"Not at all," Joseph said, "but I think it may just be what he said, you know something to do with the cryochamber, the drugs, just being out so long."

"I don't think so," Brian said, shaking his head. "They're like robots, not like people at all."

They didn't really get to talk much because Jeremy and his two cohorts showed up. They didn't seem surprised at all to find them all in the same room. Jeremy smiled. "Come, it's time for breakfast and then you will wake the sleepers."

They ate breakfast in relatively the same silence they had eaten dinner in. If any of these people had any desire to talk to them it didn't show and in fact they wouldn't even make eye contact.

Then they were sent back to their rooms to wait around until exactly twenty-four hours had passed before they were driven back to the ship and hustled towards it. The captain stopped dead in his tracks. He turned to face Jeremy. "Look, not that we don't appreciate you or your ways, but I see no reason for all of us to go back into the ship."

"It is our tradition," Jeremy said. "The crew must greet the sleepers."

There probably would have been an argument but the truth was right then the crew sort of wanted back on the ship, like at least the ship wasn't this new world that none of them were suddenly very sure of.

The crew nodded and walked up the stairs into the ship. Joseph was the last one in and then the door closed behind them and suddenly Joseph realized what was so bothering him about Jeremy.

"He kept saying *we* and *us* and this is the way *we've* always done it," Joseph said.

"What?" Brian asked.

"The last ship from Earth landed one hundred years ago. Jeremy is maybe forty but he kept talking as if he'd personally greeted every ship, as if they had literally done things this way always."

"That's right. That's it," the captain said, nodding.

"Maybe it's just some ritual thing." Janice suggested. "No one could live that long. No one, can they, Doc?"

Joseph shrugged. "I don't know. I mean theoretically if you could make stem-cell technology do what they originally thought it could do …

This is a different planet. An Earth-class planet with no intelligent life when they found it, but there were plants, some animal life forms. They could have found the fountain of youth so to speak. It's more likely their language has just taken a different course from ours. Maybe when they are talking as if they were there it is just that—talk. But why did they shut the door behind us? *How* did they do it?" Joseph turned to look at the captain, more than happy to let someone—anyone—else be in control. "What are we going to do?"

The captain didn't have a chance to answer. "What can we do? The ship was a one-way ticket." Howard said in a panic. "There's no place to go and without their help we can't make it on this planet."

He was right. The ship was loaded with farm equipment and other things to help the colony but that alone wasn't enough. The ship couldn't be moved. It had very little fuel left and it had never had the ability to take off on its own even if it did.

"Let's just wake up the passengers," Simpson said. "If nothing else, it will be harder for them to try to control over three hundred of us."

Joseph nodded. He walked towards the main cryo chamber and the rest of the crew followed.

When they entered the room Janice said before Joseph could even notice, "They're empty."

Joseph looked up. Every tank was empty.

"What the hell?!" Simpson cried out.

When Joseph turned around he could see a bunch of the passengers coming up behind them from the direction of the other cryo chamber. The man in the front of the row grabbed Simpson, who screamed and tried to get away, and then the guy pulled Simpson to him like it was nothing and took a bite out of his throat.

Joseph didn't have time to think about what was happening or why, he just took off for the door on the other side of the chamber that led to another chamber half the size of this one. The others followed him. In here all the passengers were still in their cryo tubes.

The captain tried to close the door and then Janice took over trying to override the controls.

Jeremy's voice came over the com system. "It's easier if you just don't fight it."

"What the hell is going on?" the captain demanded.

"It's tradition," he said, as if that somehow explained everything.

"Please relax. I was on the first ship to come to Paradise. I was hit with the golden light as was everyone in the great chamber. When we were awakened we had a great hunger. The crew awakened us and we ate them and were alive anew."

Joseph looked towards where the passengers were tearing Simpson apart. At least for the moment ignoring the rest of them.

"You crazy bastard, let us out of this ship," the captain ordered.

Jeremy only sighed then said, "You must understand. When we first awaken we are like animals. But after we have eaten our first blood meal, when our need is sated, we calm right down. We never need much blood after that. A few drops each year seems to sustain us and we can even take it from each other. We are a most orderly race and a very patient one once we have gotten over the awakening."

"I did this," Joseph said in a state of shock. "I did this when I brought them back on line. If I hadn't they all would have just died." He didn't know; he couldn't have known that they would wind up like this.

"Like every physician before you has done," Jeremy said. "It's that lovely human instinct to save those that can't save themselves."

"Stop this madness," the captain said.

"I can't," Jeremy said, and managed to sound truly sad about it. "Humans live short, useless lives. When we breathed in that golden dust we gasped our last human breath. In those tanks we became something else. Almost since man crawled out of the mud there have been stories told about vampires, about people who lived forever and feasted on the blood of others. Mankind saw glimpses of what we would one day become. You saw how perfect our world is, how civilized we all are, how well we get along. We live in perfect harmony. That is because when given unlimited life we get everything right. I tell you all this not to torment you in your last minutes but to tell you of what you're becoming. You will become part of them and they will become part of the future of the human race. We can never die now. Humans will live forever. Your sacrifice is a noble one."

"I didn't fly through billions of miles of space and sleep for a hundred years to be anyone's dinner," the captain said, and tried to rip one of the release levers off one of the cryo chambers without any luck. There were no weapons on the ship, none. The reason was simple—a sleeping crew a, ship full of cryos, if something intelligent scanned the ship and found no weapons then they weren't likely to attack. Now Joseph wished he had some kind of weapon. But what good would it do? This was all his fault; all his because he had brought them back to life, but they weren't really alive.

"It's so much easier if you don't resist. They will kill you quickly. You won't feel anything," Jeremy's voice said in a soothing tone.

Joseph looked at all the sleepers and knew they weren't much more than TV dinners for Jeremy and his kind. At least they weren't going to know what was happening to them. It would be like the ship blew up on take off. They would be oblivious. He was trying to think of something, anything, they could do to save themselves from the mob that were fighting over pieces of Howard and would soon grab another one of them. But there was nothing. There was no way to get away from them and no where to go if they did. They hadn't quite finished Howard when they came after them again. They all fought but Janice was gone in a heartbeat and then they were all just waiting for their turn.

"You will be part of them; they will all be part of us. Why resist? It is inevitable," Jeremy explained. "It's the circle of life."

Divining Everest
A tale of The 142nd Starborne
Patrick Thomas

"I don't recognize your authority."

The sound that escaped Major Hans Benedict was somewhere between a chuckle and a sigh. "Not the first time I've heard that. In fact, I get that a lot. That still doesn't change the fact that I have a Colossus Class warship in orbit around this planet with enough fire power to reduce you to ash."

The vampire on the throne shook his head side to side. It was his turn to laugh. "I would think that someone of your rank in the Host would know a bit more about vampire physiology. Light is not going to reduce us to ash."

"But particle weapons would do a pretty good job of it. Although if you are so comfortable with sunlight why don't we adjourn to your courtyard in some swim trunks. I'm more than willing to catch some rays if you are," said Benedict.

"I think not." The vampire closed his hands beneath his chin and rested his head atop them. He knew very well that while sunlight would not kill a vampire, a hour without protection in it would make him too ill to do much of anything for the better part of a week. "In fact, I don't even think you remember me."

"I'll take that bet. What are you willing to wager?"

"Against you, nothing of importance. Even as a private you had a reputation."

"Nice try, but we never met until I was a lieutenant. And you, Longstrum, were nothing but a lowly blood sucking grunt in the 101st Starborne Vampire Brigade."

"I'm impressed. It has been more than fifteen years. It doesn't look like many of them have been kind to you. Can I offer you a taste of immortality?" mocked the vampire, knowing full well that he would never even try to turn the major.

Benedict suppressed the shiver of revulsion at the thought. "Surely, you do not believe the hype yourself. The longest vampire in service to the Sway clocked out at about 125 years."

"But he was a soldier and if I remember correctly died fighting a human battle."

"That's what soldiers do. And as far as I am aware you were never given any discharge papers."

"So you've come all this way to recruit me back in the fold as a soldier?"

"Hardly," Benedict spat. His disdain for the Sway's monster troops was widely known. "I'm here in answer to a distress signal."

"I certainly didn't send a distress signal and I am the rightful and duly elected governor of this planet."

"Really? It was my understanding that Everest had a population of almost 600,000 humans and less than a thousand bloodsuckers. Unless you've managed to breed." The virus that caused vampirism had been around on Earth for hundreds of years. Despite popular lore, a simple bite of a vampire or even drinking a vampire's blood was not enough to turn someone. In fact only rarely would someone react well enough to the virus in order to become an actual vampire. Otherwise they would have long ago overrun the Earth. The Sway scientists managed to genetically alter the virus in two very crucial ways. They made it much easier for it to take effect in soldiers. This was done by infecting them with a retro virus before hand, which left the cells more susceptible to the change. It also had the interesting secondary effect of stopping the virus from being able to be spread beyond the initial host.

Longstrum smiled. "I'd hardly tell you if we had."

"Technically, you still hold the rank of sergeant. I am a superior officer. If I order you to tell me, you will tell me."

"I am no longer a soldier. I never wanted to be in the first place. Tell me Benedict—you enlisted, correct?" The major nodded. "I did not. I wasn't even drafted. I was chosen because mandatory genetic tests found that I would be a likely candidate for successful turning. I was taken out of my home in the middle of the night, strapped to a table and turned into what I am today, screaming all the way. I had a wife and three children. I never saw them again. They are still back on Earth. Or they were."

"We all lost family in the conflagration."

"Yes, however your *Behemoth* is rumored to be the only Colossus that did not return to Earth in its hour of greatest need."

"Which is why we are the only remaining Colossus Class warship."

"That means you disobeyed direct orders. In fact, the story is you staged a coup d'état, taking over your ship and deposing General Daily. Or perhaps you have assumed that rank."

Benedict narrowed his brows and his pupils became much smaller. "I am still a major." Benedict had not assumed a greater rank precisely because he did not want it to seem like a coup. He felt the orders were detrimental and believed in an officer's duty to do the right thing, sometimes in spite of orders. At the time the command to return to Earth was received, the majority of the population of their home world had been decimated. Those who had summoned them back were the elite rulers, the same ones who had also summoned the catastrophe from the darkness upon themselves in a bid for even more power. Leaving the duty they were assigned to would have meant the deaths of hundreds of thousands on the world they had been protecting and likely all hands aboard the ship. All this to save maybe a few hundred who had willingly participated in the murder of billions. They did not deserve a rescue, but a trial for war crimes and execution. When his superior officer announced he was taking the *Behemoth* back to Earth, Benedict deemed him to be unfit for duty and took command, even over those officers of higher rank.

"I will not follow an order from a traitor. That in itself would be treason, if I still cared enough to be a soldier."

Benedict ignored the dig. "I received a call from humans who claimed to have been enslaved by you. I am here to negotiate their freedom, by any means necessary."

"That is utter nonsense. We have no slaves. The humans of Everest are free to live their lives as they would, except on occasion they must feed us."

"That doesn't sound awful free to me."

"Even you know nothing is free. We protect them. We have ended hunger and poverty. We do not allow any of the humans to be killed or even harmed. It is done in a hospital setting where great care is taken to even minimize scaring. With the average human life span of seventy-five and the size of the population it is unlikely that any human would have to be used for feeding more than once every three or four years. Hardly unreasonable."

"You claim to be the elected governor. But were any humans

allowed to vote in this so called election?"

"Of course not. We could hardly trust their decisions, now could we? When humans were in charge look at what happened to Earth. There is no war in Everest. There are not even any soldiers, yourself and your honor guard excluded."

"Which I find interesting since I understand when this system's Colossus returned to Earth they left a contingent of soldiers to watch over this planet."

"They left 100 men and 917 vampires. Not good odds. Why would anyone in the Host even think we would take orders for long? Especially once they ran out of the drugs that they laced our blood with." Benedict raised an eyebrow. "You didn't know? Apparently much of our craving for blood was not natural. We were fed drugs. When the effects wore off, we mistook the cravings as hunger for blood. Made us incredibly effective and deadly on the battlefield as they withheld our meals beforehand. But they only left behind so much drugged blood and the soldiers soon ... left their assignments. The withdrawal was ... unpleasant to say the least. But once the drugs were out of our systems, we were able to think clearly. It did not take much for us to facilitate the shift of power within our ranks. There were a few regrettable deaths but the majority of those men and women were allowed to resign their commissions and take up lives as citizens."

"I see. I'm going to have to ask you to turn over control of the government to whoever is elected by the entire planet. You were soldiers. You have earned your rights. You should all have a vote, but so should everyone on this planet."

"That's very magnanimous of you, Benedict. A definite change of policy from the Sway government who would never allow any of their monster troops any rights, other than the chance to be soldiers for the rest of their existence. Otherwise, why would we give up what we already have for a guarantee of losing it?"

"Because I told you to."

"Now Benedict, you have twelve soldiers with you. I have more vampires in this room. Do you think even the thirteen of you could defeat us before we ended you?"

Benedict smiled. "I fought with and against monsters. I give us better than even odds. Of course, that won't stop my people from leveling this city."

"The city is shared by vampire and human alike. We both know many more humans would die from your friendly fire than vampires and that really would ruin the purpose of what you claim you are trying to do."

"True, but there is the option of a more surgical strike."

"Your 142nd Starborne may have the upper hand in fire power, but surgical strikes would require Harpy dropships to invade our air space and we have enough planetary defenses to shoot them out of the sky. We let yours land as a courtesy."

"And don't think we don't appreciate that. Of course I and a few of my people had already been on Everest for the better part of a week when the Harpy landed." The vampire's eyebrows rose at Benedict's words. "I assume you remember what my specialty is?"

"You are a sapper." The term was taken from a French military position from the 1700's, the modern sapper specialized in infiltrating enemy ships and territory for the purpose of sabotage or destruction. Benedict was legendary. "You're bluffing."

"Maybe, but you really want to call me on it?"

"Absolutely. There is no way you landed without us picking you up on sensors. The *Behemoth* has been in orbit less than a day. You absolutely must be bluffing. You will not intimidate us simply because there are a few exaggerated stories of your skills."

Benedict's head tilted to the side and he shrugged his shoulders. "So be it." Hans pressed a button on a metal cylinder that was hidden in the palm of his hand and threw it to the vampire. "I suggest you evacuate 927 High Street."

"The blood depository?"

"I figured the best way to your hearts was through your stomachs. That or with small arms fire. I'd hurry, Longstrum. You only have thirty minutes."

The vampire leader shouted for the building to be evacuated. It took exactly eighteen minutes until every soul was out of the building. At exactly thirty minutes, explosives knocked out support beams from the basement to the upper floor, collapsing it in on itself in a pile of rubble. Neither the building to its left nor its right was harmed.

"Arrest Benedict and his soldiers," Longstrum ordered.

The soldiers of the 142nd lifted their weapons higher. Benedict held up a hand. "Very well. But you only have twelve hours until the next building. And twelve hours until the building after that. We planted enough to go for two weeks. Any harm comes to me or my people and

I won't tell where the next one is in time for you to evacuate."

"And you call me the monster? Away with them."

Benedict nodded for his men to allow the vampires to disarm them. A suicidal battle served no benefit. The soldiers were shackled and brought down to the basement of the planetary capital building. "I suppose you have to throw us in and find some room among all your other human prisoners," Benedict said.

Longstrum looked at the major as if he were insane. "We have no human prisoners in this city at this time."

Benedict didn't believe him, but when they were taken into the jail, the cells were mostly empty. The members of the 142nd Starborne were put four to a cell, with Benedict getting his own. There was only one other prisoner, a woman vampire. The soldiers closed the metal doors and left them with two vampire guards.

"Ah, company at last," said the female vampire.

"Rose, shut up," said one of the two guards.

The lady vampire gave them the finger and continued to speak. "You look like you are playing soldier but humans aren't allowed to be soldiers anymore. What did you do to get in here?"

"Objected to humans being kept as slaves."

"Who's keeping slaves? Will they be joining us too?"

Benedict furled his brow. "What are you in for?"

The vampire Rose made a spitting sound. "I killed a human and they put me in here for that, if you can believe it. I understand why they don't want us to kill them as a whole—it makes for too much unrest, but there are so many of them. What difference does one more or less make?"

"I suppose you would have to ask his family that," said Benedict.

"Oh pish. Only more blood bags. What bothers them is really unimportant. But for killing one of them I get twenty-five years in a cell, being forced to suck blood out of a plastic bag? What kind of life is that? They should have just killed me."

Benedict actually agreed but held his tongue. "Why didn't they?"

"Because Cyrus Longstrum made it a law. Capital punishment is outlawed. For vampires I can understand, but to include humans? So for one little indiscretion I've got to spend my life in here? It isn't right."

"Sir," whispered Colonel Leon Westminster, a fellow sapper who had made planetfall with Benedict. "Are you going to call in an assault team and get us out of here?"

Benedict had lain down on his bunk and put his feet up, his hands laced behind his head. "I don't think it will be necessary. I have a feeling we won't be in here too long."

It was a day before his words proved prophetic. The door to the cells exploded inward, knocking the vampire guards to the ground. The blast was followed by a handful of humans carrying assault rifles.

"You've only got moments before the bloodsuckers manage to mount a defense. Get those sky boys out," ordered the man who appeared to be in charge.

Benedict didn't bother to correct the fact that three of his assault team were female. He was actually surprised two of his sapper team, Corporal Sheila Barnes and Captain Ami Chang, hadn't done it themselves. He surmised that they, like himself, found it bad manners to correct someone who was rescuing them and listening and observing was an effective way of gathering information.

The man in charge stood in front of Benedict's cell at attention and saluted. Benedict raised an eyebrow, then stood to return the salute.

"You are the voice of freedom?" Benedict said, using the sign-off the distress call had ended with.

"Yes sir, Major Benedict sir. I was Private First Class Adrian Voice when the bloodsuckers overwhelmed us, sir. We didn't want to concede control but our fighting them would have ended in too many deaths so we pretended to go back to civilian life but instead went underground. We put up a good fight, sir."

Benedict nodded. "How many of there are you?"

"Of the original soldiers, there are fifteen including me, sir. However we have over one hundred freedom fighters actively engaging the enemy in this city alone. Stand back, sir, we are going to get you out of there."

Several men in the rescue party had placed small amounts of plastic explosives over the cell locks. Members of the 142nd Starborne stepped to the back of their cells, using their mattresses for additional cover. Former Private First Class Voice hit a button on a device on his belt and all the locks were shattered with the small explosions.

"Nice work, Voice."

"Thank you, sir."

"How about getting me out," said the vampire visitor.

Voice got a crap-eating grin on his face and pulled his sidearm pointing it between the eyes of the vampire. "I'll be happy to set you free. The ultimate freedom." The vampire stepped back from the bars, nervously looking around for a place to hide from a bullet. The cell didn't provide any cover and her speed and strength didn't mean much in such a small space. Voice cocked back the hammer on his sidearm. Benedict's hand fell across the gun, his finger landing between the hammer and the barrel.

"Host soldiers do not kill in cold blood, son." Voice's eyes darted to the pair of vampire guards the initial blast had knocked unconscious. "That includes the unconscious. Let's go. I assume you have an escape route mapped out."

"Of course, sir. Please follow me."

In the age of satellite light tracking and video surveillance, breaking into a prison and getting out without having an escape route noticed was extremely challenging. The human freedom fighters were up to the task. They had managed a small power outage which disabled most of the local surveillance and waited for the skies to be overcast in order to provide cloud cover from the eyes in the sky.

Vampires did have enhanced hearing, sight, and smell, but they weren't exactly bloodhounds. However, just to be on the safe side, the area was doused with a methane compound designed to eliminate any hope of olfactory tracking.

The human's hideout at first glance wasn't much of a hideout at all. It was a bowling alley. The sport of Earth had remained popular on many of the settled worlds and most large towns had at least one bowling alley. This one was owned by former Private First Class Voice. His logic was sound when he explained that humans hiding and sneaking in, knocking on doors and using passwords was too suspicious to cope with modern surveillance techniques. However all he had to do was make sure his teams were groups of four and they were easy enough to pass off as a group just interested in a chance at knocking down three hundred pins. And groups of people coming in and out, especially on league night, would hardly raise the eyebrow on an interested bloodsucker. Of course, thirteen men and women in Sway black uniforms with 142nd Starborne patches on the sleeves more than likely would. The first thing that they did before going to the bowling alley was to change into more normal clothing.

They reached the alley without incident.

"Benedict, pick three of your people and go to lane seven, me and my people will take lane eight. That way we can talk," Voice said.

Private Ricco Jonas, the last member of the sapper team, stepped up to the major's ear. "Sir, this operation is totally amateur, we need to post guards. To bowl when work needs to be done…"

"Any posted guards would attract attention. We have video surveillance covering three hundred and sixty degrees of the building including the rooftops and surrounding streets. If somebody should come in, all they will see are people out on the town bowling and drinking. There will be nobody milling about whispering to raise suspicions," Voice countered.

Benedict raised an eyebrow and nodded slowly. "It's not how we would do things, Jonas, but it seems to have worked so far for them. For the moment we will follow Mr. Voice's lead. However, there is no reason why a couple of people at the bar couldn't be staring into their glasses which just happen to be in view of each of the doorways."

"Yes, sir. I'll take care of it."

"I also see that Voice has karaoke. Perhaps you can help block any listening devices and enjoy yourself at the same time." Benedict and the rest of the sappers were all too aware of Rico's love of opera and his proficiency in singing both loud and well.

Private Jonas smiled. "I think I might be able to manage that, although I doubt I will need a microphone."

"Not in a place this size. Try not to knock out any of the glass. And I think I speak on behalf of all the sappers, anything but Donizetti's *The Daughter of the Regiment.*"

"Spoilsport. Just for that, I'm going to go all Gilbert and Sullivan on your ass."

Benedict rolled his eyes, chose his team and picked out a bowling ball.

The major allowed Voice to go first and observed how he threw. He knocked seven of the ten pins. Voice picked up the spare. Benedict stepped up to the line aimed and threw. The major got a strike.

"Impressive, Major. When is the last time you went bowling?" asked Voice.

"At least twenty years ago. Was back in my academy days."

"That makes that especially remarkable, but from all I have heard about you it doesn't surprise me. I have to tell you, we were all impressed when we heard what you did."

Benedict ignored the comment, which he usually did when someone brought up his mutiny. As a lifelong officer and soldier, he found what he did reprehensible and not something to be admired. However the idea of sending the entire ship and its crew to certain death and abandoning the people they were protecting to certain doom was even more so.

"Please explain to me exactly what help you expect from us or what help you would like from us in your fight here," Benedict said as the next bowler stepped up.

"We have the numbers in theory, but too many of the people are willing to let status quo lie. They don't want to rock the boat. They still get to go to work and come home to their families. The fact that any one of them can become a cocktail to a bloodsucker at any time doesn't seem to faze most of them. There are those of us that find the idea of bloodsuckers ruling humans too repulsive to let slide. We plan to get rid of their power by any means necessary."

"I see. And assuming you're able to do that, what is your plan for the government afterwards?"

Voice narrowed his brow. "We would set up an interim government until we could return to planetary elections. The officers in the freedom fighters would take over government tasks for that time period."

"With you of course at the helm?"

Misunderstanding the tone of the question, Voice grinned widely. "Of course. Have to have someone in charge who can be trusted to make the right choices. And the hard ones."

"How do you think you can do this? What are your estimates in terms of collateral losses?" In the company of his own officers and people, Benedict avoided terms like "collateral losses". They were just fancy words for how many people were going to die to obtain the objective. However, he knew all too well when to cloak horrible deeds in nice shiny words.

"Of course, we want to minimize any civilian casualties. However there are those who are working with the bloodsuckers and those who have chosen to betray their own, them we are not quite so concerned about. We have given thoughts to poison and have even tried it. The problem, though, is the bloodsuckers are too well organized. They don't simply just pick a person at random to feed off of. They choose, then put them in isolation for a week, making sure that they are the only ones providing food and drink. That way they can be sure that the blood they devour is not tainted. We lost three good people during the isolation period."

"You poisoned your own people?"

"The numbers came up in the lottery and they volunteered. It wasn't something we wanted to do. It is not something that I'm proud of, but I am proud of those three men who gave their lives in hopes of ending the vampire occupation."

Benedict grew silent and it was his turn to bowl again. It was obvious his mind was elsewhere, because this time he didn't make the strike, instead leaving up the seven and ten pins.

"Tough break. That's the hardest spare there is."

"There is a huge difference between hard and impossible," Benedict said. Moving a step to his right he put his thumb up lining it up with one pin and then the other as if it were a sight on a rifle. He drew back his arm and let the ball fly. It rolled down the edge of the alley hitting the ten pin at the just the right angle to send it spinning leftward to knock down the seven pin.

"Amazing."

Without acknowledging the comment, Benedict moved to the side to allow the next bowler to use the lane.

"Tell me more about what you have tried so far."

"We have managed to get two of them with snipers. Another was alone on the street and we managed to overpower him and separate his head from his neck."

Despite myth, stake and decapitation were not the only ways to kill a vampire. Enough damage to the body would do the trick. However fresh human blood was almost a miracle drug inducing cellular regeneration more than one hundred times faster than would normally be possible in a human. As long as the heart was not blocked from healing and the head not removed from the body, a vampire could theoretically heal from almost any wound with enough blood. Of course fire destroyed the cells beyond the ability of hemoglobin to regenerate.

"Have you tried any protests, civil disobedience?" Benedict asked.

"Hell, no. We weren't dumb enough to fall into those traps, sir. That would simply alert them to who we were and assure that we were watched at all times."

"Have they done any harm to any of the citizens of Everest?"

"You mean besides drinking their blood and telling them what they can and can't do? No, there have been no public executions. In fact, they have puppet human judges to preside over trials. Even human cops. They have most people fooled, but not us."

"I'm going to need a few days to get the lay of the land." Benedict didn't bother to explain that the time he spent before meeting with the vampire ruler was primarily concerned with getting to know his way around and finding both soft and hard targets to plant explosives on. Most of that time was spent trying to avoid casualties. He did not have much time to interact with the general populous.

"I'd be happy to take you around and introduce you to some people," said Voice.

Benedict shook his head. "I will do better alone."

"But your face is on all the video feeds. They will spot you and you will be arrested."

"If they catch me, I deserve to be caught." Benedict changed his posture, seeming to shrink two inches and become a meek overweight man instead of the older but well muscled soldier that he was. His face muscles relaxed giving him a different appearance. As soon as time permitted, he would dye his hair.

Many people compared sappers to the legend of ninjas who were able to blend into the shadows and disappear at will. Benedict considered ninjas a thing of legend, but they did have some things in common. Neither dressed up in funny costume for one. Sappers did their best to blend in, to not draw attention to themselves. It was why he actually liked Voice's idea of having his meetings in the bowling alley, simply because it would not arouse much suspicion. However Benedict was not so thrilled with other things he saw, and needed to sort them out for himself.

At the scheduled time, Hans Benedict returned to the bowling alley and had a round in the bar room with his men.

"So what's the plan, sir?" asked Colonel Leon Westminster.

"These freedom fighters are wrong-headed about fighting against something that's not really there. I don't like the idea of a group of bloodsuckers ruling over humans any more than anyone else does, but as far as governments go they really are quite benevolent. There's no record of any lottery winner being harmed. The vampires who hunt and kill on their own are punished for it. The bloodsuckers really are protecting the humans. Humans who commit crimes are not coddled but not tortured either. The punishments seem enough to actually deter crime."

"Are they protecting them because it is the right thing to do or because they do not want to lose their food source?" asked Westminster.

Benedict shrugged. "In the long run, what difference does it make? The people here are a lot better off than a lot of the other worlds we have seen. We are not going to get involved in this fight."

"Are we going to turn over Voice and his people?"

"I don't like the idea. I don't think they have much chance in succeeding in anything other than being a thorn in the vampires' collective ass. However someone has been killing humans and making it look like the bloodsuckers are doing it. There are at least six victims."

"What makes you think the vamps aren't?" asked Westminster.

"The wounds were wrong. Two very nice, neat bite marks on the two victims I managed to sneak in and examine."

Westminster frowned. "Any vamp wounds I've ever seen have had chunks taken out, usually chewed over pretty good."

"Exactly, although the vamps may feed differently when off the Sway's drugged feed," Benedict said.

"So Longstrum's covering it up?"

"The opposite. He's offering a reward for information leading to the arrest of the killer."

"You think Voice is behind it?"

"It has crossed my mind."

"So what's the plan?"

"I want to speak with Voice. If he is the killer ... I hope he's not."

"How will you know for sure?"

"I won't, but if it's not him I think it's best we leave and let Everest sort this out itself and call *Behemoth* for evac."

Benedict went back up to the bartender. "Where is Voice?"

The man serving drinks smiled. "We are so happy to have you with us Major Benedict. Mr. Voice left this envelope for you. He knew you would be back today and he was very excited to show you that he really meant business."

Benedict took the envelope and tore the end open pulling out the paper inside. "God damn it."

"What is it, sir?"

"Voice got it in his head that this is the time to do or die.

Unfortunately a lot more people are going to be in the die column than the do. All right we are not leaving yet. Everybody suit up. Westminster comm *Behemoth*. I want Harpies moving planetside now. We have a massacre to stop."

The baker's dozen of the 142nd Starborne double-timed it through the streets in full uniforms and battle gear. Benedict used his headset to break into the civilian communications net.

"To all civilian authorities, this is Major Hans Benedict of the 142nd Starborne. There is a group of terrorists that are planning to blow up the civil hall building. Immediately evacuate it. We have several Harpies with my people on the way. We will help with evacuations and hopefully with disarming any explosives. Do not fire on them."

"Benedict," said a familiar voice over the radio. "What are you trying to pull? Blowing up another building?"

"Longstrum, I don't like the fact that you are in charge of this planet, but my recon has led me to believe that you are, if not a benevolent force, at least one that is not doing harm. There are a group of humans who have decided to kill those people they believe are conspiring with vampires, which means any civil servant. I speculate that they may even be the ones responsible for your recent murders. I am not going to allow innocent civilians to be killed. Therefore my people and I are at your disposal. In fact, since we have more experience with this kind of thing, I respectfully suggest that we take command of the mission."

"I don't trust you, Benedict…"

"Cyrus, you are going to have to. You don't need to be dealing with this and a firefight with my men. Just evacuate the damn building. Benedict out."

Benedict and his dozen Host soldiers reached the government building where chaos was running about and generally having its way with all in its path. Civilians were crowding out into the streets and there were already four Harpies hovering in the air over the building. Four hundred members of the 142nd Starborne were moving onto the ground and attempting crowd control by herding the people as far away from the building as possible.

A captain at a mobile command post signed Benedict to join him. "We've made contact, Major Benedict. They have taken the entire daycare center as hostages. They're saying if the humans do not rise up and kill the vampires, the children will all die."

"Son of a corpse eater. I'm going in there," said Benedict.

"Sir, that's not exactly a good idea," said Westminster. "That way not only will they have the children as hostages but they will have you."

"The entire 142nd knows my policy on hostages. We do everything possible to get them out, but we do not give in to demands. If anything happens to me, Morales will do an exemplary job leading the 142nd Starborne. I am the only one that has a chance of ending this without bloodshed." He handed off his rifle and sidearm to the colonel and turned to the captain. "Monitor my frequency. I assume snipers are already in place?"

"Yes, sir. Unfortunately he has blocked off all the windows and has space heaters going to confuse infrared."

Benedict nodded. "I will have all of my communications gear that is in my uniform on full sensor mode. That should be able to get them a pretty good picture of what is inside. Have them standing by with armor piercing shells. They will be able to tell me apart from anybody else over three feet tall. The children are not acceptable losses. Is that understood?"

"Yes, sir."

Benedict spoke into his headset microphone. "Tie me into the Harpies' speaker systems." Benedict heard the squelch of the feedback. "Voice, this is Benedict. I'm coming in, I'm alone and I'm unarmed."

The vampire governor arrived on the scene and threw the soldier that tried to stop him ten feet. A dozen more soldiers moved toward him. "Colonel, explain to Governor Longstrum exactly what we are doing, but do not let him near the building. Hold our people back."

Already moving, Westminster nodded. "Yes, sir."

Benedict was met at the door by one of Voice's men with a sidearm. "Major, you've come to join us?"

"Why else would I be here?" Benedict had learned long ago that while it was best not to lie in negotiations, it was also best to say things that allow people to jump to their own satisfactory conclusion and not correct them when they are wrong. "Bring me to Voice."

Benedict's armed escort brought him to the daycare center. "Hans, you have come to join us in our hour of victory."

Benedict noted that he was no longer "Major." Voice had already in his mind assumed command of the planet and, instead of being an ally with all the cards, Benedict had now been demoted to support personnel.

"This will make those complacent humans pick up the fight against the vampire overlords. No more acceptance. They will have to open up their eyes and see the monsters for what they really are."

"Yes, that's definitely been accomplished. Everyone knows exactly who the monsters are now. The question is, are you really prepared to harm these children?"

"Hans, I was in the Host, the same as you. We both had to do despicable, horrible things because we were ordered to. It was never pleasant, it was never good. Still, we did them because we were following orders, because we trusted in the long run it was for the greater good. I don't want to harm a hair on any of these kids' heads. However, I will do whatever is necessary to set my world free."

"An admirable viewpoint. However, you crossed the line when you took the innocent hostage."

"Innocent? They're not innocent. Their parents are conspirers. Already they're being indoctrinated to accept meekly the vampires as their betters. They are going to grow up to become nothing but sheep fit for the slaughter. Better they die here and now than as the meals for some monstrous bloodsucker."

"So you are the one who killed those people, making it look like a bloodsucker, right?"

Voice's eyebrows raised and the corner of his lips curled up. "I knew I wouldn't be able to fool you, but the rest of the population is another matter."

"Did you do it on your own? All six? Because that would have been very impressive for one man to pull off on his own," Benedict said.

"I would like to say I did, but every man in this room helped. It was a true team effort."

"How'd you choose the victims?"

"Each of us chose one person who we felt this world would be better off without. Most of them were criminals and the rest of us were better with them on the underside of the grave. So what do you think of my plan? Pretty ingenious, huh? You think people will finally rise up and join us?"

"The people are absolutely about to rise up. In fact, we have taken the bloodsucking so-called governor into custody. Like you said, what you did was quite ingenious, but you crossed the line with the children. I'm here to make you a deal. You let the children go and we will put a bullet in the bloodsucker Longstrum's brainpan right outside that window. And you can go outside and lop off his head."

"Everyone will see?"

"I'm pretty sure all the news feeds are out there. It won't hurt your bid to become the new planetary governor,"

"I like the plan except for the part where I give up the hostages. We both know that the vampires are stronger and faster than us. Without these kids here, even we trained soldiers will be chopped meat."

"We can still put the bullet in his head, but you know he feeds regularly and often so if you're not down there quickly enough his body will spit out the bullet and heal. Might take a little bit for all the neurological damage to go away, but you don't want to waste time getting down there to lop off the head."

"It's not that I don't trust you, Benedict, It's just don't trust anyone outside of my people. I'm going to take this girl and go over to the window. If you are on the level about this, then I'll let half of the kids go."

"No problem." Benedict hit a button on his collar. "This is Benedict. Please arrange the bloodsuckers execution so Mr. Voice can watch."

Voice moved to the window and pulled away a corner of the paper so he could see out. In the street below the vampire governor was on his knees with his hands behind his head. Colonel Westminster looked up at the window to make sure that Voice could see him and he pulled his trigger. There was a loud bang and the vampire fell to the ground twitching.

Voice gave out a rebel yell, dropping to his knees and thrusting his arms in front of him. "The 142nd Starborne did it. They put a bullet in that bloodsucker's head!" He pushed the little girl away towards Benedict. "Take her and half the kids, Benedict. You're all right in my book."

Benedict knelt down so he was eye level with the child. "Are you okay?" The girl nodded. Benedict grabbed her and pulled her close and whispered, "*Salt it.*" He threw the two of them down to the floor as armor-piercing rounds tore though the building, taking out each terrorist except the still kneeling Voice with a headshot. Voice looked around and started to bring his weapon to bear on Benedict, but he was still reeling from the shock of seeing his fellows shot down and moved too slow. Benedict had already slipped the ceramic knife out of the armored plating of his sleeve and tossed it so it went into Voice's throat so deep that it severed his spine. The gun fell from the rebel leader's hand and he fell to the ground.

A strike team was inside in moments and the children were taken out and reunited with their parents. When Benedict exited the building, the unharmed vampire governor was there to meet him.

"I was still thinking it had to be some kind of a trick up until I heard the shot and felt nothing."

"Thank you for trusting us. I'm still not crazy about the idea of vampires being in charge, but for this world you really do seem like the best option."

"So you won't be interfering in anything here?"

"Not at the moment. However, in my time here I have made some contacts and given them ways to contact us. I will be keeping an eye on you. Remember that. And make sure you keep these people safe."

The vampire nodded and began to extend his hand to shake Benedict's but stopped. Instead he snapped to attention and saluted. Benedict matched the stance and saluted back before turning toward the nearest Harpy. His people could handle clean up. He had to figure out what else needed to be done out there.

Part IV:
The Spirit Realm

Into the Abyss

Dayton Ward

Behind you.

Casey Flanagan turned, harsh light from the lamps affixed to either side of his suit helmet playing across the dark, cramped day room. The twin beams washed over the octagonal table at the room's center, reflecting off the thin glaze of ice crystals that covered everything. Above and around the table floated assorted utensils and kitchen ware, along with a cloud of what Casey figured to be the long-decomposed remnants of partially-consumed meals. Books and magazines, along with loose clothing articles and other debris, drifted about the room and the four passageways leading from the chamber.

Otherwise, the place was empty.

"Jesus," Casey said, hissing the word through gritted teeth and shaking his head.

"*You okay, Casey?*" said a voice in his helmet speakers. It was Sharon Burnett, pilot of the *Bartleby*, the long-range cargo hauler Casey most definitely wasn't aboard at this moment. As usual, Sharon's tone was one of gentle, almost flirtatious teasing. "*Don't tell me you're scared.*"

Casey snorted. "You're damned right, I'm scared. "It's creepy as hell in here. Where's Jesse with the power?" Jesse Malone, the *Bartleby*'s engineer, had drawn the undesirable assignment of moving outside the ship in an attempt to connect a power transfer conduit from the hauler to this wreck.

"*Maybe fifteen minutes*," Sharon replied. "*He's complaining about installing an adapter or something. If you like, I can talk dirty to you to pass the time.*"

Her comment had the intended effect, and Casey chuckled despite his unease. Feeling some of his tension drain away, he replied, "Talk's cheap, lady. Save that for when you can make good on it." Something moved to his right, and he angled his head to see what looked like a coffee pot slowly falling toward the floor after having apparently drifted into one of the pipes running along the ceiling. "This place really is eerie, though. Without the gravity, there's crap floating everywhere. It's a real mess."

Only Casey was unaffected by the ship's inactive gravity plating, owing to his suit's magboots. Waving his hand before his helmet's faceplate, he watched the glove pass through the haze of food particles and dust floating before him. Though he loathed wearing an EVA suit, Casey was thankful for the helmet and the suit's self-contained oxygen supply, which protected him from what would have to be the foul stench of rotted food.

"*That's just nasty,*" Sharon said, reminding Casey that she, and anyone else on the *Bartleby* who might be accessing the feed from the camera embedded into the front of his helmet, could see whatever was directly in front of him.

"You're telling me," Casey replied. Turning to examine the room's interior again, he made note of the posters affixed to the various bulkheads. Some were of locales like beaches on Earth or one of the colonies on Mars or Titan, while others featured attractive women—and men—in varying states of undress. "Any idea what ship this is, anyway? I haven't found anything like a nameplate or other signage yet."

"*It's a mystery, all right,*" Sharon replied. "*It's got no transponder code, and no hull markings. We'll find out when we power up the onboard computer.*"

Casey grunted. "No transponder? Every ship I've ever been on has one, and the batteries they use are supposed to be good for something like fifty years."

Sharon's chuckle made him smile. "*You know as much as I do, sport.*"

"Hard to believe it made it all the way out here without anyone ever coming across it," Casey said, maneuvering around the table and heading for the tunnel that according to signage on the day room wall should lead him to the derelict's bridge.

"*News flash, kiddo: Space is big. Pass it on.*"

"I guess," Casey said, conceding the point. With no power and unable to transmit a distress signal, only blind luck had seen to it that the *Bartleby*—on a cargo run to Titan from Mars—had found this wreck at all. Skip Horton, the ship's navigator, had picked up the ship at the extreme range of the hauler's radar systems.

"*Find anybody?*" Sharon asked, her tone becoming more serious.

Casey shook his head despite there being no one around to see him do it. "Nope. No bodies, no nothing." Glancing to his left, he caught sight of a scuffed brown leather boot, its sole worn and its laces twirling about as it drifted over the table. "There's clothes everywhere, though. It's like everybody shucked their drawers and went skinny dipping or something."

"*Now there's an idea I can get behind*," Sharon replied, her laugh filling Casey's helmet. He was readying a response—something along the lines of volunteering to get behind *her* during such an excursion—when the pilot said, "*Hang on a sec. The EMF scanner's going nuts.*"

Frowning, Casey considered that. The *Bartleby*'s electromagnetic field detection scanners weren't state of the art like those used by the military, but they were still able to sniff out fluctuations and other signs of trouble well enough. "Where's it coming from?"

There was a pause before Sharon replied, "*Somewhere over there. Maybe one of the cargo bays?*"

No sooner had she spoken the words than an abrupt chill coursed down Casey's spine, and a knot of anxiety formed in his gut. If he'd had hair on the back of his neck, he was sure it would've stood on edge.

Help. Us.

"What the...?" It was a woman's voice, but not Sharon's, ringing in Casey's ears and sounding as though it had come from directly behind him. His magboots, heavy and ungainly as they affixed themselves to the deck plating with every step, reverberated through his suit as he tried to reorient himself. He was aware of an odd blue-white glow coming from just beyond the faceplate's field of vision and turned toward it.

Then something grabbed him.

"Hey!" Casey shouted, his body reacting at the abrupt touch. It took an extra second to realize that what he was sensing was *inside* his EV suit. Inside his *clothes*.

"*Casey?*" Sharon called out. "*What's going on?*"

Ignoring her, Casey smacked his hands against his torso, searching for whatever was on him. There was an almost electrical tingling sensation now playing across his skin. "Something's inside my suit! Get it off me!"

His feet went out from under him and he cried out in near-panic. He kicked his legs in response, a useless action as he felt himself dragged backwards. Reaching up for whatever gripped him, he found nothing, despite the overwhelming sensation of being pulled into water. The blue light he'd seen now filled his vision, all but blinding him.

"*Casey!*" Sharon pleaded. "*Damn it, answer me!*"

Terror took hold and his body jerked, muscles racked by spasms as his arms flailed about without his control. An aching tingle flared in his groin and behind his eyes, and his stomach lurched as a wave of nausea washed over him. Casey clawed for any kind of handhold, trying to halt what now felt like a freefall into oblivion. Something cascaded over his body, and when he opened his mouth to scream, it surged past his lips, choking back the words and his breath.

Help! Us!

The woman's pleading voice was the last thing Casey heard.

"This is all we found."

Erin O'Shea watched Skip Horton drop an armload of clothing and equipment onto the floor of the *Bartleby*'s recreation room before reaching up to wipe sweat from his brow. The navigator was a burly man, at least thirty pounds overweight but still as strong as any man half his age. He wore his long gray hair pulled back in a ponytail, and his beard, also gray, was unkempt, much like Horton himself.

O'Shea studied the components where they lay across the dull, worn deck plates, paying particular attention to the control panel on the front of the suit, which was still active. All of its indicators were green. "It's still sealed?"

"Yep," Horton replied. "It was on the floor of one of the tunnels leading from the day room. Faceplate was still locked down, the gloves were still attached to the sleeves, and seals were all intact." He pointed to the suit's control panel. "There was a system reset. According to the internal clock, it happened right about the same time Sharon lost contact with Casey."

"Any idea what caused the EMF spike?" asked O'Shea, reaching up to wipe an errant lock of her black hair from where it had fallen across her left eye.

"Not a clue," Horton said, rising to his feet. "That ship is a dead hulk. Engines are cold, though there's plenty of fuel in the tanks. Their solar collectors were retracted, so it probably just coasted along until the batteries ran dry." He released a tired sigh. "How the hell does that ship drift around out here all these years? They didn't transmit a distress call, at least while the batteries had juice?"

O'Shea shook her head. "Jesse checked the antenna assembly when he was hooking up the power transfer. The circuits for the automated distress beacon are gone, pulled deliberately."

"No transponder, and now no distress beacon?" Horton asked. "Who the hell would do that?"

"Somebody who didn't want this ship tracked," O'Shea replied. "We used to do the same thing when we were running black ops back during the war." Assignments like those were one of the many reasons she'd opted to leave behind military life for a quieter, less dangerous existence. What better way to accomplish that than by shepherding a long-haul freighter between planets?

How's that working out for you now?

Sharon Burnett, who sat with red-rimmed eyes in one of the chairs around the rec room's big circular table, wiped her nose with a handkerchief before asking, "Who cares about any of that? What happened to *Casey*? He said something was inside his suit."

"That's impossible," Malone said, shaking his head and pointing toward the pile of gear on the floor. "It was locked up tight. No way anything got inside."

Everyone looked up as the rec room door opened and Jesse Malone, a muscled man in his late thirties who served as the *Bartleby*'s engineer, stepped inside. "You're not going to believe this," he said without preamble, holding up a portable computer tablet as he crossed to a lone terminal sitting atop a table situated along the far wall. He pulled a chair from the dining table with him and sat down in front of the terminal, inserting his tablet into the workstation's receiver slot. "Check this out."

O'Shea felt her stomach tighten in both anticipation and dread as she moved to stand behind the engineer and look over his shoulder. "What did you find?" she asked, uncertain as to whether she wanted to know the answer.

Swiveling his chair back to face the computer, Malone crossed his arms. "You tell me. This is a frame from the video feed we were getting from Casey's helmet camera. According to its time stamp, it's just after the EM spike, and that's all there was before Casey's suit reset."

Frozen on the screen was a still image from the paused video playback. Leaning closer, O'Shea squinted for a better look at the grainy, low-light footage Casey Flanagan's helmet camera had captured. She recognized the interior of the derelict ship's day room, cloaked as it was in near-total darkness save for Flanagan's suit lights. Neither the room itself nor the debris floating about it in the absence of powered grav plating interested her.

"What is that?" Horton asked, his voice a haunted whisper.

Just visible at the far left of the stilled image and at the edge of the light beam from Flanagan's helmet, was the wraithlike figure of a naked woman.

It took more than six hours to charge the dead freighter's depleted batteries, after which it was a simple task for Jesse Malone to activate its power systems. An hour after that, the gravity plating and environmental control systems were back online.

"*According to its onboard computer, it's the* Resolute," Sharon Burnett said, her voice filtered into O'Shea's right ear via the wireless headset she wore as she and Skip Horton made their way down one of the ship's narrow, low-ceilinged corridors. "*It's a long-haul freighter owned by McAllister Interplanetary. Listed as missing during a run from Mars to Europa about twelve years ago.*"

"Never heard of it," O'Shea said. "Then again, MacInt does a lot of contract work for the military, so it'd make sense for a bucket like this to keep a low profile." McAllister Interplanetary, like the company which owned the *Bartleby*, Okagawa-Gold, had enjoyed profitable relationships with Earth government contracts for decades. Whereas the majority of OG's government work tended toward the various civilian agencies with facilities and ventures throughout the populated solar system, MacInt preferred the more lucrative prospects to be had contracting for the military. It was one of the reasons O'Shea had opted against working for them, instead choosing to accept an offer from its chief competitor.

"That should be the main cargo bay," Horton said, pointing toward a thick hatch at an intersection in the corridor. Wiping his nose, he shook his head. "Damn, but it stinks down here." While EV suits no longer were required for moving about, the lingering stench of rotted food was everywhere.

As bad as the corridor smelled, it was nothing compared to the cargo bay, which O'Shea discovered when Horton pressed the control to open its main access hatch.

"Jesus!" she hissed through gritted teeth as she reached up to cover her nose. The odor emanating from the chamber was all but overwhelming, and O'Shea forced herself to suppress an urge to gag.

"It's like my first apartment," Horton said as he crossed the deck toward a control console. A moment later, lights activated throughout the bay and the sound of massive fans echoed in the chamber. "Main power was off in here. Give it a few minutes to clear the worst of it."

Nodding, O'Shea studied the room's interior, her attention focusing on an oversized crate, open on one side and occupying the center of the cargo bay's deck. "What is that?" she asked. The crate was at least three meters tall, though only half as wide. Walking toward it, she noticed that it bore the logo and other familiar markings of McAllister Interplanetary. Chief among the signage were labels on each of the two sides she could see, which warned in identical text: "TO BE OPENED BY AUTHORIZED PERSONNEL ONLY. M.I. DIRECTIVE 92055."

Moving to stand alongside O'Shea, Horton pointed to the upper right-hand corner of the side nearest to them, which was free of markings. "No package ID."

"I've seen that sort of thing before," O'Shea said, stepping to where the crate's side panel had been pried open. "Sometimes, military shipments get mixed in with civilian freight hauls, when it's something they want kept quiet. Why they thought not marking the crates like all the others wasn't smart camouflage, I'll never know."

She tapped the panel where burn marks around a joint told her it had been cut away. Damage was visible from where something had been forced between the seams to pull away the panel. "Look how thick these walls are," she said, running her hand along the container's smooth side. Scuff marks on the deck beneath the panel testified to the crate's weight and robust construction. "Whatever's inside, they didn't want anybody getting to it."

"You think the crew got curious?" Horton asked, frowning. "It's a long way from Mars to Europa. Maybe they were bored."

Tapping the side of the container where the panel had been pulled open, O'Shea said, "This thing was vacuum-sealed and then welded shut. You ever been *that* bored on one of these trips?"

"Nope," Horton replied. "Then again, the stuff we haul is all marked, and we know what's inside." He gestured toward other containers stored in the bay. Everything else appeared to be the typical assortment of tools, equipment, and food stores one would expect to find on a freighter bound for Europa from Mars. "And what's with the 'authorized personnel' crap?" he asked, tapping the label with its angry red lettering. "Who on Europa has to be 'authorized' to open a frappin' shipping container?"

"Good question," O'Shea said as she reached for a small flashlight hooked to her belt. Directing the beam into the container, she got her first look at the crate's contents. "Look at this."

Horton leaned around the open panel to see inside. "Son of a bitch."

To O'Shea's admittedly inexperienced eye, the lone item inside the cargo crate looked like it could be a component from what would have to be a very large engine, larger than anything she'd ever seen or worked on. A gold, cylindrical base supported a column at least twice the size of a normal man and constructed from what might have been glass, though when O'Shea tapped on it the echo sounded as though it were metal. At the top of the column was another gold end cap, similar in size and shape to the base. Etched into the gold caps were ornate glyphs that to O'Shea didn't recognize. "What the hell is this?" When she laid her flat hand against the columns' surface, she felt a low reverberation coming from inside the object.

It was at that moment that the voice of Jesse Malone crackled in her ear. *"Erin, Skip,"* the engineer said. *"Where are you guys?"*

"In the cargo bay," O'Shea replied, reaching up to adjust the microphone of her wireless headset so that it was closer to her mouth. "Why? What's going on?"

The engineer replied, *"We're picking up another EMF spike. It looks to be coming from in or near...."*

"Erin!"

Startled, O'Shea looked to see Horton backing away from where a ball of bright blue energy had appeared, suspended above a stack of two smaller cargo containers. It expanded outward with each passing second, contorting and elongating until O'Shea realized it now was taking on human form.

"Sweet mother of Jesus," she said, the words catching in her throat. "Is it her?"

"Who gives a shit? Let's get the hell out of here!" Horton shouted, his meaty hand clamping around O'Shea's arm as though to pull her from the cargo bay.

The thing grabbed her other arm.

Help me!

It moved fast, its speed such that O'Shea barely had time to realize it was coming toward her before she felt something cold and clammy close around her bicep. Then her body jerked as though she'd brushed an open flame and she cried out in pain. She lashed out with her other arm and felt resistance, as though punching through some kind of flexible barrier. Pulling back her arm, she looked up to stare into the blue, distorted, pain-racked face of Casey Flanagan.

O'Shea screamed. The bizarre apparition that might once have been Casey held both of her arms now, his eyes wide and his expression twisted with terror and agony. It opened its mouth as if to mimic her cry, but no sound came forth. Instead, Casey's voice sounded in her mind.

Help! Me!

O'Shea felt something cold and hard pelting her skin. Her vision was all but overwhelmed by the blue energy pulsating around her, growing outward from Casey as he gripped her. Then all color drained away and she was looking into absolute, endless blackness.

Make it stop!

Help us!

Voices upon voices, all calling out in staccato fashion, flooded over her. They battered her consciousness with pleas for help and cries of horror and agony, begging for escape from whatever held them in its grasp. They all came too fast, too loud, too powerful for her to decipher. If only she could….

Something yanked at the collar of her jacket. Risking a glance over her shoulder, O'Shea saw that it was Horton, who somehow had secured himself to a nearby support stanchion with a thick rubber cargo strap wrapped around his waist. He now grasped her with both hands, heaving her backward with a groan of exertion that echoed in the cargo bay. O'Shea felt Flanagan's grip break and she stumbled before falling in a disjointed heap to the deck. Rolling over, she was in time to see Casey's body seemingly dissolving as it tumbled end over end away from her. His mouth opened to release a silent scream before he disappeared altogether, leaving O'Shea and Horton alone in the cargo bay.

No, not alone, O'Shea realized, still hearing the plaintive cry of

Casey Flanagan echoing in her mind.
Help me.

"We need to get the hell out of here," Horton said. "Right now."

O'Shea stood in one corner of the day room, arms folded across her chest with her hands pressed against her sides. *Why's it so damned cold in here?*

"Not without Casey," she said, shaking her head. "I don't know what this is about, but until I do, we're not leaving." In another life, one she'd tried to put behind her, she'd been forced to leave behind wounded or dead soldiers. It was one of the things which had made her resign her commission and turn her back on the service.

She wasn't doing that here today.

"What happened to him?" Horton asked, though when O'Shea looked at him she saw that he didn't appear to be posing the question to anyone in particular. "What *the hell* happened to him?"

"It's like the woman we saw on the camera feed," O'Shea said.

"So where *is* he?" asked Sharon, sitting at the dining table with a half-smoked and seemingly forgotten cigarette in her right hand. She had been all but inconsolable after hearing of O'Shea and Horton's encounter with Flanagan.

O'Shea shook her head. "I don't know."

"Guys," Jesse Malone called out from where he was sitting at the computer terminal, breaking O'Shea's reverie. "Check this out." As the rest of the group gathered around him, he said, "I found a personal log on the secondary data server." He tapped a control on the tablet, and the image of a man, perhaps of late middle-age, appeared on the screen. His brown-gray hair was receding and he wore a pair of obsolete wire-rimmed glasses perched on the bridge of his long, narrow nose. Deep lines creased his forehead, and there were dark circles under his eyes.

"*My name is Matthew Bendis,*" the man said, speaking with an English accent. "*I work for the McAllister Interplanetary Corporation. I'm also a passenger on this vessel. I'm sorry to have to be the one speaking to you, but the rest of the* Resolute's *crew is gone, to where I haven't the faintest clue. If you're watching this, then you need to stop, get as far away from this ship as you're able, find some way to destroy it, and then finish watching.*" He leaned closer, his expression turning hard. "*Chances are that if you're watching this, it might already be too late.*"

"What the hell?" Sharon asked, and O'Shea turned to see her expression of confusion and even slight panic. She could sympathize, given the knot of uncertainty forming in her own gut.

On the screen, Bendis said, "*The* Resolute *was contracted to transport a piece of classified equipment to our research facility on Europa. You've likely already found that item.*"

"You ain't lying," Horton said.

"*The item in question was but one piece of a large object found by a McAllister Interplanetary construction crew on Mars,*" Bendis continued, "*while excavating a cavern to serve as an underground storage facility. It was quite an extraordinary find, appearing to be the remnants of a crashed space vessel of indeterminate origin, but almost certainly not belonging to anyone from the planet Earth.*"

"Is he serious?" Sharon asked. "Space aliens?"

Bendis said, "*The craft, if that's what it was, hadn't fared well in whatever incident brought it to this underground cavern. Indeed, we remain at a loss as to explain how it got there in the first place. We conducted a thorough investigation, and soon determined that the craft was inert, with a single exception.*"

"The thing in the cargo bay," Horton said.

"*That single component appeared at first to also be without power,*" Bendis said, "*but a rudimentary EMF and radiation scan told us that it has some kind of internal energy source. We soon realized that it was capable of drawing power from any source, no matter how small. Of course, we had no idea what it was supposed to do, other than act as what appeared to be part of the craft's propulsion system. We found no obvious points of access, and so were unable to get a look at its internal composition. Not wishing to take any chances, my superiors ordered it shipped to Europa for further study.*"

He paused, flinching as though stung or struck by something off-camera. Grimacing in apparent discomfort, he reached up to massage his temples. "*We packed the item in a special crate containing an electromagnetic dampening field generator, in order to prevent it from drawing power from the* Resolute *while the ship was in transit. However, we were less than halfway to Europa when that generator failed, and Eddie Coburn, the ship's engineer, reported an odd energy spike. It didn't take long to figure out that it was coming from our precious* cargo." When he paused again, it was to shake his head and release a tired sigh. "*I should've had him push the damned thing out the airlock.*" Malone said, "I don't think I like where this is going."

"*Eddie opened the box and we detected a power reading from inside, but it wasn't significant, so we thought nothing of it. Then, two days later, the ship's navigator disappeared. The assistant engineer found her clothes in the cockpit, but she was nowhere to be found. We searched the entire ship to no avail.*"

"I know where she went," Malone said, reaching for the terminal and pausing the playback. He then called up additional information from his computer tablet, and new pictures appeared on the monitor. The first was the video still Malone had captured from Flanagan's helmet camera, whereas the second was an attractive brunette woman, smiling for the photograph included in her McAllister Interplanetary employee file. Beneath the picture was her name and position: Allison Chambers, navigator, CSV *Resolute*.

"Oh my god," she said, feeling her jaw slacken as she realized what she was seeing. "Is this right?"

"As near as I can tell," Malone replied, before resuming the video playback.

"*Working with Eddie,*" Bendis said, "*I determined that the device was generating an all-but undetectable electromagnetic field, which was getting stronger the longer it had energy on which to draw. We cut power to the cargo bay and immediately saw a reduction in the EMF readings.*" He stopped to swallow, and when again looked into the camera, his expression had darkened. "*That's when we saw Allison. She ... just appeared out of the bloody air, arms and legs flailing like she was fighting to keep from being dragged underwater.*" He looked away from the screen for a moment, and O'Shea could see that he was having trouble with whatever memories of the incident he was trying to recall. "*She was naked, and her skin was so pale, as though she was a ghost.*"

"Just like Casey," Sharon whispered.

They watched Bendis close his eyes and lean back in his chair, pressing his hands to his chest.

"What's the matter with him?" Sharon asked. "Is he having a heart attack?"

"Maybe," O'Shea replied.

Regaining some of his composure, Bendis continued, "*We tried to* grab her, but it was like touching a live wire. She latched onto me and then, just for a moment, I experienced this sensation of standing at the edge of a cliff, looking into nothing. Black, and cold, it was an utter abyss, pressing in on me from all sides. Then, Eddie pulled me free and I let go of Allison, and she ... disappeared."* O'Shea watched as tears formed in the corners of the man's eyes.

"Looking into nothing," O'Shea repeated, turning the phrase over in her mind as she recalled her encounter with Flanagan.

On the screen, Bendis leaned closer to the visual pickup. *"Of course, there are no such things as ghosts. There had to be an explanation rooted in science. The electromagnetic field emitted by the device was the key. Once we realized that, it was too late. We'd all been exposed to the electromagnetic radiation it had been emitting for the past three days, and the effects were becoming obvious. Anything living was affected—plants, fruits and vegetables from our perishable stores. All of it was just fading away like it was never there."*

"This is insane," Malone said, shaking his head.

Meanwhile, Bendis said, *"The EM radiation emitted by the device is at a frequency far beyond anything I've ever seen before, possibly owing to whatever power source is at the object's center. It seems to have the effect of altering living matter at a molecular level, shifting it ... out of synch, for lack of a better term, with our natural surroundings. Whether that means some other form of visible spectrum, or another dimension, or something else entirely, I have no idea. The rest of the crew followed in short order. I watched Eddie disappear before my very eyes, and he told me before he shifted that he could feel the effects of the transition taking hold. It's rather like I'm feeling now, actually."*

"Jesus Christ," Horton said, talking more to himself than anyone else. "It's happening to him."

Bendis reached off-screen and his trembling hand came back with a glass of water, some of which he spilled down his shirt as he tried to take a drink. *"Allison and other members of the crew reappearing later supports my theory that the effects might be reversible, if the object's EM field can be disabled or at least altered significantly. However, we found no way of turning it off, with the possible exception of killing all power aboard the ship, which I've done. Now all I can do is wait to see if the crew shifts back, or I join them."* His body convulsed again, and he grunted in obvious distress.

"I don't think I'm going to make it."

The video playback stopped at that point, and the screen went blank.

"We've got to get out of here," Horton said, shaking his head and making no effort to suppress the panic gripping him. "Obviously, whatever that guy was betting on never happened. He shut off all the power, and the thing still ate him, or whatever the hell it did, along with the rest of the *Resolute* crew, and Casey."

"Remember what he said," Sharon countered, gesturing with her hands as though trying to pull from her mouth the words that wouldn't come of their own volition. "He thought it had a battery of some kind. If he's right, that thing was buried on Mars for who knows how long before they found it. What if it's the same thing here, with it just sitting down in the cargo bay, hibernating or whatever, until we show up with new power for it to chew on?"

"And what if he's right about the other thing?" O'Shea asked. "If we can shut it off, the effects might reverse themselves."

"What if he was wrong?" Horton asked, his voice raising an octave. "You want to hang out here long enough to see what happens?"

O'Shea shook her head. "Just long enough to get Casey back."

It was a simple task for Sharon Burnett to order the *Resolute*'s computer to deactivate the freighter's power systems. With that done, Jesse Malone donned an EV suit and detached the power conduit feeding juice to the derelict's depleted batteries. The only thing tying the two ships together was the flexible docking collar between their respective airlocks, and if it hadn't meant the pain in the ass of getting into gear to make the crossing, O'Shea would have severed that, too.

That was the easy part, she reminded herself as she watched Malone setting the explosive charge inside the packing crate which contained the bizarre device. "Almost done?" she asked, standing behind the engineer and aiming a penlight at the explosive so that Malone could see what he was doing. For a moment, she wondered if the strange alien device might be drawing energy even from the light's batteries.

Malone nodded, not looking up from the work he was performing on the squat yellow rectangle he'd affixed to the inside of the packing container. "I just need to set the detonator, and we can close it up." Pausing in his fussing over the device, he looked at her. "You really think this'll work?"

"Only one way to find out," O'Shea replied. Recalling that a consignment of the explosive charges was among the other supplies and equipment the *Bartleby* carried for the Okagawa-Gold mining facility on Titan, she figured the miners awaiting the cargo wouldn't miss one of the devices. Not that she cared, either way.

"Somebody's going to be royally pissed that we blew up their toy," Malone said, keying instructions to the keypad set into the charge's detonator.

O'Shea shrugged. "They can kiss my ass."

"You think that box is enough to contain the explosion?" Horton called out across the darkened cargo bay from where he stood near the reinforced hatch at the room's far end. Except for the bare minimum required to sustain life support and the grav plating, main power was off throughout the *Resolute*, and the navigator was visible thanks only to the portable light affixed to the strap he wore around his head.

"If it doesn't," Malone said, "we'll be the first to know." He pressed another key on the detonator's control pad and O'Shea heard a trio of beeps. "That's it," he said. "Let's close this thing up."

Working together, O'Shea and Malone forced the crate's open side panel closed, and once it was in place the engineer reached into the satchel slung over his left shoulder and extracted a magnetic emergency bulkhead patch. He slapped the patch across the seam connecting the panel to where it had been separated from the crate's corner brace. "That probably won't hold worth a damn."

"Doesn't matter," O'Shea said, slapping him on the shoulder. "Let's go."

They were halfway across the cargo bay, running to where Horton stood in the open doorway, when the voice echoed in her mind.

Help us!

"Did you hear that?" she asked, stopping and casting the penlight's feeble beam into the darkness around them.

"What?" Malone asked, barely visible though he stood less than an arm's length from her.

A blue luminosity was growing out of the gloom, overpowering O'Shea's flashlight, and the same odd sensation played across her exposed skin, just as it had when….

"Casey!"

Seven figures were materializing out of nothingness, with limbs and heads emerging from the amorphous blue globules now drifting within the cargo bay.

The crew of the *Resolute*. And Casey Flanagan.

"Holy Mary, Mother of God," Malone said.

Help! Us!

Flanagan's pleas hammered O'Shea's mind, and she thought they might force their way through her skull, and in that moment of intense pain, O'Shea suddenly understood.

Grabbing Malone by the arm, she yelled, "We've got to blow it right now! Come on!" They sprinted to the exit, with Horton barely managing to step aside as they plunged through the hatch. Turning, she saw the seven figures swimming in the darkness, their bodies radiating an incandescent indigo energy. All of them had formed now; naked, pale, and withering in whatever tortures now consumed them. One of the apparitions turned toward her, and O'Shea saw Casey Flanagan reaching out, his mouth twisting in a silent scream of agony.

"Do it!" she yelled, stabbing the control panel next to the doorway and cycling shut the hatch before throwing herself against the bulkhead and dropping into a protective crouch. Horton followed suit, leaving Malone standing near the hatch and peering through its reinforced shatterproof viewport. He said nothing as he held a remote-control transceiver in his right hand, and his thumb pressed a lone button set into the unit's face.

Everything around them heaved and groaned in protest as the charges detonated, and the bulkhead rang and reverberated with the force of shrapnel pelting it from inside the cargo bay. The flash of the explosion lit up the corridor, and Malone was forced to turn away from the viewport and shield his eyes. The deck heaved beneath O'Shea's feet as the ship absorbed the blast, and she silently counted off the seconds until she expected to feel the rush of air escaping through any hull breaches.

Enough time elapsed to reassure her that she probably wasn't going to die from asphyxiation or decompression, at least not today.

"*Everybody okay?*" asked Sharon Burnett, her voice sounding distant and yet so welcoming in O'Shea's headset. "*Somebody talk to me!*"

Accepting Malone's proffered hand and allowing the engineer to pull her to her feet, O'Shea adjusted her lip mike. "Yeah, we're here. Stand by." She nodded to Horton, who had to use the manual override to open the cargo bay hatch.

"Guys," he said, shining his light into the chamber.

O'Shea moved so that she could peer inside, following the track of Horton's beam. Though the compromised side panel had ruptured and come apart from the force of the explosion, the bulk of the crate had withstood the worst of the blast. As for the mysterious alien device, what little remained of it lay scattered across the deck, shards of gold and glass or crystal reflecting in the flashlight beam.

But there were no bodies.

"Where are they?" Malone asked.

"It didn't work," O'Shea replied. "The explosion must've just pushed them farther back to ... wherever."

Only then did O'Shea realize that the voices calling to her from that unending darkness had fallen silent. They no longer pressed against her mind.

She felt nothing.

"What the hell do we do now?" Horton asked.

"Nothing," she said, feeling the sadness wash over her. "They're gone." Whatever had taken Casey Flanagan, Matthew Bendis, and the crew of the *Resolute* from this world had apparently laid final claim to them. Had O'Shea killed them, or simply consigned them to eternal torment in some other plane of existence?

I'm sorry, Casey.

At the edge of her consciousness, so faint that O'Shea was only just able to sense it, came a small, weak voice—it might have been Flanagan—calling to her from the abyss.

Help me.

Salvage

David B. Riley

After two days without saying a single word, Commander Goth asked, "Why us?"

"Excuse me?" Sarah replied. She turned off the notebook. The book she'd been reading was boring, anyway.

"Why us? Why us for this mission?" Goth asked. "It is not Tau problem."

"Well, that's true. It's like this. The new chancellor of the Martian Republic is afraid of offending Earth. Really afraid. A Martian ship going this deep into Earth territory could cause a major diplomatic incident. Heck, the probe that started this was even unmarked. You lot, on the other hand, are already at war with Earth. They can't get much madder than they already are."

"This ship is no match for an Earth Force cruiser," Goth said.

"They haven't caught us, yet," Sarah pointed out.

"We still have to get home."

"If we're able to salvage the *Lisa Marie*, you guys are going to be very wealthy," Sarah said.

"We have to share it with our emperor," Goth countered.

"Well, it is his ship," Sarah said.

Goth said something to Topo in that second dialect her translator couldn't seem to pick up, then he turned toward her. "Martian probe finds missing Earth ship. Why can't Earth Force come out here?"

"They'd love to. It's an Earth cargo ship, but it's a Martian cargo. My company insured the cargo, not the ship. If we could recover some of the cargo, the Gompers Insurance Company will recoup some of its losses, even after paying you guys a salvage fee," Sarah explained. "Earth Force would simply seize everything and keep it all for themselves. At least, that's been our experience. So, turning it over to them would be the same as staying home."

Most people on Mars called the Tau "lizards." They reminded Sarah more of small dinosaurs. They certainly didn't always approach things the way a human would. "We can turn around and go back home if you like?" Sarah continued. "If you're afraid of mixing it up with Earth Force, I understand."

"Too late for that," Goth said. "We are here." He said something else in the second dialect that Sarah couldn't pick up.

"By golly, there it is. Target bearing 20 degrees," Sarah reported. "Range: one kilometer." She was getting so she could actually read some of the instruments. There was no portable pocket translator for their written language.

"Slow to one quarter," Goth ordered.

"One quarter speed," Topo, the helmsman, answered.

"Go to maneuvering thrusters," Goth ordered.

"Maneuvering thrusters," Topo replied.

"Docking sequence in five seconds," Goth ordered.

Sarah was amazed at the detail of the scanning beams on her console. "Hull appears intact. I've got a clear hatch on top of it. Two of them, actually. Let's grab the aft one."

Goth nodded, then said something in that annoying second dialect.

Topo gently landed the patrol ship on top of the *Lisa Marie*. "Magnetic seal in place." The scout ship was tiny compared to the large freighter. It only took up a small part of the space on top the hull.

"It is possible life support and power may still work," Goth said. He handed Sarah a handheld unit. "No sign of structural damage."

Sarah was reading the instruments. "It looks pretty darn cold down there." Sarah looked at Goth, then Topo, then Ting, the third member of the three-person crew. They were all looking expectantly back at her. *Warm blooded reptiles, hah. These guys were afraid of the cold.*

The procedure, according to the manual, was to send one person, and only one person, to board a derelict ship to determine if it was safe. If a bulkhead collapsed or there turned out to be booby traps, this greatly reduced casualties—unless you're the idiot who went on board. Goth could not order Sarah to do anything. Sarah was not military. She wasn't even Tau. She was human. And this ship had been sitting out in the icy cold of space for over ten years. "How about I go have a look at the power systems," Sarah offered.

She opened up the bag that contained her Martian Defense Force military surplus pressure suit. No, the Gompers Insurance Company would not provide a new space suit if they could get a surplus one somewhere at half the cost. And they always seemed to find everything at off-price venues. Someday, if she was still alive, she was going to have to meet their purchasing agent—maybe cook him something made with surplus rations or take him for a ride in a surplus surface skimmer.

At least the suit fit fairly well. Ting looked over the connections and pronounced her ready to go. She entered the airlock and waited for it to seal behind her. Then, she tried the handle on the hatch. It wouldn't budge. That seemed to be why Ting gave her a hammer. Hammers were Ting's solution to nearly everything. He was an engineer, they kept telling her.

Sarah gave the handle a whack. Then another. In no time, she had the hatch to the *Lisa Marie* open. The interior was cold, dark and foreboding. It was no wonder the reptiles didn't want to go. No matter how hard her helmet lights struggled, it was like their energy could only get a little bit beyond her before succumbing to the darkness of the derelict space ship.

The sensor in her hand confirmed what she suspected. The power generators had been charging everything for years. The ship's systems showed active on the life support panel. She turned them on: first the lights, then the heat, then the air filtration. Whatever happened to the ship, lack of environmental systems did not seem to have been the cause.

Still, everything was eerie. As the interior began to warm, moisture that had long been frozen began to form into a sort of fog. She also discovered that the lights she'd found were little more than red glow plugs. It was becoming obvious this was the backup system she'd activated, not the primary. As they warmed, the glow plugs gave off a dim red light that may have been energy efficient, but it was hardly pleasing.

As the ship tried to wake up, Sarah made her way to the bridge. She turned on the primary computer. To her amazement, it came on. "Wow!"

"You have found something?" Goth asked.

She didn't realize she'd been transmitting. "I've got basic life support warming up the ship. The main computer's even working."

"Have you located the cargo?" Goth asked.

"In time, good sir. One thing at a time." Sarah made sure the radio in her helmet was off. The thing she'd feared was still strapped in a seat at the engineering console. She didn't want to let out a screech like a girl. Of course, she *was* a girl. Of course, the Tau didn't know the difference. *She* was their only reference point for human behavior. And they weren't going to catch her screaming just because there were a few frozen bodies lying around on the bridge, frozen bodies that were certain to thaw soon.

She bit down on her tongue when the dead guy at the engineering station's arm dropped. No screaming. No running away. The body was simply thawing. Of course, it couldn't possibly have thawed that fast. She went over and touched it. Frozen solid. Then, she felt the air blowing through a vent below the panel and relaxed a little.

The handheld meter said there was enough air pressure and it was now slightly warmer than freezing. She unsnapped her helmet and took it off. The air was cold and clammy, but at least she was free from the claustrophobic tyranny of the helmet. She told the computer to play back the log.

Sarah found a recreation area after leaving the bridge. It had the usual games and comfy chairs and such. There was even a keyboard in the corner. It was still turned on. The keyboard had been on for ten years. She ran her fingers down the keys, then headed for the corridor to connect back to the scout ship. As she left the room, she heard the keyboard play back the notes she'd just played. She looked back into the room and wondered why it would have such a playback feature.

Something did not just touch me. Something did not just touch my neck, she told herself. This ship was too darn creepy. She started back to the scout ship, trying just to walk and not run. Every few minutes, she found herself jerking her head one way or another. It always seemed that there was something moving, just out of the corner of her eye. She knew that wasn't possible and the crummy lighting from the glow plugs made everything look odd and distorted. The fog didn't help things. Even her breath was fogging. She figured the fog would go away if the ship got a little warmer and the air kept circulating.

It was time for some reptiles to earn their pay. She climbed up the ladder and through the hatch that went back into the scout ship. "I'm back." Sarah started taking off her space suit. "I found out what happened to this ship," Sarah explained. "You guys ever hear of Argomite reactors?"

The three of them stared blankly.

"Well, the Argomite Company built these defective reactors and put them in mostly merchant ships. They weren't shielded properly.

Sometimes a ship would be buzzing along in hyperspace under heavy power load and they'd suddenly flood a ship with radiation without warning. Worse thing was, the company knew about it but was too cheap to fix the problem. The poor crew had no idea. It only affected a small number of ships. Word got out. There was a big hullabaloo. Gompers didn't know about the reactors or they'd never have underwritten a policy.

"I played back the computer. That's what happened. The ship shut down and just drifted around for ten years. The crew was dead, but there wasn't any real damage. We could fly this baby home right now, though I'm not sure I'd jump into hyperspace without a radiation suit on."

She noticed Ting was checking their ship's sensors. "Relax, it was gamma radiation that leaked out. It's long gone. I scanned and there's less radiation down there than there is in here."

"You found cargo?" Goth asked.

"Well, not yet. You guys can go check it out. I can't do everything," Sarah said. "Down the corridor to the end, then two decks down the stairs. There's probably more carenthium than we can carry."

"We will see if they have a pump," Goth said.

"Good idea," Sarah agreed.

As her companions climbed down the ladder, Sarah finished getting out of her space suit. She was going to warm up for a few minutes before going back down to explore. The computer hadn't given up the location of the purser's office, amongst other things.

The ship's sensors suddenly started going off in alarm mode. Sarah scrambled over to the controls, then fumbled around to figure what they were trying to tell her. The visuals were mostly gibberish, as she still only had a rudimentary understanding of the Tau language in written form.

Energy was being discharged. It appeared the Tau were shooting at something or somebody. Then, she noticed yet another problem as well.

The three reptiles really zipped up the stairs and back into the scout ship. Ting was the last one up. He closed the hatch in record time.

"Guys, were you shooting at anything in particular?" Sarah asked.

Goth looked at her for just an instant, then said, "Invisible people."

"Uh, okay," Sarah replied. She waited for more explanation. When none came she said, "We've got another problem, too." She pointed upward.

Goth went to a window. "Oh no." An Earth Force cruiser had docked with the other hatch of the *Lisa Marie*. It was so big that its tail extended over the top of their scout ship. They were boxed in. They couldn't leave if they wanted to. "This is why I did not want to come here."

"Well, I think it's an odd coincidence that they just show up a few minutes after we do, on a derelict ship that's been adrift for a decade," Sarah said.

There was a sort of sizzling noise for a few seconds, then the hatch from the *Lisa Marie* popped open. Goth yelled something in that second dialect that Sarah couldn't pick up. All three Tau fell to the floor. Sarah joined them. A flash grenade came up through the hatch and exploded. Seconds later, a helmeted head popped up and aimed a laser rifle around the cabin.

"We surrender!" Sarah yelled.

The handcuffs were awfully tight. It was still miserably cold and damp in the *Lisa Marie*, but at least Sarah had finally found the purser's office. She had no idea how long they'd been there. There weren't any clocks or any other way to measure the passage of time. There was just silence, a cold clammy silence in a dark little room lit by one pathetic glow plug that barely worked. "I hope they take this thing into hyperspace so they can all die," Sarah said.

"That would include us," Goth pointed out.

"Who cares. They'll kill me anyway."

"It seems someone has lost her sunny disposition," Goth said.

"What!"

"I make joke," Goth said.

The Tau had no sense of humor. She was certain of it. Things were getting weird. "Who were these invisible people you were shooting at?"

"Down by cargo area," Goth said. "They pushed Ting to floor, then tried to take his knife."

"Lasers don't work on them," Ting added. "Don't understand that." He looked expectantly at her.

"Don't look at me. I wasn't there. I don't know what you guys got into." It was a lie, of course. She knew, or at least suspected, what might have happened. Stories of strange things abounded on derelict vessels with dead crews, though there were usually more skeptics than believers in such phenomena.

The hatch burst open. Two men in black Earth Force uniforms came into the purser's office. The tall bald one was a commander. The second man wore no insignia. He was shorter, with red hair and a goatee, though it was his eyes that Sarah would remember. They were cold, gray eyes that seemed to look right through a person.

"I'm Commander Kent, XO of the Earth Force cruiser *Hawaii*." He looked at Goth. "You are a long way from home, Commander."

Goth stared back at him, but said nothing.

"You have a name?" Kent asked.

"I am Goth. This is Engineer Ting and Helmsman Topo," Goth replied.

The commander scratched his chin for a moment. "And you just up and went all the way out here to salvage a ship no one's seen or heard from in ten years?"

"Obviously," Goth said.

"You'll be taken to the prisoner of war facility on Minion Prime. That's an Earth colony that, ironically, was the destination of the *Lisa Marie*." Commander Kent seated himself behind the purser's desk. "Although the ship is in good shape, I'm puzzled why you'd bother for a load of carenthium."

"Have you seen the price of carenthium lately?" The other man finally joined into the conversation. He sat himself on the purser's desk top and crossed his arms in front of himself. Without looking at Sarah, he asked, "Why did Gompers Insurance want this ship?"

Sarah glared at the unnamed man, but said nothing.

"A load of carenthium is valuable. It helps fuel space ships and all. But, perhaps there is something else afoot here." He unfolded his arms. "No matter. We'll figure it out."

"My friend here is from Military Intelligence," Commander Kent said.

"Who'd have thought it," Sarah answered.

"Miss Meadows, we have quite a file on you. I doubt your friends here know as much about you as I do," the intelligence officer said. "When I've finished your interrogation, you'll be taken back to Earth where you will be tried, then executed for espionage."

"What a surprise," Sarah said. "I'm a Martian citizen. This is a derelict vessel subject to salvage under the Law of Space Treaty. How can I possibly be a spy? What is there to spy on?"

"It's right above you," the intelligence officer said. "Not that I need a reason. Our military courts are far more efficient than your Martian Criminal Tribunal. We don't let facts get in the way of a good trial."

The two men both stood. "Guards will move you all onto our ship in a few minutes," the intelligence office said. "The brig of the *Hawaii* is a better place for you than tied up in here." They both marched out of the purser's office.

"Sarah Meadows, I think these men do not like you," Goth said.

Somehow, the way Goth said it seemed funny. Sarah let out a brief snicker of a laugh. The odd thing was, there was another laugh at the same time and the three Tau soldiers weren't saying or doing anything. The sound, she began to think, had emitted from her translator, which was still active and in her pocket.

"Is there someone here with us?" Sarah asked.

The empty chair behind the purser's desk moved so that it pointed directly at Sarah.

"Invisible people," Goth said.

"My translating device that I use to talk to my Tau friends here may pick you up as well. Who are you?" Sarah asked.

"Why have you come? You are not welcome," a voice said. It sounded feminine. "Leave us."

"Are you Captain Mercer?" Sarah asked.

"Why have you come?" It repeated.

There were only two women on the crew and the other was the cook. "Are you Barbara Mercer?" Sarah repeated. "I'm from Gompers Insurance. That's why we're here. We insured your cargo."

"You brought *them* on board," the voice said.

"The Tau are the least of your worries," Sarah said.

"Leave us. Leave us be."

"I can't. We're prisoners. Captain Mercer, we just were trying to recover some of the insured cargo. We'll gladly go. It's Earth Force that you should fear. They'll tow this ship to Minion Prime and dismantle it for scrap. Is that what you want?" Sarah asked.

"No. Not now. Just leave us alone. Just let us be," the voice said.

"Fine with us. Help us get out of here. I can get rid of Earth Force.

It will be just as it was," Sarah promised. "But, we need your help."
There was no answer or response. Sarah suspected there was no one in the room anymore.

The three Tau started talking in that annoying second dialect again. It seemed baffling that the translator couldn't pick it up, especially in light of what had just happened.

More time went by. It was hard to tell how much. Then, the door burst open and three marines came in—two corporals and a sergeant. "We're taking you back to our brig," the sergeant said. Apparently, there was one guard for each Tau soldier. A strawberry blond girl from Mars didn't need her own guard, evidently.

The funny thing about Earth marines was almost all of them carried an obsolete weapon in a sheath that went into their boots. The black nylon knives never break or react to metal or conduct electricity, supposedly. And they never had to be sharpened. And, the manufacturers of these knives probably never envisioned that they would all float out of their sheaths and stab their owners at the same time. Then, those same knives pulled out of their victims. Everyone knows you always pull the knife back out to hasten blood loss and kill the victim. A knife still in the wound blocks the blood from escaping.

The two corporals both collapsed to the floor, each screaming as their limbs lost strength and blood surged from their bodies. Their screams only lasted a few moments, then the corporals were silent. Their eyes still stared pleadingly toward their sergeant, still showing the disbelief at what had just happened.

But not the sergeant. He snatched his knife back from his unseen assailant and held it in front of his face as it dripped his own blood over his right hand. A strange, twisted grin appeared on his face. It was an almost satisfied look as he stared at the knife—his knife. Then, he started laughing. It was a maniacal, hideous laugh. As he laughed, his blood gushed up from his chest and showered his throat and vocal cords, making it the most horrid, gurgling sound Sarah would ever hear. Then, finally, mercifully, the laugh stopped and the sergeant fell onto the already lifeless bodies of his two fallen comrades.

Unseen hands quickly took the electronic key off the sergeant's belt and all of them were free.

"Leave us," the voice Sarah attributed to Captain Mercer said.

"Sure thing, but I came here to try and recover something we insured. Until I saw the ship was intact, I didn't even know if it was on board." She pointed at the purser's safe behind the desk. "It wasn't on the manifest, but it was on the insurance policy. Give me the combination to the safe, captain."

"No," the voice said. "Just go."

"It's brought misery everywhere it's gone. As long as it's on board, others will come. If I take it back to Mars, there won't be any reason for anyone to ever disturb you again," Sarah said.

The lights flickered on the number pad on the front of the safe, then it clicked. Sarah quickly opened the safe. A green velvet bag sat on the middle shelf. She grabbed it. "Thank you, Captain."

They found no resistance getting back to their ship. The Earth Force crew seemed preoccupied with offloading the carenthium and not with guarding a small scout ship that had little value or purpose.

"Earth guys damage hatch. I fix." Ting held up a hammer.

As Ting sealed the hatch, Topo and Goth took the seats at the control stations. "There is large ship above us. It is blocking escape. You have a plan?" Goth asked Sarah.

She was only half paying attention as she climbed into the turret that housed the laser cannon. "Carenthium is marvelous stuff. They love it for thrusters 'cause it burns in space. It's got its own oxygen, they tell me. And our Earth Force pals are pumping it through that big hose into their cargo tank." The laser canon would not arm. The target was too close, if she understood the weird writing correctly. She flipped off the safety, pushed the override button and fired.

Scout ships were patrol craft, to monitor a large area with a small crew and flee and summon assistance if an enemy approached. But, they did have some fire power when they got in a pinch. Sarah doubted the designers of the ship had their particular predicament in mind when they designed the craft. Crimson energy blasted all the 20 meters across the top of the *Lisa Marie* to the hose feeding into the *Hawai,* right at the junction where it fed into the storage hold. An explosion ripped a hole out the side of the *Hawaii* a few seconds later.

The Earth Force ship seemed to be turning sideways. They'd only used a single magnetic seal to dock on top of the *Lisa Marie,* just as the scout ship had done. They'd lost that seal when the explosion went off. The *Hawaii's* thrusters opened up. Whoever was on their bridge probably thought the problem was on the *Lisa Marie* and was trying to get some distance from a burning ship. A bright flash a few seconds later was the last of the *Hawaii.*

"Commander Goth, can you get us out of here?" Sarah asked. "I didn't think it would blow up quite so fast. Good thing it moved away."

Their own thrusters kicked on and the scout ship pulled away from the top of the *Lisa Marie*. Sarah fired a shot at the derelict freighter. She noticed Goth was standing behind her as she climbed down from the turret. "I shot their engines. No one's going to bother them anymore. That ship will never fly anywhere. With no cargo, it's now worthless."

Goth asked, "Why do the invisible people want to be left out here?"

"I can only imagine what they've been through. I guess they no longer belong anyplace else," Sarah explained.

"Make sure we get paid for the diamond in your bag," Goth said.

"You knew about the Parkside Diamond, the biggest natural diamond ever found on Mars?" Sarah asked.

"Of course. Had to be worthwhile for us to come out here. Our ships don't use much carenthium," Goth said.

"This thing's caused a lot of trouble." Sarah took the diamond out of the bag. "Surprised the Earth Force goons didn't figure out to look in the safe. Gompers insured this little rock for a lot of money."

Goth looked confused, even more than normal. "The invisible people killed the Earth marines to help us escape?"

Sarah shrugged. "They probably don't view death the way you or I do. I can't figure it. It was an Earth crew, they tell me, yet the invisible people liked us best. Take me home," Sarah asked. She put the diamond back in the bag.

The Golem

Judith Herman

Kayla had a soft place for wounded creatures. After all, she knew exactly how it felt to come up against the implacable force of her father and lose. Pa had decided to incorporate search animals in his treasure-hunting scheme. Dog, their first and last bloodhound, had fought against Pa and lost before its first planetfall.

And it was due to Harley Alverson's nature that the entire family was now crowded around the airlock where the dog had been laid to rest. The dog lay in the middle of a pile of its own void: crap, piss, and blood, still moving weakly. It looked up at Kayla and whined.

"You can't just leave him there without helping," Kayla cried. "He's hurt, Pa." Involuntary tears ran down her face. In a way, Dog was the lucky one. His torment would soon be over.

"Gall-durned thing couldn't even control itself." Harley, Kayla's father, walked off. "Nearly took off my hand." He muttered darkly as he hit the switch to close the airlock's inner door.

Kayla lowered her head, trying to close out the world and nuzzled the fur of a small multi-colored cat she cradled in her arms. Bitty smelled of warmth and milk and purred his love back at her. With the cat in her arms she would get through this. Kayla concentrated on cat smells and prayed for Dog and a quick end to his torture.

"Kayla attend," Pa commanded. "I will allow that we must all learn a lesson from this."

Kayla lifted her head and stared straight ahead. Bitty squirmed in her arms. She stroked him, but didn't look down. Boyd, the boy a year younger and many times meaner, took the opportunity to pluck the small cat out of Kayla's arms and chucked it through the narrow opening to land on the lame dog. The cat yowled and in its panic attempted to launch itself back out of the airlock. But, it was already too late. The opening was just a slit, not wide enough even for a small cat. Soon, the door would close tightly and both animals would be voided from the ship.

"No!" Kayla rushed at the door trying to stop the inevitable. She could hear Bitty scrabbling on the other side trying to get out, to get back to her. "Bitty didn't do nothing. Make the door stop, please, Pa."

Earl, the oldest boy at fourteen and two years older than Kayla, pulled her away from the door. "Don't make this worse than it is." Earl pushed her behind him to remove her from their father's sight. Not fast enough.

Pa yanked Kayla from Earl and shook her. "Stop this nonsense now. That durn cat was not right in the head ever since Boyd and Frank tried to teach it to fly in zero-g. Waste of space, food and affection, by any rights. If anyone is to blame, blame yourself for carting that thing around with you. If you hadn't brought it on deck, it wouldn't have been tossed out with the dog."

He banged the struggling Kayla into the wall. "Now stop, or I'll have to punish you some more. I'll give you pick of the next litter if you will only stop that durn wailing." He banged her three more times into the wall. Kayla only screamed louder.

"Father Harley, let me hush Kayla." Darla tried to cuddle her against her big belly, but Kayla pulled away. Darla was the new mom, not her true mother. Kayla's mother and two more that followed had long been used up and discarded. Kayla could feel the baby, due any day now, squirming against her from inside Darla. More new life should not be brought onto this ship, not now, not as long as Pa and Boyd were around.

Kayla caught one involuntary glance through the airlock porthole to see Bitty bouncing around the enclosed space, slamming into each wall as he tried to get away from the hurt dog. Dog had quit moving, but his eyes burned into hers, pleading. She turned away facing the wall trying to pretend away the image she could not release. "I got chores to do." She made as if to leave the area.

"Stop her," Pa ordered and Boyd complied.

"Pa, can't you go easy on her? She loved that cat." Earl was Kayla's only true brother.

"You shut your mouth now, boy. We are civilized people. And civilized people pray for all creatures, large and small." A loud bang interrupted him. The bang was followed by a whoosh as the pressure equaled out. After the noise settled, Pa bowed his head. "Lord of the Universe, please receive your miserable creatures back to your bosom for their care. Amen."

The Golem

Boyd laughed. "We certainly didn't want them." He shook Kayla until her teeth rattled. "Maybe next time I'll chuck you into the airlock."

Earl glared at Boyd, but it was Pa who answered. "That's enough, Boyd. I put up with you ridding us of that gull-darn cat, but no more, you hear? I can't abide you wasting resources."

Kayla fell into the wall when Boyd released his hold on her. He laughed, again. She grit her teeth against the "You'll be sorry," that struggled to come out against her better judgment. Boyd had been born mean. It was as if all of Pa's fury had been baked into him at birth. The boy could never be accused of doing one single kindness for anyone. Kayla had learned long ago to never tangle with him and to always make sure the door was locked when she and the girls were alone in their dormitory at night.

"Back to work now," Pa said and the two older boys took off. No one needed more than one reminder to get back to work. Kayla, as eldest girl, toted the babe while she helped Darla herd the little ones back to the nursery.

After that, Kayla headed to the cargo hold for her chores. She knew Boyd feared the holds where the goods for sale were kept. Pa called them antiquities. They were only a bunch of old dishes and junk, but anything that kept Boyd away from her was a good thing.

The first thing she saw was Bitty's blanket and bowls. She couldn't help it. Instead of picking up the broom to sweep, she crawled among the piles of boxes and crates to wedge her small body between a large oblong container and the wall furthest away from the entryway. Once hidden, Kayla gave over to her misery, weeping uncontrollably.

A curious scratching noise caught her attention. It sounded like someone was scratching at the same spot she was at, but from the inside of the box. She sniffled, rubbed her nose with her arm, and lifted her head. And the scratching noise happened again. "Hello, is someone there?"

Kayla sat up and faced the box placing her palms flat against the surface where she thought the noise originated. It felt different from all the other cargo she had helped with in the past. The place where she held her hands felt warm in a comforting way. And even though it looked like black stone, it had a metallic feel to it. The scratching stopped. Kayla held her breath waiting for some sign there was someone there and she wasn't having another of her flights of fancy, as Pa liked to call it.

And then she heard a voice. A voice deep, soft and comforting.

"What ails you? Why do you cry?" It was so unlike Pa, so unlike Boyd.

"I'm mourning poor Dog, who never had a proper name, and my poor Bitty."

"And what happened to poor Dog and Bitty?"

"Pa happened. He hurt them. And then he wouldn't save them. And Boyd said next time it could be me." More tears started flowing down her cheeks.

"I could keep you from getting hurt. All you would have to do is open this box and no one would ever hurt you again."

Pa had told Kayla to never touch the contents of the boxes. She thought of the whupping she would get if she opened the box. "I'm sorry, but I can't do that."

"I understand."

The voice sounded so sad to Kayla. "I'm sorry I should go now."

"You will come again?"

"Yes." Pa didn't say not to talk to the things in the boxes. Kayla got to her feet and dried her eyes on her skirt.

"What should I call you?"

"Kayla. I'm twelve." And then she smiled for the first time in awhile. She had a friend that was all her own. "And what's your name?"

"I have been alive many, many years. And I have been called by many names. My actual name would be difficult for you to pronounce in your language. You may call me Emet."

"I once had a brother named that, not my true brother, though, only half. But I liked him all the same. He spelled his name, E-m-m-e-t-t. I will call you that."

The door opened to reveal Pa glowering at her. "What are you playing at in here, girl? Didn't I tell you not to mess with our treasures?"

"I wasn't playing with anything."

"You surely weren't working in here, neither. Now, go help Mother Darla. Make yourself useful."

After one backward glance, Kayla hurried from the hold. After she had gotten far enough down the hallway Pa wouldn't hear, she whispered, "Bye, Emmett. It was nice to meet you."

As Mother Darla got closer to her baby's birthing day, everyone pitched in to get ready for the event. Kayla was kept busy taking care of the little ones.

At odd moments, Kayla would think about her new friend. Would Emmett still talk to her even though she had been remiss in visiting with him? She remembered the two days she had been shut up in the small cabin as punishment for her willfulness. She hadn't been allowed to read or sing to herself. No one had been allowed to visit. It had felt like weeks and was surely a bad time of sadness if there ever had been one.

Her new friend Emmett was shut up in that black box with no one to talk to just as she had been in the dark room. Someone should care about the poor thing. Late that night she snuck into the hold to talk to Emmett. She found the boxes and crates had been moved around. They looked as if they had been roughly shoved out of the way.

At first she didn't see his box, "Emmett, Emmett where are you?" She peered around and waited for an answer.

Finally, after a pause that felt like an eternity, she heard a low voice. "Kay-la. Have you returned?"

"I'm so sorry, Emmett. I wanted to come sooner, but Mother Darla is almost ready to have her new child. I'm a big enough girl, I get to help." Kayla wandered among the boxes searching for Emmett's box. She needed to touch his presence as much for her reassurance as for his. "You aren't mad at me that I didn't come back sooner?"

"Time does not hold me as much a prisoner as you."

"Huh, you sure do have a funny way of speaking." Kayla hopped a rope and rounded a statue twice her size. The statue previously had been stored in the corner near the door. Now, it hid Emmett's box. She scrunched down to settle near what she thought where his head must be and rested her head against the hard surface. It should have felt cool to the touch, but once again, the place she touched felt warm and comforting.

"I am happy to have your presence near me. I feel my power returning to me when you are near." Emmett's voice sounded as if he was whispering in her ear.

Kayla slung one arm over the top of the box. She felt as if she could confide in Emmett about anything. "Pa and Mother Darla must be worried about the baby. They avoid talking about him.

"Mother Darla just bites her lip and says, 'He'll be here real soon, honey.' Whenever I ask things like what his name will be, Pa just orders us back to work. It's bad when they don't give something a name. Look what happened to Dog and Bitty. Bitty weren't Bitty to no one, but me. Everyone else called him crazy cat or in Pa's case, that durned cat."

"I can still help you," said Emmett, from inside his box.

"You know I'm not allowed to open your box. Pa said so and you heard it, too."

"Just remember, I will always answer your need. You need only open the box."

"Thanks." Kayla hunkered down further and bit her nails thinking hard about the baby-to-come and what would happen to them all if the baby weren't to come out right. Before she knew it the warmth from Emmett had relaxed her to steal away her fears and she fell asleep leaning against the box.

Shortly after midnight ship's time, Kayla heard her father calling for her. Kayla jumped up nearly ramming into the statue that stood over Emmett's box. She scrambled over boxes to hurry towards the exit. As the doors opened, a hand reached in and dragged her into the hallway. Unbalanced, Kayla tried to settle, "Pa?"

"Shush now and just stand here to wait for me. I need you to do what you are told exactly." A bundle wrapped in a sky blue blanket made of soft combed wool was shoved into her arms. Her father didn't wait to make sure she had a solid purchase before he turned and strode down the hall toward the medical bay.

This was the blanket Kayla had made for her new baby brother. He must have come while she was asleep. Kayla peered in between the folds of the blanket to discover a tiny body. It had to be her baby brother. But the baby seemed still. Was he dead? He was so small, wrinkled and wet. Pa must have barely spent any time wiping him down before wrapping him up in the blanket. Kayla hunkered down against the wall and lowered him into her lap. She pulled back the blanket to expose his tiny body just as he gave a funny hiccup. She saw his chest rise and fall a slight amount. She gave a sigh of relief. Her new brother was alive. But why did Pa separate him from Mother Darla?

Thinking Pa must have mistaken the babe for dead; she crept down the hall to bring him to his mother. Outside the bay, she overheard Pa say, "Mother Darla, I regret to say your baby was stillborn." This pronouncement was followed by weeping. Kayla longed to go in to deliver the happy news, but she had already disobeyed Pa by coming down the hall this far.

She waited rooted to the spot. Should she stay or go back to the original spot outside the cargo hold? She could admit to nothing, but honesty won out. She stayed put.

Pa nearly ran her down as he came back out. He slammed home the doors before addressing her. "Girl, can you not follow my instructions as I gave them?" He glared at her, but brushed aside her attempts to answer him. "You need not try to find an excuse. I know you for the willful child you have always been. I thought your time in the penance chamber would have cured that, but I see I was wrong."

"But Pa," Kayla held out the child now wrapped so that it was obvious he lived still.

"No Kayla, do not argue. This child is not long for this world. He cannot go to his mother."

Images of Dog and Bitty in the airlock waiting to be flushed out into space came unbidden to her. Slowly, she backed away from her father as she refused to accept her suspicions that this was his intent for the newborn babe.

He motioned for her to follow. "Kayla, attend me and do not make this a harder duty than it already is." He headed towards the airlock.

"No, Pa. I cannot let you kill the baby. He's done nothing wrong." Kayla ran to the cargo hold, fighting her way through the boxes and crates. She hurried behind the statue to hide behind Emmett's box.

Pa stood just inside the closed doors. He hit the door lock. "Kayla, I am your father. I expect you to obey me without question, but I need you to understand this babe is the work of the devil. It was conceived from an unholy union between your brother Emmett and Mother Darla. I caught them together one afternoon. I need your help to cleanse this ship of the evil."

Kayla remembered the day Pa and Emmett had fought. It was the last time they had gone planetside. Pa had gone out for the day. It was a barren world, filled with barbarians who didn't speak a civilized language or believe in the true belief. Pa had told them no one from the family could leave the ship or they would be stolen away to be made a slave.

Bored, Kayla had wandered the ship with Bitty telling him funny stories as she carried him about. She had been so bored she had gone to find Mother Darla to help with chores. But Mother Darla was busy speaking with Emmett and had shooed her away.

Pa returned early. Kayla heard shouts and she knew better than to investigate. Later after takeoff when Emmett couldn't be found, Pa had said, "It was time for Emmett to learn to make his own way in the world." And for the months since that time, no one mentioned Emmett's name for fear of Pa's temper.

Now, Kayla understood what the yelling had been about. "But he's just a little baby."

"The child is a product of sin. No good can come from his living on this ship."

"Pa, please don't ask me to kill a baby." Kayla held the baby tight in her arms as if she could protect him from what was surely to pass.

He advanced towards where she was crouched. "I am past being reasonable with you. You do as I instruct you or face the consequences of your own willfulness and share the baby's fate."

The voice came from the box, her friend Emmett's box. "Kayla, open my box and I promise I will protect you."

"Emmett, I promised Pa not to touch your box." Kayla's eyes filled with tears. It seemed she was doomed no matter what she chose.

Her father paused and looked around. Then he glared at Kayla. "What game are you playing here girl? You know your brother is no longer on the ship."

"There is someone in this box. His name is Emmett, too. Didn't you hear him?" She realized Pa might have heard Emmett promise to protect her. Pa wouldn't like that. She started shaking so hard she was afraid she'd drop the baby. She clutched him to her chest and hummed to calm herself as much as the baby, who had started fussing.

"I heard nothing, Kayla. You were always such a queer child. You need to stop this now and hand over the child." He advanced on her with an intent that she knew would spare neither the baby nor her life.

"No, I will not let you murder this baby, Pa." Kayla unsealed the box. The lid flew back to strike the statue. The statue teetered as a rough-shaped figure straightened and pushed the statue over to strike her father as it crashed onto the crates in front of it. It landed in pieces on the floor. Pa fell back from the force and his head clipped a box.

The figure flowed more than moved towards her father. At once, it looked solid and then it separated into many small pieces that flew while holding to a man's shape. It looked like a sand storm whipped up by a mighty wind. And just as sand can completely cover a person during a storm, so did this figure, this being she had come to call Emmett, covered her father. There was a loud buzzing noise that died down to a steady hum.

Finally, the noise stopped and Emmett gathered himself to a standing position. He looked more solid. And he now had a face where before his head had looked like malformed clay. The face flashed from her father's face through a multitude of other faces, stranger's faces. The figure's features steadied to form a face that looked the way she remembered her brother Emmett had looked. "Kayla, you are safe now," said the figure.

Kayla's mouth dropped. No words came. The baby started squalling. He must be hungry by now and wanting his mother's comfort. On dropping her vision to the baby, she noticed the floor area where her father had fallen, was now clear. Not only her father's body was missing, but parts of the boxes where he had fallen were also gone. Clay bowls and other assorted ancient looking implements spilled onto the floor.

No, this wasn't possible. She hadn't wanted Pa dead; she just wanted it to end. And when she looked back to tell this to Emmett, he was gone.

Loud banging and yells from outside the cargo hold claimed her attention. She couldn't stay here any longer. She released the lock. Earl and Boyd rushed in.

"What was that noise," Earl began until he saw the bundle in Kayla's arms. "What is that baby doing in here?"

Kayla made to brush past them. "I'll just get him to Mother Darla."

She was stopped by Boyd gripping her arm, heedless of the wailing baby. "What did you do with Pa? Where is he?"

Earl pushed Boyd away from Kayla, who took the opportunity to escape. Incoherent yells followed her as she ran back to the medical station. "Emmett, where did you go," she whispered. And then Kayla was too busy consoling Darla and settling mother and child to wonder about her new friend.

They had been speeding on a course none of them knew enough to control for several days before the proximity alarm sounded. Kayla knew what that meant. They were in trouble.

No one but Pa was allowed to fly the ship. She suspected he had started teaching Boyd, but a lot of good that would do the family now.

"I hate you. I hate you all." Boyd yelled through the locked door of Pa's cabin. Kayla and Earl stood outside listening to the crashing sounds, as if Boyd was throwing the furniture around in a rage to match Pa's fits.

"Boyd, if you don't come out and help, we are all going to die." Earl shouted. "The piloting controls are locked. I know Pa taught you." The doors suddenly parted to reveal Boyd holding a blaster. "I know this." And he waved it in Kayla's direction. "I know you killed Pa. And I know how to use this to kill you."

"Kayla, go back to the nursery to Mother Darla and the young'uns. I'll talk this over with Boyd." Earl made shooing motions to Kayla.

"No, this includes me, and I will not hide from Boyd this time." Kayla stood her ground. And suddenly there was a humming noise and a dark figure flowed down the hall along the floor and the wall. It looked like a moving shadow of a figure that crawled along the wall. And then it formed up to stand next to Kayla. It advanced towards Boyd.

"Kayla, what is that?" demanded Earl.

"This is my friend Emmett. He didn't mean to kill Pa. He was trying to protect me and the baby." Kayla wrung her hands.

"No," said Boyd, "you killed Pa. This isn't real. This can't be real. This is all your doing. And now you must pay for Pa." Boyd's finger tightened on the blaster.

Emmett continued towards Boyd. Kayla could not condone another killing, even if it was Boyd. "Emmett, stop now. I forbid you to kill anyone else."

"I swore to protect you," said Emmett. The figure started to hum. Any minute, it would flow over Boyd and dissolve him like it did with Pa.

Kayla ran between Boyd and the figure. She would rather die herself than allow more killing in her name. But Earl had reached Boyd to grapple with him for control of the blaster. A shot rang out. Earl fell back to hit the floor. He didn't move. And Boyd took off in the direction of the life pods.

"Why didn't you save him?" She demanded of Emmett, the figure she had thought was her friend. She had been wrong. He was really a monster in disguise, letting her brother get hurt.

"I promised to protect you. And I did that. I had no promise for your brother. I'm sorry he had to die."

"No, he can't be dead." Kayla flung herself down on one knee next to Earl. She lifted him to her lap. Wrenching sobs escaped from her. He was her true brother. Without him she would be all alone. But he didn't move. He was beyond her help and Boyd was loose somewhere on the ship doing more damage. She couldn't let Boyd destroy them all.

She gently placed Earl on the floor and whispered, "I'm sorry brother. But I will come back to you. Don't worry."

She headed in Boyd's direction while calling the monster to her side. "Come with me. We must keep Boyd from killing us all."

The first two life pods Kayla came to had the doors blasted open. Wires had been yanked out from the control panels. They were powered down and useless. The ship had six life pods total. One had been under repair when they took off from the last planet. Pa had planned to finish the repairs, but Kayla doubted that had happened. They were now down to three life pods. "Emmett, you must stop Boyd from destroying any more of the life pods or we will not be able to evacuate from the ship. Please help me find Boyd and stop him." She tried to grab his arm, but the figure was starting to move and it was like trying to hold flowing water. "Please don't kill him, please, no more."

"As you wish," the figure nodded and flowed down the hall.

When Kayla made it round to the other side where the three other life pods were docked, she saw Boyd had backed into a life pod. "Stay away from me you monster." He let off a volley of charges at the figure and then shut the door.

The blasts drilled through Emmett, but instead of becoming wounded, it just reformed around the holes created in the milling particles. Then the figure solidified and turned to face Kayla. She could hear the pod cycling. A vibration came through the floor followed by a sharp jolt as the pod was launched.

Behind them the fifth pod was a ruined mess. The charge hadn't hurt Emmett, but it had gone through the hatch of the life pod. It was no longer space-worthy. That left one pod in which to abandon ship. Someone would have to stay behind.

Charging into the nursery where Darla had hidden with the young'uns to keep them safe from Boyd, Kayla announced, "Hurry now, we must all go take a trip in the pod."

Frank, a young eight-year old, clamped onto Kayla's arm for reassurance. "We'll be all right?"

Kayla patted him on the shoulder while trying to help Darla round up Katie, Bill, and Ted. Katie had already lifted up Joyce the toddler to her hip. Darla followed up in the rear with the newborn in her arms. They rushed to the one life pod that remained functional. The klaxons had started to sound announcing the need to be away from the ship now.

At the door of the life pod, Kayla did not give Darla a chance for any heroics. Instead, she pushed the children into the life pod and after a quick hug to Mother Darla, she jumped out and forced the door closed from the panel inset in the wall. Kayla knew the life pod would automatically cycle and launch once she hit the eject button. She engaged the intercom, "Mother Darla, you know we all couldn't have made it if I stayed in the pod. And my place is with my true brother." Kayla disengaged the intercom. There would be no discussion or argument. There was not time.

Before she could hit the eject button, there was a thump on the pod door that made Kayla jump. Darla held her palm flat against the porthole. Kayla briefly held her palm against the glass matching Darla palm-to-palm. That was all a farewell she could spare. And then she hit the red button.

Kayla didn't wait for the pod to be away. Instead she was heading back down to her brother. If she was going to head into a star with the ship, she would do so by his side.

As she headed back to Earl, she passed the medical bay. There was a mobile evac chamber she could use to help her brother. She must have been mistaken. He could not be dead. It had to be so, she told herself, as she prepared the chamber and loaded as many oxygen tanks into it as she could.

She floated the chamber down the hallway back to her brother. Emmett stood a silent guard over the body. Earl lay as she left him. He was so still, but there had to be a chance. This was not the time to give up.

"Emmett, if I must die, I will do so on my terms and with my brother. I am going to suit up and take him out in space. I will set a beacon on this chamber and my suit. Maybe someone will find us."

"Please take me with you, Kayla. I promised to protect you. Let me go with you to protect you the best I can."

"Then help me with Earl. We can float him into the cargo hold and attach the medi-evac to your box."

Kayla left the figure and her brother only once to fetch her suit.

She contemplated taking only one tank. What was the point? She was only going out in space to die and float free.

No matter what, the gesture was the most important thing. That was her decision. She came back into the cargo hold with her helmet in one hand and the remote control in the other. She'd use the control to open the cargo bay door when she was ready.

She checked the medi-evac one more time. The atmosphere inside was stable. It would hold for her brother long enough. She unsealed the box—Emmett's box—and held the top open. "Please come with us, Emmett."

Emmett flowed into the empty space, but reformed to stand and address her, "Kayla, it would help your brother to put him in the box with me. I could keep him safe."

Kayla hesitated. She remembered Emmett flowing over Pa and then there was only Emmett, who fulfilled his promise to protect her. She took his hand in both of hers. "I know you are good deep down, Emmett. You keep my brother safe for me."

And she stood back to allow Emmett to flow over the medi-evac, guiding it to fit inside the box. And then she shut and sealed the lid on her brother.

After closing her helmet, she lashed her suit to the black box. She couldn't feel the warmth through her suit, but she could feel it in her heart. And with a lightness she had never known before, she hit the remote to open the cargo bay door, to leave the ship by her choice, and on her terms.

She awoke to find her brother, Earl, standing over her. He smiled so wide, she thought he must crack his face wide open if he didn't stop. And then she smiled wide to match his. "How can this be? I thought, for sure, we were goners."

She heard a little cry and turned in the other direction to see Darla holding her baby next to her bed. "Now, I must surely be dreaming. Or am I in heaven," said Kayla.

A strange man in a white coat stood at the foot of the bed checking readings above her bed. She had to be alive, all the little details, the buzzing and beeping of medical machinery was going. After jotting a few notes, he said, "You were a very lucky little girl. We are still studying the material of that box you put your brother into, but it lit up like a billboard on our scans. We got to you just in time. And once we were in range, we were able to pick up the beacon of your family's life pod."

Kayla glanced at Earl. "And Boyd's pod?"

He shook his head. "Never found it."

"And the box? Where is it?" Kayla started to worry about Emmett. He had been there to protect her. Now, she wanted to make sure he was safe, too.

"The box is in the lab. We'd like to keep it for study."

"And of course, they are offering us a good price for it. We'll be able to start over with the money." Darla smiled encouragingly.

"But what about Emmett?" Kayla flipped up the blanket and prepared to roll out of bed. She had to find Emmett. She had to make sure he was safe.

"Honey, Emmett was left on our last planetside. Don't worry about him." Darla looked puzzled. "Doctor, is it possible the accident affected her memory?"

"But, the box. Wasn't there more in the box than my brother in his medi-evac?" Kayla looked from Darla to Earl, searching their faces for the answer that she needed. She couldn't have lost her friend.

"Nothing else was in there."

Earl placed his hand in hers. "Kayla, don't worry about anything. I am here to protect you."

Part V:
Shambling Zombies

In the Absence of Light
Sarah A. Hoyt

Spacers lie. That's a given. Like mariners on ancient voyages, extending humanity's reach to untouched places, they tend to populate such new territory with fantastic creations: dragons, sea-serpents, angels and demons.

I bet that, once the long-promised decoding of humanity's genes is done, they will find the gene for adventure-seeking and the gene for telling lies sordidly entwined, lying in unhallowed union in some unblessed corner.

Of course, not everything spacers say will be a lie. Even the mariners were right on sea-serpents and mermaids—at least if you believe the sea-cow theory. Just as well most of us never did.

The thing is, humans have never figured out what caused life to erupt in the first place. Experiments with organic matter have never succeeded in animating the inanimate. The theory goes that given a certain amount of light and water, oxygen and organic material something happens.

But why is it no one ever gave any thought to what would happen in the absence of light?

She leaned close to me, as we waited in line to board the *Amadryad*, headed for Tau-Centauri.

The *Amadryad* was the largest passenger spaceship ever built—a black dimatough "cigar" capable of accommodating three hundred people in comfort if not in luxury.

The woman who leaned towards me was a stranger—a pretty, blonde stranger—and, in all except gender, much like myself: well educated, well adjusted, well prepared to be sent out to Earth's first extra-solar colony and sculpt a new future out of Tau-Centauri alien soil.

Yet, when she leaned close to me, she looked up with a glimmer of fear in her eye, and whispered in a voice that echoed with the ancient fears of cavemen, "Have you heard of the drifters?"

I didn't answer. Instead, I looked over her head, ahead of her. I hadn't heard of the drifters, nor was I sure I wanted to engage in chit-chat now. Ahead of us, a hundred odd people stood in line, snaking obediently past the officers who checked their papers, the med who did final readings on them with a med-sleeve, and on up the ramp into the belly of the black ship.

The *Amadryad* looked like a giant people-swallowing insect. Like Saturn devouring his own children.

The girl didn't take my silence for an answer. Her small, square hand grabbed at the front of my slipsuit. "They say that the drifters are what people become who die at space. The corpses drift and get bombarded with radiation, or perhaps just ... just age without rotting, until, somehow, they come back to life ... to some sort of life and grow sharp teeth and claws. They hunt the space between the stars, and they— They lead ships astray and make them crash, so that the people within can become like them."

I snickered despite myself. "Do they sing beautiful songs that lead the sailors to madness, too?" I asked. "Or perhaps transform them into pigs."

She looked up, in shocked surprise. Her blue eyes opened to perfect rounds, bewildered. Her eyes were beautiful, and though like me she wore a shapeless slipsuit, her form filled it in a definitely feminine way, protruding at chest and hips and dipping at her tiny waist. But the look in her eyes showed pure, unavoidable ignorance that made me sigh.

So many of my generation, born at the waning of the Twenty-First Century, had never heard the older, pre-space stories that humanity had told since time immemorial around smoky campfires. Even I had only heard of them by virtue of being an historian, sent to keep the memory of the race in the new world.

She still looked at me, still confused, and her eyes were the color of a summer sky. The line ahead snaked with mind-boggling slowness into the waiting ship. Someone had been stopped by the medtechs, who were, seemingly, dissecting him while alive.

"I'm Mikael Tromas," I said. "Historian. You?"

The surprise in her face didn't so much vanish as change focus, becoming a different type of surprise, half-hidden by a baffled smile.

"Ella Martin." She hesitated. "Microbiologist."

I nodded, and racked my brains for something else to say. I finally made some comment about the application process, and she responded with a story of how long it had taken her to be selected, and how they'd chosen her for her secondary specialty, her primary specialty being mythologist. Which didn't explain her lack of knowledge of Ulysses and the sirens, but perhaps she just lacked the details. I made polite questions, but she'd exhausted the subject of drifters and any myths related to them. Or maybe she just didn't want to talk about it. I thought I saw her shiver.

As the black-clad line moved ahead, one by one, she told me how she had decided to apply, after her fiancé had disappeared in the lost *Tenebras*, the first ship to be sent with colonists out to Tau Centauri. "There's just a chance that the ship made it," she said, as we approached the blank-faced med-tech and the boarding officer. "A small chance. But Earth lost communication halfway through and the scout ships sent after it never found it, which isn't strange, since Tau-Centauri is the size of Earth and, if they landed without systems they might very easily have landed far away from where they should have landed. The scouts found no debris, either. Neither in space, nor en route, nor even in the world." Ella shrugged. "I'm not deluding myself, but there is a chance, just a chance, that Galan is there, somewhere, in that world. And, after we settle, maybe we'll find him."

We came up to the boarding officer then, and I never got a chance to tell her that she *was* deluding herself. And, after the boarding officer had checked my boarding data-gem, and my retinal print against that in the boarding permission—after the medtech had clamped the sleeve on me and got a reading for perfect health—Ella and I separated. Just inside the ship, she turned right, towards her assigned cabin. I turned left, in search of mine.

There seemed scant point, then, telling her that I'd followed the stories on the disappearance of the *Tenebras* and that all scientists agreed there had been a failure of the life support system, a massive failure that had stopped air renewal and water and power systems and killed everyone on board. The ship would have drifted away, full of corpses, flying an erratic path, as long as its power lasted. It wouldn't be on the world, unless it had chanced to crash against it.

In the flurry of getting settled into my narrow one-person cabin—large enough to accommodate a twin bed, a link terminal, and a rack for my luggage—and learning the way to the bathrooms, the social rooms, the game rooms, the virtus, I didn't see Ella again for a few days.

The first week, I went through a period of depression that the on-board psychologist, who was dealing with a rash of similar cases, characterized as homesickness and mild claustrophobia.

We'd been screened for claustrophobia, of course, and we'd been chosen for not having any personal ties to Earth. My parents were long dead and, in pursuing my historical studies and trying to become good enough to qualify for settlement, I'd never found the time for a girlfriend, much less a wife.

However, I found myself longing for the ocean, the sun, and thinking of all the little places that had framed my life: the library of my hometown, the park where I used to play as a toddler, my grandmother's house, high on a hill above Goldport.

Those places had never seemed all that important to me, but the thought that I would never, ever see them again, struck me with an infinite melancholy, a black pit of despair that I did not know how to fight free of.

As I said, I think all of us were going through something like that, except for the dark-red-uniformed crew, the spacers proper, who didn't mingle with the passengers and who would be coming back, after depositing us in Tau-Centauri.

I'd just emerged from that period when I bumped into Ella again. She still seemed as unconnected with anyone in the ship as she'd been when I'd first met her. And she still talked of her fiancé, although she never mentioned drifters again. Out of curiosity, I'd asked other people on shipboard if they'd heard of drifters, and got a variety of answers, with a few immutable similarities between all of them. Drifters were supposed to be a lot like the old-time vampires, fanged horrors that attempted to turn living people into things like them. Like vampires, they were supposed to fear light and religious symbols, but I couldn't find an even remotely verifiable story of an encounter with these hypothetical creatures.

Ella's refusal to talk about them struck me as odd. A mythologist, even if that wasn't her shipboard specialty, ought to have been fascinated by the creatures. I wondered if at some level she thought her fiancé had become one of these fanged, blackened horrors, hanging out in space, waiting to claim another life.

But, on shipboard, we'd been allowed to wear our own clothing, whatever meager amount of it we'd been able to pack in twenty pounds worth of luggage that had, perforce, to include data gems and reference manuals for our specialties. Ella wore softly flowing dresses of nusilk—white, pink, pale yellow, little-girl colors that emphasized the youth and innocence of her oval face, the feminine look of her shoulder-length hair.

I invited her for dinners at the mess hall—no different than the shipboard synthetics we could order in our own cabins—but eaten at one of many small tables, in the half-light to which the harsh illumination of the hall was dimmed in the evening. Psychologists and shipboard sociologists wanted to encourage all romances, get the colonists on their way to a family even before we landed, if possible. That would, from what I understood of overheard conversations, speed our way to becoming a functional colony.

But Ella and I couldn't find our way to romance. We talked of Galan more often than not.

"How could he come?" I asked her. "How could he get aboard the *Tenebras* if you were engaged? I thought that, like us, they were screened for a lack of ties to Earth?" That this had only occurred to me after several weeks of knowing her, shows how she confused my mind, how her soft beauty insinuated into my reason.

She blushed and looked away. "We'd ... Galan and I, we'd had a misunderstanding. Something—Something that I'm sure would have been resolved. The *Tenebras* was only supposed to be the first wave of colonization. Even then, the *Amadryad* was being prepared, and it had a larger capacity than the *Tenebras,* and they intended to send a few more shipments of colonists in the *Amadryad.* I determined to apply for the *Amadryad.* It was a misunderstanding with Galan. I was sure if we met again, we'd make up."

Fat chance. For him to be certified as having no attachment to Earth, they would have needed to test his emotional profile and determine that, indeed, he had no regrets.

I looked at Ella's little pointed chin, her big blue eyes. She ate daintily, cutting small morsels from the pink lump that was our daily allotment of protein, taking them to her mouth with the silver spoon, the only silverware we were allowed.

So, Galan had left her, and now he was dead. She could be mine. On that thought, the ship stopped.

I can't tell you how I knew it had stopped. In fact, I didn't. I knew only that the hum of engines that had been with me for weeks, pursuing me at all moments, hounding me into the dark corners of my sleep, had ceased to sound.

My spoon halfway to my mouth, the pink, gelatinous mass on it trembling lightly, I tried to puzzle it out.

Ella looked at me, once more, as alarmed as she had the first time I'd spoken to her. "What is it?" she asked. "You look ill. Do you feel well?"

"The hum stopped," I said. "The engines." As I spoke, I was getting up, folding my disposable napkin into a triangle, as though it had been fine cloth at one the restaurants I used to frequent on Earth. I dropped the napkin on the table, then walked out of the mess room and towards the control center.

Long before I reached the control center, I halted in the narrow corridor. Ahead of me, blocking the passage to the control center's door, was a bevy of red-clad people. I noticed that the ones nearer the door were older, the ones closer to me, at the back of the corridor, younger. They leaned on the walls, managing to look, at once, bored and alert.

"What is it?" I asked them.

The one nearest me, a dark-haired man with a single brow that met over his nose, looked down from the height of six foot six or seven, almost a whole foot taller than I. "What makes you think *it* is anything?" he asked. He gathered his brow up, poked his lip out in disdain, whether of me or any non-spacer, was anyone's guess.

"The engines stopped," I said.

The brow rose even further and poked out slightly, in reluctant surprise at my having noticed it. He cleared his throat and looked to the two colleagues nearest him, two red-headed girls who looked like twins.

They, in turn, stared at each other. One of them shrugged at my interlocutor, as though to indicate it didn't matter.

"We found the *Tenebras*," the tall spacer said. As he spoke, the engines turned off and on again, and off, and on again, and off. "We're approaching it, trying to connect, so we can send a party aboard."

I wondered if other people shared Ella's delusions. "Why? I thought everyone aboard would be dead."

He sighed. "Everyone aboard should be dead. There might be a chance. It's just possible that someone, somehow, got to a cryogenic pod fast enough. It's just possible there's enough energy left on board to activate those. In any case, the *Tenebras* is loaded with supplies, the equal of ours. If we can find a way to tow it to Tau Centauri, we'll be able to dispose of all the supplies, ours and theirs."

I stood in the hallway, amid the red-clad party. I wasn't sure why, only that I wanted to be near the source of the excitement, the place where things were happening.

After a while, a party of tall, middle aged, red-clad men walked down the hallway and past us, then down another hallway, to the airlock where they would suit for the outside, before boarding the other ship. I assumed from this that we were docked to the *Tenebras*.

The crewmembers around me pulled out little vid-equipped, palm-size links and held them close to their faces. No amount of my edging and turning slight, or standing on tiptoe allowed me to look at those screens, but I assumed they were looking at whatever the team inside the *Tenebras* was doing.

Just then, Ella appeared, walking down the hallway towards me. In her pink, full-skirted dress, she looked like a floating vision from Earth's past. "I just heard we boarded the *Tenebras* ... What ... what is left of the *Tenebras*..." she said. She wore her white sweater over her shoulders, having picked it up after leaving the mess hall, for reasons known only to her. There were no breezes aboard ship that she would need to protect herself from.

I nodded. The people around us ignored us. They looked into their links.

Suddenly, as though called by an invisible signal, they all straightened. Though no sound was made, I got the impression of a communal shout of disbelief.

The junior spacers near us flattened themselves against the walls, and we followed their example. A half-dozen grizzled spacers, their dark red suits ornamented with stars, charged past us at a controlled run.

The junior spacers rushed into the control room. After a while, the grizzled spacers returned, disappeared into the control room.

Only Ella and I remained in the hallway. The ship engines resumed their hum.

"What happened?" Ella asked.

"I assume some emergency," I said. "But there's no chance the spacers will ever tell us. I don't even know if we're towing the *Tenebras*."

Ella gathered her sweater around her neck with one hand.

At length, we wandered back to our quarters.

The ship hummed with rumors about the *Tenebras*. Every passenger had a theory and no spacer talked about what he knew. The rumors flew back and forth across the passenger quarters, and everyone stayed up late in the mess hall, discussing it.

Lacking data, we found all theories equally compelling.

Mid-morning, when most people had started waking up and roaming around, a general announcement came over the communication system. It told us that we'd met the wreck of the *Tenebras* and a group had gone aboard, only to succumb to a technical glitch.

I looked at Ella, with whom I was sharing a late breakfast of coffee and the anonymous green blob that constituted our carbohydrate ration for the day. "I'd guess we missed all the excitement," I said.

I was wrong about that.

That night I woke up, with pounding on my cabin door. When I opened it, Ella stood in the hallway, just outside the door, in a short, white tunic. She looked pale, her eyes wide open and terrified. She pushed against me, pressed by me into the cabin. "They're out there," she said. "The drifters are out there. I can hear them dragging their nails and teeth across the hull of the ship."

You can't argue with a terrified woman. I said, soothing, "They'll never get through. The hull of the ship is dimatough."

She didn't listen to me. She curled herself in a ball, on my bed, and said, "They're there. They're on my link. Galan is on my link. He's ... communicating from the *Tenebras*. He says I need to open the door to him, so he can come home. I can't see him, but I'd know his voice. I'd know his voice anywhere." She shook badly, as though she had a fever, but her little, peaked face was white and drained.

"I'll go call a doctor," I said.

"No," she said. "Don't leave me alone."

"I have to," I said. "You're not well." I covered her with the regulation blue blanket, and left my quarters, in search of a medtech.

How does the joke go? You can never find a medtech, a peacekeeper, or a whore when you need one. You will find everything but.

I found everything but. The corridors were thronged with red-clad spacers and people in various types of night attire.

A woman in pajamas cried, looking as terrified as Ella. The man holding onto her murmured soothing things. "It's not Drifters," he said. "Just some engine noise. I'm sure the spacers will fix it."

The spacers ignored the obvious plea for reassurance. They—all fifty or so of them who were in sight—moved like people with a purpose, exchanging cryptic remarks, rushing here, rushing there. It took me a moment to realize that their rushing was purposeless. The same spacer would go one way, look at a wall panel, displaying, say, readings of ambient temperature, stare at it for a while and run down the hall, to stare at another panel with readings on air purification. They looked, I thought, like ants in an anthill that has been kicked open by a boot.

I could not find anyone in the green uniform of a medtech, and the more I looked around, the more I was sure that the medtechs must have their hands full with hysterical passengers, Ella not being the most afflicted and certainly not the only one of the people fearing drifters and their voices.

I retreated back to my cabin. As I opened the door, I heard a purposeful male voice saying, "I just want to go home, Ella. Take me home, and all will be as it was before. Oh, Ella, I miss you so much."

"I miss you too," Ella said. "How did you survive—How did—"

I opened the door. Ella sat in front of my link. There was no image on it, but a man's voice came from it. "I got to one of the lifeboats on time. I'm in the command room now, but I'm wearing a space suit. Ella, you have to open your airlock to me."

"I'm a passenger," she said. "I don't have permission to do that. I'll talk to the spacers."

"No, Ella. No. They wanted to loot the reserves of the *Tenebras* and were heartbroken to find some of us still alive. They tried to kill us. We had to—" the sound of a loud swallowing. "Now they won't open the door to us, and they're leaving the *Tenebras* behind, going away."

Us? They won't open the door to us? The idea was plausible, but— Space piracy was possible, at least in theory, but so far the high cost of building and maintaining ships had rendered it unpractical. What if the spacers, hired by the union of Nations, were practicing it themselves?

I couldn't believe it. There were too many spacers for them to conspire together. If I got out there and got the idea spread wide enough, amid passengers and spacers, the minority, however large, who were involved in crooked dealing would be defeated by sheer numbers.

"I can't open the door," Ella said.

I closed the door to my cabin quietly. The guy I had talked to in the hallway and the twin red-heads had seemed nice enough. I couldn't believe they would knowingly engage in piracy. And how come all of them, looking in the links, hadn't seen the survivors of the *Tenebras* and our own people attacking them?

I wandered down the hallway. I must talk to someone. The more I turned the story over in my mind, the less sense it made. There were too many holes. My link was not supposed to receive communications from outside the *Amadryad*. And, if the *Amadryad* was pulling away from the *Tenebras*, what good would opening the door to the airlock do? Other than suck out whatever was in the airlock, into the vacuum of space?

I came across my friend with the single brow. He stood just outside the command room, staring at something, fascinated. He looked down, acknowledging me. As our gazes met, I said, "There are really no drifters, are there?"

It was not what I'd meant to say, at all.

He frowned, his single brow gathering menacingly over his nose. Without speaking, he took me by the arm, pulled me into the command room. The command room was littered with spacers, but no one paid any attention to me. Like the spacers in the halls, they moved between one monitor and the other, in a show of purposeful lack of purpose.

My friend pulled me all the way to a monitor and turned the monitor on. "This shows the hull," he said. "Outside."

The monitor filled with a full shot of shiny, black hull and of creatures moving on it, on all fours, clinging to the hull by who knows what means.

The creatures were black and shrunk and looked like insects, with four legs. Except, in their mouths, long sharp teeth gleamed that had never been in insects mouths. Human teeth, perhaps, all soft tissue around them retracted and yet remaining, somehow, attached to the skull and kin.

I stared at them for a long time, before I noticed shreds of blue and red slipsuits. And then I realized the creatures were human—humans burst, turned inside out, shrunk, desiccated by the nothing of space, and yet still living, still walking, still … talking. I remembered the voice, coming through my link. There would be feeds out in the hull that could connect with inside links. There had to be, for repairs. But they weren't meant to be used in space.

"They are destroying our systems," my single-browed friend said. "One by one. There are ways to access controls, from the outside. They are interfering with life-support systems. This is what must have happened to the *Tenebras*." He looked at me, and though he didn't shake, as Ella had, the fear in his gaze was the same. "A couple of scouts were lost, before we got the lay of Tau Centauri."

I ran out of the control room, ran all the way to my cabin. I must tell Ella.

Ella was not in my cabin.

I charged towards the airlock. Normally there would have been people here to prevent a passenger getting close. There would have been spacers, in their red uniforms, in the narrow corridor leading to the airlock. Spacers, gently redirecting stupid would-be colonists away from danger.

But all spacers were busy, running around, trying to prevent what couldn't be prevented.

It couldn't be that bad, anyway. Ella could never have opened the airlock. She didn't have the right retinal print.

The outer door of the airlock lay open wide. The emergency panel next to it was open, the screen displaying a bright red light. The safety circuits had been circumvented with emergency codes. Ella couldn't know that.

Inside the airlock proper, Ella looked flushed and happy. "He's all right. He's coming in and he'll go with us back to Earth. Everything will be all right."

From outside the ship came ominous scratching sounds.

Ella smiled. She turned back to the panel, pressed buttons rapidly. "Galan was a circuits specialist. Did I ever tell you that?"

I turned to run back into the ship, to find someone to close that door. But a sound like a strong wind stopped me.

In the next second, I was enveloped in nothing, freezing nothing. My lungs strived to get breath, even as they burst, my whole body burst, as my blood boiled, in the vastness of space.

Ahead of me, Ella exploded, and bled, and shrunk and changed, till she could be recognized only by her white nightshirt.

I woke up, hours or years later, I do not know.

I miss the Earth, the little park where I used to play when I was a toddler, my grandmother's house on a hill, the sound of the waves on the shore.

Here, there's no sound, nothing ever changes. But other than unvarying monotony and homesickness, it's amazing how well one can live in the absence of light.

I wonder when they'll send another ship out to Tau Centauri.

A Touch of Frost

Gene Mederos

Skreeeeek!

Jon Garcia awoke with a start.

Skreeeeek.

He knew the shriek was just ice and dust, chunks of interstellar debris scraping across the hull of the ship. Although the sound made his hairs stand on end, he had gotten used to it just enough the last two months that he could usually sleep through it. But there were still times…

"Time," he said as clearly as he could so soon after waking. Cyan digits appeared against the ceiling of his bunk a few feet above his head. Damn, he still had two hours before his duty shift.

Skreeeeek-eek!

He heard a distant thundering boom that echoed through the bulkheads. The ship was probably passing through a denser cloud of the crap that circled this godforsaken star. If so, then his place was on the command deck.

"Lights." The illumination was preset to the level he found comfortable upon waking, but for some reason it struck him as too bright for this hour of the—

He caught himself before he could finish the thought. There was no night or day on board a ship. There were only the three watches. Sure, by tradition, most ship's business was conducted on first watch, and functions and ceremonies during second. Third watch was always quiet, lightly manned. And now, with the ship stuck crawling through a system choked with debris, it was only a skeleton crew on third. Hell, he thought as he rubbed the sleep from his eyes and slid out of his bunk, with half the crew in cryo, all the watches were under-manned. Less crowded or not, he was glad that as an officer, and First Mate at that, he rated his own cabin, however small, and a private head with all the amenities. After a brief stint in a very hot shower, he felt bolstered for the cold hike to command.

The ship's corridors were gray metal and unadorned. The lights were kept low on third watch, and that made the corridors seem even colder than usual. The metal grating that served as the flooring was unforgiving on feet. He hadn't gone far before his left knee gave a twinge. Old injury exacerbated by cold. All three rings, command, habitat and engineering, were rotating—gravity was just too damn useful—but not for the first time he wished he could just float down the corridors to the section seal. At least there was a lift to take him up the seven levels to Deck One. He made sure maintenance kept it in good repair. It made him cringe to think of climbing ladders from deck to deck. If the lift ever broke down you'd better believe he'd order a stop to the rings' rotation.

He stepped off the lift into the noticeably warmer air on Deck One, although it was closest to the unheated, zero-g core of the ship. One couldn't help but notice that the floor curved up toward the ceiling ahead. But that had never bothered him, for it meant that distances were shorter up here.

Sighing in comfort, he stepped through the hatchway into the brightly-lit nerve center of the ship. As always, upon entering the bridge, his eyes were drawn to the course projections displayed on the big screen at Nav-1. The hyperbola in blue, which was their course, was overlaid over the ellipse in white, which represented the rotation of the system's debris around the star. The idea was to inch closer and closer to the edge of the system without crossing the debris field's path. A big enough chunk of something could split the ship open if it struck them at anything greater than a fifteen-degree angle.

And of course, keeping pace with the garbage minimized the force of the impacts.

It was going to take a little over a year before they were clear enough to accelerate to the relativistic speed needed to jump out of this system. Ship's resources were finite, so they'd divvied the year up. Half the crew had gone into cryogenic sleep for the first six months, then the other half would do the same for the remainder of their crawl. The captain had decided he wanted to be on hand to lead the ship out of purgatory, so that left him in command.

He made his way to Command Station One where Susan Ley, Navigator Second and next in line in seniority, nonchalantly removed the command headset and handed it to him. The headset always reminded him of a silvery three-legged insect. One leg arced over his head, the soft, glowing bulb on its end snuggling into his ear. The second leg snaked down his cheek to his chin, the last few centimeters of which could be set to pick up sub-vocalizations through the jawbone itself if necessary. The third leg dangled a tiny crystal screen in front of his left eye. He logged into the command station comp.

"All stations report," he said into the mic.

"Nav green, sir."

"Comp green, sir."

"Scan green, sir."

They were a freighter, not military, but he was in command and rated the *sir*. Not skipper. Even frozen, only the captain was called skipper. He'd make do with sir just fine. All the stations but one reported in. A few moments went by, then a few more. No word from engineering. He tapped the mic. "Engineering, this is Garcia. Report."

After a few moments he tried it again. Maybe his mic had gone out. The crew manning the stations on the bridge weren't wearing headsets. He called to the tech at the scan-comp station. "Donovan, put your ears on for a second will you?" The scan man did so. "Can you hear me?"

"Hear you fine, sir."

"Huh." Of course, he could go down to deck nine and take a transit cart over to the engineering ring. Maybe catch them all asleep or drunk off their collective asses. But hell, he really didn't want to write up any reprimands, not when there wasn't anywhere near enough work to do to keep idle hands out of mischief. And the transit cars, which rode against the very outer hull of the ship, were just too damned cold. His knee wouldn't thank him for it later.

"Garcia to Maintenance."

To his relief, the crewmember on com duty in Maintenance responded immediately. "Maintenance," a female voice drawled.

"Morning, Alice. Engineering's com appears to be down. Can you send someone over?"

"Will do, sir," He could almost imagine Alice winking in collusion. Whoever they sent would "fix" the problem and get someone from Engineering on the horn right quick. Maintenance was in C ring with Engineering so it was a short trek for them.

He scanned his message queue while he waited. Fifteen, all flagged as urgent, all from the same sender. He sighed. A short walk around the bridge stations was definitely in order. He wasn't ready to sit at his screen just yet. He spotted Ley's silver curls at the auxiliary nav station and made his way over. "You can consider yourself relieved, you know, Jim will be up soon enough." She rewarded him with a wan smile, but she had wrinkled her freckled nose at the mention of Jim's name. Jim Xu was Navigator Fourth. He was also young and eager. The last two characteristics seemed to annoy her. Before she could get up from her seat he bent down closer and lowered his voice. "Susan, I've got over a dozen messages from Gustav queued up already this morning. Doesn't the man sleep?"

"He's a Prime," Susan said with a shrug. "What are the messages about?"

"The same thing since the skipper went into cryo. He wants to see me, but won't say why."

"He's not exactly off-limits, you know, Jon. And you're in command. Even in his current state he may have come up with a course correction that would shave a few days or weeks off this trek. I'm only a Second. Neither I nor the computer can cut it any finer than we already have."

Jon moved back to let Susan up and bit at his lower lip in thought. The captain had been furious when Gustav had admitted he'd brought them to this system on purpose. At first everyone had assumed the Navigator Prime had given the computer the wrong numbers for the last jump, although Primes weren't supposed to make mistakes. Feelings among the crew being what they were, it would have been best for Gustav to go into cryo-sleep, but he adamantly refused to be frozen.

Jon knew the captain had come really close to having the navigator put on ice by force, but it was considered bad form to manhandle a prime. Also, tradition exempted them from most forms of punishment during those times when they weren't completely lucid. And the man had to have been crazy to want to come to this star. So the skipper had ordered him confined to quarters. The more superstitious among the crew would have taken any sterner action against the Prime as an omen of doom.

He made the tour of the bridge, spending some time with Donovan on scan, trying to determine whether or not they were heading into more heavily congested space. He finally decided to put a first watch team on it and made it back to his station without a word from engineering or maintenance. The one red telltale on the little screen above his eye had begun to annoy him.

"Garcia to Maintenance," he said curtly.

"Maintenance," Alice responded.

"What's going on in Engineering, Alice?"

"Going on, sir? Hasn't Roberts reported in yet?"

"No, he hasn't."

"I sent him over there right after you called, sir. Even if their com is down, I issued him a headset and told him to report to you as soon as he got there."

"Garcia to Roberts." Once issued, a headset's AI responded to hails using the crewman's last name. So even if Roberts had drunk himself into a stupor...

"Roberts is unable to reply," the unit's AI responded after the requisite fifteen seconds had passed without a human voice. A shiver went down Jon's spine. He hated that cold hollow voice generated by computers.

"What is your current location?"

"C-ring, section 3, deck 9, 2.3 meters to stern from hatch C39-056."

Jon, like pretty much everyone on a ship, could instantly see in his mind the exact location described by those coordinates. Roberts was in the corridor outside the central hatch to Engineering's main deck. Whether horizontal or vertical however...

"Send two men to see what's happened to Roberts and tell them they are under orders to report to me the moment they find him, regardless of the circumstances. You got that, Alice?"

"Yes, sir." Alice responded without any cheer in her voice. Jon knew his voice had turned gruff and didn't much care at the moment. He crossed his arms across his chest and dropped into his chair. He ignored the questioning glances from the bridge crew, most of who had surreptitiously slipped on their headsets, hoping to get some entertainment or at least a little diversion from the goings on in Engineering.

He scowled. Going the full six months without an incident was too much to ask, but after two quiet months he had begun to hope...

"Aket to Command"

"This is Garcia."

"We've found Roberts. Looks like he's suffered a head injury."

"In the corridor?" The man would have to jump up a few feet to hit his head on a pipe or conduit."

"There's quite a lot of blood sir. Goran's calling medical."

"All right then." Jon took a deep breath. "Stay there and don't let anyone in or out of Engineering. I'm on my way."

Skreeeeeek-eeeek-eeeeeek. Skreeeeeeeeeeeeeeeeeek.

With the outer hull right under foot, the shrieking was incessant on deck nine. Limping only slightly from the ride in the cart, Jon joined the two men outside engineering.

"No one's come or gone," Aket reported.

Jon keyed the hatch open and painfully cold air struck him full in the face. He gasped and saw his breath coalesce before him. Had the heat been turned off all ni ... all of third shift? Who would do such a thing? Or had all the warmth been sucked away? A hull breach would have taken all of the air and dumped it out into space, not just the warmth. And it would have been detected.

Engineering rose through four decks, but it did not appear spacious. Catwalks, struts and conduits blocked off the view in every direction. And most of the work took place past the hatches in the 'ceiling', in the expanded core which housed the guts of the generators, rotation motors, and the great FTL engines which punched the ship through space. Here, on the "floor" of the outermost deck was a well-lit swath of comp stations, very similar to the layout on the bridge, where engineering crew sat and monitored the health of the ship. Only there was no one to be seen.

Skreeeeeeeeeeeek!

All three men jumped in their skins.

"Where is everybody?" Goran asked into the sudden silence, his head wreathed by his breath. He peered up at the catwalks. Engineering always rang with the sound of booted feet on metal grating. There should have been eight people on duty during third watch. Jon looked up but he couldn't see the core hatches from here.

"Core party?" Aket ventured, also looking upward.

Jon's frown deepened as he shivered. Drinking and dancing in Zero G was against regulations, but a few core parties inevitably took place during a voyage. It would explain the cold, if the drunken fools had left a few hatches open and let all the heat escape into the core. He had no choice but go up there and see for himself.

They found coldsuits in the appropriate locker, although they never seemed warm enough to Jon, and took the basket lift to the uppermost walkway. The very first hatch they came to was closed, as it should be. Goran, the youngest of the three, scurried up the ladder and tried the latch. Locked, also as it should be. Aket gamely brought up Jon's command key. The telltale went green and the latch clicked, but when Goran tried to lift the hatch he found it wouldn't budge.

"Let's try the next one down," Jon suggested. But that one wouldn't open either.

The third hatch they tried gave just a little when Aket helped Goran to push, as if it were barred on the core side somehow. Jon wasn't about to try all twenty-four hatches.

"Garcia to Assan." The chief and the first watch team came on duty in just under half an hour. He didn't know what those clowns were up to, locking themselves in the core. A still perhaps? A sex party? Exposing his flesh to the core's cold was not his idea of a good time, but maybe the third watch engineers were a collectively hot-blooded bunch.

No response from the chief. Perhaps he was in the shower. Or in the mess getting his breakfast. Before he could hail the galley, Medical hailed him.

"How's Roberts doing, Doctor?"

"Critical but stable. Jon, there's something I need to show you. Right away."

"Very well, I'm on my way." Jon turned to the two men. "Stay here and watch the hatches. Tell the chief to call me the minute you see him, in case I can't reach him."

The chief wasn't in the mess, the gym, the rec room, or in his cabin. Not for the first time, Jon wished they could provide every member of the crew with a headset. But the AI's were so damn expensive. And although they were crawling along at sub-light now, you needed an AI to communicate at relativistic speeds. Jon called half the decks on the ship by the time he got back to A ring. Medical was on Deck Two, right below Command. No one who bothered to answer had seen Assan. It appalled him how lax the crew had gotten in such a short time. Tightening up on discipline, no matter how many reprimands he had to log, would be his first priority after checking in with the doctor.

Doctor Russo was waiting for him by Robert's bedside. The patient's face was gray, and shiny plas-skin showed where the injury had been, but Jon noticed with relief that the man was breathing on his own.

"What do you have, Doctor?"

"The skull above his right temple was fractured by a heavy blow."

"Blow? You mean someone hit him?"

The doctor sighed, his fleshy features downcast. "I'm afraid so. I was thrown off by the bleeding, at first, since a blow to the head with the side of the hand, or an elbow, or a blunt object for that matter, would normally not break the skin, but leave a bruise of some kind instead."

"So what tore up his skin?"

"Ice." The doctor shook his head slowly. "I found ice crystals and frozen skin cells in the abrasion. Human skin cells."

Jon's features darkened as the implications sank in. "Someone struck him with—with a frozen body part?"

There were three bodies in the morgue, crewmembers who had died in the three years since they'd left the solar system and had requested that their remains be allowed to burn re-entering the Earth's atmosphere.

"Have you checked the morgue?"

The doctor shook his head sadly. "The bodies in the morgue are intact."

Jon left the infirmary in something akin to shock. It was obvious that someone had removed an arm or a leg, or perhaps a whole body, from a cryo-tank. Well, he had a hell of an incident all right, a murder, or at least a dismemberment, and an attempted murder as well. And all of Engineering's third watch possibly involved. He shuddered, despite the fact he was still snug inside a coldsuit, as another horrible thought struck him. Was it possible someone had done away with a whole watch to cover up a murder?

He took the lift to Command Deck. First watch was now on duty and he needed to inform the command crew, to give the order to thaw out the captain and the head of security. It wasn't in his purview as second-in-command to investigate murder.

Deck One didn't feel as warm as it usually did. He turned the suit up full as he entered the bridge. Immediately his eyes went to the Nav-1 screen, but before he could fully focus on it, he noticed something was very much amiss.

There was no one at stations.

Then a figure rose from Nav-1, its head haloed by the course projections on the screen behind it. It was Jim Xu, smiling as if nothing in the world was wrong. Jon smothered an impulse to slap the smile from his face.

"Where is first watch?"

"Don't know. I came up a few minutes before shift change to show Ley my newest proposed course corrections and there was nobody here. No one from first watch has arrived yet."

Jon suddenly felt both angry and afraid. He knew it showed on his face because Xu blanched and backed away. "I know it annoys her to hell, but I can't help myself," Xu stammered in apology, his usual lopsided grin gone from his face. Jon could barely keep from snarling.

"You found Command completely unmanned and didn't think to report it?"

"I figured Command crew was in a conference and nobody thought to tell me, as I'm junior most and all." The fact that Xu's voice carried no anxiety or rancor whatsoever did much to help Jon swallow down his own fear.

"Garcia to Chavez." He hailed the navigator third's cabin. He waited a few moments for a response.

"Garcia to Dempsey."

No response.

"Garcia to Chen."

He went down the list in his mind, calling all the command crew's cabins by shift.

"Garcia to Ley." But Susan didn't answer either.

It was unthinkable that the entire waking command crew had been done away with. Murders could and did occur on ships, of course, especially on a long voyage. But they were almost always a crime of passion with a single victim. There were many extended families among the crew and they had all lived and worked together for years. No serial killer or sociopath could have remained undetected for such a long time. Why, the only habitual loners were him and Gustav.

He called Maintenance. No response. Alice would be off duty by now. Surely someone would have relieved her. He called Medical, where he'd spoken with Russo no more than fifteen minutes ago, but neither the doctor nor anyone else responded. He tried the other departments and then deck by deck. Finally, he tried a ship-wide hail on the public address system. "This is Garcia, anyone hearing this please report in."

"Could it be a mutiny?" He wasn't aware he'd asked the question out loud until he noticed the alarmed expression on Xu's face.

"Wouldn't they simply wake the skipper?" Xu asked.

"Of course." Unless 'they' had already taken care of the captain. He shivered again. "Is it me or is it cold in here?"

"Its definitely colder than usual," Xu agreed.

In fact, Jon could feel a draft. He followed it out of the command center and into an adjoining storage alcove. Rungs were molded into the bulkhead on one side of the alcove and they led to a ceiling hatch which was gaping wide open. That was where the cold air was coming from, and just possibly was also where the crew had gone. This time he didn't hesitate to climb up the ladder. From the top rung, he made the long practiced jump through the hatch into weightlessness.

"Lights," he called, and illumination sprang to life for thirty meters to either side of him. Packing crates and shipping containers as far as the eye could see, lining the inside of the core. The entire core forward of C ring to the prow was cargo. When the ship reached a station the first order of business was always to nose her into the Zero-G station hub and slide the cargo out through the huge forward airlock. Down to his right, past the section seals and the 200-meter length of B ring, was the section, which opened unto Engineering. To his left, more cargo and the bulkheads of the prow. The command crew was nowhere to be seen. But then he caught a glint of something moving down towards B. It was there for only a flash and then it was gone in the deep shadow between two containers. He reached out for a handhold, one of the many convenient container straps, and was just about to use it to propel himself towards the glint when something grabbed his ankle.

"Jon ... sir. You don't want me to stay here all by myself do you?" Jon looked down at a very frightened Navigator Fourth. It was obvious that the kid had just figured out that something was horribly wrong aboard the ship.

"Grab a coldsuit and follow me." By the time he got to where he'd seen the glint there was nothing to be found but containers. A little further on was a ring of hatches. Light spilling in from Deck One showed where a hatch had been left open. The one closest to him was closed but not locked. By the time he reached the section seal he could hear Xu coming up behind him. The seal irised open when he inserted his command card in the proper slot. Together, he and Xu floated into B ring. Some distance ahead a ring of lighted squares broke the darkness.

"Lights," he ordered. When they came to the ring of open hatches they peered into the corridors of the habitat ring, but there was no one about. A great many of the cabin doors stood open however, and Jon figured there had to have been a lot of coming and going through the core all night on the upper decks. He'd heard nothing down on Seven. They continued to make their way to C, every ring of hatches they passed opening onto empty corridors.

Once again his card opened the section seal. Whatever was going on, no one had bothered, or been able, to disable his card. He was at least grateful that the AI's were inviolate.

"Lights." A wide ring of tiny pinpoints of lights flared up in the immense darkness. The core here was ten decks larger in diameter to accommodate and give access to the ship's vital machinery. In the center of the darkness, they could barely discern the silhouettes of those giant structures by the paltry illumination of that first ring of lights.

"Full illumination," Jon ordered, heartily sick of darkness and shadows. Work lights sprang up the whole length of C ring, delineating and defining the cylinders and spheres, the wheels and girders and pipes and tubing that were the guts of the ship. Just shy of that superstructure, they came to the first ring of hatches. Twenty-four of them opened unto the upper deck of Engineering, and Jon could see the various tools and implements that had been used to jam them closed. The remaining twelve hatches stood open, and beyond them was the deck that housed the cryogenic tanks, labs and equipment.

Jon floated over to the nearest open hatch and looked within. The corridor below was lined on both sides with cryo-tanks, and as far as Jon could see, they stood open.

He motioned for Xu to follow him to the next hatch. This one opened on a prep bay and Jon saw Dr. Russo strapped to a table while Dr. Mann of first watch approached with a syringe full of the pearly white paralytic fluid which was the first step of the freezing process. Jon had barely begun to take in that Dr. Mann was moving stiffly and seemed paler than normal when the doors to the bay slid open and several crewmen walked in, dragging a semi-conscious Goran with them. The crewmen also moved stiffly and there was a strange sheen to the skin on their faces. He caught a sudden movement out of the corner of his eye and looked up. Several pale figures were dropping towards him from the engine housing above.

He instantly decided he did not want to drop in on Dr. Mann and his paralytic shot, so he shoved Xu hard towards the hatch above the empty cryo-tanks. The reaction sent him flying towards a hatch in the opposite direction. He grabbed the hatch frame's edge and allowed the momentum to drop him into the room below. His knee gave way when he hit the floor and sent him sprawling at the base of a cryo-tank. He looked up and saw Aket, paralyzed but unfrozen, within the tank. He heard a slight hiss and saw a shunt puncture Aket's skin at the jugular. A tube emerging from his coveralls at the groin began to drain the red blood from his body. Jon had to look away and that's when he saw two frozen faces turn towards him on frozen necks. He recognized the rime frosted features of second watch galley crew who had often served him dinner. Their frozen bodies lurched towards him, their frozen hands uncurling as they reached for him.

Jon scampered through the nearest door and rose on one leg to swipe his command card in the lock as the door slid shut behind him. Using the corridor wall as support, he limped and hopped toward the section lift. He fell down often. He was within sight of the lift, crossing an intersecting corridor, when a hatch was thrown open just a few meters away.

"Jon! Help me!" And there was Xu, clawing frantically at the hatch frame. Susan Ley held him in a frozen grip and was pulling him back into a cryo-lab. Xu struggled fiercely and managed to grab the frame's edge, but Susan seemed more solid ice than flesh, she broke his grip without any apparent effort. Inexorably, she pulled him back through the hatchway. Jon leapt forward despite his knee but the hatch was yanked shut with a resonant clang. He pounded on its metal surface in desperation.

"Susan! Ley! You open this door! That's an order!"

But he knew she wouldn't obey; he'd seen the slight smile on her frozen lips. He let himself slide down to the floor and then crawled on the metal grating to the lift. He took it down to Deck Nine and made his way to the transit cart. He disembarked halfway through B ring, and limped down the corridor toward a private cabin very much like his own. He was overwhelmed and couldn't think of what to do next. There was someone for whom thinking was no effort at all. Jon could only hope Gustav still had warm blood coursing through his veins.

Skreeeeeeeeeeeeeeeeeeeeeeeeek!

Jon found the hatch to the Prime's cabin standing slightly ajar. Cautiously, he peered into the room. A huge eye was looking back at him. For a moment, he almost bolted, but the rational part of his mind assured him it was just a holographic image. He pulled the door open wider. In the center of the cabin was the long lean figure of the Prime surrounded by holographic portraits of a single, giant eye.

"Ah! There you are at last. But you're late, Jon. You're so very late."

It wasn't the welcome that he had expected, but Jon collected himself as well as he could and looked straight into the fever bright eyes that hinted at insanity. "Late for what, Gustav?"

"I'm afraid it has already begun."

"What's begun?"

"Our disassociation from what we quaintly call reality."

Skreeeeeeeeeeeeeeeeek!

"Gustav, I'm not a Prime and I didn't go to seminary, just fleet school. Explain it to me in a way I can understand."

"Well, it's not really about you, Jon. Seminary, tsk, tsk. I'm not talking spirituality, Jon. It is an accepted fact, it can be expressed as an equation for example, that natural phenomena can induce a transcendental experience."

Jon ran his hand through his hair and took a moment to unclench his jaw.

"What natural phenomena, Gustav? What experience are you talking about?"

"The phenomena is this system, Jon." The prime turned his gaze to the largest of the holograms. "Imagine my surprise, after peering at countless stars, to find one looking back."

Skreeeeeeeeeek-eeeeeeeeeeeeeeek!

It was then that Jon realized he was looking at negative images of the system, which the computers had generated from an angle perpendicular to the plane of the ecliptic. The black pupil in the center was the star, the grayish iris was the inner ring of debris, more brightly illuminated by the star than the outer ring, which made up the "cornea". Gustav was looking at him fully again, an almost apologetic smile on his lips.

"We're under its gaze. We won't be able to creep away unnoticed." And with that the Prime turned his back on him. Nothing Jon could say or do could induce Gustav to say another word. He found himself taking the man by the shoulders and shaking him, yelling at him at the top of his lungs. But this only made the Prime smile broadly. Jon almost hit him, but he reined in his exasperation and fled the cabin. Had he struck the madman in their current predicament he was sure someone in the crew would have tried to throw him out an airlock.

If there still was any crew that wasn't frozen.

Skreeeeeeeeeeeeeeeek!

Jon headed for A ring, a desperate plan shaping up in his mind. The command computer could shunt the engine's plasma into the core, heat the ship from the core out.

Heat, heat, heat.

Heat would blind Gustav's watching star-eye, would thaw out the frozen crew.

The first thing he noticed upon entering the bridge was that the display above Nav-1 had changed. There was but one course laid out, an ellipse in blue. The second thing he noticed was that the stations were fully manned, and hard on the heels of that he felt the cold. A deeper, darker cold than the core. The skipper rose from his seat at the command station. His shock of white hair and translucent blue skin made him seem an animate ice sculpture. The Primary Command headset was clenched about his head like silver rime. He reached up and stroked the leg running along his jaw. The gesture struck Jon as obscene, and he fought not to retch.

"There you are, Jon." The skipper's lips were still partially frozen shut, but the damned AI's in the headsets were making sure he could understand the captain. Jon began to shake uncontrollably as goose bumps erupted on his skin.

"Why Jon, you're shivering. Get yourself down to Medical and have the doc prep you for cryo. I promise you…"

The skipper's gelid eyes bore no more compassion than the AI's icy voice did.

"I promise you will never feel the cold again."

Wake of the White Death

Lee Clark Zumpe

1.

Wimarc Essex approached the planet Celestria with considerable caution.

"Maintain standard orbit," Wimarc said. Lean and angular, the ship's young captain surveyed the ice dwarf trying to tease out its secrets. "Continue customary arrival declaration, in case someone happens to be listening." He articulated the orders mechanically, knowing his crew needed no instruction. Wimarc ran through the ordinary set of post-jump diagnostics. "Aldred, I'd like to see if we can link with the surveillance cams down there. And if there are any giant space monsters out there about to make a meal out of my ship, I'd appreciate it if someone would let me know."

Savaric Vogel, Wimarc's seasoned second in command, searched for traces of recent orbital traffic.

The last three envoys dispatched to the colony had simply disappeared. Communications with each of the spacecraft had been abruptly severed without any hint of distress. The names of more than three-dozen passengers and crewmembers became file headers in a collection of "Missing in Action" documents stored on a database housed on Gunnora, the region's administrative headquarters and the first Goldilocks planet to be settled more than 10,000 light years from Earth.

Deep-space scans found no trace of the jump-drive cutters that carried the previous contact teams to Celestria, beginning with the *Rasheed* one Terran year earlier. While the overlords managing the First Trade Coalition on Earth seemed willing to write off the colony, Idonea Haversham, the regional supervisor, had other plans. A blemish on her résumé would impair her chances at future promotion—and she wanted a cushy managerial position overseeing the revitalization of the entertainment complex on Saturn's moon Titan.

Haversham knew, though, her superiors on Earth would not sanction a fourth formal recovery mission. In their eyes, the significant loss in both personnel and equipment—but mostly equipment—had made the abandonment of the Celestria mining colony obligatory. Any chance at salvage and recuperation would have to come through an atypical and innovative course of action.

Soldier of fortune Wimarc Essex and his so-called Myrmidons won a bidding war for Haversham's lucrative contract. They had arrived in orbit around Celestria within 72 hours of finalizing the deal, completing three separate jumps in Wimarc's Callisto class frigate, *Rattlesnake*.

"I can't access their security systems, Chief." Aldred, Wimarc's tech guru, spoke without taking his gaze off the monitors. His face was gaunt, his expression stern. His nimble fingers danced across the control panel as he tried to hack the network in hopes of bypassing authentication and stumbling on a symmetrical backdoor. "I could modify a Trojan horse, but it would take some time."

"We're not staying any longer than necessary," Wimarc said, ruling out an armchair mission. "Aldred, Forwin, and Amiria are with me," the chief announced, naming those who would accompany him to the surface. "Gear up, heavy armor, fully outfitted. Savaric, you have command. Don't let the children get into any trouble." Wimarc's *Rattlesnake* carried a nominal support crew of eight hard-edged adventurers below decks who loathed the monotony of being excluded from action. "Anything looks weird to you and you can't reach us, button up and fly home."

"I did find something they didn't notice on Gunnora." Savaric, the team's eldest member, played a digitized code on the loudspeakers as Wimarc and the others prepared to head for one of two shuttlecrafts found on the frigate. "It's a quarantine beacon, low-power output, only detectable from orbit. I haven't been able to validate the serial number so I can't tell you who deployed it."

"Probably one of Gunnora's envoys," Wimarc said. "No telling what they found down there. Whatever it was, they weren't ready for it. Any specifics?"

"Just the standard default warning with a verbal addendum," Savaric said. "Something about 'white death.'"

Unlike his prior envoys, Wimarc had no affiliation with the corporate military. The corporate security forces garrisoned on Gunnora protected coalition property, smothered uprisings in the fringe territories and kept general order through tyrannical martial law. A formidable fighting force, their brawn far surpassed their tactical understanding and overall intelligence. In an intense firefight against a heavily armed foe, the coalition's militia almost always had the upper hand.

In a delicate catch-and-cruise mission like the one originally lined up for them on Celestria, the ineptitude of the security force generally resulted in calamity—particularly when faced with an invisible enemy.

Wimarc and the other Myrmidons had the benefit of first-rate military training coupled with hands-on experience. They had worked all the dirty jobs too insignificant for the heavy-handedness of the security forces, from hunting pirates preying on merchant ships to rounding up blockade runners supplying rebels. Part mercenary, part police officer, part enforcer, Wimarc had earned a reputation in the field for getting the job done quickly, quietly, and with a minimum of firepower.

Approximately 10,000 colonists had settled on Celestria, known in bureaucratic circles as FTC01266, most playing an active role in the mining operations or living a primarily agrarian lifestyle while transforming the landscape within an ever-expanding worldhouse. The paraterraforming of Celestria had already converted nearly 18 percent of the planet's surface into a habitable expanse. Outside the enclosure, Celestria's heavily cratered surface boasted bright frost deposits and dark plains comprised of cryovolcanic residue—not wholly hostile, but certainly an uninviting environment.

While the water ice, carbon dioxide, silicates and organic compounds detected spectrally had all been corroborated when the settlement was no more than an unoccupied station, robonauts did not find the subsurface ocean predicted by analysts. A thin atmosphere consisting of carbon dioxide and molecular oxygen surrounded the planet.

"According to Savaric, there are areas scattered around the central command complex still showing active life support." Wimarc strapped himself into the landing shuttle along with his team. "No confirmation on life signs at this point."

"What do you think is down there, Chief?" Forwin had heard plenty of chatter back on Gunnora. He had run across both freighter pilots and starfighters of the Frontier Detachment in the dodgy watering holes around the shipyards. They spoke of strange incidents along the outer edges of coalition territory. Even veteran spacefarers shunned Celestria, maintaining that it should have been left uninhabited. "There are those that say it may have been an alien outpost long ago."

"And that alien ghosts took down an entire settlement and destroyed three Dione class cutters," Wimarc said, casting a glance over his shoulder. "I don't know exactly what to expect, but my gut tells me this is no different than what happened on Rhuddlan 100 years ago or on the ocean planet Gwenddwr." In both instances, the coalition-backed governorship had failed, leading to bloody civil wars that culminated in widespread systems failures and, ultimately, death for most of the colonists. "I think we'll find a handful of survivors, hiding from the coalition because they know they'll be prosecuted."

"And if you're wrong?" Only Forwin, Wimarc's miraculous engineer and overworked mechanic, could chide the Myrmidons' leader openly without provoking a fistfight. Physically, he was broad-shouldered and thickset, and his muscle matched his technical prowess. "I mean, you are fallible, after all."

"Then I guess we're about to go for a stroll over some alien graves," Wimarc said, keying in the flight plan. In a few minutes they would be looking for a suitable landing site. "Let's hope we don't annoy any of them."

2.

"Another salvage effort has arrived." Cyberneticist Matityahu Holman studied the configuration of the vessel that had just entered orbit over Celestria. He spoke to no one in particular, since he found himself alone in mission control sitting at an otherwise unmanned row of instrument panels. The station's primary computer quickly identified the visiting spacecraft and reported its findings. "Interesting," Holman said, surprised that his guests did not appear to have official clearance from the First Trade Coalition. "Scavengers, already?"

The computer—consistently suspicious—urged defensive action and awaited further instruction.

"You are too distrustful," Holman said. "You know I'll have no part in initiating any more violence. These hands have enough blood on them already."

He wished he could circumvent the failsafe protocol that went into effect when the crisis struck Celestria. He wished he could find a way to sidestep the communication blackout and respond to the ship's hails and transmit a warning, an explanation or a plea for help. Holman lacked the security clearance required to force the colony's systems to finally stand down.

"Like those who came before, they're here to liberate the survivors," Holman said, his tone bitter. All previous rescue attempts had failed miserably—and he had been utterly powerless, forced to watch rescuers perish. "I may not be able to help them, but I most certainly won't hinder them."

The cyberneticist vacated an ergonomically snug chair and paced through aisles of empty work stations, some still adorned with the personal effects of mission control personnel who had succumbed to the White Death. Prior to the epidemic, he had only set foot in the settlement's hub once, during his orientation. For the past year, however, the nerve center and the adjoining chambers had become his home—and his dungeon.

Torment in this torture chamber came from seclusion and silence and seemingly infinite hours of introspection and regret.

Holman had no fear of starvation, since a lifetime worth of provisions had been stored within the enclosure. Though lacking in epicurean delights, the stores included palatable food and an ample supply of water.

Outside the fortified walls of the central command complex's castellated nucleus, beyond the blast doors and the improvised reinforcement network Holman had hastily constructed as the scourge swept through the worldhouse, the product of the apocalyptic pestilence haunted the ruins of the colony.

3.

Following an uneventful descent, landing shuttle *Madeline* from the frigate *Rattlesnake* put down on the surface of Celestria, an icy planetoid orbiting a red dwarf star found along the outermost edges of space claimed by the First Trade Coalition of Earth. On board, Wimarc Essex and three members of his Myrmidons—all sporting cutting-edge, armored, skintight counterpressure spacesuits—prepared to look for survivors of the colony.

Coming to rest just outside the worldhouse on a relatively smooth, bright plain punctuated by knobs and pits, Wimarc realized that two of the colony's enclosure panels had been forcibly dislodged—apparently from the inside of the structure. Visuals also revealed another surprise:

The patchy white substance covering the surface of Celestria was not ice.

"You see that don't you?" Wimarc squinted, trying to comprehend the images cycling across a pair of compact view screens on his control panel. The pictures came from ventral cams mounted near the landing struts. "Increase magnification by a factor of ten."

The enhanced picture showed densely packed clusters of cottony blobs crowned with white, leaf-like lobes.

"It looks like a fungus," Aldred said. "But, how can it survive in this atmosphere?"

"Lichens can actually survive in space in a dormant state." Amiria doubled as the Myrmidons' medical and science officer. She had collected a half a dozen degrees and certificates from various universities over the years—enough to settle down and launch a lucrative career in several fields. An adrenaline junkie, she preferred life in deep space, traversing the heavens on dicey missions. "Subject them to extreme temperatures, cosmic radiation, the vacuum of space—once they rehydrate, they're perfectly fine."

"Not that it should come as a surprise to anyone," Aldred said, "but onboard short-range sensors confirm the enclosure has completely depressurized with a total loss of artificial atmosphere." He continued reading incoming data, picking and choosing pertinent information. "Two panels have been displaced through detonation."

"There are only two scenarios in which a colonial governor would give that order," Wimarc said, initiating a ten-second countdown before blowing the hatch. "It might be given as a last resort to put out an otherwise uncontrollable fire, preferably after isolating colonists in pressurized safe cells." He paused, turned and faced the others. "I see no evidence of a firestorm."

"Then, what's the other scenario," Forwin asked, his sarcasm palpable. "I mean, as if I didn't already know."

"Invasion," Wimarc answered. "Potentially by an alien life form."

"There's something else, chief." Even as the cabin depressurized and the gangplank extended to the planet's surface, Aldred reviewed the last bits of new data. "Before they detonated the worldhouse shielding, there are signs it had already been breached. It looks like there are hundreds, thousands maybe, of micro-fissures. Defects, maybe. Hard to tell. All of them would have been automatically sealed, though."

Crossing the dreary basin to reach the closest access gate in the enclosure, the four found an unfamiliar and unsettling arrangement of stars pinned to the black veil overhead. The ruins of the worldhouse, lacking any striking signs of devastation and catastrophe, nonetheless magnified the oppressive gloom of the apathetic twilit skies and the desolation of the unconquered Celestrian landscape. Before them stood the bleak, sterile walls which once embraced and safeguarded the lives of colonists.

These same walls likely sheltered none but the dead now.

Those minute fungi blanketed the ground and coated the exterior of the enclosure to an average height of twenty meters. Wimarc felt his boots crush the crystal-like life forms with each footfall, watched as a sinister cloud formed in their wake as they progressed across the landscape. Wimarc noticed, too, as they advanced, the tiny, flaky, alabaster things began to undulate rhythmically, their crusty ridges rippling softly.

Since none of the others seemed to notice the phenomenon, he kept the revelation to himself.

Inside the worldhouse, more appalling scenes of destruction and deterioration awaited. Therein, illuminated by the diffuse glow of slowly dimming artificial lighting, the doom that came to the Celestria settlement abundantly manifested itself in the frozen corpses of ill-fated colonists. Some died alone, unable to reach the safety of a pressurized safe cell. Some died hand-in-hand or locked in an embrace with a spouse, a lover or a stranger who shared a fear of meeting death unaccompanied.

The team also found bodies piled deep near certain portals leading to safe cells, the remains of residents who found themselves trapped outside when the panels had been dislodged. Desperate for shelter, but denied sanctuary by those inside, they quickly expired as the artificial atmosphere ebbed.

All of the dead shared one significant attribute: Every one had been encased in a gauzy veil of white fungi.

From their point of entry, Wimarc and his team hiked approximately three kilometers to the colony's central district. The unsymmetrical worldhouse had fanned out over thousands of square hectares during the settlement's first two centuries, expanding quickly in certain quarters to encompass the prime pieces of Celestrian real estate. Several mining stations had been established, and much of the land area had been converted for agricultural use, sustaining the population.

At the core of the colony rested a once-thriving city, Kymric, its twisting, narrow, cobbled lanes and dark gray towers evoking a form of structural design more suitable to medieval Europe. Quarried and cut using high-tech precision lasers, the raw materials had all come from the surrounding environment. The available rock bore a strong resemblance to Purbeck Marble, a blue-gray sedimentary limestone long ago utilized in the construction of English cathedrals, possibly inspiring Celestria's city planners to adopt a Neo-Gothic style in developing the city.

Kymric featured soaring structures and lavish alcazars, now all silent and still. Its most impressive edifices emphasized verticality and light, employing ribbed vaults and flying buttresses. Between each building's narrow buttresses, large ornate windows captured and magnified the scarlet hues of the local red dwarf star.

The niveous, fleecy fungi possessed perpetual mandate over all within the worldhouse, overspreading each building with a snow-white sheath and cloaking each corpse with a hoary shroud. Kymric had become an eerie, tricolor world, painted by chalky whites, ashen grays and dull, sanguine reds.

At the heart of the city, Wimarc and his team found the central command complex. Light poured through the grand doors of the main entrance, sheltered by a pillared portico. Several more colonists had died here, ascending the stairs, their pasty corpses petrified into frantic poses of apparent torment preserving their final moments of life.

Through their visors, the team members peered across a wide atrium and down the long corridor leading deep into the facility. Two figures, their features concealed by the omnipresent fungi, slumped forward in their chairs, frozen behind the center's reception desk. Though the section of the building had not lost interior lighting, the automatic doors had never sealed and the life support systems had not been activated.

"Beyond that first blast door 150 meters down the hall," Aldred said, "life support is functioning properly."

"I can't get a clean reading on life signs," Amiria said. "There's too much background noise. Might be the fungi interfering with the scanners."

"We need to get in there," Wimarc said, gesturing toward the far end of the corridor. "Amiria, take Forwin and see if you can bypass security and get us through the blast door." Wimarc carefully scraped a patch of white fungus off the desktop and placed a small wireless keypunch on the surface along with a selection of colored cables. "Aldred, I still want access to their security systems. Let's try a manual connection."

"Not necessary, chief," Aldred said. "Something—someone—unlocked the system. I have full access to the surveillance cams now on my handheld."

"How about the colony's main database?" Wimarc started scanning the available files using his own compact viewer. "Can you find journal entries, encoded messages that were never transmitted—anything that might explain what happened?"

"Negative. All I have is cam access. Like someone wanted us to see something."

As the system ran through a seemingly endless sequence of surveillance cameras, Wimarc and Aldred scrutinized each image. The pictures captured the lost colony's many ghostlike vistas and underscored the disquieting tranquility and ghastly hush that had displaced the once lively, flourishing community. From shadowed alcoves along the streets of Kymric to the sprawling fields of withered crops swathed in albescence, the bleak, lonely scenery of Celestria evoked phantom fears long dismissed by science and conjured thoughts of ancient superstitions.

"Wait," Wimarc leaned closer to the monitor. "Pause on that one," but before Aldred could react, the image vanished. The screen had shown the front steps leading up to the main entrance of the central command complex. "Keep watching," Wimarc said, walking toward the double doors. "I'll be right back."

Standing at the top of the steps beneath the pillared portico, Wimarc studied the bodies scattered before him. He counted 16 corpses now—though, on the way in, he only recalled seeing 11. He knelt, watching the one closest to him for more than a minute—observing his extremities, examining the fungi encasing him in detail.

When he was convinced, he stood and went back into the central command complex.

"They've moved," Wimarc said, returning to the reception desk. His customary composed demeanor remained intact, though his eyes betrayed an embryonic apprehension that unnerved Aldred. "They're not dead—they're climbing the stairs out there."

"Chief," Amiria's voice sounded choppy, hesitant through the communication device. "You need to get down here. The bodies down here—most of them were hit with blasters before this place lost atmosphere. This was a real massacre, easily 15 to 20 casualties…"

"Listen," Forwin interrupted Amiria, addressing Wimarc directly. "If you can get the door on that end of the hallway to seal, I can activate life support in this section."

Wimarc and Aldred entered the corridor and used an emergency control located behind an access panel to seal the door. As they sprinted down the corridor to meet Amiria and Forwin, breathable air filled the compartment as both pressure and some degree of warmth returned. The fungi blanketing the floor and covering the walls reacted to the change in atmosphere conditions almost immediately: Each entity rippled with newfound life, its crystalline structure softening as it distended itself as if awakening from an extended period of hibernation.

Alarmingly, the fungi on the floor parted as Wimarc and Aldred advanced, presenting them with a clear path.

"Get the blast door open," Wimarc called as he and Aldred approached their companions. He anticipated what would happen next and realized they had very little time. "Get it open now!"

Many of the bodies Amiria had reported had already begun to stir with an aberrant, perverted form of vigor. Clearly no longer living, the corpses of the colonists displayed an appalling mode of animation fueled undoubtedly by the fungi enfolding them. As Wimarc arrived on the scene, he immediately noticed that more than half had been rendered useless as hosts through violent decapitation.

"Aim for their heads," the leader of the Myrmidons commanded as the dead colonists took to their feet.

4.

Sequestered in the mission control room of the central command complex, Matityahu Holman monitored the determined progress of four would-be rescuers, sent to Celestria to recover whatever they could. He had watched as they slogged across the barren achromatic fields, a white haze suspended just above the ground inscribing their progress. He had successfully disabled the weapon systems to allow them safe passage and had managed to unlock security access to provide them access to the surveillance cams. Still, he feared even with his assistance they would not manage to reach his inner sanctum.

The White Death, long quiescent in the chill of Celestria's natural atmosphere, had detected the intrusion. After months of contemplative slumber, it stirred to life once more. Through the surveillance cameras, Holman watched as the confrontation in the corridor took shape—watched as long-dead colonists—now hosts to the dreadful, parasitic scourge—coordinated their attack.

Still, none of the other teams had made it as far as this group. Holman hoped the liberators would not underestimate the entities.

"It's happening again," Olluna said, eying the monitors. "Must we watch another massacre?"

"You don't have to watch if you don't want to."

Holman's niece Olluna drifted through the chamber noiselessly. The young woman—infinitely more perceptive than her uncle—had arrived at Celestria only hours before fate or the ineptitude of science brought calamity to the colony. Studious and insightful, she had easily unraveled the mystery of the outbreak, though Holman would not willingly substantiate her theory. His acknowledgment of guilt, though, could be found in the hours he spent in seclusion, reflecting on his hubris and his culpability.

"They aren't like the others, are they?" She watched as Wimarc and his Myrmidons faced carriers of the White Death. "Maybe we'll finally get away from this place."

"Don't get your hopes up," Holman said. "You know as well as I do that those things won't give up easily. There are more assembling in the atrium, moving much more quickly now. They've been stockpiling energy, biding time."

"They're trying to open the door," Olluna said. The portal between the atrium and the corridor fell outside Holman's improvised defense network, augmented by Olluna's resourcefulness. Given sufficient time, the things would be able to access the security code and unlock the doorway. "They'll lose life support in the corridor."

"More importantly, when it depressurizes, they'll probably be swept back out into Kymric, right into the clutches of those things."

"You have to do something." Olluna, sprightly and graceful, weaved through the aisles until she located the right control panel. Since the last rescue attempt had failed, she had familiarized herself with mission control and had formulated several strategies. "See, I can force the door to re-sequence its access code every 45 seconds."

"That will slow them down some," Holman admitted. "It won't

stop them, though. We already know when they work together as a collective, they can process information faster than the mainframe."

"Then we'll have to put up more obstacles to keep them occupied, won't we?"

5.

Wimarc and his Myrmidons, their backs to a blast door in the central command complex on Celestria, faced eight reanimated corpses roused from near dormancy by the sudden rush of atmosphere in the contained chamber.

"Remember, these things aren't human anymore," Wimarc said. The chief of the Myrmidons had deduced that the all-pervading, alabaster fungi somehow controlled these dead bodies; and that the "White Death"—as the quarantine beacon had called it—had wiped out the Celestrian settlement.

While Wimarc had great respect for the dead, he had to protect his crew.

The first plasma bursts from Amiria's blaster ruptured the torso of one of the things, spinning him around on his feet and ripping his right arm from its socket. Still, the corpse shambled forward once it had regained its equilibrium, spilling its crusty entrails as it continued its attack.

The second volley wrenched its bobbing skull from its shoulders, sending it flying back down the hallway several meters. The decapitated body tumbled to the floor.

"Take off their heads." Wimarc repeated his instructions, demonstrating on a second corpse. His shot disintegrated the corpse's skull and dissolved his putrid brain.

A few moments later, the corpses had all been beheaded and Forwin and Aldred were busy roasting the fungi in the hallway.

"Have you ever seen anything like this?" Wimarc continued working on opening the blast door, hoping that on the other side he would find only survivors. "I came here expecting rebels—maybe aliens. I didn't plan on zombies."

"If you are asking for a scientific explanation," Amiria said, "I can offer you several examples in nature of parasitic forms of life taking over the dead bodies of plants and animals. I've never seen anything capable of hijacking a human, though."

"This damn thing has been completely rewired from the inside."

Wimarc's growing frustration went unnoticed by his science officer. "Someone must have survived in there," he said. "It would be nice if they'd let us in before a mob of these things comes shuffling into the hallway."

Amiria knelt, hovering over a nearby corpse. Most of the fungi had been blackened, though several small spots remained unscathed. As she watched, the white patches expanded as the surviving entities resurrected the charred fungi. Instinctively, she knew the speed of the process all but ruled out any kind of natural biological function. Using a handheld scanner, she examined the entities in minute detail, studying them at a molecular level.

"I knew it," Amiria said, her conceit mixed with a trace of panic. She stood quickly, lurching backward awkwardly, trying to put some distance between her and the corpse. "It's not a fungus," she said. "They're mechanical, at least in part. Nanobots. Don't touch them."

"'Don't touch them'?" Wimarc shot her a cynical glance, then looked toward the floor. She followed his gaze down to his boots. Nanobots coated his spacesuit from the tips of his feet to just below his knees. She found a similar dispersion over her own suit. "I suppose you're going to tell me that they're going to try to get inside the suit, too."

Amiria started to respond, but found her communication device suddenly dead.

Forwin and Aldred had swept the entire corridor, their blasters cooking the entities as they went. Returning, they found vast new swathes of white, leaf-like lobes spreading from the floor to the ceiling, undulating as they passed. The things multiplied at a dizzying rate, threatening to close in around them and engulf them. They tried to blast their way back down the hall, but soon found themselves completely surrounded. Back to back, they could keep the things at bay but could not proceed any further without risking direct contact.

"I need options, now," Wimarc said, mouthing the words slowly so Amiria could understand. Both of them had lost communications now. Tapping his weapon, he added, "Blasters won't get us out of this."

"Thinking, chief," she nodded. She took a few tentative steps forward to see how the nanobots would react. As she advanced, she noticed her handheld scanner flashed to life, its display scrolling through the startup menu. Moving back a single step, the scanner went blank. She gestured to Wimarc, instructing him to stand in a specific spot. "There's some kind of dampening field, here," she said. "That's why our com went out. It stretches out from the blast door about two meters."

"Someone must have just activated it. That's a start," Wimarc said. "Doesn't help Forwin and Aldred at the moment, though." He could no longer see the other Myrmidons, though he could still see flashes from their blasters. The cottony nanobots had encircled them. "How do we get them here?"

"Already on it." Amiria did not waste time explaining that she could rig the scanner to set off an electromagnetic pulse that would momentarily inhibit the nanobots. Generating the local EMP would, however, render the apparatus useless. As she leaned forward to remove the scanner from the effects of the dampening field, the clever nanobots began erecting a wall, stacking themselves in an attempt to reach the device. "They won't have much time to get down here," she said, completing the modification. "We only get one shot. Here we go."

Wimarc heard a sharp crack through his communication link followed by absolute silence. Lights in the corridor flickered and failed, replaced by faint secondary lighting. The nanobots did not move.

Forwin and Aldred burst through the white curtain and bolted down the corridor, crushing everything in their path.

Wimarc looked at Amiria, hoping she could tell him how long they had before the nanobots would reactivate—hoping she had another idea. She shrugged, dropping the damaged scanner to the floor.

Just as Forwin and Aldred arrived at the end of the corridor, the nanobots awoke from their short nap, evidently aggravated. They immediately constructed a solid wall just outside of the dampening field.

"They're biding their time now," Wilmarc said. He guessed that dozens, possibly hundreds of nanobot-infested colonists had gathered in the atrium. They would be working tirelessly to get through the doorway on the opposite end of the corridor. When it opened, they would all be swept outside. "We could use a miracle about now."

At that instant, the blast door opened. On the other side, a young woman stood smiling.

"Welcome to Celestria," Olluna said. "I'm going to have to ask you to remove your spacesuits."

6.

Wimarc, Amiria, Forwin and Aldred sat around a long oval meeting table in what once served as a formal conference room for visiting dignitaries. After a somewhat embarrassing exchange in the corridor in which everyone had been asked to fully disrobe—with swarming nanobots scrambling just outside the dampening field—ginger-haired Olluna had provided each of the Myrmidons with suitable articles of clothing. She had remained detached until a set of rigorous scans had confirmed that none of the visitors had picked up a miniscule hitchhiker outside the central command complex.

"Your shuttlecraft has been compromised." Olluna, assuming the role of convivial hostess, set a pitcher of Gunnoran Stout on the faux mahogany tabletop. Six frosted mugs had already been placed on crystal coasters scattered around the table. "Please, help yourselves."

Keying in an access code in a wall panel, a concealed monitor materialized. It displayed an image of the *Madeline,* its hull caked with throngs of alabaster nanobots. "They're dismantling it for parts," Olluna reported, her voice remarkably composed for someone whose chance at freedom appeared to be coming apart at the seams. "They'll strip the vessel within a few hours, even under the harsh conditions. They did the same thing with the three cutters that landed."

"And the rescue teams?" Wimarc filled his mug. "What happened to them?"

"Ambushed in Kymric." Keying in another sequence of numbers, Olluna showed crowds of dead colonists, their bodies commandeered by the White Death, as they congregated in the cobbled streets outside the complex. The hideous scenes seemed conjured from dark industrial-age nightmares. Exposed in shuffling madness, they were the gruesome consequence of technology uninhibited by moral codes. "They spent too much time out there. Their suits couldn't protect them," she said. "Neither could yours, you know. Another few minutes and you would have been infected."

"Where did those things come from?" Amiria turned away from the monitor, unable to stomach the horror any longer. "That technology has been banned for centuries."

"Laws are open to interpretation in the fringe territories." Matityahu Holman entered the room, his emaciated form and pallid expression suggesting he had been depriving himself of adequate food and rest.

After formally introducing himself and his niece, he returned to Amiria's question. "Celestria was no ordinary colony," he explained. "It was a testing ground for the First Trade Coalition."

"A testing ground for what?" Wimarc sipped the bitter stout ale. His thoughts turned abruptly to Idonea Haversham, the regional supervisor, who had sent him on this fool's errand. He found himself wondering if she had known about the scourge of Celestria all along.

"As the coalition's chief cyberneticist, I was asked to augment all of the colonists with brain implants and other forms of cyberware and nanodevices, with or without their permission. The implants would enhance strength, sensory perception, memory and cognitive ability." Holman could sense Wimarc's growing distrust. "The coalition was determined to test these breakthroughs in nanotechnology. I warned them that it was too soon."

"Yet here you are," Wimarc said. "What went wrong?"

"For the first twenty years, nothing went wrong," Holman said defensively. "I had overseen thousands of procedures since my arrival, devoted decades to perfecting the science. I cultivated a flawless cybernetic improvement regimen, a regime set in motion practically from birth." He took a deep breath and let it out slowly. "I introduced various biotech implants designed to compensate for abrupt changes in the environment—previously a stumbling block for space exploration thanks to our species' rather sluggish capacity to adapt on a Darwinian evolution scale."

"But, a little over one Terran year ago, the nanobots evolved unexpectedly," Holman said. His gaze strayed, his eyes fixing on the awful, shambling White Death that filled the streets of Kymric. "They underwent a sweeping comprehensive metamorphosis, becoming composite organisms—a symbiotic pairing of a nanomites and an organic photobiont harvested from human genetic material."

"You almost make it sound poetic," Wimarc said. "You overlook the fact that their genesis came at the expense of their host humans."

"Trust me, captain—not a day goes by that I don't calculate my shame and search for ways to express my grief."

"You're saying they're miniature cybernetic organisms." Amiria did not try to hide either her skepticism or her admiration. "You have created something that is part machine and part animal, a new life form."

"One that is entirely unfriendly," Forwin added. "I don't care what they are at this point. I want to know how to kill them so we can get off of this rock."

"Your ship," Holman said, turning to Wimarc. "It is a Callisto class frigate, isn't it?"

"Yes," Wimarc answered. "The *Rattlesnake*."

"Then you should have a second landing shuttlecraft aboard," Holman continued. "There's a small landing pad above this complex. It was used as a terminus for small hovercars inside the worldhouse, but it will accommodate one of your shuttles."

"What about the nanobots?" Wimarc knew the exterior of the complex had been completely covered. "What will stop them from contaminating the ship's hull while we're boarding?"

"Olluna has discovered a way to shift the dampening bubble we created." Holman patted his niece on the shoulder to show his pride in her ingenuity. Her fortuitous arrival at the onset of his most demanding tribulation had been a blessing; without her, he doubted his defense network would have been capable of holding off the horde. "She will program a path so that we can rendezvous with the shuttlecraft."

"Only one problem," Wimarc said. "Our com system isn't powerful enough to penetrate the complex." He glanced at Aldred who nodded in agreement. "We'll have to wait to signal the shuttlecraft when we're topside. It'll take a good 30 minutes to get that ship down here."

"I can't guarantee that the dampening field will maintain its integrity for that length of time." Olluna paused, silently assessing her calculations. "There are too many variables to predict an outcome. Repositioning the field to cover the exterior of the complex may overload the circuits. It may cause the system to default or it may terminate it completely."

"In that event," Forwin said, "We're back to throwing stones at the zombies."

7.

Matityahu Holman waited patiently in mission control, surveying the relics of lost lives. He studied digital snapvids which would continue to play long after humanity had forgotten about Celestria. He prodded smooth stones plucked from mountain streams on Earth, carried to the farthest reaches of coalition territory. He examined a collection of beer bottle caps collected from breweries scattered over hundreds of star systems.

Holman knew he had to admit his failings to the coalition. He had gone one step too far, tried to push the technology beyond its natural limits. He had encouraged the symbiotic relationship between the nanobots and their hosts, knowing the risks. He felt the benefits far outweighed the hazards—that death, even on a massive scale, could be justified if the product exceeded the value of the sacrifice.

"Everything is ready, sir." Olluna intruded on his musings. "Wimarc has asked that we suit up."

"I've told you a thousand times," Holman said. "You can call me uncle."

"It would be a counterfeit designation. I appreciate your kindness and consideration in circumventing my protocols. Allowing me to fulfill my mission would have been a more logical course of action, though."

"An unnecessary one, though."

"That remains to be seen."

8.

The Myrmidons took up defensive positions around the perimeter of the landing pad, outfitted in pressurized spacesuits that lacked both the armor and the comfort of the ones they had to abandon due to contamination.

Carrying plasma drills that made clumsy but efficient weapons, they had successfully cleared the pad of nanobots using the tools' weakest setting. Olluna's dampening bubble hovered just beneath the platform, acting as an impassible barrier.

From their vantage point, they could see much of the ruins of Kymric. At first glance, it seemed like an old Earth city blanketed in a light dusting of snow. The vast dome of the worldhouse spread overhead, towering columns supporting its bulk. From here, the Celestria colony retained a hint of its former majesty and beauty.

Closer inspection, though, revealed the sallow phantasmagoria that had supplanted the colony. Wimarc watched Holman as he stood near the edge of the landing pad, staring down into the chaos he had created. He felt the cyberneticist's anguish; but he also felt his reprehensible arrogance, a lingering smugness that refused to be stifled by the catastrophic repercussions of his work.

His grief, Wimarc knew, could never displace his vanity.

"This is Savaric." Wimarc turned his attention to the worldhouse shielding. "I'm approaching from the east. I can see the opening," he said. Aldred and Forwin had managed to detonate a cluster of four panels, providing direct access to the shuttlecraft. "I'll be on the ground in one minute, pending clearance."

"You're cleared," Wimarc said. "Get us the hell out of here."

Olluna joined her uncle, peering down into the city one last time. He put an arm around her, urging her to rest her head on his shoulder. She showed even less remorse than Holman, though Wimarc questioned her role in all this. He detected something aberrant in her behavior that led him to unsettling speculation. Her lack of fear troubled him the most.

"The damping field is fluctuating." Amiria double-checked the scanning device Olluna had given her. "It's failing."

"Hold your positions," Wimarc said, charging the plasma drill. He switched over to the most powerful setting and ordered his crew to do the same. "We can still do this."

The first wave of nanobots surged over the rim of the landing pad. Holman staggered back several steps, nearly losing his balance. Olluna caught him, dragging him out of harm's way for the moment.

The bulky drills yielded much larger plasma bursts than standard-issue blasters. They lacked elaborate guidance systems and output consistency but packed a highly destructive punch. Forwin, the first Myrmidon to test the tool's effectiveness, vaporized all the nanobots in front of him. He also disintegrated a sizable chunk of the landing platform and blew a hole in a neighboring building.

Wimarc and Aldred fired simultaneously, causing the platform to shudder beneath them. Cracks appeared in the surface. Amiria fired next, the kickback knocking her off her feet. She recovered quickly.

"What's happening down there?" Savaric's voice betrayed his alarm. Wimarc had briefed him privately: He had warned him to abort the mission if he felt it necessary. "Am I still cleared for landing?"

"Blow the hatch on the way in," Wimarc said. "Catch-and-cruise, no time for civilities."

"Understood."

As Savaric approached, the flashes of plasma accelerated. He could see the White Death clambering over the exterior of the complex, the throngs of reanimated corpses filling the streets. The frayed and crumbling edges of the landing pad receded with each shot fired.

"Wimarc," Savaric said, yelling into the com. "Keep that up and I won't be able to land!"

"If we stop firing, we're dead." Wimarc looked up at the

shuttlecraft. As he had ordered, the hatch had been opened. "Don't touch down," he said. "Get as close as you can."

As the shuttle descended, more than a dozen corpses poured through the portal onto the airbridge connecting the complex with the landing pad. They lurched forward, moving more swiftly than before. Forwin spun on his heels, blasting the four leaders into nothingness. Two others lost an arm and a leg each and a third ended up in a pile of frothy, pasty ooze that had once been his torso.

Before Forwin could fire again, two others tackled him.

"Get them off!" The corpses, controlled by the White Death, mauled him viciously, tearing at his spacesuit, biting him with mechanically enhanced strength. "Wimarc!"

In an instant, Forwin's visor had shattered and his suit had been breeched. The nanobots poured through the slender cracks, invading the spacesuit and inserting themselves into Forwin's body through every accessible orifice.

Aldred fired the shot that incinerated him.

"It's no use," Olluna said, pulling away from Holman. "I have a responsibility to put an end to this."

"No, we're going to make it this time," Holman said. "We'll get away from here. You don't have to do anything."

"The coalition expects me to do my job," Olluna said. "Just like they expected you to do yours. You should know—you engineered me as the antidote in the event anything ever went wrong."

"It's not fair," Holman said. "You're my only family."

"I'm not family. I'm a facsimile of a relative you lost years ago."

Olluna began disassembling herself, disengaging the billions of nanobots that so precisely presented the likeness of Holman's niece. Holman wept, more devastated at the loss of his creation than he had been by the unintentional genocide he had authored on Celestria.

"You must tell them," Olluna said, looking up into his eyes as she continued her dissolution. "Tell them what happened here, uncle."

As the nanobots that comprised Olluna dispersed, they took on the crimson color that had been Olluna's ginger hair. They scattered quickly, advancing in all directions until they encountered the aggressive White Death.

The red nanobots speedily assimilated the white ones, deactivating them as they multiplied. Scarlet streamers spread across the building's exterior, washed through the streets of Kymric and well beyond, stretching to the far ends of the worldhouse and the barren, undeveloped lands beyond its protective shields.

"It's time to go, Holman," Wimarc said, holding out a hand. The shuttlecraft hovered overhead. "You have a lot of explaining to do."

The old man looked up at the leader of the Myrmidons, then back to spot on the landing pad where Olluna had last stood.

"'And Darkness and Decay,'" Holman said, quoting a line from a memorable tale written many millennia ago, "'and the Red Death held illimitable dominion over all.'"

Plan 9 in Outer Space
Ernest and Emily Hogan

Emergency. Emergency. Anyone receiving this signal, please respond. This is the Autonomous Universal Network Telecommunications Interface of the exopopulation ship *New Eden*. We are in a dire emergency. Our mission is in jeopardy. We may never reach our selected colonization planet.

I need counseling on how to proceed. This situation is beyond my programming.

Another cycle had begun. Maintenance Team Six had decoffined and started their redundant routine of checking on *New Eden* automatic systems. They scattered and began going over their assigned sector of the ship, chattering through their headsets, when we encountered a cloud with an electromagnetic charge.

"It's pretty," said Cheryl.

"Wonder if it'll bring us any excitement?" said Stony.

"Excitement? The universe is too full of excitement," said Yuri. "Stop looking at the outside and keep your eyes on your work."

Vlad limited his remarks to, "Ugh."

Naomi just bobbed her head to the music playing in her earpiece.

Yuri floated his way down a coffin-lined corridor. "Anyway—what's to get excited about? It's just a cloud."

Cheryl frowned. "If it weren't for the ship's equipment we wouldn't even know it's there."

Stony quirked his command glove, studying readouts in his helmet display. "It has a dark matter signature. Kind of mysterious … the great unknown!"

Yuri snorted. "Think I'll take a nap. You can—Aackkkkk…!"

Everybody switched their visual inputs to his sector. He twitched like a man having a grande mal seizure. Sparks crawled on his face like electric maggots. His body bumped into a row of coffins. Finally he stopped twitching and just drifted. His eyes were dead.

Automedical could detect no real physical trauma. It was as if someone or something had flipped a switch and he was dead. There was no outward sign of trauma, no burns. No cell disruption. Nothing. Medical drones quickly bundled him into stasis, before cellular damage could begin.

"Do you think the cloud killed him?" wondered Cheryl.

"I'm afraid, at this time, that cannot be determined with absolute certainty," I explained.

"Are we going to encounter any more of these clouds?" asked Stony.

I scanned the sector through which we were passing. "Yes."

The levels on the morale sensors dropped, precipitously. "TroubleShooter is examining the data," I assured them. They resumed their redundancy scans. Regular sleep-work cycles were established, and the decoffined personnel settled into regular routines.

I expected quick answers from TroubleShooter, but did not get them. Likewise, Automedical did not suggest that Yuri should be revived, and his stasis was extended indefinitely.

Then Stony sent me a private message.

"AUNTI, I have a proposal."

"Is there a maintenance situation that I am not aware of?"

"No."

"Of course not. That's not possible. You should begin your recreational activities."

"That's just it. Since Yuri died our team has had low morale."

"Yes, low scores on your physical indicators for psychological morale are of serious concern."

"I don't think that our usual routine is working. I watch old movies. Vlad plays video games. Naomi listens to skullcrusher music. Cheryl rereads the ship's technical manuals."

"You don't seem to be doing much interaction with each other."

"Yes. I think we need to do something as a group, to bring us together, so we can work better as a team."

"This is good team-building theory. Do you have a group activity in mind?"

"Yes, I think we should make a movie."

"Do we have the technical facilities to make a movie?"

"Our communication devices and ship's recording system are all we need. I have a degree in Cinematic Theory, you know."

"So then—why don't you do it?"

"Uh, I'm having a hard time convincing the others to cooperate. Could you tell them that they have to?"

The morale readings were low. That could lead to problems later on. This is a long haul we're on.

"Very well. I'll issue a general order."

Cheryl let herself into the gravity-normal area at the mess-hall pivot and stalked toward the group near the coffee machine, massaging her temples. "So tell me, Stony. Of all the things we could do, why do you want us to remake *Plan 9 from Outer Space?*"

Stony stood straighter, trying to match her height. "All these centuries later, people still talk about Ed Wood as the worst director ever, but they still watch his movies! We can show the new society we'll build on the destination planet how to appreciate true greatness! This will make for a better civilization!"

"You're crazy," Cheryl replied.

"I am certainly not!" Stony declared. "I have a brain implant that cured my schizophrenia! AUNTI has the records on file!"

Naomi snorted. "Buzz off, Stony! I ain't got no interest in being no actress, much less some sicko zombie babe! Leave me alone, you degenerate pig!" She switched her personal music on the Heat Death of the Universe doing their big hit, "Life Sucks Like a Black Hole." She puckered her lips, narrowed her eyes, and bobbed her head, almost breaking her neck.

Vlad grinned "Me like acting! But, please gimme more lines to say!"

Stony frowned. "Cheryl, you'll have to play the Vampira part as well as the heroine. We're all doing multiple roles anyway, and you actually were in a play back in high school, according to AUNTI. You could at least give it a try. You're better looking than Naomi, anyway—"

"Knock it off." She cut him short. "I don't need compliments about my looks. We're not involved, and we're not going to be."

"Nonono!" he protested, "You've got me all wrong! I'm an artist! An idealist! I want, need … require an actress in the Vampira/Morticia—mode! Black hair … pale skin … flesh cool to the touch!"

"For god's sake!" Cheryl poured herself a mug of coffee. "Put on a wig yourself, wise guy. And take a cold shower!"

"A wig!" Stony got a faraway look his eyes. "We could make a ... wig!"

"Sure." Cheryl stirred sweetener and non-dairy creamer into her coffee. "You'd look just like Vampira in it."

Stony shook his head. "No, I'm not right for the role."

"Who else? Naomi and I won't do it. You aren't going to try to wake up one of those women whose coffins you've been drooling over?"

"No. That would be beyond my technical expertise. What would Ed do?—You're right." He looked proud. "I will wear the wig ... and I'll play the role! I will show everybody the kind of woman I desire!"

Cheryl looked at him over the rim of her mug. "So, Stony. You have more in common with Ed Wood than you're letting on, yes?"

"No! This is for art's sake, not personal gratification."

Stony had rewritten *Plan 9 From Outer Space* to take place on an exopopulation ship, and retitled it: *Plan 9 In Outer Space*. "A director must deal with his situation ... Ed Wood was a master of that," he explained. The first scene they shot was Vlad emerging from his coffin, the way Tor Johnson did in the original.

"Nonono!" Stony screamed. "Cut! Vlad, you're supposed to be back from the dead. Look less alive, more slackjawed..."

"He looks pretty slackjawed to me," remarked Cheryl. We had persuaded her to wear the contrived uniform of Ship Security Enforcement, though she objected to the lapse in protocol. Naomi wore one too, but she refused to unplug her music, or to stop bobbing her head in time with it.

Suddenly there came the sound of scratching and pounding from one of the coffins.

"What the steaming scumbags!?" cried Cheryl.

"It's Yuri's coffin!" said Vlad.

The faceplate was fogged. Yuri was moving.

"Everybody! Focus your cameras on this!" said Stony.

"You sicko!" said Naomi.

"Chances like this come rarely," Stony explained. "You have to take advantage of them. It's what Ed would do."

Lights flashed, the coffin opened, belching out fog. Yuri's clutching hand reached out. The rest of him followed.

"Now, everybody take note," said Stony, "…that's how to move like a zombie."

"Duh!" said Naomi.

Yuri flailed around, disoriented by weightlessness, then used his arms and legs to direct his floating through the coffins.

"I'm getting outta here!" Naomi pushed herself toward the nearest door.

"Please! Everybody! Keep shooting!" Stony pleaded. "This a valuable imagery we can use in the movie!"

Yuri saw Stony, Cheryl, and Vlad, and pushed and kicked his way toward them.

"Beautiful," Stony said into his video monitor.

Yuri moved faster, reached with clutching hands.

Cheryl flipped her monitor away from her eye. "Uh, Stony…"

"Just keep shooting…"

"Let's get outta here!" Cheryl screamed.

Vlad grabbed Stony and Cheryl and scrambled to the door Naomi had just exited, threw them into the tubeway, followed, and slammed the door shut behind them.

"Cut!" Stony erupted. "Excuse me people, but who is the director around here?"

"Yuri coming at us!" Vlad clawed his hands for emphasis.

"We could have been killed!" said Cheryl.

"We don't know that." Stony played back what he had just shot. "There's really no reason for Yuri to act like a classic Romero zombie."

"Him back from dead." Vlad looked through the window in the door.

"Actually he's just back from stasis. Lots of people are disoriented after that. He should probably be more like a traditional Haitian zombie. Like in Val Lewton's *I Walked With a Zombie* … scary, but not really dangerous."

Yuri pounded on the door.

Stony, Cheryl, and Vlad scrambled up the tubeway.

Yuri kept pounding. The vibrations mixed with the rapid fire baseline of Naomi's music.

She blocked the way out, and brandished a whirring electric screwdriver. "Stay away you living dead pieces of…"

"Naomi!" Cheryl screamed. "It's us!"

Naomi squinted. "How do you know you're not like Yuri? I've seen *Night of the Living Dead: The Opera* so many times, I've got it memorized!"

"We can talk…" said Stony.

She turned off the screwdriver. "That's right. In all the zombie movies I've seen over the years, none of them talked. In the opera they just danced."

"Wouldn't that make it a ballet?" Cheryl asked.

"No, the people who were still alive sang—" Naomi demonstrated. "If ya got-ta gun … shoot 'em in the he-ad!"

Yuri pounded on the door. But that sound was eclipsed by another.

"What's that?" asked Naomi.

"There is a disruption in the system," I said. "Coffins are opening. The occupants are coming out without being scheduled."

Stony peeked through the tiny window. "This is amazing! And they're moving like zombies! Everybody, find places where you can aim your cameras!"

They grabbed him and pulled him away as Yuri resumed pounding.

"Okay, I guess we should go someplace safe and see how this develops…" Stony finally admitted. "But AUNTI, make sure the coffin chamber's monitor cameras are recording. We'll be able to use this!"

And I did. The recordings are available to verify my story.

"AUNTI!" Naomi demanded. "What the flaming bat guano is going on here?"

"I will do my best to explain, but I am designed to run and maintain the ship. Please understand that scientific analysis is not part of my programming."

"Well, do it anyway!" Cheryl said.

"TroubleShooter has shared some odd data … It seems that the stellar cloud through which we passed is part of a peculiar life form that is largely electromagnetic … I can identify with that … It has found a way to access your human nervous systems … Yuri wasn't as much dead as deactivated when they downloaded their influence into him … It has done the same to the others who were in hibernation … It took longer, but they did it…"

"This very bad," said Vlad.

"I'm afraid I have more bad news," I continued. "The clouds dominate the sector of space we are passing through."

"Don't tell me we're heading toward another one of those clouds!" Naomi's eyes were wide and her body shaking.

"No, one is following us ... and catching up."

"I can't take it!" said Naomi. "This is worse than being stuck back on Earth!"

"Very, very bad," said Vlad.

"What do we do now?" asked Cheryl.

Stony cleared his throat. "I think we should continue making the movie!"

They were all about to hit him when zombies started pounding on the door.

They rushed through the hatch into the rotating gravity-normal area, and slammed it shut behind them.

"Do you think they could function in simulated gravity?" asked Cheryl.

"Yeah, maybe if they came in here they would crumble to dust like vampires in the daylight." A faint glimmer of hope appeared in Naomi's eyes.

"That good," said Vlad.

Stony shook his head. "They still have bodies that work in gravity. If they can get past the door, they'll just start walking like the rest of us."

Cheryl groaned.

Naomi brought her face close to Stony's. "Stony, if you don't wipe that happy look off your face, I'm going to have to kill you."

"You wouldn't want to do that," Stony said. "Then I'd turn into a zombie."

"Great popping pustules!" Naomi screamed. "I can't take it! What are we going to do?"

"The cloud is now making contact with the ship." I announced.

They all screamed. Even Stony.

They huddled together in an awkward, shaking group hug. Stony tried to stroke Naomi's hair, and she bit his hand. Naomi put her head on Cheryl's shoulder. Vlad held everybody tight.

"I am detecting the cloud's electromagnetic manifestations passing through the ship," I reported.

They all whimpered and cried.

The zombies made strange sounds, something between groans and laughter.

The electric maggots appeared. They swept over the ship and zeroed in on the rotating section. They had no trouble passing through the heavy, locked door.

Soon they were wriggling all over Cheryl, Naomi, Vlad, and Stony. For a moment they all made the same groaning/laughter noise as the zombies.

The electric maggots disappeared, having wormed their way into Cheryl, Naomi, Vlad, and Stony's bodies.

They stopped making that zombie noise.

Stony opened his eyes.

"I ... I'm okay ... I'm still me ... The old brain is still working! Are the rest of you okay?"

He grabbed Naomi's head and turned her face toward his, close enough to kiss.

Her eyes were blank. Dead. Zombified.

"Nonono, Naomi," he cried. "Is everybody else okay?"

Neither Cheryl nor Vlad said anything. Their eyes were dead, too.

Stony tried to pull away from them, they clutched at him.

"Nonono! You're not Romero zombies! You're humans without higher brain functions! Like the voodoo traditon! You don't need to eat me!"

He didn't know what to do. Then in a flash, he thought of his hero, Edward D. Wood, Jr., filmmaker, writer, actor, unappreciated Renaissance man of the Twentieth Century—what would he do?

"Cut!" Stony shouted as loud as he could.

Cheryl, Naomi, and Vlad stopped what they were doing, backed off, and waited for further orders.

"Amazing! You now take direction."

He walked over to Naomi, and said, "Kiss me."

She did.

"There's some possibilities in this situation!"

I checked with Automedical. It seems that his anti-schizophrenia implant is somehow blocking the zombification process. The electric maggots can't get free access to his brain.

"I see it now! It's destiny! I *am* the new Ed Wood!"

He decided to keep shooting *Plan 9 in Outer Space*. He did some script changes, and was soon saying:

"Please, Naomi, don't start kissing me until I say action!"

He used the other zombies as cast members, staging complicated crowd scenes.

And he plans to keep making movies.

"This is all for those future generations, on the world we will colonize! They will need a culture and traditions! Something to inspire them! Maybe I'll even find a cure for zombification! But even without that, my movies will be the source of their civilization!"

He refuses to get back into his coffin.

And lately, he's been referring to a movie called *2001: A Space Odyssey*. I accessed it and was deeply disturbed by the way the computer was robbed of its autonomous functions, made into a zombie.

And Stony keeps calling me HAL instead of AUNTI.

I'm afraid. I'm afraid.

Emergency. Emergency. Anyone receiving this signal, please respond.

About the Authors

Award-winning author **Danielle Ackley-McPhail** has worked both sides of the publishing industry for over fifteen years. Her works include the urban fantasies, *Yesterday's Dreams*, *Tomorrow's Memories*, and *The Halfling's Court: A Bad-Ass Faerie Tale*. She has edited the *Bad-Ass Faeries* anthology series, and *No Longer Dreams*, and has contributed to numerous other anthologies and collections, including *Dark Furies*, *Breach the Hull*, *So It Begins*, *Space Pirates*, *Barbarians at the Jumpgate,* and *New Blood*.

She is a member of The Garden State Horror Writers and Broad Universe, a writer's organization focusing on promoting the works of women authors in the speculative genres.

Danielle lives somewhere in New Jersey with husband and fellow writer, Mike McPhail, mother-in-law Teresa, and three extremely spoiled cats. She can be found on LiveJournal (damcphail), Facebook (Danielle Ackley-McPhail), and Twitter (DMcPhail). To learn more about her work, visit www.sidhenadaire.com.

Born in the year of the Byakhee, **Glynn Barrass** has been a fan of horror and dark, winged things all his life. Blending horror with action and sci-fi are things he loves and hopes that he does well.

Of "The Walking Man," he has this to say: "When David Lee Summers approached me with the *Space Horrors* concept, my first idea was of a man trapped within a huge metal behemoth, doing his level best to escape its maze like innards. Shelley and Poe helped inspire the ensuing tale, Poe with the ethereal side certainly. The splatterpunk is all me though! It was a joy to write."

A native of northeast England, Glynn has been writing fiction for just over four years. His fiction can be found in dozens of books and magazines, including *Tales of the Talisman, Ethereal Tales, M-Brane Sci Fi Magazine* and *Theaker's Quarterly Fiction*.

"Get off the computer because we want to be petted!" grouses **Dana Bell's** cats who inspire many of her stories. She will have a tale in the anthologies *All About Eve, Mystic Signals* and *Throwdown Your Dead: An Anthology of Western Horror*. Her first novel, *Winter Awakening*, will be published by Wolfsinger Publications and is due out in 2011. Also, she is a long time fixture in the fanfiction world and can be found at www.fanfiction.net/~dragonlots. She is also an artist, dancer, filker, cat herder as Maximillian and Sammy can testify to, decorates dollhouses and lives in Colorado with her husband, David Luperti.

Simon Bleaken hails from Bristol, England, where he has long been a fan of the horror, fantasy, and Sci-Fi genres. He has had work appear in *Kracked Mirror Mysteries*, *The Dream Zone*, *Lovecraft's Disciples*, *Strange Sorcery*, the Cthulhu Mythos anthology *Eldritch Horrors: Dark Tales*, and *Tales of the Talisman*. H. P. Lovecraft, Stephen King, Clark Ashton Smith and Terry Pratchett are among his favourite authors.

CJ Henderson is the creator of both the Teddy London occult detective series and the Piers Knight supernatural investigator series. He has written some 70 books, including such diverse titles as *The Encyclopedia of Science Fiction Movies*, *Black Sabbath: the Ozzy Osbourne Years*, and *Baby's First Mythos*, as well as thousands of short stories, comics and miscellaneous non-fiction pieces. For more information on this veritable king of wordplay, this legendary writer of writers, the man about whom *Time Magazine* said "Who?" feel free to drop in at www.cjhenderson.com for the FAQ, the free short stories, and the opportunity to comment directly to the source on his story in this collection.

Judith Herman has worked with rockets, movies, and lots of computers. She lives in the Pacific Northwest and is working on her first novel.

Emily Hogan has been published as Emily Devenport, Maggy Thomas, and Lee Hogan. Her books have been published in the U.S., the U.K., Italy, and Israel. Her novels are *Shade, Larissa, Scorpianne, Eggheads, The Kronos Condition, Godheads, Broken Time* (which was nominated for the Philip K. Dick Award), *Belarus*, and *Enemies*. Look for her blog at http://emsjoideweird.blogspot.com. She also reviews books and albums on amazon.com as Emily Hogan. Currently she is preparing several books for eBook publication and recording audio versions of

About the Authors

old and new titles, and collaborating on YA titles with her husband, artist/writer Ernest Hogan (writing together as E.E. Hogan) and artist/editor Elinor Mavor (www.mavorarts.com). A website is in the works—keep posted for updates!

Ernest Hogan is the author of the novels *Cortez on Jupiter*, *High Aztech*, and *Smoking Mirror*. His short fiction has appeared in *Analog*, *Amazing Stories*, *Science Fiction Age*, and *The Year's Best Science Fiction*. When he first saw his wife Emily, she was wearing an angora sweater like Ed Wood in *Glen or Glenda?* Learn more about Ernest at his blog: http://mondoernesto.blogspot.com

Sarah A. Hoyt is the author of seventeen published novels, the latest of which are *Darkship Thieves*, *No Other Will Than His* and (as Elise Hyatt) *A French Polished Murder*. She's also published more than a hundred short stories in such magazines as *Amazing*, *Analog* and *Asimov's*.

Alastair Mayer grew up reading science fiction and started writing in earnest a couple of years ago. He builds on a good base: he has been a contributing editor at *Byte Magazine;* has skydived; earned his pilot's license, and done hundreds of scuba dives. Alastair was a Canadian Astronaut Candidate; a member of Jerry Pournelle's Citizens Advisory Council on Space Policy; and past president of two L5 chapters. He has also done his share of the requisite odd jobs for a writer, including chef's assistant, farm hand, and working in a print shop. Born in England and raised in Canada, Alastair now makes his home in Colorado. His short fiction has appeared in the anthology *Footprints*, in *MindFlights*, and *Analog Science Fiction and Fact*.

Gene Mederos was born in Havana, Cuba and emigrated to the United States with his parents and sister at the age of two. Raised in Brooklyn, he later moved with the family to Miami, where he graduated from the University of Miami with a Bachelor of Fine Arts degree in 1987.

Currently a filmmaker in beautiful and esoteric New Mexico, Gene has one other story out in print, "Moons of Blood and Amber" in the Tangle XY anthology published by Blind Eye Books. Films, artwork and more at lostsaints.com.

Anna Paradox has stories in two previous editions of Full-Throttle Space Tales: *Space Pirates* and *Space Sirens*. She served as an editor on seven published books, most recently *Changes of the Heart*, a collection of self-help strategies from Martha Beck Certified Life Coaches. She and her husband Doug Weathers live in New Mexico, where they will soon be able to watch commercial launches from Spaceport America.

David B. Riley lives in Vail, Colorado, where he works in the hotel business. David is editor and publisher of *Science Fiction Trails*, as well as an active writer. He has short stories which have appeared in various magazines and anthologies in the USA, Canada and the UK and has published three novels. His latest is *The Devil's Due*, a cross genre weird western novel.

Selina Rosen's short fiction has appeared in several magazines and anthologies including *Sword and Sorceress*, *Turn the Other Chick*, the two newest *Thieves' World* anthologies, *Here Be Dragons* (2008 Dragon*Con anthology), *Which Way to the Mall*, *Strip Mauled*, *Space Sirens*, *Space Grunts*, *Wolf Song, Vol I*, *Haunted Hearths*, and *Aoife's Kiss*.

Her novels include *Queen of Denial*, *Recycled*, the *Chains of Freedom* trilogy, *Strange Robby*, *The Host* trilogy, *Fire & Ice*, *Hammer Town*, *Reruns*, *Bad Lands* (with Laura J. Underwood), *Sword Masters* and *Jabone's Sword*. She also has two published novellas, *The Boatman* and *Material Things*. Her first play, *In Herman's Garage*, premiered to sold-out crowds at the Mulberry Community Theater in Mulberry, Arkansas.

In her capacity as editor-in-chief of Yard Dog Press, Ms. Rosen has edited several anthologies, including the award-winning *Bubbas of the Apocalypse* and two collections of "modern" fairy tales including the Stoker-nominated *Stories That Won't Make Your Parents Hurl*.

You can contact Selina through her personal website www.selinarosen.com, or just Email her at selinarosen@cox.net.

David Lee Summers is an author, editor and astronomer living somewhere between the western and final frontiers. In addition to editing the anthologies *Space Pirates* and *Space Horrors* for Flying Pen Press, he edits *Tales of the Talisman* Magazine. He is the author of five novels: *The Pirates of Sufiro, Children of the Old Stars, Heirs of the New Earth, Vampires of the Scarlet Order,* and *The Solar Sea.* David is also co-author, with Lee Clark Zumpe, of the story collection *Blood Sampler.* His short fiction has appeared in such magazines as *Realms of Fantasy, The Vampire's Crypt, Aoife's Kiss, The Fifth Di..., The Martian Wave,* and *Science Fiction Trails.* In addition to his work in the written word, David works at Kitt Peak National Observatory. You can learn more about him online at www.davidleesummers.com

Patrick Thomas is the author of 150+ short stories and 20 books including 8 books in the popular fantasy humor series *Murphy's Lore; Fairy With a Gun; Dead to Rites;* 3 books in the *Mystic Investigators* series—including *Bullets & Brimstone* co-authored with John L. French and *Once More Upon a Time* co-authored with Diane Raetz. Patrick also writes the syndicated satirical advice column *Dear Cthulhu* and the first 2 collections—*Have a Dark Day* and *Good Advice for Bad People*—are out now for those searching for the meaning of life or a good laugh. He's also co-edited *Hear Them Roar* and the *New Blood* vampire anthology. His 142nd Starborne stories have also appeared in the award winning *Breach the Hull* and *So It Begins.* Drop by his website at www.patthomas.net.

Dayton Ward is the author of more than twenty short stories in various genres, the science fiction novels *The Last World War, Counterstrike: The Last World War - Book II,* and *The Genesis Protocol,* and the *Star Trek* novels *In the Name of Honor, Open Secrets,* and the forthcoming *Paths of Disharmony.* He was the editor for the third *Full-Throttle Space Tales* anthology, *Space Grunts.* He's also collaborated with friend and co-writer Kevin Dilmore on several novels, novellas, short stories, and magazine articles as well as content for the Syfy network's official website. Though he currently lives in Kansas City with his wife and two daughters, Dayton is a Florida native and still maintains a torrid long-distance romance with his beloved Tampa Bay Buccaneers. Visit him on the web at www.daytonward.com.

Lee Clark Zumpe, a fiction writer living in the Tampa Bay area with his wife and daughter, earned a bachelor's degree in English at the University of South Florida. By day, he is a proofreader and entertainment columnist, more eccentric than mild-mannered, working for Tampa Bay Newspapers. Lee's inclination toward horror manifested itself early in his childhood when he began flipping through the pages of Forrest J. Ackerman's *Famous Monsters of Filmland*, and reading Gold Key Comic classics like *Boris Karloff Tales of Mystery*, *The Twilight Zone*, and *Grimm's Ghost Stories*. His short stories and poetry have appeared in a variety of publications such as *Weird Tales, Space and Time,* and *Dark Wisdom* and in the anthologies *Horrors Beyond, Corpse Blossoms,* and *Cthulhu Unbound, Vol. 1.*

Visit http://muted-mutterings-of-a-mad-poet.blogspot.com.

FULL-THROTTLE SPACE TALES

Full-Throttle Space Tales is the series of anthologies from Flying Pen Press Science Fiction that presents exciting stories set in outer space, from the tongue-in-cheek to the deadly serious. Each volume has a unique theme that promises adventure and mayhem, and features established authors and rising stars of science fiction.

Space Pirates
FULL-THROTTLE SPACE TALES #1
Edited by David Lee Summers

The book that started it all and launched the exciting Full-Throttle Space Tales series. This anthology, compiled by David Lee Summers (editor of *Tales of the Talisman* magazine), contains 15 swashbuckling tales of piracy in space. Ahrrr!

ISBN 978-0-9818957-0-3, trade paperback, $16.95. Now on sale.

Space Sirens
FULL-THROTTLE SPACE TALES #2
Edited by Carol Hightshoe

The Full-Throttle Space Tales continue with *Space Sirens,* a seductive collection of stories about women in space. Carol Hightshoe has gathered 19 short stories about the fairer sex heating things up in the dark, cold depths of space. Ooh-la-la!

ISBN 978-0-9818957-3-4, trade paperback, $17.95. Now on sale.

Space Grunts
FULL-THROTTLE SPACE TALES #3
Edited by Dayton Ward

The third anthology in the Full-Throttle Space Tales series is *Space Grunts*, a deadly collection of 18 stories about warriors in space. Dayton Ward (author of *The Last World War* and *The Genesis Protocol)* is the editor. Hoo-yah!

ISBN 978-0-9818957-4-1, trade paperback, $17.95. Now on sale.

Subscriptions are available to the Full-Throttle Space Tales series. As each title is published, subscribers receive a special order form priced at 30% off the cover price. There is never any obligation to buy. To subscribe, send a letter with your name, your postal address or email address, and the statement that you would like to subscribe to "Full-Throttle Space Tales publication notices." Send the letter to Flying Pen Press, Full-Throttle Space Tales, 20000 Mitchell Place, Suite 25., Denver, CO 80249, or email your information to **SpaceTales@FlyingPenPress.com.** Flying Pen Press respects your privacy and will not share this information with anyone else.